# STONE AND HONEY

CHRISTINA ZEMPI was born in Malakasa, Attica, and is a nursery school teacher. She lives and works in Athens. She is married and has two children. She has written poetry, short stories, fairy tales, and plays for children's puppet theatre and children's parties, material which she uses in her teaching. *Stone and Honey* is her first novel.

IRENE NOEL-BAKER is a psychologist, a translator and a poet. She grew up in Euboea, Greece. Her recent translations from Greek include psychoanalytic works, history, architecture, short stories and novels. Her translations of Plato are published by the Aldeburgh Bookshop.

# STONE AND HONEY

CHRISTINA ZEMPI

Translated from the Greek by Irene Noel-Baker

Arcadia Books Ltd
139 Highlever Road
London W10 6PH

*www.arcadiabooks.co.uk*

First published in the United Kingdom by Arcadia Books 2016
Originally published by Okeanida as *petra kai meli* 2013
Copyright © Christina Zempi 2013

The English translation from the Greek
Copyright © Irene Noel-Baker 2016

With grateful thanks to the Ouranis Foundation for their assistance in funding this
translation, and to the International Writers' and Translators' Centre of Rhodes.

ISBN 978-1-910050-80-4

Typeset in Garamond by MacGuru Ltd
Printed and bound by TJ International, Padstow PL28 8RW


ARCADIA BOOKS DISTRIBUTORS ARE AS FOLLOWS:

*in the UK and elsewhere in Europe:*
BookSource
50 Cambuslang Road
Cambuslang
Glasgow G32 8NB

*in the USA and Canada:*
Dufour Editions
PO Box 7
Chester Springs
PA 19425

*in Australia/New Zealand:*
NewSouth Books
University of New South Wales
Sydney NSW 2052

For my husband Chrístos,
for my daughters Constantína and Ioánna,
for my parents.

### The Poisoner

*One Easter Sunday I got up*
*to bake my pies and burnt them all*
*so wretchedly, that I went off*
*to find my father: 'My pies are*
*spoiled, it's a bad sign'.*
*'You silly thing, don't worry now,*
*you have buns in your apron*
*and red eggs in your pocket.'*
*On the road I met my husband*
*and my brother-in-law; I stopped*
*and asked if they had seen*
*my brother Kalapóthos.*
*'We left him at the sheep-pen, milking,*
*making cheese, eating and relaxing.'*
*Down at the sheep-pen when I arrived*
*I heard him gasping his last breath.*
*'Tell me, Kalapótho mou, who*
*did this? Let me take revenge.'*
*'How can I tell you, it was your husband*
*and brother-in-law who did it.'*
*I dragged him home but on the way*
*he stiffened dead. I left him there,*
*inside a church, and went along*
*to Tzimova, and bought an ounce*
*of soulima to poison both*
*the killers. Then home again*
*I went, and cooked, and threw the bitter*
*soulima into the dish and*
*called them in to come and eat.*
*At the first bite their eyes rolled back.*
*Did they not know I'd take revenge?*
*When it was done I went to find*
*their father and I told him all:*
*'I did to them what they did to*
*my brother, and I paid them back.'*
*Did you ever hear such a thing?*
*A Christian woman, burying*
*both husband and brother-in-law,*
*on the same holy day of Easter?*

Anargyros Koutsilieris
*Moiroloya tis Manis,*
Bekakos, Athens, 1997

# Abandoned Towers

'SOME PEOPLE FIND THESE abandoned towers depressing, but I like them,' said Effie.

As fitting symbols of human vanity, I like them too. A tower on four floors, turned into a crow's nest. I hope it collapses into a heap of stones for snakes and lizards to live in and maybe provide jobs for archaeologists sometime in the future. My mother bores me rigid with the history of that bloody house and the *moiroloy* – laments – she collects religiously wherever she can find them. From books, old magazines, local newspapers. She records them at village funerals with a microphone tucked in her bag. Old women in black, droning on endlessly like the crows in the ruined towers. 'The *moiroloy* frighten me,' my mum admitted. 'It's the truth those pursed lips keep locked away until the pain of death brings it out.'

I like old towers. You can take a girl you fancy to those deserted houses and no one would ever think of looking for you there. So you can get on with whatever you want to do in peace, petting, kissing, and if you're lucky, shagging. It's the only glory there is left to these buildings. I often thought of doing it before, but never dared to. Because of my mother always telling me to 'be careful, be careful' and I don't like to upset her when I'm down here. She has enough worries, she stresses about me when I'm in Athens and she doesn't want any more problems here, the old ones are enough, she says, though for some people problems are in their character, their system attracts them and I am one of those people. Everyone knows it. Mothers advise their precious sons to stay away from me, because I'm 'bad company', and their daughters not to take 'risks'. I am dangerous, and I'm proud of it. Any boy who comes near me will risk smoking weed, popping pills and shooting up, despite the fact that I've never tried those things myself, and girls risk losing their virginity prematurely, even though I haven't yet lost mine. With a reputation like mine, it was a big deal getting Effie to come and meet me alone here, and even more of a big deal that she trusted me, and let me touch her.

We clamp our mouths together and seek out the smooth skin under our T-shirts and we both go too far. She flouts her mother and father, and it isn't easy to flout Mitsikoyiánnis, a civil engineer with an office in Areopolis, a local councillor in the municipality of Oetilus, a local bigwig and sworn enemy of my mother. Hardly likely to take kindly to my making out with his daughter! And in his own friend's house what's more … Me! The bastard! And yet again I have disobeyed my mother, the 'general'. She made me promise to stay away from the girls in the village and in particular Mitsikoyiánnis's daughter. I couldn't care less if I never got within a mile of the others, I could always find a willing summer tourist, pert nipples peeping through T-shirts, suntanned legs strolling lazily along the cobbled streets, calves, thighs, knees naked in the sun, but I knew the instant I made that promise to my mum that I would never keep it.

I read somewhere that smoking is genetic and though I'm not an expert I agree, because nicotine doesn't suit me at all. I hate it as much as my mother does. But I like the conspiratorial, secret side of it, and it suits my purposes right now. Effie has already tried it and given up, but I never did. I have to live up to my bad reputation somehow, and to find an excuse to hide with her behind walls and ruined buildings, of which there are plenty, luckily, where we live. I bought a packet, and that was the excuse for our first time alone together. Our first touch was behind the church wall, when, to hide my nervousness, I offered her a cigarette and lit it for her – I had practised earlier, obviously – as politely as an English lord, and more so. It was windy and we had to find shelter, so we got pretty close. Her girly scent wrapped itself around me, her hair tickled my nose and although I was terrified, I knew from that moment that I wanted to lose my virginity with her. And they could all go and stuff themselves, Mitsikoyiánnis and my mother and everyone else.

For a whole year Dimitris, my mate from Athens, had been bugging me to go along with him for my 'baptism of fire'. He had already done it many times, and there's no denying it, experience *is* everything. *Pappoú* told me directly that it was high time, that he would give me the cash, and not to tell my mother. I said no. Don't ask me why. Why should I have to prove my manhood in the arms of poor foreigners called Anoushka or Gabriella or Vanessa, who tell you they were medical students back home, and will now sell you a fuck cheaper than a bottle of olive oil – which has gone right down in price by the way, even in the Mani which produces the best in the world. I have absolutely no desire for it and I'm not sure I could rise to the occasion.

Mitsikoyiánnis's daughter is no walkover. Her friend Soula would be more up for it and I know that; she 'seems as one long since prepared', as Cavafy, peeping out from my mother's books, would say. My evil reputation draws her like a magnet. Her virginity has become an unbearable burden to her, and she wants to get shot of it as quickly as possible and move on, but I don't feel like helping her with that, so I suggested it to my friend Vassilis: 'Don't be a wanker, go for it,' I said. He's considering it.

I'm crazy about Mitsikoyiánnis's Effie … I think of her and start to sweat, I long to see her, to touch her. Because of her, I fear nothing and nobody except my inexperience, but I'm encouraged by the thought of Adam and Eve. They were totally inexperienced, and yet they managed an original sin, and so what if it cost them their paradise. I don't care what it costs me, no price is too high where she's concerned, and what's the use of a paradise if you don't even want to be in it?

So as I said, I love old towers, and in particular this one here, standing alone, still upright, scary in the silence, with its own little ghost, like all self-respecting old houses. And I'm not referring to myself, though I am about to turn into a ghost, standing in here waiting for Effie with a hard-on, like an ancient satyr on a postcard rack outside a kiosk. Okay, maybe not quite so well endowed! Old people and children in the village talk about a strange light appearing every so often through its little windows. The light goes up the four floors of the tower, one by one, they say, to carry up the rocks and boiling oil, perhaps. Probably illicit lovers, or an illegal immigrant finding refuge, and it has set people's imagination going. Whoever it was, I owe them a favour, because it means that Effie and I are completely safe. It's unlikely that anyone will come here. Mitsikoy-iánnis is far away in bed, and my mother, even if she was suspicious, is afraid of the house for her own reasons, which have nothing to do with ghosts. Only the moon, like a large orange ball, watches me kiss Effie – tracing the circumference of her face – her eyes, wide open as she looks deep into mine, and then closed in expectation. I like the way we take it step by step, exploring and discovering one another, preparing ourselves for the inevitable. She may not have completely comprehended it, but I feel sure – I'm plucking up my courage for what's about to happen, and it's coming closer by the hour.

This tower has a long history. It was built on the highest point in the village, eight minutes' fast walk from my mother's and an awesome rival to our house, which guards both the entrance to the village and the pass, in both directions, from Sparta and from Areop-olis. The two towers keep a lookout over the entire region, and above all they keep an eye on each other. The floor we're on and the first two floors of this monster here were built around 1700, but its two top floors were built much more recently, when the war with the Anastasakaíoi was at its peak. First they raised it up a floor to equal ours, and then they built another level to make it taller, and leaving absolutely no doubt that they intended to defend what they owned: basically olive oil and water. Generations back we used to kill each other over a single olive tree, a strip of turf, a spring with barely a drop of water. But this was an open threat. According to the unwritten rules of our region, my clan gave their enemies fair warning: If they didn't scale down the height of their tower along with their ambitions, there would be war. The others replied, like true Spartans: 'Molon lavé' – if you want it come and get it. They didn't use those words exactly but their meaning was plain enough.

My people started the murders: they ambushed and killed the doctor, Piéro Anastasákos, on his way to the priest's sickbed. It was a set-up, naturally. Then the elders of the clan met, here in this house, and decided on the best way to wash away their shame and satisfy the women of the family, who were baying for blood. As a result Spyros Haritákos was sentenced to death and killed in his field, next to Ay' Ilía's church, while he was napping under an olive tree in the afternoon heat. He wasn't actually the one who started the killings, but they decided on him instead of his father, Vassilis, who was a lazy good-for-nothing. By contrast Spyros was a man known for his discretion, and well respected throughout the length and breadth of the Mani, and the Anastasakaíoi wanted to hit at the Haritakaíoi where it really hurt. But they underestimated us. The wife of the murdered man demanded vengeance; she refused to come out of her house until the black mark of shame besmirching her honour and self-respect had been removed. If the men of the family didn't have the balls for it, she would do it herself, with her own bare hands. The Haritakaíoi wouldn't stand an insult like that. There followed more of the same, from both sides, until all that was left of the warring clans were the two towers, symbols of their power and greed. Due to the latter, we lost the former. It is difficult to work and make your land flourish if you're hemmed in by gunslits, expecting death to strike you at any moment, and trying to be invisible, like the lizards who nest in the stones. The survival of their men was the women's only concern, while they worked like dogs to bring in the food for their families. What an irony! To owe everything, even the food on your plate, to women, busily weaving your destruction on the loom of fate, and whose only concern was the death of the enemy!

*How proud they were*
*the men of our clan*
*now they're yours for the taking*
*Traitors and cowards*
*ruins washed down the river by the first flood.*

That *moiroloy* wasn't sung for us, or for the Anastasakaíoi. But it fits us like a glove. There was hardly anything left, and I don't just mean stone ruins. Faced with the threat of extinction, the elders of the two families, three generations back, were forced to capitulate. A *psychikó*, a truce, was agreed with the intervention of the Nikolakaíoi, a good family, whom both sides trusted and respected. They didn't quite fall into one another's arms, but it had become clear that if our feud continued there would soon be none of us left. We had the same number of dead on each side, the same number of graves, no one looked weaker than the other, less worthy, more cowardly. My great-grandfather made a truce with Anastasákos's grandfather, they shook hands, and for a generation we were at peace, without any loss of dignity; more likely they all felt relieved. For one generation only. The dance of death, as my grandfather used to say, is ever with us, and it will always find a way to start its bloody game again from the beginning.

Effie and I were lying on the millstone, while the first stars of the Mani night winked at us over the house of our old enemies, and the moon gave us its blessing to get on with it, and do what women and men have always done, since the beginning of time, when they're alone together. I was certain that the time had come, she wasn't resisting, the stone was hurting our backs but neither of us minded. I took off her top and touched her naked skin. She shivered, like the sea beneath the wind's caress.

And then suddenly a stranger appeared at the door of the tower, silent as a ghost. I couldn't see him properly in the dusk; I only noticed that he was tall, with short hair, wearing jeans and a dark shirt. The moon lit up his grim face, completely unknown to me.

I was terrified. I had heard about weirdos who steal up on couples, rape the girl, rob, and sometimes kill them. Not here in the Mani, obviously, but you never know. Effie was my first concern – to protect her from the stranger and get her to run back home to safety.

'Having a party, are we?'

The guy was *xénos*, a foreigner, you could tell by his accent, the way he said the word 'party'. He must be a homeless immigrant, working somewhere nearby and using the house to sleep in. He didn't look Albanian, they aren't that tall, maybe Bulgarian or Romanian. He kept his distance, which was just as well. By God I would have gone for him if he had tried to touch Effie. I would have hit him, though he was no pushover – huge, with wide shoulders and hands like sledgehammers. But he didn't move a muscle; he gave me time to tell Effie to get dressed and go, and to convince her that I'd be all right. She went down the path by the millstone. I only breathed again when I was sure she was safe. I looked more closely at the stranger, who for some unknown reason, despite his stern expression, seemed amused.

The only thing that worried me was that if he was from around here he might shop us, and if anyone blabbed to Mitsikoyiánnis, my mother would find out, and then there would be a fuss. Effie would be in for it, and who knew when I would see her again. I tried to play it cool. I had managed to button up my trousers and swallow my frustration after the almighty let-down.

'Who are you? Don't you know that this is private property?' I said, in a pathetic attempt to scare him off.

'That's what I thought,' he said, as if I had no more right to be there than he did.

It was an awkward situation. He evidently wasn't going to be scared away by a kid. So I changed tack.

'Look, buddy,' I said gently, 'it doesn't bother me you being here, and I won't tell anyone. You can stay as long as you like, no one ever comes here. Only do me a favour ...'

I was overcome by the strange notion that he was able to read my thoughts. He actually smiled. He was laughing at me and the blood rushed to my head, but I didn't want to play tough – the guy had the upper hand. There were two people who might object to his being in the tower: one was Uncle Nikifóros, but he was away in Athens with his wife critically ill in hospital. The other was Effie's father, Mitsikoyiánnis, and if he were to find out, there would be no hole small enough for us to hide in. So I swallowed my anger and tried to think.

'Don't tell anyone you saw us here. I don't care about myself but I care about the girl. So please ...' I pleaded, like an idiot. I even dug my hand into my pocket and offered him what was left of yesterday's wages. Twenty euros. He didn't take it. He just smiled wearily and rubbed his eyes.

'I don't care what you do,' he said. 'Only don't come back here until I've gone, I need some peace and quiet.'

He promised not to say anything to anyone. He didn't care about the place; he was just passing through. What concerned him, he went on, was that I seemed to be getting on pretty well with her, meaning Effie, and that in his opinion I was asking for trouble. He put his hand into his pocket and took out a box of condoms, which he handed to me.

'Never go into battle without your shield,' he said. 'Haven't you seen the statue of Leonidas in Sparta? Sword unsheathed, but shield firmly in position.'

I admit I was so stupid I didn't even think why a Romanian would know about Leonidas. Something else struck me: Get a load of these refugees! They have nothing to eat, nowhere to sleep, and yet they don't go anywhere without their condoms! I spent the whole of that evening thinking about it. We parted like two friends who had shared a secret, we even shook hands, which made me thank my lucky stars I didn't have to fight him – he had an iron grip. And if I hadn't been freaked out by what he said at the end, I might even have liked him. But just as I was about to jump out of the tower, he called me back.

'Hey kiddo!' I turned round, clutching the condoms. 'How old are you?' I told him I would be sixteen in November and he smiled oddly.

'She's sweet, your bird,' he remarked, 'but she's not right for you. Forgive me for saying so, but you need someone older for what you're after.'

It pissed me off that he had an opinion about everything. About me, and about Effie, and about what exactly we were doing together. I told him to bugger off, and jumped off the roof of the old chicken house and on to the mound outside the tower.

It was hot and my T-shirt was clinging to my skin. There was no breeze at all, which is pretty rare in our wild and windy part of the world. Not a breath was stirring, and that does your head in. If I hadn't been in such a hurry to talk to Effie and reassure her, I would probably have noticed the unusual activity in old Dimákos's house. I didn't notice anything, I only thought of her, mad with worry, waiting for a call or a text. The moon had risen further, lighting up the lines of rock that merged into the distant coastline, and I just managed by the light of it to send her four words: 'Don't worry, all fine.' I didn't dare phone her, I didn't know who was with her or how she would explain the call. I would wait till she had a chance to phone me.

There was no point in hurrying back home; *Pappoú* knew I was never home before one or sometimes two o'clock. I usually hung around with Vassilis and the others outside the church, bantering and fooling about. They would probably be there still, but I didn't fancy seeing them. I would have to explain where I'd been, and somebody was bound to have noticed my being away with Mitsikoyiánnis's daughter the same time every day. Definitely Andreas, Kosmas's son, who misses nothing, and who has inherited his father's peculiar talent for being insatiably curious about other people's affairs. If he even got the smallest hint of what we were up to, we were done for. He would have no qualms in giving us away. He's never forgotten how I threw a stone at him and cracked his skull five years ago, when I was ten and he was thirteen. He is a complete loser, which is why he made the mistake of underestimating me because of my size. But none of that counts when the other guy is a shit, and you're driven mad with fury, and at that moment I wasn't frightened of anything. He was lucky to get away with just a broken skull, three people had to hold me down. If anyone says a word against Marináki I go crazy, and he had the cheek to call my mother a whore in front of everyone. He, of all people. They all had a go at me after that. And who got the blame? I did. The bastard, who else?

Obviously, no one dared mention Marináki's name after that. And whatever my mother says, *Pappoú*, my Grandad Haritákos, with the wisdom of a man who's been in prison, said I did the right thing. Because you either have the balls and show it, or you just sit there and let people fuck you over.

I like walking at night here in the Mani. The darkness gently covers the sharp lines of the rocks, the sun that scorches you all day long has gone, the air, even when there's no breeze, like tonight, brings down sweet scents from Taygetus. It clears your head, you see things as they are, you can dream, despite the stress you're under. I went back home and waited for the telephone to ring. *Pappoú* had cooked aubergines *imam* and they were delicious, but I had no appetite, not until I'd spoken to Effie and made sure that everything was okay. *Pappoú* wasn't yet back from the *kafeneíon*. Their card game was probably dragging on, and so much the better – the last thing I wanted at that moment was people asking questions.

The phone rang just as I turned on the television to get the sports news on NET – not much of it, since it was summer. I grabbed my mobile from the kitchen table. Effie's voice, frightened, sobbing. She was trying to tell me something, talking so quietly that I couldn't make it out. She obviously didn't want to be overheard and we weren't getting anywhere, so I cut her off quickly.

'I'm coming over, go out into the back garden.'

We met and she told me that when she got back home she had found her mother in a state, annoyed with her for having disappeared all afternoon, and asking where she'd been, so insistently that at first she thought she must know. But it turned out not to be about her. Effie's father has a small construction company, which relies on people coming back to the village to do up their old family houses. They might build a couple of rooms on a small piece of land or maybe renovate an abandoned tower. But who wants a holiday house when they can barely afford to live? Her father had counted on building a new hotel, using some of the old village towers. It would be a big asset to the neighbourhood, and though his company is small, they do an exceptional job in restoration, and he has the experience. He renovated the Anastasákos's tower, where I've been meeting Effie. But the construction industry is going through a crisis right now, the big companies from Athens smelled money and came down on the hotel project like crows. A French company got in on the act and it was they who eventually got the job.

As I said, I'm not too fond of Mitsikoyiánnis, but I do admire him for staying put in the Mani, when it would have been so much easier to leave. He loves this place a lot and he is the best at restoring the towers, because the history of the Mani is his passion. A romantic at heart, stubborn. And honourable, despite the difficulties. If it had been anyone else, he would have oiled every wheel in the municipality instead of keeping well out of it for ethical reasons. He has the old-fashioned, straight way of thinking: the truth is the truth and a lie is a lie, black and white sorted out, children should be born after their parents get married and so on. And he doesn't think much of bastards with unknown fathers like yours truly.

So Mitsikoyiánnis had missed his chance with the hotel. And

Effie's mother, who did the interior design for her husband's business, was upset about that. Despite the lecture, Effie was relieved that her secret was still a secret. Then her father came home and they were all sitting at supper when his phone rang, and the bomb dropped.

The person on the phone was Odysséas Anastasákos, Mitsikoyiánnis's best friend, who had left years ago for America. The last remaining member of the 'enemy' family. The stranger in the tower house! As Effie told me this piece of news, the church bell started to toll mournfully, but I hardly noticed it then. It's nothing unusual in a place where there are only old people left.

The moon had risen fully, a gentle breeze blew Effie's hair back to reveal her face. At last, a breeze! She had tears in her eyes and was frantically looking at me for help. She had a point; the man in the tower house was no stranger after all. He would probably be in and out of their house and be invited for meals, and might even stay with them till he'd cleared the cobwebs out of his own house. There was nowhere to hide, the guy would talk, and probably with great satisfaction as soon as he found out who I was.

Far away on the horizon you could make out the dark sea. People would be strolling about the alleyways of Areopolis and settling down for a drink at the Xemóni. Up here it was silent except for the sounds of the night, an evening like any other, broken only by the tolling bell. Effie told me that Odysséas Anastasákos had proved everyone wrong and had finally come back in time for his aunt's funeral! There had been talk of his arrival for over two weeks. When his aunt went into hospital the rumours multiplied: 'He has to come now,' they all said. I didn't think so, because if he had really wanted to come he would have caught the first plane back as soon as he heard Dimákaina was ill. That's what you do for the people you love. What's the point of kissing a corpse? They said he delayed it because he was up to his eyes in work, as if the old lady would wait till he was free before throwing in the towel.

Dimákaina never expected him to come back. Whenever they

talked about him the tears came to her eyes and she would sigh 'my poor lost boy' as if he were dead. And when she heard his voice on the telephone: 'I can hardly tell if it's him any more,' she would say to my mother, and I would leave the room as fast as I could. I didn't want to hear about him, I didn't want to feel sorry for him, I couldn't. How can you bear it, Marináki, how do you still have time for him, even now? That evening was when I first told her to get married, while she was correcting her Ancient Greek papers with a red pen and putting marks with a ring round them at the top of the page.

'Why don't you get married, *Mamá*?'

If you think of all that's been written about the full moon, from ancient times till today, and how much it apparently influences people's lives, then it's hardly by chance that Anastasákos chose to come back on the night of the full moon. The breeze had dropped as suddenly as it had started, my clothes were sticking to my body, my brain froze and there was no way out. I had to act fast, this very evening, because tomorrow the creep would see us both at the funeral and there would be hell to pay for Effie, and all because of me. I told her not to worry, to have faith in me and that I would sort it all out. She very much wanted to believe me, and convinced herself it was all okay. If only I could have done the same.

'But how are you going to talk to him, Alexi, at the funeral with all those people around you?'

She was right. The house would be packed with people, it wouldn't be at all easy to get him alone, but I didn't let my uncertainty show. Girls, my grandad says, are like the tender shoots on the olive tree; they get easily broken.

'If I have to, I'll put it in a *moiroloy*,' and I started up:

*Poor old Anastasáko*
*with your great big tower*
*and your shedloads of dollars*
*why did you come back here*

*just as my sweetheart*
*was giving me a kiss*
*on your old millstone?*
*You should have stayed in* xenitiá
*eating and drinking and getting smashed*
*and living it up with all that cash*
*instead of coming over here*
*to smash our …*

I emphasised what I meant with the familiar hand gesture and, despite being worried, we both laughed. We risked a quick kiss.

'Don't be afraid, I'm not leaving you,' I whispered into her parted lips.

And it's true, she shouldn't be afraid. I didn't know how, but I would sort everything out. I had no choice, or I would never see her again. Her father wouldn't allow it. I went off to Dimákos's house. I felt my feet dragging as I got nearer and my optimism vanished. Why should the guy keep our secret? And how could I ask him such a thing amongst all those people. What would I say to him?

\*\*\*

The wooden gate to Dimákos's garden was wide open, as was the front door. The familiar scene of the wake, with the men outside and the sound of the women's lament coming from within. In the front yard the foreigner stood out from all the others and now that it was light I could see his features clearly. So this was Odysséas Anastasákos! His grey hair made him look older than he was, but he was well preserved and impressive, mainly due to his height and build. Broad shoulders, enormous hands. Fiery black eyes in a face that reminded me of hermits on the icons in church. I laughed inwardly at the thought. Who had ever heard of a hermit with condoms ready to hand? He was having a fine old time, the creep, even on a day like today! He was surrounded by a group of men in the garden, and why wouldn't he be, after so long abroad. Mitsikoyiánnis, his best friend when they were boys, Effie's mum's brother, Pantelis Leoúsis, Pavlákos the former cop, Kosmás the café owner, also known as 'the antenna' because he always had the gossip, and a few other old men. The foreigner looked ill, he was rubbing his eyes again, like he'd done up at the tower, and he wouldn't leave his old man's side.

I went up to offer my condolences to old Nikifóros. A cicada was energetically rubbing its wings together in all the glory of the Maniot summer, which increased my embarrassment. What was I supposed to say to the old man who had lost his wife and was left alone, with no children, and his nearest relative living in Boston? I stammered the usual clichés and went in to pay my respects to the dead, surrounded by village women dressed in black, in the certain knowledge that I belonged nowhere. I was too young to sit outside with the men and obviously I wasn't going to stay inside with the women. For a moment I thought of phoning my friend Vassilis, but I banished the thought, because then I would have had to explain my meeting with Anastasákos at the tower and to admit to my secret meetings with Effie. Not that he isn't okay, but when two people have a secret it's a secret. That's a saying of *Pappoú's*: Kolokotrónis was hiding, so they say, in a sheepfold, and the shepherd took him food every day, until one day the shepherd brought his *koumbáros* along with him. Kolokotrónis swiftly got his things together and made himself scarce, because, as he said: 'When two people share a secret it's just two people. When three know it, the whole world knows it.'

So I sat outside in a corner on my own. I don't know what I was waiting for. To go up to Anastasákos? No way. You could hear the *moiroloya* from inside – I felt weighed under by the atmosphere in the house, you could breathe the grief in there. I was fond of Dimákaina! I've known her since I was three years old, when my mother brought me down to the Mani for the first time. I can remember that when

I sat on her lap she smelled of fresh bread, and her eyes misted over when she looked at me. She loved me going to her house, and made me *díples, lalángia* and buns, and best of all she was never angry when I chased her chickens, she didn't mind when I played with Canello the dog and she even let me try milking the goat. She made a fuss of me and she called me *koróna mou,* even though I was a bastard. My throat was burning now and I couldn't stop the tears.

Effie's mother brought out a tray of bitter coffee and everyone took a cup. I took one too although I never drink coffee at that time of day, but the circumstances demanded it and anyway it gave me something to do with my hands. The grown-ups were smoking. I didn't dare to, it would be too provocative, and my mother would find out. And all hell would break loose. I've no idea how long I stayed there in the corner, lost in my thoughts, until I felt the for-eigner's enormous hand on my shoulder. I leapt up in surprise.

'Young man, go over to the *kafeneío* and bring us a bottle of cognac.'

He eased me towards the exit, where no one else could see or hear us. The guy was evidently no fool; he knew I wanted to talk to him. But he looked annoyed and my knees buckled under me.

'Say what you have to say and be off,' he said. 'I told you I wouldn't tell anyone about the girl, so why are you hanging around me?'

I had no room for manoeuvre. I would do anything for Effie, but I hated having to plead with him. Me. With him.

'Mr Anastasáko,' I said hurriedly, 'the girl you saw me with is Effie, the daughter of your friend Mitsikoyiánnis. Please don't say anything to him – she's almost dead with worry. And anyway she's not to blame, I …'

He looked me straight in the eyes. All my life I had wondered what his eyes were like, and the sound of his voice. I was a bit upset, but I needed to hold myself together and persuade him to keep his mouth shut, and I had to do it quickly. Nothing else mattered. I decided to tell him everything in one go, now that I had the courage.

'There's something else,' I said, as steadily as I could. 'I need to introduce myself. I'm Marina Haritakou's son.'

Later, on the way home, I sat down on a dry stone wall for over half an hour, thinking about the catastrophe. I didn't dare phone Effie. What could I say to her? That I'd gone to plead with the creep not to give us away and ended up punching him? I could still feel his beard against my knuckles and the contempt ringing in my ears when he pushed me away like something disgusting that's hardly worth touching, let alone hitting. I would have preferred him to hit me. It would have hurt less. It all happened so quickly, once I told the foreigner who I was. He said something that drove me wild and made me lose my cool completely, because he was way, way out of line. He said: 'At least you're more honest than your mother.' When people are rude about Marináki I go mad. My fist flew at him before I had the chance to think about the consequences and I landed a punch on his chin. I don't regret it. Nobody talks about my mother like that without paying for it. He wasn't expecting it, he almost fell over in surprise, but he's a lot bigger than I am and he grabbed me by the arm with that pincer he has for a hand.

'I could beat the living daylights out of you,' he hissed under his breath.

I didn't try to get away; I knew I'd only look like a coward and make a fool of myself. If he wanted to carry out his threat I wouldn't be able to stop him, but I wasn't afraid. Christ, I was furious. All the feelings I'd kept hidden away for years, anger, misery, frustration, had finally overwhelmed me, and the only thing I was concerned about was crying and further humiliating myself. I didn't cry. Not then. I cried afterwards on that stone wall on my own, when, over and over, I recalled his expression of disgust as he pushed me away.

'Get out of my sight.'

What a creep!

I don't know how long I would have stayed there if my mobile hadn't gone off. I was certain that it was Effie before I saw her name on the screen. I answered her glumly. I had no idea how to protect her the way I'd promised. Should I go and see her father? Maybe the *xénos* had already spoken to him and all hell had broken out. Or to my mother? Or my grandad? I plucked up the courage to tell Effie the worst, but before I had the chance, she herself told me that Anastasákos had actually called her on the landline at home and had set his conditions. He wanted to see us both at the tower. Now!

I waited for her, certain that it was all going to go terribly wrong. I suddenly felt the unbearable burden of all those years of waiting. Years, while Anastasákos had been getting rich and cruising with condoms in the pockets of his jeans, more casually than he carried his cigarettes, and barely remembering, I'm certain, that somewhere on the planet there was a corner called the Mani. I felt old, definitely older than him, even though he was about fifty and I was only fifteen. I felt guilty for having been naughty as a kid. I was a difficult child, angry with my mum that I didn't have a dad, and as a teenager I broke Andreas's skull, and hit a cop at a demonstration. For those things I felt no guilt at all, only relief. But I did feel unbearably guilty when I said that thing to my mother once when we were arguing: 'I've no idea what you thought you'd gain by having me.' And the reply I got was silence, a bitter silence. And I feel bad for all the other times I've behaved towards her like a complete prick.

Now I'd given up pleading with him, come what may, and the die was cast, as Caesar said, and I didn't care any more. We found him sitting on the big millstone with a lighted cigarette, a little star describing its orbit from his lips and back. Poor Effie was a tragic sight. After all, she'd been caught practically naked in the arms of a boy, by her father's best friend – as if that were a crime, as if it weren't the most natural thing! I squeezed her hand to give her courage. The guy must have decided, for his own reasons, to keep our secret. Otherwise why would he call us up here? We waited in silence while he kept us in suspense, the creep! He didn't speak until he'd smoked the cigarette, stubbed it out on the millstone and thrown the butt away into the long grass. I wished it'd still been alight when he threw it, and it had caught fire and burnt him alive there on the millstone. He and his shitty house.

He didn't speak the way most Greek Americans speak, using English words with Greek endings – Gringlish – but proper Greek, with only a slight foreign accent. Now it felt as if he was stripping us naked with those burning eyes of his.

'I'm going to do you a favour and not tell anyone, if you do something for me in return.'

I tried to keep my cool. He had a nerve! I had no intention of joining in his little game. He didn't know anything about me, or what I was capable of – bastard descendent of the Nyklians, with the blood of murderers and brigands flowing in my veins.

'Tell us what you want,' I snapped, 'we didn't come here for a party.'

Instead of getting angry, he smiled, an ironic half-smile.

'You're plucky, considering your position. If her father hears about it, you'll be strung up on the belfry. And your family won't be too happy about it, either.'

'What d'you want?' I asked, cutting him short, since he wasn't saying anything I didn't already know.

He rubbed his tired eyes again. He looked ill. Pale, unshaven, great black rings round his eyes. In any other circumstances I might have felt sorry for him, but this was Odysséas Anastasákos, and I had no pity for him. He was a pain, and a big one. His coming back would set off an entire chain reaction, first and foremost with my mother, whom I didn't dare think about.

'I want you to promise me you'll cut out taking risks,' he said wearily. 'Exchange messages, hold hands, even give one another a kiss once a year on Easter Day to celebrate the Resurrection. You're too young, especially Effie, but you too, since you evidently hadn't thought about contraception. What would you have done if she'd got pregnant? Did you consider that at all? Your actions have consequences, and you're old enough to know that. I won't say a word to anyone, if you give me your word that it won't carry on. I can't collude with two kids making a fool of my best friend, do you understand that?'

Why did you come back? I wanted to shout at him! Why can't you really be lost and dead! Instead you came all this way to lecture me, as if I don't have enough to deal with. I didn't feel like arguing with him, and he knew that very well, but a Haritákos never leaves without a fight, 'out of duty to the guns', as the saying goes.

'We want to go on seeing each other,' I insisted, 'in broad daylight if necessary, and be able to talk. We wouldn't have come here alone if her father wasn't such a stick in the mud and didn't blow up every time he sees us together. I'm like a red rag to him. Why don't you speak to him, and then we'll give you our word.'

'I'd be upset too if you were trying to shag my daughter,' he cut me off. 'Why else would a person like Yiánnis forbid you to talk to each other? And who am I to tell him what he should allow his daughter? I'll see what I can do, but I'm not promising anything. What I do promise, however, and you can be sure I mean it, is to tell him right away if I think you're making a fool of me. And as long as I'm here, I won't let you out of my sight. Off you go now, I have to go next door.'

Effie and I said goodbye to each other there at the millstone. The guy wasn't about to shop us, but that hardly made her feel any better. She was, I think, very embarrassed. Her eyes were full of tears and I held her close. I can't bear sentimental crap, but I had to say it to her. I was worried Anastasákos might get to her somehow, and try to put her off me. He'd be bound to hear all about me from Kosmás, as soon as the funeral was over.

'I love you, Effie. Don't take any notice of him. If I just wanted to fool around, there are any number of girls I could be with. But I'm here with you, because I love you.'

I was shaking, though it wasn't cold. She clung to me and cried.

I wanted to cry too, but I couldn't because she might have broken down completely. She needed to feel that I was strong, even if I wasn't. I stroked her cheek and whispered sweet nothings. How all those words came to my lips I have no idea, I patted her like a baby. I wasn't going to let that creep separate us, no way. The thought that he would probably be at Effie's house after the funeral, and might poison her with all the usual rubbish about me made me even more determined.

'I don't mind that we didn't do it, it isn't important. I don't mind waiting. The fact that you love me is the only thing that matters. Don't listen to them, *moró mou*. Without your love I'm as lost as Anastasákos.'

'Of course I love you, Alexi, otherwise ...' She didn't go on, but I knew what she meant: 'I love you, that's why I come with you to the tower. I love you, that's why I kiss you in lonely places, that's why I was within an inch of letting you make love to me on the millstone, that's why I let myself be humiliated when Anastasákos caught me half-naked in his house.' And I didn't even see him coming! I'm biting my lip now to stop myself crying again. Effie is burning inside me, burning ... Nothing else matters, not the creep, or her father, or my own mother. I'm in despair, and yet I'm crazy with joy. In my despairing joy I finally think about what happened today. Dimákaina was dead, and her lap, which used to smell of warm baked bread, was about to be covered with earth. Her 'lost boy' was back now. He had barely set foot in the Mani and was already making my life difficult.

When I got home I met *Pappoú* at the door just as he was going out to the wake.

'Your mother phoned, she's coming home tomorrow.'

'Anastasákos is here too, I saw him just now at the wake.'

'He's most welcome,' was my grandfather's cool reply.

No, he's most unwelcome! There had been so much going on that I hadn't even told my mother he was back. Should I call her now? She would be fast asleep. Should I wake her? I decided it was better not to. She might not get to sleep again, and it's harder to cope with problems when you're tired. She had that advantage over Anastasákos. She slept; he never slept. She had told me he'd had a hard life, that he had nightmares ever since he was a child. Judging by the black rings under his eyes and his habit of rubbing them, he clearly still had a problem. So what did it mean, his coming back? Nothing good, I was certain of it.

# Aretí

I WAS FEELING ANXIOUS and as usual I couldn't sleep, so I got up.
Lou didn't even notice, she was fast asleep and had stopped worry-
ing about what I do at night when I'm awake. I put on the creased
suit I'd left in a crumpled heap on the chair, put my tie in my pocket
and went out. It was raining. Constant rain is the bane of a Boston
summer – you can't step outside without an umbrella. When I got
home I had a bath and then sat at my computer to take another look
at the data John had sent over. We'd agreed there was an error somewhere, but I couldn't find it, and neither could he. I only noticed the
message on the answerphone an hour later, at five in the morning,
twelve noon in Greece. It was brief. 'Call me as soon as you can,
Odysséa, it's urgent.'

I lifted the receiver with a tightening of the stomach: something
had happened, the message was left at eleven our time, that is six in
the morning over there. I phoned Yiánnis who told me that *Thía*
Aretí had been taken to Athens, and the doctors weren't optimistic.
Uncle Nikifóros was desperately worried. Maria, Yiánnis's wife, was
taking them to Athens, but she couldn't stay; she needed to be back
in the Mani. She would try to visit them again as soon as she could.

Aretí had been fighting cancer for years, she wouldn't hear of going
into a private hospital for the care she deserves, and her coming over
to Boston was out of the question. 'I want to die in my own country,'
she had said. I couldn't bear to think of my aunt dying and never
hearing her voice again. My homeland only exists in the sound of her
voice: 'Are you eating properly, *koróna mou?* You've forgotten about
us over there, and I want to see you before I die.'

Left to myself, I probably never would have made up my mind to go, but now events had taken over and I needed to get back. There was so much to do before leaving, because I wouldn't know how long I'd be gone. I went into the office with a splitting headache. And my dizzy spells were back. I asked Lou for a coffee and called everyone into the boardroom. John wasn't in yet and wasn't due to come in at all, I'd completely forgotten. Their daughter Ellen, my 'niece', had played in a big concert the previous night, with the Boston Symphony Orchestra, no less, and we were celebrating with a dinner tonight.

The vision of ethereal Ellen in a long formal skirt and white lace top, with her fair hair tied back, holding her violin, banished my gloomy thoughts for a while. It wasn't a small thing for the child to be chosen at such a young age, only fourteen, and to play with one of the best symphony orchestras in the world.

I postponed my phone call to the Petersens till after nine. Lou informed me that no one else I wanted to see was in yet either, except for Takanki, the Japanese. I have the feeling that something's going on between him and Lou and I hope it's true – it's about time she moved on from me. I told her so yesterday that she has my blessing. I meant it for the best, but she was hurt, I could see.

'Are you in such a hurry to get rid of me, Odysséa?'

'Surely you should be in a hurry to get away,' I replied, with a bitter smile.

While I was waiting for Takanki, I looked again at the data John had sent me and spotted the error – it was right there staring me in the face. I had drunk my first cup of coffee and was on to my second, my brain was beginning to clear. My uncle didn't have a mobile, he wasn't a fan of technology, so I couldn't reach him on the telephone. I'd told Yiánnis that I would come to Athens as soon as I possibly could.

By a quarter past nine the others had arrived at the office and I told them I was planning a trip away. Lou looked surprised. I shared my workload between the five of them and told them John would be in charge. I sent them away quickly. I had very little time. When I told Lou about the phone call from Greece she offered to come with me, but I said no. I didn't want anyone with me. Each person's hell is his private affair. We could take a trip together some other time, there'd be nothing for her to do, trailing around hospitals and cemeteries. At that last word, the fear, lurking since I'd heard Yiánnis's message, homed in on me, and Lou left me alone. She understood.

I didn't phone John after nine in the end, since I was going round there anyway for supper, and I didn't want to spoil their evening. I sent an armful of flowers to my niece early in the day: 'Congratulations, minx.' My present – one of the four hundred or so Stradivariuses in the world – was an investment in her future, and I was planning to give it to her that evening. Maggie would be bound to complain that I'm spoiling the child. I could make up something about tax exemptions for money spent on charitable causes, and maybe hint that I won it at an auction. John would never buy that, of course, he knows me too well. I would never bid for a violin, especially since I couldn't tell a Strad from the fiddles they play at *panegyria* at home.

At twelve, I ate a small sandwich, splashed water over my stinging eyes and phoned Yiánnis.

'Isn't there a phone I can reach them on?'

'Where? In the corridor of the Evangelismos hospital?'

'Jesus Christ, Yiánni! Couldn't you take her anywhere else?'

'You know what they're like, Odysséa. They said she'll get a bed in the morning. The hospital was taking emergencies, and they didn't have anywhere to put all the people. We gave the doctor something. As soon as she gets on to a ward, Maria will phone you and give you the number.'

'Whatever the time!'

'Whatever the time, but hurry and come. I don't want to frighten you, but …'

At half-past seven that evening I picked Lou up from her house, and we rang the Petersen's bell a little before eight. I was wearing a suit again, in honour of Ellen, and Lou looked very beautiful, in a décolleté evening dress. Her shoulders shone like alabaster, her hair was dead straight, black and thick. Why couldn't I love this woman? I was insane, I knew it, and when I saw her like that I recognised the fact. The Strad was resting in my arms, in its case, inside a white box with a pink bow, to make it more of a surprise.

Ellen opened the door and flung her arms around my neck. Lou gave her present first, a small box from an expensive jeweller in town. I recognised the make, I had bought our wedding rings from there and the rock I gave her when I proposed. Now that we'd 'separated' my wedding ring was locked away in the safe at my bank and Lou had hers somewhere. I had asked her to keep it, along with the engagement ring; it would always represent my love for her. I loved her as you love your sister – except that you don't sleep with your sister – or the way that you love the familiarity of your own home, a place where you can wander about just as you like, half-naked, naked, wearing slippers.

Lou had bought Ellen some earrings. She tried them on and admired them in the mirror, and then she picked up my box, feigning nonchalance.

'It's clothes,' she said, playing our usual guessing game.

'Wrong.'

She looked at me searchingly.

'Shoes?'

I shook my head.

'I don't know, I give up.'

'All right, open it.'

She opened the parcel and took out the case. Then she let out a cry. The name Stradivarius was clearly visible on the instrument and she knows me well. I would never buy a fake. She held it in her hands with extreme care and lightly plucked at the strings, her eyes shining.

'Play something, *sousouráda*, play something just for me.'

'I'll play a piece that suits you, uncle, better than anything I know,' she said, and picked up the bow.

I don't know what it was she played. We all listened in astonishment. It was a very melancholy piece and she was right, it did suit me. The sorrowful music floated through the house like a *moiroloy*.

Ten days passed before I left. Things kept cropping up at the last minute, but in the end there was no choice, I had to get on the plane. A bed had been found on a ward for my aunt, but it wasn't easy for us to communicate by telephone – one phone between six patients – as it was constantly engaged. In the end I spoke to my uncle. 'She asks for you every time she opens her eyes,' said Uncle Nikifóros. 'She wants to tell you something, I don't know how aware she is, she doesn't understand me a lot of the time.' I hated to think of them thrown on to that ward without a relative to help them. Yiánnis was having problems with his business, and he depended on it for his livelihood, so he couldn't just leave everything and rush off to Athens, to be where I should have been. He and his wife had already done so much.

I landed at the new airport at the end of June, early in the afternoon, and went straight to the hospital in a rented Mercedes like the one I drove in Boston. Lou had organised everything to perfection. She booked me into the Intercontinental just in case, but there was no need for it. As soon as I arrived in her room the old lady knew I was there. She opened her eyes when I came in, as if she'd been waiting. Then she embraced me, just as she had done to comfort me when I was a child. Her arms were thin and wasted now from her long illness. She looked at me lovingly and wept.

'Forgive me, *koróna mou*.' The frantic clutch of her hand loosened; she let her head rest in my arms and passed away.

We called the doctor, and the nurses ushered us outside. I saw white-gowned figures bending over the tiny heap of bones that was once Aunt Aretí. They attempted to resuscitate her, but it was too late. Uncle Nikifóros broke down in tears. It was the first time I had ever seen him cry. I hugged him and kept saying 'forgive me' again and again, just like my aunt had done. My only living relatives in this world, abandoned in this hideous place, while I was giving a three-million-dollar violin to a fourteen-year-old girl.

I found an undertaker's office, or to be exact it found me, and made arrangements for the funeral the next day. Then we set off for the Mani.

My uncle had changed, there was almost nothing left of his once-proud figure. And he must have been thinking the same about me.

'You've gone grey, *koróna mou*,' he said, and when I nodded he just stared out of the window in silence, and I could tell that he was trying to hide his tears. I wanted to cry too, but I couldn't. My head was throbbing and my eyes were hurting, I hadn't slept for almost forty-eight hours and I felt as if all my past nightmares were coming to life.

We made the journey almost without stopping, with the bitter taste of nausea and grief in our mouths. Coming down on the approach to the Mani I saw that old sign: 'The Mani cannot be divided.' Some things don't change even after seventeen years, or after thirty-seven, or ever.

At the entrance to the village a little curtain waved cheerfully at me in the breeze from a window on the third floor of the Haritakos's tower.

I parked next to the old man's house. There were things to do. His house to be prepared, the priest told, the bell rung to let the village know that Aretí had died. She deserved to leave us with respect and dignity, as she had lived her life, even though she had worked like a dog with barely a change of clothing, as the saying goes. She had never asked for anything and always gave generously of everything she had: cakes, sympathy, *synclino*, eggs, affection and love.

Inside, the house was already spotless, presumably Maria's work. The first to hear the news and come running was Pavlákos, the ex cop. I left my uncle with him and went next door to my own house, to splash some water over my face. As I walked along the path by the millstone the dry grass around the threshold was almost as high as my waist. It looked just as abandoned as when I had first returned all those years ago, and I felt just as destitute. I turned on the tap in the bathroom and let the water run clear. I stumbled over the tables in the sitting room on the way out, which served me right for having the electricity cut off. Luckily I found my mother's old paraffin lamp and lit it, and it was then I saw two kids fooling around in the yard. How could I have guessed that the boy was her son and the girl Yiánnis's daughter, both of them quite evidently determined to go all the way that evening.

Some things never change, but children, it seems, do. I was the same age as this boy when I first left for America, and I wouldn't have dared go off alone with a girl like that. Not that we didn't all want to. This lad in my garden had his mother's doughtiness and all the pluck of the Haritakaíoi. You can say what you like about them, but wimps they are not. He must have known that Yiánnis would go ballistic if he found out they'd been together at my house this evening, and it obviously wasn't the first time.

I could see the boy clearly in the light, and now that I think about it, he was very tall for a Haritákos. They tend to be of medium height and stocky, whereas this boy was tall and slender, like a young cypress, a beautiful boy, with his mother's pearly smile and the same dimple in his cheek. With all the arrogance of youth. Like in Savvópoulos's song: *eimai dexarcheis, sas yamó ta lykeia* – I'm sixteen, and you can go fuck your schools. He clearly cared for Yiánnis's daughter, and I was touched by his self-sacrifice in trying to protect her. There was something in his eyes. A provocative look that seemed to come straight from my own haunted past. Because of that, I didn't feel like mentioning it to Yiánnis, not just because everyone was sitting up at my aunt's wake right next door, but because of the boy. Nonetheless, he looked like he needed a talking to, and I gave it to him myself.

The *moiroloy* had begun next door and I went to rejoin the wake. I had grown up with the *moiroloya*. When my father died, my mother, tearing her hair and scratching her breast over my father's lifeless body, gave me to understand then and there, and with complete certainty, that there was no life beyond the grave. It was all here on this earth, death, hell and paradise, here, all of it. Because if there had been another life and my father had gone somewhere else, no power, not God, nor the devil, would have stopped him coming back to help her in her grief. Her sobs and the *moiroloy* she sang for my father still keep me awake at night. Or they wake me up when I'm asleep. Which is rarely.

*Where can I find you, where*
*is the mountain, where is the cliff*
*to hurl myself down on the black earth below*
*and shatter my heart for you …*

Now Potítsa had appeared on the terrace, like a ship under sail, and I knew that we were done for. We were in for the entire Anastasákiad, beginning with that old lament of my mother's. I prayed fervently that someone or something would stop her. But of course she carried on regardless, taking her place beside the dead woman. No one in the Mani would ever stop a chief mourner.

But she didn't begin with my mother's *moiroloy*. Instead she began with a lament for Vassilis, Aretí and Nikifóros's dead son.

*Come on, get up now, Aretí*
*I've a few words to say to you*
*of things that happened long ago*
*to comfort us a bit while you*
*go off to find your Vassilaki,*
*who's waited thirty years and eight,*
*and left old Nikifóros here alone.*
*He wants his mother's kiss*

*he wants news of his father.*
*Vassilis mou, get up and look,*
*here she is, here comes your mother.*

The other women joined in, relatives and fellow villagers, but I could tell that they were angry she had come and taken the lead without asking anyone; she was always a renegade, was Potítsa, and always uncompromising. She and *Thía* Aretí had been my mother's best friends. Potítsa, whom no married woman in her right mind would allow over the threshold. But my mother, Fotiní, wasn't afraid, she trusted her husband. And she was right, my father never looked at another woman. For women like Potítsa he had nothing but the profoundest disdain.

*Let it out, Aretí, let out a cry*
*and tell Fotiní to come out of Hades*
*and stand like a star at the gate*
*and see that her boy has come …*

Now she was remembering my mother, and I prepared myself to listen to my entire life story issuing from her lips. Like my namesake Odysseus hearing his own life story sung by Demodocus, on the island of the Phaeacians. Except that in Greek tragedy there's always a *deus ex machina* to rescue the situation.

*Ah Fotiní, zargana mou*
*get up and look at your darling son*
*his hair's grown white*
*in that lonely* xenitiá …

Potítsa went on. I would dearly have loved to be in the wildest *xenitiá* possible at that moment, the foreign city where my life had cast me among strangers, not remembering, not hurting, not existing! I wanted to cry out from my innermost being. Instead I found myself whispering to my neighbour: 'She could have left that last bit out.'

'She's right, you have gone grey,' someone else replied.

I turned round. I knew who it was without looking, I remembered her voice well, but it wasn't just her voice. It was my blood, churning through my veins, my body that remembered her. The tips of my fingers had touched that neck. Marina Haritákou! There I was looking again into her astonishing brown eyes that go dark and then golden, depending on her mood. 'I look at you and I feel drawn like a moth to a flame,' I had said once, and it was true. There'd been nothing left of me by the end but the tiniest drop of dignity, and I'd paid for that all my life.

I was somewhat comforted by her seeming even more at a loss than me. Apparently her son, for his own reasons, hadn't told her I was back, and she could barely conceal her surprise and shock, whereas I maintained my customary mask of indifference. I had spotted the little curtain waving in her open window earlier, and I'd met the boy in my garden, so I was more or less prepared to see her at some point. With impressive coolness, she offered me her condolences, and before I had a chance to ask her why she was in my uncle's house on this day of all days, with my family in mourning, I saw her go and hug my uncle. She whispered who knows what to him, and then the old man let himself go, like a little child, and wept. She clearly wasn't just any village woman coming to grieve and pay her respects to the dead. She seemed to be a member of my family now, and a loved one. I had obviously missed a few episodes.

Later, when the two of us sat drinking coffee in the silent house, feeling as though at any moment the door would open and Aretí would come in, the old man bowed his head as if in shame and told me that all the while he was in Athens by the side of his dying wife, Marina was the only one who stood by him, no one else. She sat up all night next to my aunt, sent my uncle home so he could have a wash and lie-down, and took him food every evening. And before she went to hospital, whenever Aretí needed X-rays and doctors, she stayed in Marina's house in Athens. He drank her health with water, as they say, every day he held her dear. Nikiforos told me this one morning, a few days after the funeral, when I was staying with him. My house next door had needed a thorough clean, but more than that, Nikiforos needed me and I needed him, and I didn't want to leave him on his own, not this time.

It seems that they had bumped into Marina Haritákou on the ward at the Evangelismos. She was with a seventeen-year-old girl from some orphanage and by coincidence they had been put in the same room. My uncle hadn't slept for two nights, so Marina sent him to her home in a taxi. Her father was there, old Michális Haritákos, and so was the boy, a bright, lively lad, about seven or eight at the time. Haritákos was clearly besotted with his grandson and proud of his achievements. He was top of his class at school and had been swimming since the age of four. The house was full of photographs of the boy; toys and books everywhere, no sign of anything from the past.

'Up till then,' my uncle confided to me, 'I'd assumed that Haritákos had taken it badly that his daughter had a child like that, unmarried, you know. Nowadays you take no notice of these things, but for us it's a big disgrace. However, I was wrong. And then I saw it from his perspective. He had lost his own two sons, and his old lady, and spent years in prison. And then suddenly this boy appeared. 'Nikifóre,' he said to me, 'I wasn't expecting a gift like this to come now, at the very end of my life.'

After that the Haritakaíoi had looked after my uncle like a member of the family. They did everything I didn't do. They put him up in their house, he slept in Marina's room, the boy made him coffee in the afternoon, spilling half of it on the way but never mind. Meanwhile the poisoner stayed over in the hospital by my aunt's bedside. 'It's no trouble for me,' she would say, 'I'd be sitting here anyway to look after the girl.'

'What was her relationship with that girl?'

'Nothing. Marina works in an orphanage, without pay. She spends hours there. The girl had no one else, and Marina…'

'Maybe she was atoning for her sins.'

My uncle bowed his head again and I felt I shouldn't have said it. He answered me in the words of Christ even though he isn't religious.

'He who is without sin cast the first stone. Michális and I talked a lot about old times, about you, and things that had happened more recently. "I don't mind about any of it," he said, "I don't want to remember. I only care about one thing. The boy."'

So that was how the Haritakaíoi had wheedled their way into my family, the boy must be in and out of my tower house all the time, and his mother in and out of my aunt's, taking my place. I had no right to condemn anyone for anything, no one takes your place if you're there to defend it, and no one was expecting me to come back, not even my aunt. I think she knew I couldn't face it. I didn't have the courage. In fact I wonder why she so insisted on seeing me. You don't expect to see a person who has been lost and dead to you for years. And I had been dead for years. Killed off one morning seventeen years ago at the tower house. By the poisoner!

## Koutalídes me méli

THERE'S NO FUNERAL WITHOUT laughter and no wedding without tears, as they say, and so we were standing there chatting at the wake, when my old teacher came up in conversation in the context of Marina's adolescent son. Apparently Yiánnis knows all about him and his daughter Effie, although he doesn't know how far they've gone.

'You were the same at their age. Anarchic!' he said. 'Do you remember Yioúli Petrea sending you out of the classroom? Poor Petrea still remembers you.'

Sure she remembers me, and she hadn't forgotten my insult. She'd harboured it like a true Maniot. I had loathed her Ancient Greek lessons, and except for maths and physics and chemistry, I didn't open a book. Mr Kostákos, my maths teacher, asked my father to persuade me to try a little bit with the other subjects: 'With a brain like his it's a shame not to study.' That evening, after dinner when he was smoking his usual cigarette, my father told me very seriously that I would definitely be going to university, I wasn't going to get out of it, so I might as well try a little harder, and save us all the expense and the bother of retakes. It had never crossed my mind that I might leave the Mani, I loved the village, my friends, my father's hard work as a farmer. And I knew that to study I'd have to go to Athens, which required money, and we didn't have any to spare. I remonstrated, but he wouldn't listen. 'Hardly a problem,' he said. 'When I was young we had problems – war, starvation, civil war, and during my grandfather's time we had the vendettas. Do your best, and don't worry about anything else. Just get away and live a better life. That's all I wish for you, my boy.' So I promised I would try.

That afternoon at school I was so bored I couldn't keep still.

Yioúli Petrea had been telling us about a speech in *Antigone*, whose authorship is disputed by scholars. Antigone protests that she would never have defied the law to bury her brothers, if it had only been her husband or child who had died. She could always find another husband and have another child, but she would never have another brother, since her parents were in Hades. Would Sophocles have ever written anything so harsh and so hard to digest?

Petrea then read out the famous *Moiroloy of the Poisoner,* which I had heard before from the lips of my grandmother, who was a great storyteller. The woman is lamenting the death of her brother-in-law, her husband and her brother. The first two have killed her brother, and she then poisons them both to avenge her brother's murder. She stays to watch them as they die, and then she goes to her father-in-law, with no qualms at all, and confesses her deed. 'I did what they did, and I got justice.' In this tradition there is no love greater than the love of a sister, said Petrea. But I didn't pay any attention, I was only a kid and it seemed highly unlikely that my mother would rate my father and me less than she rated Uncle Sarándos, her brother who left for America years ago and forgot all about us. Only years later did I realise how wise were the words of Sophocles and the poisoner's *moiroloy*. I was forewarned and I ignored it, although my poisoner didn't do me the favour of killing me outright. Instead she chose to poison my life. If I hadn't met her I might have come to love Lou as she deserved, I wouldn't have hurt her so much, I might have had children and a family. It might have been my own daughter holding her Stradivarius in the Boston Symphony Hall.

Anyway, that day in the *Antigone* lesson I was unbelievably bored.

'If I take some burning oil up the tower, will you persuade Petrea to walk under it?' I asked Yiánnis, who was sitting next to me.

He nudged me to shut up, the teacher was looking at us, but it was too late.

Petrea left her desk and walked over. She was short, round and spectacled, and her face looked very comical when she was angry.

'Is Anastasákos bothering you, Yiánni?'

My friend was always Yiánnis, and I was Anastasákos, the only child in class she called by his surname. There was an ancient Odysséas Anastasákos in fact, a distant relative of mine, who had taken part in the battle of Verga against Ibrahim and had left his bones there – there is even a *moiroloy* to prove it. But why should she care about that? I knew she disliked me, and with reason: I loathed both her and her lessons, I was provocative to the point of delinquency. I didn't hide it. I was fifteen.

My friend tried to cover for me. 'No,' he said, 'he was just asking about the translation.' Naturally she didn't believe him. She peered at me through her glasses. 'Really. Have you decided to do a translation, Anastasáko?'

I didn't answer either yes or no. I wasn't a diplomat, I'd been taught by my father to stand up to bullies, even if they were teachers, but I had also promised him not to get into trouble. For the next three years, I would do everything possible so that I could study maths. But this teacher had other ideas.

'When I speak to you, I want you to look me in the eye and answer me, Anastasáko.' Then she gave me a lecture about people who go to school and show no interest in it, which is their right obviously, but they had no right to bother other children who have goals and who are there to learn.

'So? I asked you a question,' she said finally.

I admitted that I had no intention of doing the translation, I had no desire to waste my time on this useless subject, the hunting season was about to start, and it made more sense to catch partridges, at least you could eat them, whereas being forced to recite a dead language had no point in it at all.

'I know teaching brings in your groceries, miss,' I said as an afterthought, 'but you'll get them anyway, whatever I do, so don't pretend that you care about me.'

There followed a deathly hush, and I couldn't believe what I'd just said. She pointed to the door.

'Out!' she said, white with fury. 'How dare you insult the language of your ancestors in that way, useless boy! And tomorrow I want to see your father, here. First thing!'

I gathered my books together in silence. My friend was staring at me in astonishment, and so was Kalliroe, the girl who sat in front with the little mole on her neck a couple of centimetres below her ear. I used to gaze at her for hours. That memory is etched in my brain far more than any lesson, more even than the games of football in the playground. Now everyone's eyes were on me as I left and slammed the door behind me, and the crash sounded like an explosion in the silence of the autumn afternoon.

When the bell rang, Yiánnis came out and found me sitting at the bus stop, taking deep breaths to calm down. I was staring at an army of ants, carrying off the last seeds in time for winter, one after the other, in an endless line. Carefully I stretched out my foot to block their way. I didn't want to squash any, and after struggling to get over it, they made a diversion and continued on the same route towards their goal. The anthill. I bent down and picked up a stick and began playing with the minuscule creatures, creating obstacles for them, which they stubbornly bypassed to continue along the same predetermined journey to its end. Even if I squashed some of them – I knew because I'd done it before – nothing would change, neither the route, nor the goal. Even if a mountain popped up in front of them they would go round it or just over it, nothing would stop them. Tiny creatures. Heroic.

My friend was staring at me in silence.

'Look, Yiánni, how like ants we are,' I said. 'It's easy enough to crush an ant if you're big enough. But people aren't ants, and when a person is crushed there are consequences.'

I remember the ramshackle bus juddering up the steep rocky hills to the villages, the sun burning through the windows, autumn now well on its way and still no rain, the sea under a haze, indistinguishable like a light grey cloud through the dust. The bus was full of children talking and laughing, some standing in the aisle, others sitting, nobody had heard of seat belts and safety regulations then – the very existence of the bus was a luxury, giving us access to school, even in a region as remote and inaccessible as the Mani. I didn't feel like talking, but Yiánnis asked me: 'What will you say to your father, Odysséa?' I thought for a bit and said, 'I'll tell him about the ants.' His father, Kostís Mitsikoyiánnis, was strict and liable to beat his son for much lesser things than being thrown out of the classroom. My father on the other hand had never raised a hand against me. It was my mother who lashed out at me if I was naughty when I was little, and she could still catch me. Later I would jump out of the window and run away until she calmed down. I was no less in awe of my father because he never hit me. I was afraid of him, I respected him, and I loved him.

Nine of us got off the bus at the village square. Me, Yiánnis, Kosmás the son of the *kafetzi*, Sotíris Haritákos, Pantelis Leoúsis, the two Kaloyeroyiánnis boys, and Athena Dimakitsa and Maria Petropoulitsa, who were the only girls. There was no one waiting for us at the bus stop except for Pantelis's sister Maria, known as the *kolaoúzo*, the limpet, because she never left his side. It was the olive season, the adults were all away picking olives, and we went along to help them after school, before it got dark. All, that is, except Kosmás, who went to help his father in the *kafeneíon*.

That day I jumped down from the path by the millstone, opened the door – never locked until I locked it when I left for America – and went into the cool kitchen. My mother had left a covered plate of food on the table. Fried cod with greens. I sighed with relief that it wasn't chickpeas again. I made short work of my food, but the misery stuck in my throat like a fishbone.

By this time my parents had picnicked under the olives, and were hurrying to pick as much as they could before nightfall. And now my father would have to waste a day of harvesting to go to Areopolis and see my teacher, leaving my mother to thrash at the trees on her own. What use is one pair of hands? The answer I suppose depends on whose hands you're talking about. My mother worked tirelessly all day long. I think it must be from her that I inherited my inexhaustible energy. She got up before us, prepared our breakfast and the lunch we took with us – usually cheese, olives and bread. Then she woke us up and went out to see to the livestock: chickens, goats (three) and a pig. While we got dressed and ate, she made our beds, washed the dishes, drank her tea on the run, stuffed a piece of bread in her mouth and went out with my father to work.

After your mother dies, it hurts to remember the smallest things. That afternoon, once I'd eaten, I left the plates where they were on the table and went straight out again. I could have washed them, could at least have carried them to the sink so she wouldn't have to deal with them when she got back. It didn't occur to me though. It was women's work and she would do it in the evening when she'd finished with the men's work that she did all day. I found them down in the fields, my mother separating the olives from the leaves, sacking them up, heaving them away, my father picking from the higher branches where she couldn't reach. The sweetest image in my world was the smile that lit up my mother's face whenever she saw me coming back from school. And she had a beautiful smile, my mother: '*Kalóstone*! Look who's here!' I took the sack from her and shook it well to settle the olives and make room for more, tied it and lifted it on to my back.

My father finished with the ones high up, jumped down off the tree on to the rocks, lit a cigarette, inhaled luxuriously and then asked me: 'How was school?'

If it's to happen, let it be quick, I thought to myself.

'Petrea wants to see you at school in the morning,' I said all in one breath.

I remember the way he looked at me, and then threw his cigarette on to the ground.

'Grab the end of that canvas, will you,' he said. I knew what that meant. Work first. We could talk about it all later, after dinner. We set to, to get the rest of the daylight. When we got home I went up to my room on the third floor of the tower to do my homework. My mother made coffee, which they drank together by the millstone. It was their favourite time of day, sitting there sharing the silence as it grew dark, now and again exchanging a word or two, about work and everyday difficulties, the eternally low price of olive oil, when would the goats have their kids, how much did we owe to the Agricultural Bank and to Kosmás the *kafetzís*, who kept a grocery store along with his coffee house. In the summers when the tourists arrived, my father would work in his shop. That way we had some extra income, because the livestock and the olives weren't enough for us to live on. We planted anything that would grow in the meagre earth between the rocks: we had beehives, farm animals, olive trees, we worked from dawn to dusk every day and barely managed to keep on top of things. During my last three summers at home, my father's friend who owned a sweetshop employed me too, as a waiter, and my mother was left to manage everything else on her own. That was my friend Miltiades's dad, who had married a girl with this sweetshop in Gytheio. My father called him the 'son-in-law'.

'How are you, son-in-law?'

'Worse than a flayed fox.'

Miltiades was two years older than me; we worked together and competed for speed and tips. When the day's work ended, we skimmed stones over the water to see whose went furthest and bounced most often. He always won, and I had to hold back the tears, because I was an only child and hadn't learnt to lose.

At that time I felt my parents' love wrapped around me like a bright aura, but I'd never seen them touch each other, or kiss each other. All that was out of bounds when I was with them – I guess it happened behind closed doors in their bedroom, and it must definitely have happened, since apart from having me my mother was pregnant five more times. Instead of caresses, my father gave her tender looks and silences, and his one and only compliment: 'Ah Fotiní, you're a magician!'

That evening after my quarrel with Petrea, while my father went as usual to the *kafeneíon,* my mother prepared dinner, took care of the animals, swept, dusted, did the washing, and got out clean clothes for the morning. By the time my father got back, the table was laid, the food ready, the house clean. On a plate, hidden behind the bread basket, were *koutalídes:* spoonfuls of batter, fried to a golden crisp in olive oil, and covered with honey.

It was thirty-four years ago and I still remember that silent dinner, struggling to swallow my lentils, which didn't go down easily at the best of times. I was afraid and deeply ashamed. I had promised not to get into trouble and I hadn't kept my word, and that, to my father, was an unforgivable sin. He wouldn't punish me, he only had to purse his lips scornfully for my world to fall apart, and for me to feel and believe that I was useless. Petrea had already said I was, shouting it out in front of the whole class that afternoon.

We finished eating, he pushed his plate away, and I knew that the moment had come – impossible to avoid one's fate. I handed him his packet of cigarettes and his lighter. He lit up and inhaled deeply.

I told him everything word for word, it never occurred to me to lie to him. I wouldn't stoop that low and I wouldn't dare. Lies have short legs, he always said, meaning that sooner or later he would find out and then God help me! Nothing was worse than telling a lie to get out of a scrape. It wasn't manly, he always said.

My father told me to go to Yioúli Petrea the next day and apologise.

'I can't do that, father,' I said boldly. 'It wasn't my fault. However hard I try she's always so sarcastic, she just doesn't like me.'

He was secretly proud of me for saying that, I think, but still determined to tell me off.

'So you try, do you? Have you done that translation?'

I hadn't done the translation and he knew it. I bowed my head, it was hard not to cry, but I didn't. My father didn't like me snivelling like a girl. He lit a second cigarette to give me a chance to swallow my pride and come to terms with my defeat, and then he said: 'Maybe you don't try hard enough. Now, when you go upstairs to finish your homework, I want you to prepare for this Petrea woman's lesson, so that when I go and see her tomorrow I can tell her you're trying. You'll apologise to her, whatever you think of her lessons. It was wrong to say that she only does it for the wages. Do you understand me? No wage is worth being spoken to like that. I want you to give her the apology you owe me, for not trying as you said you would. And don't worry, she won't be sarcastic to you again.'

I took it, willing or not, and he patted my head with his enormous hand.

'Don't bother about stupid things that don't matter. You have a goal, and that's to study. Don't let anyone put you off your goal, you owe it to yourself to succeed.'

'Like the ants? They aim for the anthill and they don't let anyone stand in their way.'

He laughed.

'Like the ants.'

I was about to get up when my mother, who'd been watching us in silence all this time, put the plate of honey *koutalídes* on the table in front of us.

'Come on, let's sweeten things up a little,' she said, and my father gave her one of those looks he reserved only for her.

'Ah Fotiní, you're a magician! Come on, my boy, the bitterest things are sweetened with honey.'

Ah, those *koutalídes* with honey, and the bread dunked in oil, the sweet fried *lalánges, díples, kayianás* with salted ham, all those tastes from my country, so closely connected in my mind with my mother's caress and my father's calloused hands. People don't know how to eat over there in *xenitiá*, they don't dip their bread in oil, they don't know how to caress you with a look, how to communicate in silence, to share a crust, and laughter and tears. It was dreadful in the beginning to be so far away on my own, living with my aunt, the *Americána*, who knew so well how to make you feel unwanted and out of place. I deserved it, after the calamity I brought down on us, I deserved that and everything else I got. I was no good, I was worthless, useless, a liar, a deserter and a coward. But still, there's truth in that saying of my father's: 'Even the bitterest things are sweetened with honey.' Perhaps that's why, even now, in my most stressful moments, I dive into a shop selling Middle-Eastern sweetmeats and stuff myself with syrupy cakes!

# Potítsa

'WHEREVER YOU GO IN THE WORLD, you may forget all the others but you'll never forget me!' Potítsa, my mother's best friend, whose long blond hair was tucked into a headscarf that kept slipping off, who always forgot to do up the buttons on her shirt. It was my last week, the day before I left for Athens to fly to America. Miltiades's father had undertaken the bleak task of getting me to the airport. I tried to dissuade him but he insisted. It was his last duty towards my parents, he said, to put me on the airplane and get me safely away. My mother, before the tragic accident that took her life, and that of the taxi driver bringing her back from Gytheio, had prepared everything for my flight. Now there was nothing to do but leave.

I was lying on my bed on the third floor of the tower, feeling as 'miserable as a beached mackerel,' as my mother would say, and allowing *Thía* Potítsa to guide me once more along the mystical paths of pleasure and ecstasy. I had lived through a tragedy worse than anyone knew, even Potítsa. I might perhaps have coped with the deaths of my parents, I think, as something unavoidable, but the burden of my own guilt was unbearable and I was close to a breakdown.

She was as white and inviting as a loaf of new bread, her body all curves, her breasts nudging open her shirt, eager to hold me in her arms, which smelled of wild roses and mint. I lost myself in the turmoil of Potítsa's passion and, ashamed as I am to say it, I forgot my misery. If only for a while.

'You're so beautiful, *Thía*,' I whispered boldly once I had eventually found my voice, four days after she first took me by the hand and led me up the steep stairway leading to my bed. The most erotic image I could ever bring to mind many years later was the sway of her shapely legs as I followed her, trancelike, without the will to resist. Aunt Potítsa! It was thanks to her that I learnt where to find my only consolation – apart from syrupy cakes – when things got tough.

'Do you like me, *koróna mou*?' I liked her very much! She often came by our house, and I couldn't help looking at her. 'Your son's a little cockerel,' she would say to my mother. 'His mouth still smells of breastmilk,' was my mother's brisk reply, while my grandmother looked daggers at Potítsa. 'That devil woman you keep bringing will close your house,' she would say afterwards. My mother never exchanged one cross word with her mother-in-law in all those years of living under the same roof, but my grandmother didn't like Potítsa, and wasn't keen on her coming and going. 'In our day women like that were tied across a donkey and led around the village.' A woman's honour in the Mani was seen as protecting the honour of the entire family. Leading her around on a donkey would have been the least of it. Women like Potítsa were sometimes butchered like lambs in 'honour killings', looked upon leniently in court.

But Potítsa had no reason to be afraid. Who would be likely to kill her? All the men in her family were dead and her husband, Ilias Nikolakos, was terrified of her. She had three sons, all younger than me, none of them her husband's, so she told me herself. Lías was impotent – he had never touched her. Apart from their wedding night when she had waited for him in their bedroom with the lamp turned out, a virgin wearing her bridal nightgown, the sheet pulled up to her neck, frightened and excited about the miracle she would know when it came. He solved the small 'anatomical' problem with his fingers so that she wouldn't be able to prove anything afterwards, and to give him the bloody sheet to bear witness. And he never laid a hand on her again, neither to caress, nor to clout her. The first because he didn't want to, and the second because he didn't dare.

I had learned Potítsa's story from mutterings at home, scattered conversations here and there, and obscene talk in the *kafeneíon* led, as always, by Kosmás's father. Afterwards I heard it from Potítsa's own lips in stages, during my last week at home, when she was teaching me how to make love in the tower house. And later, on my first trip back, when she spoke more frankly, because the intervening years and my age made it easier. It was like many other stories of women in small communities with well-kept secrets.

Lías Nikolákos was comfortably off. He had his own oil press and land, whereas Potítsa was penniless, the eldest of five girls with no father. But she was the most beautiful woman in the village, maybe in the whole of the Mani, and so no one was surprised when Lías asked for her. She said yes and was grateful, never dreaming she would be so lucky. Not only would she have plenty to eat, she would be able to help her mother and her sisters.

The engagement was announced with three rifle shots into the air, and lasted for eight months, long enough to prepare for the wedding. The bridegroom paid for everything, even the wedding dress, and Potítsa lived as in a dream, with a new life to look forward to, and a man she believed loved her, because why else would he have wanted her? All through the betrothal there wasn't a single stolen touch to treasure, and not one tender look, but she was too inexperienced to have a clue what her marriage would be like. 'A smokescreen, to hide the shame of the Nikolakaíoi.'

At this point Potítsa digressed. It had been clear to everyone that she hadn't been coming to our house for me, still smelling of breast-milk as I was, nor was she leaving her shirt unbuttoned for my sake, nor did she let her skirt ride up accidentally on purpose to reveal her beautiful knees and shapely thighs for me. However hard she tried to hide it, as they say, 'coughs and lovemaking can always be heard'. She didn't have a cough, but what she felt for my father could not be overcome, she confessed as much to me on that first evening when we got together.

'You're like him,' she said, 'but different, you were born to change lovers. He didn't give me a single kiss, I want you to know that. His life began and ended with your mother.' It was then that she told me about my parents' relationship, and the story of their betrothal, as told to her by my mother Fotiní. Fotiní had loved my father since he was a boy and had cried in secret because there was no hope of him noticing her, the daughter of Layákos the drunkard, with no dowry, just a few 'roots' of olive, and a brother gone to America who had forgotten all about them.

My father was twenty-one when they married, and had just left the army. My mother was eighteen. Spring, sixteenth of March, the eve of my father's saint's day – Alexios, Man of God, and a big anniversary in the Mani, when we celebrate the beginning of the Greek rebellion against the Turks. Not our rebellion, because the Mani was never under the Turkish yoke; it had always been free and unsubdued. It was almost dusk, the day giving way to a purple evening, and as usual Fotiní stood waiting for him on his way back from the fields. She wore a flowery dress, and she was blushing with shame, because she had made up her mind. With the smell of damp, dewy earth in his nostrils, he got down off his horse and they spoke for a while in full view in the middle of the road. He was tall, with broad shoulders and a moustache, and she a delicate figure, with her hair tucked under her white scarf. There was a ruined stable nearby and Alexios pulled her inside. First he took off her headscarf, and Fotiní's long, black hair tumbled down to her slender waist. They didn't say a word, they just rolled together on the ground and she didn't hesitate for an instant, she wasn't afraid. His breath smelled of cigarettes and mint, and his hands of cloves. She was smooth and soft as clay. Afterwards they sat silent and shy on the ground, and when my mother started looking for her dress, without a word, asking for nothing, and without the usual womanish excuses, he took her by the hand.

'Let me look at you, let me take my fill of you,' he said, because she was a beautiful sight, Fotiní, with her long hair, so beautiful that he never tired of looking at her, not even when she was pregnant with me and swollen like a balloon. She didn't speak, she only smiled at him sadly, because she loved him very much, but she believed it to be a love without hope. She didn't ask him for a thing. Silently she dressed and left. Potítsa didn't know what he did after that, but I think I know. He lit a cigarette and stayed there for a while, naked, feeling his body where she had touched him, breathing in her scent in the ruined stable. Then he got up, dressed, and found his horse waiting patiently chewing grass by the side of the road. It had grown dark by now, but tonight it seemed as if the darkness had colours in it: the red of her blush, and the black of her hair, and the white of her breasts he'd been passionately kissing just now. He had already made up his mind.

The next evening my mother was out at Potítsa's, and when she got back she found her father talking to someone in the yard. Surprisingly my grandfather was sober. Alexios knew the old man's habits and took him from the *kafeneíon* before he had time to get drunk.

'I want to talk to you, Uncle Thanássi,' he said. 'Not here. At your house.' Usually Layákos would stay at the *kafeneíon* until it closed, and only then drag himself drunkenly back home. There were times when he didn't make it to the house, and then my mother, forewarned by the jeers of the other children, would run and pick him up and heave him as far as his bed. Wife and daughter would take off his shoes and cover him, amid his loud drunken laughter, swearing, vomiting, and finally snoring. My mother carried the shame with her all her life. However much she loved her father and worried about him, she disapproved of him deeply.

On that day my grandfather was sober enough to guess what was going on and he didn't dare believe it. His family had fallen on hard times after years of vendetta, but it was still a noble family. Alexios was an honourable man and a hard worker, a man who was not afraid of life, took hold of it and squeezed it dry. So Fotiní would never lack her daily needs. Layákos may have been an alcoholic, but he wasn't an idiot and he immediately saw that something was up. Normally there would be a matchmaker, but the bridegroom was clearly in a hurry and he wasn't a person who ignored the conventions. So he must have a reason.

At that moment Fotiní came home. Layákos called to her sharply to come over and she obeyed, blushing. He could tell from her expression exactly what had happened.

'Alexis has asked for you, what do you say?' he asked her curtly.

My mother didn't hesitate. She looked at them both boldly, turned away from the old man as if he wasn't there, and looked at my father.

'Why?' she asked.

'Because I want to live with you, Fotiní, for the rest of my life.'

'Out of duty?'

'Out of love. If you want it too.'

'All right. On one condition.'

Alexios frowned. He liked her courage. Anyone else would have leapt for joy. He liked her hesitation, and he knew that whatever it was that had thrown her into his arms on the previous evening, it certainly wasn't flightiness.

'What is it?'

'I want your word, as a man of honour, that you will never get drunk.'

'I give you my word.'

'Thank you. Because if I ever see you drunk, it will be over between us.' My father looked at her and then at the old man, and nodded.

Layákos bent his head in shame. Normally he should have raised hell to find out why the young man was duty-bound to ask for his daughter in such a hurry. Instead he made the sign of the cross and told his wife to bring out some wine. That evening he touched the glass to his lips but didn't drink, for the first time in many years. He didn't want to make his daughter feel ashamed again, and he couldn't bear the way she looked at him, with pity and contempt combined.

'I want to see you happy,' Layákos said, 'and then I can die.'

Prophetic words. For the six months of their engagement he didn't touch a drop, then one week after the wedding he was thrown off his mule, hit his head on a rock and was killed.

My parents were rarely alone while the betrothal lasted. Once the wedding was over, and they had locked the door behind them on the second floor of the tower, they embraced and made love again. Only then, safely held in his arms, did she ask him, sadly, 'Why did you marry me?'

He gestured towards the bed. And smiled.

'For this … is it so little?'

'I thought you liked Potítsa …' My mother knew she was quite ordinary-looking compared to Potítsa. 'For years I've thought you wanted her.'

My father just chuckled.

'She's a temptress and she's not for me. I like girls who live from the heart. I've always wanted you, from that twilight when you were carrying sacks with your mother and I stopped to help you. You were wearing a white headscarf and it came undone, and I saw your hair. Let me kiss it before I die, I said to myself. But I wouldn't have had the courage to do what you did.'

In the morning according to custom the mother-in-law looked at the sheets, but she didn't find what she was expecting. At breakfast she noticed my mother blushing, while my father slurped his coffee loudly, smiling into his moustache. Fotiní left the room and the old lady understood.

'But when …?' she started to ask.

'That's not your affair,' her son retorted. Then he added, with the kind of expression I remember well: 'And you watch your tongue with Fotiní!'

After this diversion, Potítsa told me the rest about her own marriage. During the first year, endless days of unceasing work in the house, the oil press and the fields, and nights lying awake, her husband with his back to her in bed, and she wondering what she had done wrong. Of course she was convinced that if Lías didn't desire her it must be her fault. When she saw Fotiní pregnant with her first child, she was overcome with anger and grief that she would never feel a child kicking in her belly. Then for the first time she thought that perhaps it wasn't her fault. Not completely.

That was when the Cretan turned up. Tall, dark, with a dashing moustache, eyes like fire. He was a labourer in the fields and in her husband's oil press. Laughter and song on his lips. He'd been in some trouble back home and it's true he was hot-blooded and quick-tempered and always getting into fights at the *kafeneíon*. When he looked at her she felt naked, as if he could see through her clothes, and at first she bowed her head in shame and disappeared. He didn't miss much, and he asked about her at the *kafeneíon*. 'That wife of Nikolakos's looks unwatered to me.' My uncle overheard and told him to be careful, we don't take kindly to that kind of thing over here. He knew it, they didn't take kindly to it back home in Crete either – that was why he'd packed his bags and left. One day when he found Potítsa alone at the oil press, he plucked up courage and sang to her. He was always making up *mantinádes*:

*I see your beautiful white neck and it makes me lose my mind.*
*One little kiss from your sweet lips and then just let me die.*

Revenge is a dish best served cold. This one hadn't cooled down all that much. A year after her wedding, Potítsa began to understand just exactly what had happened. She had been made a fool of in the worst possible way. She had been insulted and used, and things were unlikely to change. Her mother-in-law kept giving her dirty looks, as if to say 'A year's gone by and she's infertile,' and so Potítsa made up her mind. Every evening the Cretan brought fodder for the animals to the stable, filled the mangers and then went away singing softly and whistling. At that time of day Lías was always out at the *kafeneíon*, and her mother-in-law was at the cemetery lighting the oil lamp at her husband's grave. So one day Potítsa waited for him, sitting on a bale of hay with her headscarf off, the buttons open on her blouse for the first time, her skirt up to her knees. She could hear the sheep bleating and smell the fresh-mown grass. Her breasts were as firm as a young tree in bud and when he came inside, their eyes met in silent agreement, he shut the door behind him and fell on her.

At dusk, Potítsa stood before the mirror in her bedroom and smiled at her reflection for the first time since her wedding day. She combed her hair and changed her clothes. It wasn't so much the moments she spent in the arms of the Cretan, it was the taste of retribution that sweetened her mouth. They saw each other at every opportunity. Brief, hurried meetings in the little caves above the village, in the stable in the evening, even in the church of St Ilías. 'I thought God would strike me dead!' she told me.

After three months she was late. She announced her pregnancy proudly during dinner, looking at Lías challengingly over her glass, but just as she expected he didn't say a word, and his mother's genuine delight made it clear that she had no inkling of Lías's peculiarity. Afterwards, in the bedroom, with her hands on her hips, she waited for the storm to break. 'Whore!' whispered Lías, but he only whispered it. 'If you asked me when did I loathe my husband with my whole soul, I can tell you, it was then. Before that I felt sorry for him, I hated him, but I didn't detest him. If he had grabbed me by the hair there in front of his mother and laid into me, as I deserved, if he had shouted "Whore!" out loud, for my mother-in-law to hear it, and for the whole village to hear, he might have won just an ounce of respect from me. But he was a frightened rabbit, he wasn't a man, not in bed, nor anywhere. "You have a choice," I told him. "Either you accept both me and my child and we say nothing, or I go to your mother and tell her everything." And do you know that in the end Lías was perfectly happy. He had a wife and a son, and a well-kept secret that no one ever found out.'

The Cretan was the first lapse, but he wasn't the last. Lías wasn't slow in working out who had sprung him an heir, and he dismissed the Cretan quietly with no fuss. Although the man liked Potítsa well enough, she wasn't worth crying over. He went to neighbouring Messenia to find other Potítsas and wait until things had calmed down in his village so he could go home.

*Free as a bird I'll fly away however much I love you,*
*as passion comes and passion goes, quickly I'll forget you.*

Potítsa didn't miss him at all. The child she was carrying was by now the centre of her world. And when it was born and turned out to be a boy, there was a great celebration. Whereas before she had been a silent, tireless ghost around the house, she now had an opinion about everything. Her mother-in-law thought highly of her and could see that Lías wasn't much use, although she was unaware of his lack in the bedroom. And then, when the old woman had her first stroke, there was no one left for Potítsa to fear. Her husband trembled before her. She had a fling with Kostí Mitsikoyiánnis, and when Lías dared mutter about what people might say, she threatened to give him *soulima* – poison – to drink, or to murder him in his sleep.

So there was nobody to rein her in! It's one thing to be an innocent virgin who's never known a man, it's quite another for a woman who's known sex suddenly to be asked to live like a nun. Mitsikoyiánnis's wife smelled a rat and one day she leapt out at Potítsa from some bushes and shoved a gun between the buttons of her shirt, which by now were completely undone. 'If I see you anywhere near my husband I'll make so many buttonholes in you, you'll never do them up again.' Touché! It was quite an ambush. At that point Kostí Mitsikoyiánnis swiftly withdrew, because Potítsa was lovely, but not lovely enough to risk losing a wife and children. And Potítsa did likewise, because she had a son to think of who was Lías's heir.

After her stroke, Lías's mother was bedridden for three years, and Potítsa cared for her like a daughter right to the end. Meanwhile she was constantly changing lovers. She had affairs with quite a few men from the village, and some from Areopolis and the neighbouring villages, and my father, who had called her a temptress, proved to be more than accurate. He said it without thinking, he saw something in that woman that she herself wasn't aware of yet. Was he afraid of her rare beauty? I don't know. But it's a fact that my father was the only man completely oblivious to her charms and the only one she really longed for.

'When he danced at the *panegyri,* he looked like an eagle with wings outspread,' she said. 'His hands were broad and calloused from work, and I dreamt of him touching me with those hands. At night when I slept with other men I shut my eyes and pretended it was him touching me, and when I was alone I cried in desperation and often I prayed I would die. Because he wasn't just some stranger, he was the husband of my friend Fotiní and I couldn't bear it. The evening he was killed, I was rolling out the pastry for a *pitta* and Haralambis was stirring the flour and getting it all over the place – I couldn't bring myself to scold him, he's so pretty, that little one – when the two older boys came in and told me what had happened. The floor seemed to rise up and I fainted, and when I came round, my children were shaking me in terror and Haralambis was trying to open my eyelids with his fingers. I thought I had killed your father through my wicked thoughts, because I couldn't have him for myself. I was convinced that everything you and your mother suffered was my fault. You have his eyes, his hands, his figure. It isn't hard for me to imagine that you are him.'

I don't know what Potítsa was dreaming of those afternoons during my last week at the tower house, when she taught me about love with gentleness and wisdom. I know that I forgot the tragedy I'd caused, just for a while, when I was close to her. The pain, the guilt, the desperation. Nothing can keep my Furies away for long, not Lou's love, nor my success at work, nor the money of which I have plenty, nor Ellen's smile. That's why I can't sleep. Most people find redemption of some kind. For Potítsa it's the grandchildren she chases after with a spoon to keep them well fed, for Kastrinós it was death, for Haritákos prison, and for his daughter her stroppy son, who defends her from the slander of the world, dealing out punches and throwing stones at people who insult her. Only I drag the curse of loneliness and sleeplessness with me to a foreign country, among strangers, because my own people still frighten me. I don't want their pain, or their pity, or their forgiveness. And love was nothing but a lie, a vengeful trick. *Soulima* from the hands of the poisoner.

# The Funeral

THE HOUR BEFORE DAWN is the hardest time at a wake, when the hours you have left with the person you love are so few and yet you want it to be over. Your eyelids keep closing, your limbs feel numb, you ache all over and you long for the sunrise. It's the hour when you realise how mortal you are and despite your great grief you need to eat and to lay your weary body down somewhere, because life goes on. Another reason for my feeling mortal was that sitting opposite me was Marina Haritákou, my poisoner. There were hardly any women in the house now, and just a few men in the garden. The *moiroloya* had been over for a while. Potítsa had stopped her Anastasákiad in the middle, due to some kind of inexplicable sensitivity to do with Marina Haritákou. They had been whispering to one another and I suspected it might be about me, but that seemed far-fetched.

Marina left soon after dawn, and I watched the hem of her long skirt caress the back of her legs. I remembered the feel and taste of them despite the years, the feel of velvet, the taste of ripe peach. She'd been driving all night, she told Maria. She had gone to the hospital, heard that Aretí had died and set off right away. My uncle apologised to her for not having let her know. But he had been in such a state and we had left almost at once to get things ready here. 'It doesn't matter,' she replied. 'I'm glad you weren't alone and that Odysséas was with you. At least he came in time to see her.' And I felt her eyes on me, dead black at first, and then golden, with the hint of a tear. For Aunt Aretí? For me? For herself?

Things have been difficult for her too. The lad is illegitimate, she's bringing him up on her own and he isn't the easiest boy in the world, as I discovered. Apparently Kastrinós didn't have a chance to recognise him as his son. Either that or he didn't want to. I read about Kastrinós's death in the Greek newspapers. I don't usually take much interest in them, but it's impossible not to notice news like that. After all, I knew him – we shared the same woman – and to die in such a violent way, say what you like, I was curious. But I can't say I was sorry.

But why should Nikifóros apologise to Marina Haritákou? And why had she raced to the hospital for my aunt? And Potítsa, stopping a *moiroloy* when she was only halfway through – which if she'd finished it would have spread throughout the entire Mani from east to west? How that woman managed to win them all round I had no idea. And why couldn't they pay for my aunt's health care? For seventeen years, since my first visit back, I ensured that my relatives at home would want for nothing. I sent more money, every month, than they could spend in two lifetimes, and yet I came back to find them left on that disgusting ward? Yiánnis had no idea why the old couple didn't have a cent, he told me, and he himself had wondered how I could have abandoned them like that. It's insane. My uncle just shrugged his shoulders when I asked him: 'That's what your aunt wanted, she wouldn't hear of us touching the money, she kept it aside.' Yiánnis thought her illness must have affected her mind. The last metastasis, in fact, was in her head. I asked my uncle why he didn't tell me on the telephone. I could have sent him some money secretly. But he just bowed his head, as if he was to blame. 'I'm ashamed, my son, to have caused you so much worry.'

\*\*\*

We carried the coffin on our shoulders to the grave. The whole village followed us to the cemetery, relatives and friends from all around, and Marina Haritákou on the arm of her son. He is already quite a lot taller than her. He leans over her protectively. She radiates the tenderness of a mother to an only son. Still beautiful! Women in the north tend to pucker up, like the kippers my mother fed us with greens, whereas our Mediterranean women broaden with age, like ancient wine jars. Maggie has already started drying out and has had a little Botox. And Yiánnis's Maria has put on at least ten kilos. Marina alone, like a female Faust, has done some deal with the devil so she can go on tormenting men! Dressed in black, a short-sleeved blouse and a narrow skirt to the knee. Her hair, which I remember leaving her forehead free, now has wisps across it, maybe to hide the odd line, but anyway it suits her. She has it tied it up to keep cool, and her neck, soft as a flower stalk, the same as ever.

We all went to the *kafeneíon* for coffee afterwards. The boy shook my hand to offer his condolences, with a squeaky voice and challenging eyes. He kept his distance from Yiánnis's daughter. I had felt his gaze on me all day, boring into me as though he was looking for something, and he wasn't just being provocative – there was something like compassion in his eyes. They sat down and the boy's grandfather, Haritákos, joined them. A shadow of the man I remembered thirty-four years ago, who could 'pick up a stone and wring it' as they say in the Mani, but in better shape than when I'd last seen him, seventeen years ago. Now he was well turned out, clean, and looking adoringly at his illegitimate grandchild. I had definitely missed a few episodes!

Potítsa sat down with them at the next table. Haritákos had been another of her lovers, like most of the men in the village. Kosmás the *kafetzis* served them in a manner that clearly suggested all the sinners of the village were gathered right there.

The heat had taken hold for good. We were all dripping with sweat from walking along under the burning sun, my uncle wiped his face with a paper napkin and I was having one of my dizzy spells. I wet my face with ice water from a bottle. My eyes grew dim and for a second everyone around me seemed to vanish. I heard someone nearby calling the boy by his name and I froze. I turned to look at him and was met by that same insolent and provocative gaze.

'Alexi!'

What the hell was that supposed to mean? How much perversion can a woman's mind contain? I tried to catch her eye, but she wouldn't look at me. Maybe she was avoiding me or she didn't care. I don't know.

\*\*\*

I had gone to find her, in her little house in the Plaka, in that quiet pedestrian street, the car horns sounded from far away and the scent of nightflower took me back to my childhood at the tower house. I rang on the bell but nobody answered, the house was deserted. I sat on the step. I didn't care how long I had to wait, one hour, two hours, three, four, the whole night. She came forty minutes later, counted by the beating of my heart. I heard the sound of the motorbike on the pavement. She took off her helmet, her hair poured out as though it were alive, a chestnut-coloured cascade, and she combed it through with her fingers. The streetlight lit up her lovely forehead and her eyes, flashing with fury. I got up and helped her push the bike into the yard; she didn't speak, she was angry and tight-lipped, waiting. There was no way I was backing down this time, and yet something made me feel cold with fright. It was the life waiting for me in Boston, in Athens, in the Mani – there was no life for me without her. I fell into the deckchair in her little garden. There was a table with a pot of basil on it.

I was never good at sweet-talking women, I never said more than was absolutely necessary, but at that moment fear loosened my tongue. It was the first time I had wanted someone so much, the first and last time, and I didn't have the words to say it, but I had to speak because she wouldn't give me another chance. I told her I loved her and asked her to marry me. I didn't know exactly what I meant by the first, I didn't have another to convey the turmoil I was in, but I was sure what the second one meant. It meant evenings drinking coffee at the millstone, gazing out in the twilight beyond the cypress and the olives to the wrinkled face of the sea. It meant sharing silences together, and nights behind the firmly closed door, breathing in her hair, counting the seconds with her breath, warming my frozen soul next to her body. It meant breakfasts of *koutalídes* and honey. It meant commitment – genuine, willing and equal. I had never said such things before, ever, to anyone. I had never felt like this.

She was standing in front of me like the stone statue of a goddess, without a trace of emotion. I couldn't bear it any more. Suddenly I was sure that she would never forgive me and it was unjust, unjust and wretched, all for one, stupid meaningless night. My voice was breaking, I couldn't help it. '*Melénia mou*, forgive me! Don't spoil what we have, just for something that's over and will never happen again! I want us to live together, to have children, a son, for sure, and to call him Alexis, my father's name.'

*\*\*\**

I felt dizzy. Potítsa was saying something in a loud voice. That she's living in Athens with her son and daughter-in-law and they don't get on. Potítsa isn't an easy person, and she keeps interfering in the couple's affairs. Yiánnis's daughter avoided my eye. I expect she wishes the earth would open and swallow her. I shall have to put things right and see what I'm going to do about her and the boy, now that I've got myself involved in their little romance. Kosmás has a son too, older than Marina's. He helps his father in the shop just as Kosmás used to, and he's just as keen as his father to stick his nose into other people's business. Some things never change. Kosmás told me Marina's boy hangs out with a bad crowd in Athens. Apparently he hit a policeman at a demonstration and nearly got arrested. He was recognised by another policeman from Kardamyli who naturally didn't arrest him – he would never shop a fellow Maniot – but he told everyone down here about it. And when the guy told him off for hitting a policeman who's only doing his job, the boy shot back at him quick as a flash: 'You should be ashamed of your job, toadying to anyone in power.'

Pavlákos, the former cop, was there after the funeral. He's fond of the boy and sat at their table. The boy seems to respect him despite his being a cop. Then there was Pantelís Leoúsis, the brother of Maria, whose daughter, Soula, was sweet on young Haritákos. The boy seems to have inherited his mother's gift of attracting the opposite sex like a magnet, and the girls have a point: he is a good-looking lad, with a toughness that makes him seem older than his years.

After the coffee Alexis left with his mother. She offered her condolences again to my uncle and me, and went out of the room with everyone's eyes on her. She reminded me of Potítsa, walking proudly down the road with all the men sighing after her. But this one is more provocative, as if to say 'I know what you're thinking and I couldn't give a damn'.

And then they all turned round and looked at me. Most of the faces are unfamiliar, the older generation have all gone to their maker, the children I don't know, and my old acquaintances have changed unbelievably, as, no doubt, have I. They know my story, the tragedy I carry with me and my humiliation at the hands of Marina Haritákou. I don't know what they expect from me, all these years later. I am unimaginably tired, the sweat is dripping into my burning eyes and I feel dizzy. Old Haritákos gets up from Pavlákos's table and comes over to mine. He sits down next to me in silence, as if he wants to make something clear – to me, and to everyone else. He leans over to me when they've all gone.

'You saw my grandson, Odysséa? He is my whole life.'

I look at him, and his eyes have misted over. Of all the things that have passed between us, what I did to him, what he did to my father, and what Marina did to me, there's one thing that tortures me. It's on the tip of my tongue and I can't swallow it. I almost spit out the words: 'Why did you call him Alexis?'

He bows his head, avoids looking me in the eye.

'It was what my daughter wanted. I told you, the boy is my whole life. I would give up my life for him, like your father did and more. I would kill again if I had to. If it meant he could live.'

And then he looked up. He's an old man and frail, but he means every word. And it's a warning. All these years later, and I'm back where I started. Me and the Haritakaíoi.

'I have nothing against the boy, Uncle Micháli, or against you. We said all there was to say when we last met. It's not the time or the place for this kind of talk.'

'Any time is good to prevent an evil,' said the old man. Then he slapped me on the back in a fatherly way and left.

Nikifóros and I came back alone to the empty house. 'I feel as if she's just about to come out of the kitchen,' he said, and it was true, as if the shadow of the dead woman still lived and breathed. I helped him into bed. 'It will do him good to sleep,' I thought. But his eyes won't close and nor will mine. He refused the sleeping pill I offered. 'I don't want to stop the pain, I don't want to stop thinking of her, my son. All those years together in this house, in this bed. We shared so much, the least I can do is to cry for Aretí, now that no one can see me except you.' He cried, and I cried with him.

# Xemóni

'I DON'T MIND IF YOU SMOKE,' *Pappoú* said under his breath, in case my mother heard him, even though she wasn't in the house. 'But if I catch you taking drugs or drinking, God help you! Let's get that clear.' And then he looked at me earnestly: 'You're better off dead than living with those devils that kill you every day.'

First he gave me one of his cigarettes and then he elaborated his theory.

'Doesn't it strike you as odd that they're so keen on banning smoking?'

No, it didn't strike me as odd, it had gone too far. People had got used to smoking in hospitals, in the actual wards with the patients, in schools, everywhere, and no one had any respect. Things had to be brought into line.

'If they care so much about people getting ill,' he went on, 'why don't they provide doctors for them, even in the smallest village? Why don't they employ enough nurses? There wasn't a single person in the Evangelismos to look after poor old Aretí. Nikifóros and your mother had to nurse her themselves. Why don't they pay the pharmacists properly for the medicines they give out? Why is that?'

I didn't understand what he was driving at, but even so he had my attention. I shrugged my shoulders. How should I know?

'The people who make up these laws don't care about you, they only care about keeping their comfortable jobs and paying their supporters, and that doesn't mean people who vote. Don't just look at the cheese, keep an eye out for the trap. You've got a brain, put it to work, don't swallow everything that other people tell you.'

'You've lost me. Can you explain?'

'With pleasure. Doesn't it strike you that while they're fanatically cracking down on us smokers, they allow drugs to be sold in the street as if it's no big deal at all? Even though both using and dealing are supposedly imprisonable offences.'

'That's true. Why do they do it then?'

'I'll tell you,' he said dragging on his cigarette and then throwing it on the ground. I was still holding mine. I didn't see the point of lighting it, since Effie wasn't there to see me. 'Imagine a group of crack addicts injecting themselves. How does it look to you? A bunch of kids completely out of it, barely conscious and out of control. Now imagine a similar group, having a little smoke, talking, expressing their feelings, complaining about the government and anyone else they can blame, standing up for their rights. The cigarette is anarchic, just by its very nature, it brings people together, it stops you feeling lonely, it generates ideas. That's why cigarettes are against the law: to make all you young people take to crack and drink, to become losers, to stop looking around you. That's the only reason they care. And then there's all the money to be made out of those losers. I've been there and I've seen it, in prison – addicts who would sell their own souls, sell their mother and their father, give away everything they have just for one single hit. Do you understand me? There's just no point in living through that kind of humiliation. I lost both my boys, you know that, and it's left a wound that isn't going heal, ever. But when I saw young lads in prison slowly melting before my eyes like candles, from those evil drugs, I thanked my God for sparing them that at least.'

I understood, of course. Today's lesson was 'yes' to cigarettes, 'no' to drugs. *Pappoú* always had weird ideas, but I have to admit that quite often he hit a bullseye. Prison had made him wise, as my mother would say. Apparently he was known as 'the philosopher' in prison, due to his many theories about life.

'Will you tell your mother?'

'Are you crazy?'

We laughed conspiratorially. If my mother found out she would just give me that look that makes me feel foolish, and say three words: 'So you're smoking.' It wouldn't be a question or a statement, but somewhere in between. And then she'd say nothing and go on with her jobs, the crease between her eyebrows deepening, and I would feel so guilty that I'd have to quit smoking, and then the kids at the Xemóni would give me a hard time.

It's an old *kafeneío* in the main square at Areopolis and I work there in the holidays to help my friend Nikos, who is its only full-time employee. The place is owned by Petrouléas, a friend of my mother's from university. He worked all the hours possible and turned it into a coffee bar, and it's become the most popular place in town. It's called the Xemóni after those remote, lonely towers that guard the wilderness. Lonely is the one thing it isn't, I think, as I rush around feverishly to keep up with the orders. I like working there. I'm saving up to buy a moped. Assuming I can persuade my mother. I've been on at her but so far the 'general' doesn't show any sign of backing down. 'When you're eighteen,' she says, 'you can get your driving licence and I'll help you buy a second-hand car. For now you're still underage.' As if I would be the first person to drive a moped without a licence. And the bizarre thing is that on this subject she has *Pappoú*'s support.

'I thought you were supposed to be on my side,' I moaned to him.

'Not on this. She's afraid for you, and she's right. Haven't you seen the accidents that happen every day? Don't push it, she's got enough on her plate.'

However, hope springs eternal. If I had my moped now I wouldn't have to cadge lifts to Areopolis when my mother is in Athens. I'd go swimming any time I felt like it, and now that we have the Anastasákos problem and we've lost our refuge at the tower house, me and Effie would be able to get away on the moped, even if it is pretty risky. She usually comes down to Areopolis on Saturday evening, but this evening with Dimákaina's funeral it's out of the question, and who knows when I'll see her.

The Anastasákos problem is complicated and the only solution is for him to buzz off as soon as possible. He looks so cool and so tough, so apparently casual and yet those piercing eyes of his don't miss a single thing. What's going on in that head of his? What is he thinking, I'd like to know. With his flashy suit and his expensive watch, and the Mercedes waiting at the door. It screams money and power from a long way off and he makes no effort to keep it hidden. His movements are all so calculated and so sure, and his words even more so. And the way he just stands there, as if he's used to ordering people about and being listened to, both here and in America, I imagine. How idiotic can you be to mistake a person like that for a homeless immigrant? Or was I just too freaked out by the reality?

'I've never met a more unfeeling person,' I had said to my mother.

'Don't be taken in, he's suffering. He loved *Thía* Aretí very much.'

'Then he hides it very well.'

'Yes, he hides it, all right.'

There was just one moment when the impassive face of the *xénos* looked as if it might crumple He was walking in front of me, one of the four who were carrying the coffin, and his eyes, tired-looking, shone with tears he wouldn't let fall. He was the tallest, and he bent down to the same height as the others. With his shoulders hunched and his grey hair, he looked devastated at that moment, and if Anastasákos hadn't been the man he is, I would have felt sorry for him.

Marina stumbled as she walked, and held on to me. We both knew that Anastasákos was walking behind us and looking at us. He was supporting old Dimákos and yet he was alone – he had been away for such a long time, a lonely *xemóni* just like the rest of us, me, old Dimákos, *Pappoú*, and my mother.

***

A gentle breeze was caressing the olive trees. Two falcons were hovering in the distance ready to dive on their prey. I watched them until they disappeared behind the hills. My mother drove in silence, her mind elsewhere.

'If you weren't so stubborn and would let me get a moped, you wouldn't be in a rush now,' I said to remind her of my presence, repetition being the mother of learning and all that. She gave me a sideways look.

'It doesn't bother me.'

I regretted mentioning the moped. She had driven through the night yesterday and gone straight to Dimákos's, where she had found the creep waiting for her. I felt guilty about not warning her, but, you see, last night there was Effie, and this morning Marina only came home briefly to get ready for the funeral. She accidentally fell asleep beside my bed. She likes looking at me when I'm asleep. Ever since I was little she sometimes keeps watch all night by my pillow, and not just when I'm ill. It gets a bit annoying now I'm older. At seven in the morning she cried out 'No!' in the middle of a nightmare and woke me up. I leapt up and saw her sitting in the armchair beside my bed, taking deep breaths as if she was suffocating. I brought her a glass of water from the kitchen, put my arms around her and didn't say a word about her falling asleep in my room. 'I'm sorry,' she said. 'I only came in for a moment to look at you.' I squeezed her hand. 'Never mind that now. What did you see? Are you okay?' She was perfectly fine, she reassured me. And she couldn't remember what she had seen. Lies, obviously. On both counts!

The worst of the heat was over now. The sun was sinking in the distance over Kalamata and had set the mountains and the sea ablaze. It was the most glorious time of day. But I had a difficult evening ahead. The thing that had happened with Anastasákos was bothering me a lot, but not as much as the furrow on my mother's forehead. I felt I should speak, even if I said the wrong thing, but I couldn't say a word, Marina's expression imposed silence. She dropped me in front of the Xemóni and said she'd pick me up when I finished work at dawn. 'Go and get some sleep,' I said, and she nodded. Another lie. She couldn't sleep. My mother usually slept well, like everyone with a clear conscience. But the creep had managed to keep her awake all night.

It was busy at the Xemóni until late, when at some point the coffees, crêpes and ice creams gave way to cocktails, shots and beers. The crowd eased after three. Petrouléas slapped me on the back and told me to phone my mother. 'I'll finish off here,' he said. I still needed to sweep, but he wouldn't hear of it. He put fifty euros into my hand. It was far more than we'd agreed, but he insisted.

'What did you do about that scooter? Did you persuade your mother?'

'Nah ... like banging on a deaf man's door.'

'I'd get it for you myself, but she'd kill me.'

I said goodnight and as I was leaving I heard him say to someone in the café: 'If only I had another one like him! He does the work of three people.'

I couldn't resist turning round, and stood there with my mouth open. At the door, on his way out with a bottle of whisky in his hand, was Odysséas Anastasákos, the creep! What the hell was he doing here? He couldn't stay with Dimákos a single night without looking for entertainment. So insensitive.

'Come on,' he said casually. 'I'll give you a lift.'

He went out, certain that I'd follow on behind, and I don't know why, but that's exactly what I was doing when Petrouléas grabbed me by the arm.

'Do you know that guy?'

I nodded and ran ahead to catch up. He unlocked the car and got in without looking at me, as if he didn't care whether I went with him or not. I was annoyed with myself for taking orders like that without objecting. Well, never mind if he thinks he has me at his beck and call. It's best if the enemy doesn't know exactly who he's dealing with. The element of surprise is essential in battle, and something told me I would be needing it.

We set off in silence. It had grown cooler and he opened the sunroof.

As he held the gear stick firmly his hand reminded me of the iron giant Daedalus had made in Minoan Crete: inexorable and immovable, a sleepless guardian of the island. Talus. But you only had to pull out the nail that kept the blood inside his body and Talus would fall down dead. For the moment Anastasákos looked straight ahead at the curving road in complete concentration. The black rings under his eyes were even darker now. I couldn't take my eyes off that hand, hypnotised by its sure movements. The bizarre desire to stretch out mine and touch it became so intense that I could barely drag my eyes away.

'Your employer seems to think very highly of you,' he commented. I didn't know whether he was trying to make peace or whether he was teasing me.

'He's exaggerating.'

'He's not exaggerating. I saw you. You're quick, friendly with the customers, you don't forget. I've done that job, too, and I know.'

'I imagine I'll do well then, like you have,' I said sarcastically.

'That's up to you,' he said, and glanced at me. 'What's the story with the scooter?'

I thought for a bit, but I had no reason not to answer him.

'I'm too young for a licence and my mother doesn't want me to get one, even though I have the money,' I explained.

'She's right,' he said as we drew up in front of my house. 'You should have everything in due time. Scooter, car, gun. Otherwise …' He turned and looked at me with his flashing eyes. 'I'm sorry I said what I did about your mother.' He was determined to astonish me this evening.

'I'm not about to say sorry to you though,' I said drily.

He chuckled wearily.

'That's okay. It doesn't matter. You have a right to defend the people who love you. Goodnight.'

I contemplated his apology as the car drove away, and then went inside. My mother was waiting up for me. She drummed her fingers nervously on the table.

'Are you hungry?'

'No. I'm sleepy, but let's talk first.'

She shrugged her shoulders. She was barefoot – she likes to walk around like that in the house – sitting cross-legged with a book on the table in front of her. It was that one by Koutsilieris with the *moiroloya,* which she knew by heart. Opened at the *Moiroloy of the Poisoner.*

'Do you know who gave me a lift?' I asked her.

'I saw. Why did you go with him?'

'I just did. Curiosity.'

'Be careful!'

'Oh come on, Marináki! He should be careful. If he bothers you, he's done for.'

My mother leant back and laughed a laugh that sounded more like a sob.

'Bother me? Him? He's terrified of me. He thinks I'm like her,' she said, and pushed her book over to me.

I didn't pick it up, there was no need. I know the *moiroloy* well. And I know very well it isn't my mother.

She promised me she'd go to sleep and I went upstairs. In the light of the moon you could pick out the Anastasákos's tower, pitch black, abandoned to the ravages of time. But something told me that it wasn't deserted tonight, its master would be huddled away in there, with that bottle of whisky, like the beast in the fairy tale. My mother told me he hadn't slept properly for years, he was like a nocturnal bird of prey, at work while others sleep. No wonder he'd made so much money – catching people off their guard.

I didn't turn on the light. I sat there watching my enemy in the dark, like the men of my family centuries ago. Their house was eight minutes away exactly. 'One cigarette' or eight minutes of quick walking, and a gulf between us of graves, strips of land, wellsprings, olive trees, Marina and now Effie. I lay down on my bed and counted the planks on the wooden ceiling. That man's great weakness was also his great advantage. I needed to sleep, he didn't. I was thinking of him so intensely that I had stopped feeling tired. For years I had wondered what he looked like, how he stood, how he walked, how he talked. Would his voice be gentle, like my Uncle Vangélis's voice when he spoke to his son Niko, or would he sound bitter, like *Pappoú* when he spoke about his dead sons. I had all the answers now and I didn't like any of them. The guy was as cold as sheet metal, frostier than the frozen winter snow in that city over the ocean where he lives. His voice reminded me of a monotonous drumming on wood, level, colourless, dry. He had the air of a fascist general, accustomed to people bowing and performing somersaults when he speaks.

I think of my mother, proud and uncompromising always, struggling to earn a living, with two jobs in the winter, the legal one at the school in Athens, the illegal one at the tutorial college, and her voluntary work at the orphanage. And I think about Anastasákos too. Worms like Anastasákos, Mitsikoyiánnis and Kosmás aren't good enough to polish her shoes! But however hard she tries, she can't make herself hate that creep as he deserves. Never mind, Marina, I hate him enough for both of us! I closed my eyes and let the hatred lull me to sleep.

# Flight

I TOOK MY BOTTLE OF WHISKY and lay down on the millstone in the garden. My most intense memory of home is this stone, hard under my body. Something scuttles off to hide in the dry grass. My return has startled the creatures of the house and I stay motionless. I don't want to disturb. Strange to find myself here with everything so different and yet so much the same: the enmity the same, the hatred the same, a cycle that turns and repeats itself. Old Haritákos doesn't hate any more, he has found a meaning for his lifetime in prison, in the existence of his grandson. He has been snatched up by the future, and he's ready to kill to protect the boy. The boy still hates though, I saw it in his eyes. Never mind, maybe it's better like that, maybe fate never intended our families to be united. Look what happened the last time we tried it!

I don't have a glass, so I'm drinking whisky from the bottle, like my drunkard grandfather. From somewhere there's the scent of nightflower, *mirabilis jalapa*, probably from the depths of my memory. My mother loved the plant and she put it in a corner of the yard. When Yiánnis did up the house for me there were two things I insisted on. I wanted the nightflower in a corner of the yard, and the millstone in its place, where my parents used to sit and share their coffee and their silence. The millstone is still here, the nightflower persists in seeding itself in a corner of my soul, in the place where I've buried the past: Yiorgís, my father, my mother, Aunt Aretí and my first time with Potítsa, afternoons playing football, the little mole on Kalliroe's neck in class, my parents and me working under the burning sun, a little girl with a light blue ribbon whose eyes turned golden when she was angry and when she laughed, *koutalídes me méli*, and Melénia, the honey of my youth, love, betrayal and pain.

The memories come flooding back with the drink. Four in the morning, no sign of a light at the Haritakaíko, a cricket chirruping, an owl hooting nearby.

We had seen a cuckoo, sitting up on the roof of our house, letting out its solitary, mournful call. My mother had made the sign of the cross and spat to ward off the evil eye. She thought it a death omen and was gloomy for days. When the bird eventually flew off I happened to be looking in that direction, and I saw it fly directly to the Haritákos's house, to the highest part of the tower, and settle there.

It had been a mild winter, the calm before the storm that would sweep everything away. Everything was running so smoothly at the tower house, there was nothing to disturb our routine; our lives were like the still waters of a lake, spotless and crystal clear. After my father's visit to Mrs Petrea at school, I always did my homework, I knew the translation by heart and studied the grammar. But she had changed too. She treated me with respect and never spoke sarcastically to me again. It was as if the two of us had come to a tacit agreement.

I didn't doubt for a moment that I owed the truce to my father. Alexios had barely finished primary school, but he had a brain as sharp as a razor and commanded the respect not only of Mrs Petrea, but of everyone he associated with. I'm fifty now, and I've never met a man so honourable, hard-working, clean in all his dealings. And the fact is that my childhood years in the Mani, despite the poverty and hard work, were the happiest of my life. It was a paradise, lost because I wasn't worthy of it. If my father were still alive he would spit on my so-called success. The things he thought important I never acquired in all my years away.

In the evenings during that last winter at home we would light the fire and gather in the kitchen, where my mother put down rag mats to keep the cold off our feet. When I was little my grandmother told me stories to pass the time, but she had died years before, and now my father and I spent our time cleaning the guns, while my mother busied herself in the house. He had two hunting rifles and taught me to shoot. My mother wasn't very happy about it, it wasn't unusual for accidents to happen in the region, but I was a good shot and my father was proud of me. Very often, Uncle Nikifóros and Aunt Aretí would come round, and Potítsa, swinging her hips and shattering her hopes on the rock of indifference that was my father. She used to bring us chestnuts from her sister, the one who was married at Kosmás, a village on Mount Parnon, and we roasted them in the fire. She could give us chestnuts all she liked, but with my father there was nothing doing.

My mother was strangely accommodating, as if she felt sorry for Potítsa. They had grown up together and she didn't want to close the door to her as others had done. I wondered at her attitude, how she could risk bringing such temptation into her house. My doubts were resolved on one of those evenings, the only one that differed during that happy winter, when my father thoughtlessly threw a stone into the still lake of the tower house and unsettled its waters. All he did was to create a series of ripples in the water, but my mother didn't just call up a storm, she raised a tsunami. The cause of it was not Potítsa, but Miltiades's father, the 'son-in-law' from Gytheio, who came to the village to see his elderly parents. They got together in the *kafeneíon* – childhood friends – and without meaning to my father got carried away, lost count of the drinks and forgot his promise to my mother. I believe that he walked home knowing that he had overstepped the mark, he had broken his oath and would have to face the consequences.

We realised that something was wrong before he crossed the threshold. His footstep wasn't his usual steady tread. He didn't come in straight away; it was as if he was groping, trying to open the door and not managing it. His body swayed oddly as he came in, the words came out of his mouth all jumbled up and his eyes were bleary. No, this was not my father. Fotiní and I both stood up – I curious, she white as a sheet. She stood in front of him and looked enormous, while he seemed to shrink. 'We're finished,' she said. Just that. We both watched her go up the steep steps to the tower. He stammered something, I couldn't understand what, but the door of their bedroom shut with a bang and he was left outside. This smack in the face went some way to bringing him round. He was legless, but enough aware of the situation to see that his wife was not only angry, she had just announced the end, and he knew her well enough to take it at face value. His eyes were now quite clear, his mind was working, and he slapped me on the shoulder: 'Go to bed,' he said. My feet were nailed to the floor. I'd never experienced this before, but the thing that shocked me more than the quarrel were the tears that flowed down his cheeks. My father, weak, defeated, crying! I couldn't believe it. 'Let me help you …' I muttered awkwardly. 'Go to bed.' This time it was both an order and a request, he wanted to be left alone and I obeyed. Of course I couldn't sleep. None of us slept that evening, I'm sure of it. I lay frozen in shock under my bedclothes, she was probably crying in the dark, and he? God knows.

I got up at the usual time for school and went down the stairs with a weight crushing my chest. My father was already in the kitchen, wearing my mother's apron, preparing my milk and their tea, and had lit the fire. My father, a great big man, whom everyone rates and respects, behaving like a whipped cur. He had decided to humble himself utterly in order to keep the woman he loved and the tranquility of his home. A *Maniátissa* is a hard nut and he knew it well. When she came in, two minutes after me, with a bundle of clothes in her hand, determined to leave, her face was pale, marked with lack of sleep and tears. She stood motionless in the doorway, as shocked as I was by the sight of him wearing her apron. He didn't say anything to her, he just opened his arms and stood there waiting. Then she let go of the clothes and buried herself in his arms with a sob. It was the only time they embraced in front of me. 'I'll do whatever you want, Fotiní,' he whispered and kissed her hair. And she said: 'If you love me, don't ever make me go through that again.'

Then he winked at me over her shoulder. I quietly finished my milk and, light as a bird, left them alone. They were late going to work that day and everything got behind, but in the evening at supper we had *koutalídes* with honey again, to sweeten the bitterness of the previous night. To celebrate, my mother sacrificed our poor cockerel and stewed it with macaroni. My favourite dish.

\*\*\*

Almost two weeks had passed since the evening I had watched the portentous flight of the cuckoo from our roof to the Haritákos's roof. March had arrived, my father's name day was approaching and my mother had a thousand jobs to get done.

'Make sure the animals are spick and span, Fotiní, or there'll be gossip!' my father would say and wink at me.

'There's a stone here, Mother,' I teased as she swept the yard till there wasn't a pebble to be seen. She pretended to be annoyed with us, but she was proud of her housekeeping and we were proud of her. The house shone, there wasn't a hint of dust anywhere and her *mezedákia* were the best in the village. She shone too. On my father's name day she always wore her best dress, combed her hair carefully – with Potítsa'a help – and wore scent. And she was beautiful. Very beautiful. Smiling she would welcome the villagers who came to wish us well. The Haritakaíoi usually arrived first, Aunt Katerina dressed in her best, Uncle Michális wearing his cap, and their three children: Sotíris, Yiorgís, and their last born, Marina, seven years younger than me, clinging to her mother's skirts, little and shy, with lovely eyes I can just about remember. Then there was my Uncle Nikifóros and my Aunt Aretí, Pavlákos's family, Leoúsis's, Kosmás's, Potítsa's and Yiánnis's of course. The children grabbed as much as they could eat and then went out to play. The grown-ups yelled at us to wrap up, but we didn't take any notice, focused on football. Men and women sat eating and talking separately, different interests, different conversations, and my mother constantly on her feet, making sure nothing was missing from the table.

It was cold again that year – harsh March – and it was the eve of the great feast day. My uniform for the following morning's parade was laid out on the bed, washed and ironed, the Maniot *vráka*, a wide-sleeved shirt, with the two-headed eagle embroidered on its sleeves in golden thread, the waistcoat with gold piping and the headscarf. My mother, sleeves rolled up, with her hair tucked into her headscarf to keep it out of the way, was at the sink scrubbing a large baking pan. She was simultaneously frying little cheese pies, the whole house smelled of cooking. Earlier she had baked *lalángia* and meatballs, the delicious smells made us faint with hunger. *Díples*, covered in honey, rested in a bowl next to her. 'I've put in fifteen eggs, do you think it'll be enough?' she asked Aunt Aretí anxiously. 'Poor Fotiní, you're overdoing it. It's a saint's day, not Odysséas's wedding! Then you'll see what a feast we'll cook!' She looked at me and I looked down awkwardly. That kind of talk got on my nerves.

I tasted all the *mezedákia, a lalángi* and then a *dípla* and then on to a meatball, and from a meatball to a *dolmá* with a piece of cheese on top, then another *dípla* and back to the beginning again.

'I'm off to find Yiánnis,' I shouted, but Fotiní stopped me at the door. 'Make a little room for this,' she said and put a hot cheese pie into my hand. The last image I have of her severe face sweetened with happiness was when she looked tenderly at me as I took the scalding cheese pie and vanished, jumping off the millstone in the yard. If only my mother had known what that afternoon's outing would bring, she would have nailed down the doors to keep me safely at home. But the memory of the cuckoo on our roof had already faded.

In the evenings by the church we either played football or an old Maniot game, *stratiotikó*, where the king and his officers have to catch the brigands. Petrea said it had been played by children in ancient Sparta. Our king was usually Sotíris Haritákos, who had the charisma for it, Yiánnis his adjutant, while Thomás Pavlákos and I – less good at obeying and better at hiding – were the brigands. We hid in sheep-pens, ruins, small caves, rows of cypresses, the rocks themselves. It's a mystery that Pavlákos ended up on the side of the law. We always reserved the role of spy for Kosmás, for obvious reasons.

That evening Pavlákos and I crept round on all fours to the back of the church, and then, passing literally under the nose of King Haritákos, we snuck into the church and hid in the sanctuary. We could have stayed there for as long as we wanted, but the game wasn't much fun without the chase and the obligatory cactus fights at the end. The others had left the king unguarded, so we leaped out on him and attacked him with prickly pears, until the others got wind of it and all hell broke loose. We scattered when it got dark and everyone went home covered in spikes and blissfully happy.

I was walking back home slowly, kicking at stones, still excited about the game, and proud of capturing the king, when suddenly someone came leaping at me out of the bushes and yelling: 'Don't move! Hands up!'

It was Yiorgís, the younger son of Michális Haritákos, and he was aiming straight at my face with his father's new hunting rifle. The boy was ten years old, dark-haired and skinny, small for his age, with legs like bamboos. He had been playing with us earlier and had taken it hard when his brother Sotíris was captured. Apparently he decided to get even by scaring the living daylights out of me. I was annoyed, but mesmerised by the gun he was holding. I knew that Haritákos had paid a lot of money for it. Hunting was his passion. It was a repeater with gold engravings on the handle. A beautiful piece! Like the rifles we saw in westerns at the travelling cinema. Hardened types with faces kneaded by the sun, holding guns like this one. There was nothing more I wanted at that moment than to hold it in my hands. I had to make the kid give it to me whatever the cost.

'Is that the gun your father bought? Hand it over, let's have a look at it.'

Instead of an answer, he aimed at my face.

'I'm going to kill you,' he said.

'Don't be an idiot!'

Involuntarily I took a step back. He was only ten, but there was no doubt that Yiorgís knew how to load and shoot. We all knew how to, even from a younger age. Yiorgís burst out laughing, pleased with himself for giving me a scare.

'Are you that stupid?' he mocked. 'It's empty, you idiot. My father emptied it, look!'

He put it into my hands and I can still remember the feel of it. It was warm from the boy's hands, warm and smooth. I stroked it! I examined it! Lovingly I handled the long barrel, the gold engraving and the trigger. I was so bewitched that I almost forgot about the boy.

'I'm going to get one like this one day.'

'It's a repeater. It takes three cartridges and you can shoot without reloading,' he said, reminding me of his presence. 'Shoot at me. See what it's like to take aim and fire. Don't be afraid, its not loaded! Loser! Hey, loser!' he laughed in my face.

What is the distance between a dream and a nightmare? A moment, an eye-blink, a nothing! A tragic mistake that put two houses in mourning, reawakened memories and hatred that had been forgotten for years, and began a new cycle of blood and revenge. If I could turn back time, little Yiorgís would be alive, and so would my father. He would have grown old beside my mother, with diabetes, high blood pressure and cholesterol, and I would have grown up in my homeland, I wouldn't have run away. Instead, without knowing how, I pressed the trigger, and the cuckoo that had fluttered over my house and over Yiorgákis's house two weeks before made a deafening croak inside my head. The next moment Yiorgís was lying dead on the ground, his head limp, like the birds I had killed during target practice with my father.

For a second that seemed an eternity, I saw the calamity I had unwittingly provoked and stood there perplexed. I could still hear his voice assuring me that the gun was empty, his laughter, his mockery. I looked around me in terror and saw my father, running. He was on his way back early from the *kafeneíon* as he had promised my mother, when he heard the gunshot. And then he saw us. Me with the gun in my hand looking abjectly from him to Yiorgákis, on the ground, with his eyes open. He understood, and he wasn't a man to hesitate. He gave me one of those looks that forbid any response or argument.

'Go home and don't say a word to anyone. Not even your mother.'

'I didn't mean …'

'Go home.'

# Backgammon

IT WAS LATE AFTERNOON, the hour when the sun finally decides to stop baking the stones. A southerly wind was blowing and no one was about. I had finished my shift at the Xemóni and wanted nothing more than to dive into a cold shower. The cop was waiting for me down under the shade of the mulberry tree. He already had the backgammon board open and the pieces in place.

'Shall we play *Plakotó?* Are you coming then?'

There was no point in objecting, and anyway I was curious as to why the former cop would leave the cool of the air conditioning at this time of day.

'Okay.'

I wasn't really in the mood. I hadn't seen Effie since the afternoon of the funeral, when she came down with Soula to the Xemóni, and it was bothering me. We sat down and the cop ordered ice cream. I tried to refuse, but he wouldn't hear of it.

'I want to sweeten you up so you won't mind losing. I have these dice at my beck and call, my lad. What do you think I took early retirement for, if not to hone my skills at backgammon?'

He was right. Ten minutes after we started, he had a row of sixes and I nothing but ones and twos.

'You'd better eat up that ice cream!' he joked.

I was furious.

'I'm not playing, Mr Thomá. I haven't even had my lunch yet.' I got up to go.

'Sit down!'

It was an order! He saw that I was getting angry and he looked me in the eye.

'Please,' he said, and his look – sharp, fatherly, and with a strange tenderness – said it too. Why? The thought that he may pity me for being a bastard worries me more than all the insults from Kosmás and Andreas. 'It's only a game of backgammon, don't take it to heart. You flare up too easily. I know you're young, but you need to learn to stay cool, and not flare up about nothing. You have your whole life ahead of you, do you understand me? And each of us only has one life and one alone. It mustn't be wasted, or thrown away. Now let's move on to *Pórtes!*'

'Forget it, it's not my day.'

'You don't have the luxury of choosing your days. You throw the dice, you hope, but you play whatever you throw, got it?'

I know that I shouldn't get pissed off with Pavlákos, he likes me and I like him. I don't know why, but that's how it is. I don't like cops, but I like him. His small, clever, nimble eyes see what they should and they see what they shouldn't, he doesn't miss a thing. He never does anything without a reason, and I know he has his reasons for this game. He knows that I've been smoking in secret, and I suspect he knows why. I wouldn't be surprised if he knows about my secret meetings with Effie at Anastasákos's house. He can sense the anger and hatred in me – he senses everything I'm trying to hide.

I concentrate on the game. I lose again, but with dignity at least, I keep fighting to the end. My ice cream melts in its tub, I barely taste it. We finish with *Févga*. My luck changes and my mood changes too. I tease him for supporting Panathinaikós. When did they last win a cup or a championship? And he rags me about our defeat at Wembley, which was centuries ago. I call Andreas over and order two ouzos.

'This one's on me,' I insist. 'This is a victory that has to be celebrated.'

'I'll have a drink, you won't. You can eat the *mezedákia.*'

'Whatever you say!'

He smiles.

'That's the way,' he says. 'Life has its funny side and that's the way we need to take it.'

Pavlákos and I have played thousands of games of backgammon, very few of which I've won. We've discussed every subject under the sun. We've quarrelled about politics because he's as right-wing as they come and I'm firmly on the left. We've quarrelled because I support Olympiakós and he supports Panathinaikós. And yet we play back-gammon together. Which means that we can discuss everything and yet continue to fight our own corner.

'So. What d'you think of Anastasákos?' he asks.

I shrug my shoulders.

'You know him. What should I think of him?'

He smiles again.

'The same as you'll be in thirty-four years' time. Because you're exactly the same as he was at your age.'

I'm speechless. He lowers his voice, Andreas is listening in on us.

'Calm down. I'm not about to interfere in your affairs, you know that. I just want to say one thing. Odysséas is not a bad guy, my lad. He's a man who lost a whole series of games and won a few others. Like you did just now. Like all of us. That's how you should think of him. And maybe you should take the chance to speak to him. To get to know him better. Think about it.'

We change the subject. We talk about the likely transfers to our teams. I stay with him for another half hour.

'You must have been very good at your job, Mr Thomá. I bet no one got away from you, you would have caught them all,' I say at some point.

'Hardly! The people I should have caught and who deserved it got away. Who do you think I caught? A few poor wretches like your grandfather. Anyone could have caught them.'

'I keep wondering why a person like you would become a cop.'

'I'll tell you, my lad,' he laughed and concluded with his usual refrain. 'At first I was a cop for my ideals. And then I stayed a cop out of self-interest.'

So that was why the cop left his nice cool house at this time of day to come out into the scorching heat: he's warning me. To be the illegitimate son of the daughter of a murderer has its problems, but it has its advantages too – people expect things from you, they keep their distance, or they come closer, depending … As for Anastasákos, I don't know what it is that scares me most when he finds out that I'm his son. That he'll come closer? Or that he'll board the first plane out.

Marina has gone to Athens and the less they see of each other the better. I don't let her out of my sight. No way am I going to let him see her alone, after what he said about her. She looked grim when she left, her lips set in a straight line. I let her kiss me and I kissed her on the cheek. 'Make sure you eat properly,' she said. 'Be careful!' She always says the same thing to me, but this time I can sense she's really anxious. The creep keeps driving past our house in that Mercedes of his. He comes to the Xemóni every single evening, either on his own or with his best friend Mitsikoyiánnis, and he watches me as if I'm a robotic provider of coffees and drinks. Various people hover around him, I know them all and I know why: a fat wallet is a big draw and his is loaded with cash. Pavlákos's daughter, Evangelía, who is well known to everyone without exception, has the hots for him. Her husband works in Athens, she's a teacher, and she has plenty of time in the summer for everything. He sends her down here to be by the sea with the children and she runs amok. It's the only thing the cop's eagle eye doesn't seem to notice. The creep is fully aware of her however; he smiles conceitedly – women like him and he knows it. At night when I can't sleep I can't get his hand out of my mind. It's not the hand of a pen-pusher, it's the hand of a farmer who digs the earth – Maniot earth, what's more. The only thing missing is callouses. He must keep in training over there, to stay in shape as he does, and maybe he plays that awful game, American football, which he's so crazy about! What can you say? Each to his own.

His mobile rings at the oddest times. I see him get up from the table, he apologises and moves away talking curtly in English, giving orders one after the other. Only once when he answered he was all sweetness, 'honey' this and 'honey' that, and I stood there gawping at him, because his hard expression had softened unbelievably, as if he was a completely different person. A woman, I'm sure of it. I took him his coffee and carelessly spilled some water on him. 'Sorry,' I said through my teeth, and he had to look at me. Effie was sitting at his table with her parents and Kostís, and I couldn't resist asking when I phoned her later: 'Who is that woman Anastasákos was sweet-talking?' It was Ellen, she told me, the daughter of his friend and colleague in America, who calls him 'uncle' and whom he loves like a daughter! Imagine! He even showed them photographs, a very pretty blonde with blue eyes. 'Thank goodness she isn't here, I would be very jealous,' Effie said. She cheered me up with her jealousy, the silly thing. Who would look at a frigid *Americána*, when he has a creature like Effie? Anastasákos, most likely.

# Wreckage

THE AGE OF EMPIRE IS OVER. Whole civilisations vanished from the map because someone took the wrong decision at the wrong moment. And I changed my life in an instant. I wrecked my home along with the home of our ancestral enemies. I don't remember exactly what happened afterwards, how I got back home, how I went up to the tower without my mother seeing me. There is a gap in my memory. I was trembling and dribbling out of the side of my mouth. It must have been some form of fit from the appalling shock.

I did what he told me. As I walked away, I heard him calling me. I turned round. He was holding the boy in his arms and his look had something other than tenderness.

'Odysséa! Remember the ants,' were his last words to me.

I shut myself in on the top floor without saying a word. My mother fell asleep by the fire and waited for my father to come back.

I waited for him too in my room, my eyes fixed on the road, my ears straining for the slightest sound. His steady, heavy footsteps on the path. I still hoped. Maybe Yiorgís was still alive. Surely there was no problem that my father couldn't solve. He would have taken him to the doctor and everything would be all right.

I slept and dreamt that I was walking at Gytheio, and the sea was lapping at my naked feet when I noticed that the water was red and a sea of blood lay before me. I leaped up in fear and I was certain then that nothing was all right. Yiorgís was dead and my father … Where was my father? I went downstairs. The house was deserted, the front door open. Still dark outside. I went into the yard and saw him lying on the great millstone, his shirt covered in blood, and my mother beside him crying silently, holding him in her arms.

My mother sent me to call Uncle Nikifóros. I banged my fists on the door and he opened it, undressed and barely awake. I told him that they had killed my father. People had gathered at our house. News spreads quickly in a small place. At the tower of the Haritakaíoi, Aunt Katerina was keening over Yiorgís's lifeless body, lamenting and cursing his fate. The previous evening, after sending me away, my father had taken Yiorgís in his arms and carried him home. Aunt Katerina was preparing supper and Marina, her youngest child, just eight years old, was helping her lay the table. He crossed the threshold without hesitating. He had made up his mind to take responsibility, his grief was genuine and there was no one there to contradict him. Yiorgís was dead and I had promised to say nothing. He knew very well how quickly Michális Haritákos flared up, and how often his tongue and his actions ran away with his good sense. He knew that nothing could change what had happened. Their boy wouldn't be coming back and he couldn't let me be at risk. His last act in life was to protect me.

We carried my father into the house and placed him on his bed next to the kitchen. Crying silently, my mother laid out his body, preparing him herself for his journey. She washed and changed the man with whom she had lived for so many years, the man she had loved since she was a girl, sharing everything: the hard work, the worries, the problems, the joy and the grief. And when the time came, she dressed herself in black and went out to hand him over to Charon, crying and singing her *moiroloy.*

> *Where will I find you, where*
> *is the mountain, where is the cliff*
> *to hurl myself down …*

Michális Haritákos was arrested in his home a little while after Yiorgákis's funeral. He didn't try to escape. He left his wife alone in the hard, arid Mani to bring up another son and a daughter. She and my mother met at the cemetery, dressed in black, both lamenting at the graves of their loved ones. My mother went alone – she didn't want me to see her cry. *Thía* Katerina took Marina with her, clinging to her skirt.

My mother came back home pale and dry-eyed, but I could sense her terrible grief and she knew what I was feeling, as mothers always know. I felt her wakeful eyes on me, felt her following me like a shadow, and behind her the shadow of Uncle Nikifóros. She wouldn't let me out of her sight for a minute. And when my guilt was insupportable, and I came down the stairs at midnight, wild and determined, with my father's hunting rifle in my hand, I found my mother standing at the door of the tower house, her hair loose, barring my way.

'Where are you going?'

Where was I going? To the Haritákos's house to kill again? Or to find some corner to blow my own brains out? Or both perhaps. What I was living through had no reason, and nor had I. I hadn't yet told anyone what really happened. Not out of fear for myself, so much as out of shock and bewilderment. And because he had asked me not to. All my life I've regretted that silence. I don't know what would have happened if I had spoken earlier. Would Haritákos's eldest son have killed me instead? Would I have gone to prison? But at least the guilt wouldn't have eaten away at me like woodworm! I might have been free of it.

That evening I did speak to my mother. I told her everything even though I'd promised my father not to speak. I couldn't bear her looking at me, her eyes full of tears. I had to share my burden with someone whose shoulders could take it and there wasn't anyone else.

'There's no point in living,' I told her.

My mother, the daughter of the drunkard, who for so many years had borne the shame of her father. If I had one ounce of honour I would have kept my mouth shut, or I would have given myself up to the police. But she put her body between me and the door and kept me there. Perhaps because I didn't have the courage it would have taken to go. She sat me down and I told her.

'What did your father say to you when he sent you home?'

'To remember the ants.'

She decided my future for me then and there, without asking or giving me room to object. At fifteen you are still a child. I must go far enough away to forget everything. She would write to her brother, Sarándos Layákos, in America, and ask him to take care of me. I would start a new life and leave behind everything I loved. That would be my punishment. And my duty was to build a bright future, just as my father had dreamt for me, so that his death would have some meaning. Nothing would stop me, just as no one and nothing can stop the ants from reaching their goal. She was our sun and the centre of our world, and we always did anything she asked of us.

# *Xénos*

IN JULY 1976 I ARRIVED in New York, where my uncle was expecting me. Sarándos had married an American woman. She was a tall, bony, mean-faced aunt with money. He was the owner of three supermarkets and he gave me a job, food, a bed, and nothing more than that. His wife said outright that she had no intention of looking after his good-for-nothing relatives from Greece. They didn't have children and they seemed to me dry, sour-tempered people, empty of all feeling. All that money and they had never sent a drachma home. Very quickly I realised that if I fell into the groove my uncle had set for me, I was lost. I wanted to leave from the moment I arrived, but I was underage, penniless and I didn't speak the language. I had no choice. I got up before daybreak, worked in the supermarket, went back home and helped the servants in the house. I worked twice as hard without being paid, because I had the privilege of being a relative.

Every Thursday my aunt invited her friends for tea. She decorated the large drawing room with flowers she chose herself, arranging them in the vases with particular care, as if the whole world depended on the placing of an orchid. Poor old Antonella, the Neapolitan maid, was rushed off her feet. She had worked in the house since she was a girl, and I helped her with everything – housework, sweeping and even baking the cakes. 'Come here, *picolino*, taste it and tell me if they've turned out all right,' she would say, stuffing me full of cake. 'Come on, angel, eat it, you're far too thin!' It would never have occurred to my aunt to offer me cake. It wasn't that I wanted it, it was the difference in attitude that I couldn't understand. The women in my village always saved the best treats for their guests. You couldn't step over the threshold without being offered something. But when Aunt Bess's friends came, indolent old bags, opinionated and stuck up, she told me to disappear and not set foot in the drawing room on any account. All this was incomprehensible and insulting to me. Without realising it, I started to keep a record of the insults, one by one. I was certain that my time would come to repay them, though I didn't know how.

When I asked my uncle if I could go to school, he looked at me as if I had lost my reason, he couldn't understand why I wanted to waste my time with something so useless. For the first time I missed Yioúli Petrea, with her interminable monologues about ancient customs and her critique of *Antigone*. I missed my parents unbearably, my mother's caress, Uncle Nikifóros, Aunt Aretí, Potítsa, my friend Mitsikoyiánnis, our chats, our games. At night, however tired I was, I lay wide awake, thinking that I'd got what I deserved. This was my punishment for everything that happened. Like my Uncle Sarándos before me, I never wrote home. I didn't have the courage to speak about my life to the people I loved, or share my sadness with them.

Eventually I enrolled in a night school and went to the classes in secret. When my uncle found out he didn't like it at all. I was ungrateful, he said, wasting my time doing nothing. But there was no question of my giving it up. America was my chance, and I felt it my duty to do what my parents had asked of me.

That same evening I left my uncle's house. I was alone now in an unknown, hostile city, thousands of miles away from the place where I was born, my pockets empty, and with nothing to eat. A city where everything seemed enormous and unwelcoming, full of threatening, wretched people like me. After hours of wandering around, tired and hungry, I went to sleep under a bridge. The only thought that comforted me as I watched people wandering around like ghosts in the dark was that they probably hadn't killed anyone and so they might be less dangerous than me.

The next morning, blue with cold, I went into a restaurant run by a Greek called Zafirópoulos and I asked for a job. But I had no papers, so I was offered a plate of food and some money and told to leave. I refused the food and money. I, Odysséas Anastasákos, the last of my line, whose namesake had crushed Ibrahim at the battle of Verga, I knew that my ancestors never bowed their heads under any yoke. If it was a choice between the yoke of starvation and poverty and the yoke of my American aunt, I preferred the first. Better to be hungry and free, than fed and tethered to my uncle's manger. Come back holding your shield or lying on it, either victorious or dead!

That evening I went as usual to my English lessons and asked my teacher for help. He was a young black man and he helped me to find work in a clothing factory. The wages were pitiful. No question of national insurance. The factory was run illegally in the basement of an old building and at least 150 people worked there. Blacks and Latin Americans. I was the only Greek. They greeted me with a plastic cup of coffee and a piece of bread – I wasn't the first to keel over with hunger the minute I arrived there. It was the most delicious bread I had ever eaten. Then they put me to work. We slept there, piled on top of each other like animals. The stink of bad breath and excrement from so many people is still in my nostrils.

Another month went by like that, work all day followed by night school, when one afternoon I saw my uncle standing outside the school waiting for me. He told me he'd been worried and he asked me to come back – after all, we had the same blood, I was the son of his dead sister. I refused. He pleaded and threatened and finally he promised to put my name down at the local secondary school and pay someone to teach me English at home.

I accepted the school, but refused the English lessons. I had grown fond of the young black teacher at night school, who had helped me when I came to him out of the blue, and of my classmates, all desperate kids like myself, looking for their place in the sun. By the time school started I was able to communicate in English enough to get by. At first I tried to keep a low profile. There were often fights and I didn't want to get into trouble. I needed time to get used to things, to learn the rules. As I got better at English my confidence grew, and I soon stopped hiding myself away.

And then there were the girls! Potítsa, God bless her, had been right. I never did forget her. It was she who taught me how to use my hands and my tongue, how a caress and a kiss on a woman's body becomes a returning flame that burns you all over. She had given me a gift of invaluable knowledge, which few people had at my age. Maybe that was why Uncle Nikifóros, who never missed a trick, had waited for her outside my house that evening and handed her a huge bag of oranges. No one else guessed, they knew of her strong friendship with my mother, and she always came by with something for me: *koutalídes* with honey, or little cheese pies, or sometimes a piece of *halvá*.

I may have had problems with English, but I had no problems at all with the language of the body. Girls in America seemed to me like houris from paradise, all different colours, shapes and sizes. It was Sandy, a girl at the supermarket who told me about the night classes, who first invited me to her home. At the time my uncle had winked at me knowingly, taken a packet of condoms off the shelf and shoved them into my hand.

'Do you know how to use them?'

I knew! Aunt Potítsa had shown me. 'Remember Leonídas? You're a Spartan: sword at the ready, but the shield tight in your hand. Leonidas was no fool. Don't let yourself be taken in by some little hussy who gets you pregnant. Or worse. Diseases, my boy. Don't put your health at risk for any girl. They'll be queuing up for you, you'll remember I told you so.'

Sandy lived alone. From the one and only window in her tiny apartment, we looked out at the snow-covered city. Dirty snow at the side of the road. We ate pizza that she'd ordered and drank beer. I barely touched mine. Despite being older, Sandy wasn't all that experienced. In any case she let me take control that evening and all the evenings that followed, for about two weeks. I liked Sandy, with her boyish breasts and straw-coloured hair, and after our meetings I went home happy, to some extent, for the first time since I had left my homeland. Every evening she would ask me to stay with her for the night and every evening I said no. I didn't think about it much then, though I should have. Why would I rather see my aunt's sour face than share a bed with Sandy? Much later I realised that it wasn't Sandy's fault, and that I couldn't share a bed with anyone. My nights, full of nightmares and guilt, are my own private affair.

It lasted for two weeks, and I split up with Sandy before that snow had melted. I didn't tell her why, because there was nothing to say. The difference in our ages, I thought, explained my disappearing. She saw me by chance some time later in a café with another girl. Every time the frost makes icicles off the gutter of a roof, I remember Sandy looking at me in bewilderment and surprise, more astonished than hurt. 'I thought you were nice,' she said. No, I wasn't nice. One time back in my country I had committed a murder, and then I ran to the other side of the world to hide. I stroked her cheek and told her it was better this way. I didn't see her again.

\*\*\*

I did okay at school and applied for funding to Harvard and then, just when I had come of age, my uncle died suddenly in his sleep. All the leading members of the Greek community came to his funeral, among them Yerásimos Kafátos, a Cephalonian friend of my uncle's. *Diaólou káltsa*! A 'devil's sock' of a man. He was involved in a number of businesses, not all of them totally legal, as I found out later. My situation had been made known to him by Zafirópoulos, the owner of the restaurant where I had asked for work, and who had thrown me out into the street. Kafátos listened to my story, or to the part I decided to tell him, and there and then offered to pay some of my tuition fees. No doubt it was a unique opportunity for me, but I was old enough by now to know that nothing comes for free. So I looked at him squarely and asked: 'And what do I have to do to get this money?'

Kafátos the Cephalonian laughed out loud and slapped me on the back.

'You're no fool. Actually I did have something in mind for you, but never mind that. I like you and I'll help you, if you want to help yourself. Come and see me at the office on Monday.'

He gave me his card. I was about to leave when the Cephalonian's voice made me turn round.

'*Mikré*, if you don't have anywhere to sleep tonight, don't hesitate to come to my house. The address is on the card.'

I couldn't think why he would say that, but as soon as everyone had gone, my aunt's expression made it clear. I was no longer welcome at her house. I got my books and clothes together, kissed *Nona* Antonella, the Neapolitan woman who loved me, and Roddy, the black man who worked in the garden. Antonella was in tears. 'Where will you go, *picolino mou*?' she whispered. Roddy pressed his sister's address into my hand, in case I needed it, along with a few dollars. 'Take them, don't insult me. It's a loan. You'll give me them back double or triple after Harvard, and I've spoken to my sister about you – she'll put you up in the baby's room.' I cried for the first time since my parents' funerals.

I said a formal goodbye to my aunt and took a taxi straight to the Cephalonian's house, where I was shown into the library, an enormous room full of books, with a heavy, expensive desk and luxurious sofas. Kafátos was relaxing on one of them, drinking scotch on the rocks and reading. I peered at the book. *Das Kapital* by Karl Marx. As I said, he had breadth. He lived with his wife, about thirty-five years his junior, a classic blonde called Cathy. She was out, which was a relief because I thought she might turn up her nose at me like Aunt Bess.

He got up to greet me and smiled.

'What's up, *mikré*, did the old bag throw you out already? And I thought that you Maniots had your women on the hop!'

He laughed, asked the maid to bring in some sandwiches and a beer, and made me feel immediately more relaxed than I'd ever felt in my uncle's house. Kafátos, whose perceptions were sharp, had an even sharper tongue and with a few caustic remarks about my aunt managed to convey fully all my thoughts and feelings in deliciously risqué Greek. For the first time since I'd arrived in America, I laughed long and hard despite the gross obscenities. I wasn't used to them – we didn't talk like that at home.

'Don't hold it against her. You'll see, in a few years you'll feel sorry for her. She had the money and Sarándos had the brains and did the work. They'll soon have it off her and she'll be left with nothing, the *zourlokanéla*!' he said.

He told me to stay with him for as long as I liked, wherever I wanted, the house was enormous. We could live there together for months and never set eyes on each other. If I needed anything I was to ask the staff, he said.

The maid came in bearing two enormous sandwiches on a tray together with a beer. What with the funeral and everything I hadn't eaten a morsel. I hadn't got on with my uncle, but he had been my only relative over here. I could feel myself giving way to tears.

'He was proud of you,' said the Cephalonian. 'It was "my nephew this, my nephew that" every time he saw me. "He'll do well one day, he's made of fine stuff," he used to say.'

I always feel as if something was left unfinished with my mother's brother. As if something was left unsaid. He did try in the end. But I was so hurt by the way he had behaved in the beginning, that I never made the two or three steps it would have taken for us to get close to one another. Maybe if he hadn't died so suddenly, if we had had more time, I don't know. He took me in like you take a burden that someone suddenly loads on to your back against your will. And yet the moment I unburdened him by leaving home, he couldn't have been more concerned. Maybe he was freaked out by the responsibility, maybe he had wanted to cut all his ties with the past, and I reminded him of who he once was: an illiterate peasant, with no future under the sun.

Exhausted I went up to the room they had made ready for me. I hadn't touched the beer, which Kafátos noticed and liked. I slept deeply, but not for long. The nightmare woke me at dawn. The same nightmare that had tormented me every night since the deaths of Yiorgís and my father. The blood-red sea at Gytheio lapping at my bare feet. I woke up in a sweat as always and I couldn't get back to sleep.

I met Cathy the following morning at breakfast. She was barely thirty and drop-dead gorgeous! She smiled at me encouragingly. We were alone; Kafátos had already gone to his office in the centre of town. He had told her about me and given clear instructions. I was to be their guest, and as such I should have everything I wished. I wondered what the woman thought of having me suddenly living in her house. I soon realised that Kafátos was pretty eccentric and his wife had grown used to his eccentricities. I didn't feel comfortable, and I told her so. I wasn't used to being a guest, and I'd be happier if they gave me something to do. I didn't want to sit idle. With a smile like a toothpaste advertisement, Cathy suggested that I go shopping with her and I refused. I wasn't sure what Kafátos would think of my wandering about the streets with his wife. So I told her that when I asked for work I meant just that, and that I couldn't stand shops and shopping, which was partly true.

I stayed in the house all day, mostly reading in the library, and had lunch alone. I examined the dining room with its expensive furniture, thick curtains and precious paintings hanging on the walls. It all screamed money. And yet it was an empty house. I remembered our tower house back home. My mother and father late in the afternoon, sitting at the millstone, exhausted from the labours of the day, still in their work clothes, sipping coffee. Now and then the odd word. My father's broad, calloused hand on my shoulder as if to say 'I'm here'. He'd never actually said 'I'll protect you with my life', not in so many words, but his hand on my shoulder told me just that. And then, when it was necessary, he told me so again by his actions. My father, who never finished primary school.

It wasn't just the difference in age that made the Kafátos couple seem sad, nor the obvious advantage they took of one another – of youth on the one hand, and money on the other. Even the most self-less couples take advantage in some way. It was the hint of desolation in the eyes of the old man, and the all too evident ennui in the eyes of his beautiful wife. She's cheating on him, I thought to myself, and he knows it. I was right, as it turned out.

That summer before I started at university I worked in one of Kafátos's businesses, an underground car park. I parked cars, washed them, cleaned, filled up with petrol. It was there that I learnt to drive and got my driver's licence. During all that time I lived in his house. He liked my spirit, as he said, my hard work and the respect I showed him. And why shouldn't I? He was a stranger to me and yet he treated me like a relative, or more so. I think he also valued my keeping a proper distance from his wife. Because the Cephalonian's perceptions were sharp and he had noted Cathy's flirting and my polite indifference. I just played dumb. The lady was adorable, but New York was full of women. I wasn't prepared to disgrace myself for the sake of a romp.

In the end I got my grant to Harvard and I didn't need Kafátos's help. But he got me a room in the best wing of the hostel and thanks to his contacts with the Greeks in Boston he guaranteed me work. He advised me to start the process of acquiring US citizenship, and helped me with his contacts and his reputation. With all the money he had, he could move mountains.

'Who knows? One day you may become president,' he teased. 'We've never yet had a Greek president.'

I had left Greece in 1976, soon after the Greek dictatorship, and

I imagined Harvard to be full of students with long hair and flared jeans, painting the walls with slogans, holding sit-ins and condemning the adult world and its establishment. It couldn't have been more different. The daughter of the mayor of Boston ate with us in the canteen, the children of senators and millionaires and all the future elite of the country were gathered there. Among them were kids from home, not hopeless cases like myself, but scions of well-known wealthy, political families. To survive among those fluttering peacocks was perhaps harder for me than making it through the night alone under that bridge, penniless and homeless in New York. There were of course a few others like me, chasing after grants and working like beavers to survive. One of them was John Petersen, fourth-generation Dutch, my room mate in the hostel.

***

John and I couldn't have been more different, and at first I tried his patience sorely. Due to my Maniot upbringing I hadn't learned rudimentary housekeeping, my mother had looked after me like a prince because I was the man of the house after my father. She believed that when the time came for her to stop taking care of me, I would have a woman by my side who would go on pampering me just like she pampered my father. If it hadn't been for Antonella, I wouldn't have known how to make my bed. Also I smoked, which John detested. But despite our differences we soon became the best of friends. He invited me to his house in New Jersey for Christmas, a typical American home, which was nothing like my home in Greece, and yet it reminded me of the tower house like no other I had visited all this time in America. Our two homes had something in common which I spotted at once. I could smell it in the air. From the well-tended garden, the flowered curtains, the smells from the kitchen, to the laughter, the endearments and the teasing. It was as if something of the aura of the tower house had touched me from afar, bringing back the delight of my mother's cooking, the protective presence of my father, the silences and glances exchanged by my parents on those afternoons in the scented Maniot landscape. And when John's mother asked me over coffee: 'Are you missing home?' I found myself telling them all about the harsh land, the implacable sun, the Mani of my heart. It was the first time I had spoken to anyone about my country ever since I'd left it. The houses standing guard and keeping our peculiar homeland free all through the dark years of Turkish occupation, the hard struggle of the people, labouring in the heat, the piracy and the vendettas.

'How could a bunch of people avoid being conquered by an entire empire? It seems incredible ...' remarked Mrs Petersen.

I had often wondered what had kept the conquerors out and made the Maniots so irrepressible. It isn't the people who make a country; it is the earth that fashions them to be worthy of it. I told them a story I thought might explain it.

'It was June, the month of harvest, the men were away at Verga, the gateway to the Mani, where they had been attacked by the enemy. In 1826, the fifth year of the War of Greek Independence, it all appeared to be over. The Egyptian army sent by the sultan, a regularly army, trained and armed by the French, had fallen to the freedom fighters. It was the last pocket of resistance, and their leader Ibrahim, the son of the terrible Mohammed Ali, decided to finish us off. The Mani had by now become a refuge for anyone fleeing the enemy, and a place where they could reorganise themselves and begin another uprising. Ibrahim planned to attack Verga as a diversion, while simultaneously landing at Diro, and getting to the Mani by sea.

'The only people left at home were the old, the sick, and women and children, all busy on the *loúres* with the harvest. *Loúres* were the small strips of earth among the stones that were cultivated to ensure the food vital for survival. The enemy was approaching and the church bells rang out to sound the alarm. A horseman set off to warn the men that we were being attacked from the south, but they didn't have time to get back. So our women and children shut themselves in the towers to await the enemy, who were taken by surprise.

'Now,' I said, warming to my theme, 'the hour of the *Maniátissa* draws nigh, this formidable woman who works tirelessly night and day, in silence, without ever asking for a thing. She pulls the harvest sickle from her belt and, just as silently and tirelessly, she emerges from the portal of the tower and harvests the heads of the enemy like straw. As the women chase the enemy soldiers away, they try to throw themselves into the sea, calling on Allah to help them, in vain, because a mounted posse of our men arrives just in time and falls on them. That was the battle of Diró, which is not referred to in the official histories, and which until recently no one celebrated and few people remember. The women didn't claim any victory, and when they learnt that the battle at Verga had also ended in a victory for our side, they just picked up their sickles and went back to work in their fields as silent as ever. Because the stomach doesn't wait, it needs bread. We know that at heart, the spirit of the Mani is the strength of its women, however little we admit it and however much they humour us into thinking that we men are the ones who count. They bring us up to believe it, and God help us if we are found wanting. No quarter is given in the Mani.'

I went quiet. I'd already said more than I should have. I had admitted there, in front of them all, that I was found wanting, no quarter was given and this voluntary exile was just. I deserved it and I had no choice but to bear it. One of my ancestors was killed in the battle of Verga, his wife must have survived, I presume, and raised her children. It's my fate to live and die alone at the other end of the world, I thought, forgotten by friends and family, driven away by blood unjustly spilt. My mother had said: 'The debt has been more than paid,' but I still owed. That was how I felt then. I still have a debt to the Haritakaíoi and they owe me. No one can ever pay enough, some debts are written down and stay like that. Unpaid. Poor John tried to make a joke to lighten the atmosphere.

'Buddy, I had no idea you came from a free Gaulish village in an all-powerful Roman empire!'

His sister Emma was worried that I might feel awkward and she intervened: 'Shut up, John …'

But I didn't mind. I never mind being teased by John, one never minds a thing that's said out of love.

'I come from a Greek village. We don't have Druids or magic potions,' I replied, in the same vein.

We sat down to eat and they didn't ask me anything else, my friend had long been aware that it was painful for me to remember. His mother understood too, she served me my food with tenderness, and his father, if he hadn't been Dutch, reserved, and a man of few words, might have extended his hand in a friendly gesture, a pat on the back, let's say. That's the kind of thing my father would have done.

\*\*\*

Back in Boston, once I had got over the shock of being accepted into the university, and solved my maintenance problem by getting a job in a Greek restaurant, the Mythos, I threw myself into my studies. John and I made a virtue of necessity and studied together, since we were both aiming to do well. We both needed grants, because John's family – his father an accountant, his mother a teacher – couldn't cover the expensive fees any more than I could.

I love Boston. It was love at first sight, unlike New York, which I hated from the moment I set foot there. Boston is linked to my student years and to John, New York with my Aunt Bess and what I endured at her house. Here, in this town, I lived my life as best I could, through bitterness and joy, and made my fortune. But I miss my own land and there are times when I feel like a sick person who is being slowly devoured by worms, and who to save his life has to cut off the diseased limb. In my case the limb that was severed wasn't minor, a finger or a toe. It was an essential organ, the centre of my being, as if they had taken out a piece of my heart.

Spring comes late here, as if it's on strike. I missed home so much and I shared my thoughts with my friend. I told him about summers in the Mani, when the sun burns the stones fit to roast them. The earth in Massachusetts is like an unloved body, wearing itself out with foreplay without ever coming to orgasm, and Boston, this jewel of a town, seemed to me nothing but foreplay. He laughed at all my eccentricities and that annoyed me. Easy to laugh when you haven't lived through a summer-in-furnace.

***

In Boston that year we barely noticed that summer had arrived. Classes ended and most students went away for the holidays. But John and I had jobs that we didn't dare leave. Instead we worked longer hours and met up in the evening for the odd drink. One evening out we noticed a guy whose accent and manner immediately caught my attention. I could tell he was a compatriot and I called him over to our table. Slightly short, tending on the fat side, expensively, formally dressed, he didn't look as if he had a lot in common with us, nevertheless that drink was the beginning of a long-standing friendship.

Although he bumped into many old classmates of his from Athens, Stefanos Olympios felt more at ease with us, impoverished as we were, than with his wealthy friends who tried to impress us all with their expensive cars, clothes and women. In general terms the three of us kept well away from excess. Petersen sometimes overdid it with the drink, Olympios went overboard now and then at a wild party, and I smoked like an Arab, as they say back home, but I kept well away from drink and drugs.

During Olympios's first Christmas in Boston his sister came to visit. Andromache Olympiou was tall, slim and dark. She was so well dressed that beside her most of our fellow students looked shabby and charmless. Despite her youth she spent endless hours at the hairdresser's. She stayed at the most expensive hotel in town. We were delighted with her and the delight was mutual. In the twenty days of her stay she slept with both of us, first with me, then with John. And afterwards with many others. Stefanos seemed perfectly relaxed about it but for me it was a shock. I had different memories of the customs back home. In my particular home, the Mani, this kind of thing was a big deal, you couldn't play around with girls just like that. It was inconceivable for a woman to swap men like changing a shirt, and what's more with the blessing of her brother. 'What about Potítsa?' you may ask. But Potítsa was a special case, the exception that proved the rule. Maybe we were a bit old-fashioned, I thought, but even in Athens this kind of thing wouldn't have seemed very normal. Once more I realised that it was all a matter of money. When your purse is full, you do what you like, you don't answer to anyone. Money makes you all-powerful, you forget other values, because with the value of money alone you can buy all the others.

I laugh when I think of how careful I was at the beginning. I kept my distance, as I had done with Cathy, Kafátos's wife. I grew up in a community where the man was the hunter and the woman the prey, and the hunt excited me more than the pleasure itself. When I found myself suddenly outside the closed environment of my village in a society without restraint, I felt as if I had been let loose in a garden with every kind of exotic bird and all I had to do was to take aim and shoot freely. Sex with Máchi was one of my best experiences, maybe because she was a woman without inhibitions. Or because, as Olympios used to say, it's quite different making love in your mother tongue. Or maybe it was because she was like me: she loved men as I loved women – 'in general', as John would say. She chased after any man who took her fancy and her brother didn't show the least concern. I had no intention of spoiling her fun, but I didn't pay her all that much attention, unlike John, who was wild about her. They suit me, those kinds of women, but I don't really like them all that much, and I would never take them seriously.

My numerous and fleeting affairs were common knowledge among the Greeks of Boston. To John's bewilderment I had a lot of success with women for reasons that I knew well: 'What the hell do they see in you?' he said. How could he know that thanks to Potítsa's experience and invaluable advice, I never felt awkward with girls, because I knew what to do in bed and how to do it. Also I refused to pretend I was something I wasn't, and they got just what they saw. Why should I be afraid? I had killed a person, my mother and father were dead and buried, I had left behind everything I loved most of all, my homeland and its people. What more could possibly happen to me? I was the ant and all I saw before me was the anthill. Everything else was irrelevant.

I was always bumping into someone I knew, even in such a big city. Third- or fourth-generation immigrants most of them, and however much they tried to preserve their traditions, they were all either genuine Americans or caricatures of Americans. It was as if they lived in another universe, parallel to my own, with common points of reference, and yet foreign. The fact that I owed so much to them repelled me even more, because I hated being in debt to anyone. Nevertheless, whenever and wherever they needed me I was happy to help, regardless of the time or the money it cost me. And I was always there at celebrations, weddings, funerals and birthday parties.

When I saw Kafátos at one of these events I asked for news of my Aunt Bess. She had vanished from the gatherings of the Greek community, but he always knew what was going on and had kept up with her news. She had teamed up with a younger man and was spending all her money on him.

'Didn't I tell you they would have all her money in a flash, the *zourlokanéla*!'

\*\*\*

Stefanos went back to Athens for the summer vacation, and John said it was time for him to take a trip back home, too. I stayed in Boston despite the pleas of the Dutchman to go with him, if only for a few days. The summer rolled on slowly. I worked longer hours at the Mythos and earned more money, and from washing dishes in the kitchen, hidden behind mountains of saucepans, baking trays and piles of dirty dishes, I gradually progressed into the dining room, where I was trained by the 'maitre dee' of the restaurant.

My boss was called Jack Magnus, or to be precise, Iákovos Magnisális, a second-generation Greek from Sigri in Lesvos.

'You're a good-looking lad and you're smart,' Mr Magnus said to me one day. 'I can get anyone to work back there. Whoever heard of a Harvard student washing the dishes?'

I learned how to stand before customers with my back slightly bowed, and that the customer is always right even when he complains without reason and makes ridiculous demands. A waiter is a kind of breakwater. He hears the problem first and if he's good at his job he is the only one who hears it, the matter is dealt with there. He is the front man. I had issues with the bowing. I could never do it. I smiled formally, I was polite, I played dumb to rude behaviour, and I was particularly good at dealing with difficult customers, but I didn't bow down to them. Literally and metaphorically, I've never bowed down to anyone in my life.

And as it turned out, that summer at the Mythos marked the beginning of my future career.

While I had been working away quietly in the scullery, with a Vietnamese and an Italian, scrubbing grimy saucepans for hours on end, I noticed that provisions not only entered the restaurant but also left it before our very eyes – since as kitchen boys we were the lowest of the low, no more than human dishwashers, and no one cared what we saw. Expensive wines vanished as if by magic, exotic seafood would spoil through a series of unlucky events and although the restaurant was full of customers, we barely covered our costs. It was pure theft and many people were in on the game, including the Italian waiter, the chief of supplies, and an accountant who kept the books. I didn't feel a particular commitment to the restaurant, but I liked Magnisális. He gave me a job, he fed me for nothing, he regularly asked me whether I needed money, and I always said no: 'You should stretch your legs as far as your blanket reaches,' as my mother used to say. So when I saw what was happening I reckoned it was my duty to let him know. I had no problem in telling Magnisális about the Italian, even though he made it clear that he had links with various shady types and most people in the restaurant were afraid of him. The chief of supplies, on the other hand, was the boss's oldest nephew. Magnus had no children and was particularly fond of him. It was said that he would inherit one day, so it made no sense at all. His uncle gave him everything he wanted. Why would the idiot take such a risk just to steal from his own pocket? Then one day the Vietnamese guy nudged me just as the boss's nephew was going out of the restaurant with his pocket bulging. 'He's off to play roulette.' A compatriot of his who worked at the casino had told him. The nephew was a gambling addict.

One evening after I'd clocked off Magnisális gave me a lift back to campus. He looked worried and preoccupied and I could tell he wanted to share it, but I waited for him to speak first. He asked me about my studies, although he knew very well that I was studying economics. He was clearly agitated.

'I don't understand, my boy, how a restaurant like mine, which is going so well, stays in the red. Do you know how much money I've lost this last month?'

I told it to him straight that for a place like his to be in the red meant one of two things – bad management or theft, and I offered to take a look at the books. From his expression I could see that although Magnisális had never studied economics, he had come to the same conclusion.

'Shall we take a look now?' he said.

I agreed and he turned the car around. It wasn't difficult to find the proof I was looking for. Every evening, after everyone else had left, my boss gave me the keys to the office. I worked almost until dawn comparing the receipts with the accounts and one week later I laid out the scale of the theft before him in all its magnitude. He followed my advice and for fifteen days behaved as if he knew nothing; we didn't want to give them time to cover their tracks, or to leave the restaurant short-staffed before we had a chance to replace them. Then we broke the news to the staff and sacked those responsible. Naturally my role in uncovering the racket didn't stay secret. The Italian threatened me outright, but I told him to go fuck himself in such a way that I never heard from him again, because he realised I wasn't just another frightened cleaning lady and that he'd do better to watch out.

After that, I got out of washing dishes and waiting at table for good. I became the restaurant's financial advisor and its profits soared. Magnisális showed his gratitude by tripling my wages and said he was wiling to cover the bulk of my fees at university for the following year. He didn't need to, but he mentioned me to two or three very rich Greeks, which was useful later on when John and I set up our office. I'd thought about it for a while, and then one day I suggested it to him.

We were sitting in our room at the hostel. John was drinking an iced beer, absorbed in reading an article in the *Financial Times*, when, conquering my need to light a cigarette, I threw a pair of rolled-up sports socks at him to get his attention. He looked up from the newspaper and gazed at me with those wide, blue, innocent eyes of his, the boyish lock of hair flopping down over his forehead.

'What would you say to the two of us setting up a consultancy business for companies that need it, like what I did for Magnisális?'

# Effie

THE SEA IS GENTLY LAPPING at the Mavromicháli Palace, gilded by the first rays of the rising sun. Pavlákos is sitting in the boat, fishing. He looks up from the water and gazes around him at the seashore, the dawn, the boat, the fishing line that isn't moving at all. And finally at me.

I get on to the boat dripping with water. I don't ask whether Pavlákos has remembered to time me, it's abundantly clear that he has forgotten, absorbed in his battle with the poor unfortunate fish, and lost in the beauty of the morning. Anyway there's no point in timing me. Instead of going faster I'm getting slower, I've done so little training. If only my mother would listen to me about the scooter, but she won't. Pavlákos has a bucket in front of him, which he hopes to fill with fish, but unfortunately for him the fish don't share his wishes. We move out a little further from the shore. It's time to go – at nine I have to be at the Xemóni for work.

'I'm off *Kyr* Thomá,' I say to him and get ready to dive into the water.

'And who's going to take you to Areopolis?' he says, looking at me in surprise, as if he's waking from a trance.

'I've got a lift.'

'I'll expect you this evening to eat fish at my house,' he called out as I dived in.

It must be seven o'clock, I reckon from the position of the sun. Time flows on like water when you want it to go slowly, or it doesn't move at all when you're in a hurry.

One, two, three – breathe. One, two, three – breathe, one – Effie on the verandah, breathe, one – Effie at the Xemóni, breathe. Effie,

Effie, Effie … It's been two days since I've seen her and on the telephone she's always in a hurry, always afraid. The sea is warm as an embrace, and I need an embrace right now. It hurts. The water hums in my ears, my arms go up and down, I kick my feet with all my strength until I lose my breath, I don't stop, I haven't learnt to stop, the finish is always the wall, and my aim is to touch the wall first. But there is no poolside here, the sea has no finish, and no competitors to share my victory or my defeat, and Effie is a wall that gets further and further away. It hurts.

I had to go to Pavlákos's that evening, he phoned to make sure I hadn't forgotten and I couldn't get out of it. I regretted it as soon as I went into the house, not because of the cop, I just can't stomach that daughter of his. She's an embarrassment to her father, and I like him a lot. I can't stand him being gossiped about by creatures like Kosmás. She opened the door wearing a mini up to her navel, with far too much make-up on. I soon realised why when I saw Odysséas Anastasákos drinking his ouzo. I gave Pavlákos a look. Could he not see what was going on in his own house? He pretended not to notice, got up and greeted me warmly.

'Did you know that Alexis did 2.10 in the Nationals 200 metres freestyle?'

I greeted Anastasákos formally and he looked up and asked me, just for something to say: 'Do you take part in athletics?'

'Of course he does, and he's good,' Pavlákos replied. 'If he had someone to take him to Limeni in the mornings, before work, he wouldn't have to miss his training. We go together sometimes, but I can't cope with his timetable, he gets up at dawn.'

I wanted to strangle him. What was he trying to do?

'Did you catch these today, *Kyr* Thomá?' I asked him, to change the subject. *Kyra* Barbara had just come in with a plate of fried mullet.

'Don't say a word,' he winked at me. 'Let me pretend I'm clever at something,'

'You're too clever by half …' I couldn't help saying.

We sat down. Anastasákos opposite me and next to him Pavlákos's daughter, Evangelía, who kept leaning over and touching him. He pretended not to notice, so maybe he didn't fancy her after all. He can't have made all that money and be a total idiot.

Pavlákos and Anastasákos talked about old times and playing football and playing *stratiotikó* in the church yard, where we boys still meet to kick a ball about, smoke in secret, talk about girls and send text messages. I listened in silence while they reminisced about boring things that meant nothing to me, and I wondered why Pavlákos had dragged me over to hear it all. The cop never did anything without a reason. They talked about an evening when the two of them had managed to take the leader of the enemy prisoner, my Uncle Sotíris, dead for years now, in the *stratiotikó*.

'That was on the afternoon that you killed Yiorgís,' said Pavlákos, presumably referring to the game they'd been talking about earlier. He said it deliberately, he was pushing the conversation on, to the painful things that kept us apart.

Anastasákos nodded and looked at me. Evangelía, sitting beside him, stroked his arm consolingly, but he didn't take his eyes off me.

'Do you see why I said that your mother was right about the scooter? There's a right time for everything. If Yiorgís hadn't taken the gun, if I hadn't held it in my hands …'

His voice sounded completely steady, and if he felt any emotion he wasn't showing it. It seems that the creep is very well able to hide his thoughts and his feelings.

They were all looking at me, Pavlákos, *Kyra* Barbara, Evangelía, Anastasákos.

'There is nothing worse than hurrying to do stuff when you aren't mature enough,' he went on, fixing me with his gaze.

He was hinting at that evening of course with Effie at the tower house. He had already given Effie a lecture about it. Just the thought of it brought the blood to my head, that creep having the nerve to criticise and lecture Effie about tragic mistakes, consequences and outcomes. He had judged and found me guilty, and tried to persuade her to finish with me. There was no way!

'I'll tell you what's even worse than being in a hurry,' I said. 'It's being too late. Time is subjective. A thing that is too soon for you might be just the right time for someone else.'

We weren't talking about the scooter any more, or about the gun, we both knew that. Effie was the subject, and Marina too. He smiled.

'You're right,' he said amiably, 'except that we can't always judge our own maturity, that's also subjective, like time. And when we finally do, it may be too late.'

Pavlákos felt left out of the conversation and he changed the subject. He asked his friend about his work, which the creep didn't seem to have any interest in talking about, and he gave some vague answer. Yes, he still had his consultancy business, but he had extended into the food business with a big chain of supermarkets and another group of businesses he'd inherited and was busy developing. He still lived in Boston, which he thought of as his second home, but he was obliged to spend long periods of time in New York, where some of his businesses were based. We're talking money with wings. As for his personal life, things weren't quite so rosy. 'I got married,' he said, which I already knew from my mother and Dimákaina, 'and we separated. It didn't go well.'

'I'm sorry,' said Pavlákos.

'There's no need. Some people are lucky, like you. Others not.'

He looked at me intently for a few moments, with that fiery, X-ray look of his. Pavlákos noticed it.

'What are you looking at him for?'

'He's just like his mother,' he replied. 'The smile, the hair. But the eyes …'

I went soon after we had eaten and left him there. I could feel his eyes on my back. What on earth did Pavlákos want? We both felt awkward. He stopped me at the door.

'Who's going to take you down for your training tomorrow?' the cop asked.

'No one. I haven't planned anything.'

'Why don't you go with Odysséas? He gets up at all hours anyway and he's bored rigid away from work.'

'I don't think …' I tried to refuse.

'I don't have a problem.' The creep leapt at it. 'Unless you're afraid of me …' he smiled sarcastically.

'Me?' I was annoyed and fell for it like an imbecile. 'I'm not afraid of anyone or anything.'

'Fine, then. What time?'

'Five thirty.'

'Done. I'll beep the horn.'

I know why Pavlákos is doing this, and I'm playing along, because I want to see who this man is who did so much damage to my family. Who is this guy who left home 'contrite,' to go to the other end of the world and make so much money, whom Dimákaina grieved for as if he were dead, though he was still alive? However much I resented the thought of his company, I was overwhelmed with curiosity. What I didn't understand was why he couldn't find an excuse to save himself the bother of me.

He was in fact on time in the morning; at five thirty I heard him beep the horn and I dashed outside. As always I had my sports bag with my black jeans and shirt that I wore for work carefully folded so that they wouldn't get creased, underclothes, towels and shampoo. Anastasákos was wearing bermuda shorts, like me, and a T-shirt. He said a formal good morning and I replied. We hardly spoke at all as far as Limeni, he parked in silence and followed me down to the sea. It wasn't quite light yet and the early morning dew made your skin shiver. We were almost alone on the beach. The shops hadn't opened and only two old men were casting fishing lines near the Mavromicháli Palace. They looked at us sleepily. I was taken aback when I saw he was going to swim. Why not, he'd got up at dawn, after all, so he might as well make the most of it. The first thing I wanted was to relieve him of any obligation to me and get rid of him. I didn't like owing favours to the creep, but I'd have to find a good excuse.

I got undressed and felt his eyes on my back. I was wearing my swimming goggles. Behind me I could hear the rustle of his clothes. I knew that he was standing in his bathing trunks and I couldn't resist turning round to look at him before I dived into the water. He looked impressive despite being fifty years old. He'd worked out, and had an athlete's body, a broad chest, wide shoulders, narrow hips, without the usual rolls of flab that the routine of marriage generally brings – a man who was still ready to go for it. That Evangelía had a point and she wasn't the only one. Damn him. Even his silver-flecked hair emphasised his striking appearance. I'm usually proud of my body – I'm among the tallest in the class and definitely the most worked out from hours of training every day – but next to him I felt like a spindly branch next to a tree trunk. I couldn't help making the comparison and I couldn't pretend not to see the result, which wasn't at all flattering to me. I was so annoyed it affected my speed.

I swam as fast as I could, but the sea, like I said, has no finish, there is no wall to touch. The guy followed me for over 100 metres. During the first 50 he fought it and then he gave in. 'Where are you off to, uncle?' I called out to tease him. I carried on swimming, there was no way he could compete with me and I wanted him to know that he didn't have a hope against me. Because he is yesterday and I am the dawn that's breaking. My mood improved.

When I got out on to the shore I found him sitting on the pebbles with his legs spread out, his hair slicked back and dripping. He had lit a cigarette and his face, permanently clouded since the first time I saw him coming through the doorway of the tower house, looked like a stone mask … He was talking on his mobile, the usual orders sounded strange in a foreign language. What time was it over there? Who was staying up to keep an eye on Anastasákos's business ventures? He had completely forgotten about me, and his cigarette – it was burning away slowly. I waited patiently for him to finish so that I could remind him of my presence and that I needed to be at the Xemóni at nine, washed, dressed, ready for work. Luckily, it didn't take him long, he threw the telephone down angrily on to his folded clothes and asked: 'Ready?'

I nodded. He put out his cigarette and asked me if there was time for him to smoke another. He even offered me one from the packet but I said no.

'What, don't you smoke?' he asked sarcastically.

What kind of people there are over there, who take all his orders, I don't know. But if he was expecting me to take any from him, he was way off the mark.

'I don't smoke. If it weren't for Effie, I'd never light a cigarette.'

'So she's led you astray, has she?' he laughed softly.

'I led her astray,' I said, and I couldn't hide my anger. 'I pretended to smoke so that I could get her alone in your house. How else would I have persuaded her to come?'

'Right,' he remarked drily. 'Do you know why I agreed to bring you here today?'

'I can guess. You don't want me to see her again.'

'Bravo. You're smart, as well as being a good swimmer. I don't want you to see her again. And if you don't listen to me, you'll have both her father and me to deal with.'

My moment had come and I didn't speak at once, I tasted the words first like syrup.

'Keep your orders for your employees! Go fuck yourself!'

I leapt up and grabbed my bag. I climbed up the road to Areopolis on foot. He passed me a quarter of an hour later, pressing down hard on the accelerator while I was still ecstatically savouring my last insult, which I shouted out again as he sped past. For the first time I wasn't at work on time, I was twenty whole minutes late, and I would have been later, if the old man fishing on the beach hadn't given me a lift in his car.

# Lou

THE IDEA I'D THROWN at John along with a pair of socks some years back had blossomed, and had put out roots and leaves. We owed a lot to the Greeks of Boston and John knew it. They were the first to back us, they got us into networking with the wealthy.

Gradually we became known and the demands of our job required us to rent a bigger office in a smart neighbourhood. We sold expensive advice to companies who were going through financial difficulties. Hot air, as Uncle Nikifóros would have said, and if I'd told him how much the air is sold for, he would say I was a lunatic and call the priest over for divine unction. And yet, seventeen years since the day I left my village, a boy of fifteen, I had my own business, my own apartment and what amounted to a small fortune. And John, too. We shared everything. Sometimes even women.

That was when Lou came into my life. She turned up together with the new office. Before that we hadn't been able to pay for a secretary, we did all the admin ourselves. But later, she became indispensable. The first time I saw her, skin of alabaster, long black hair, deep black eyes, she seemed to me as precious as a porcelain doll or a rare exotic flower. She was wearing a formal suit and wore her hair loose, lightly made-up and very nervous, and she needed the work. Second-generation Japanese, she still lived with her family, her parents and two younger sisters, one of whom was handicapped from birth. Lou needed money for her sister's care and she was saving up for her operation.

I was bound to take up with Lou sooner or later. Despite our crazy work hours, she always arrived first and left last. One day I came back late to the office after meeting a client and Lou was still there. We made love, which seemed very natural for us both at that moment, and then I went home and forgot about it. But she didn't. The same thing happened many times, until John got wind of it and warned me to be careful, because she was very much in love with me. I didn't take it too seriously. I rarely saw her outside the office. She was for me a kind of accessory, like a fax machine or a computer, I'm ashamed to say, a willing embrace after a tiring day, helping me to relax and unwind. Naturally I wasn't faithful to her and she knew it. I saw other women and then came back home and couldn't remember any of them. Lou was always there, she never asked any questions, never made demands. She didn't dare, because she knew that the moment she stopped giving me a good time and started complicating my life, we'd be done. With her Eastern sensitivity she found areas of vulnerability in me that no one else could see, possibly because they weren't there. She thought I deserved to be cared for, and I took advantage of her affection to avoid tasks that bored me rigid. I didn't even hang my coat up on the peg, I threw it on the chair in front of her and she did it. She cared about me so much that John always hoped our relationship would develop into something more; she was the best girl I'd ever been with. But no. It was never more than occasional sex for me, even when, a few years later, it ended in marriage. I suppose she hoped that her feelings would one day be returned, because that occasional sex was the only stable thing in my life. I never saw another woman more than twice. But she couldn't see that my relationship with her was only stable because it was the only one that suited me. She finally understood it when I had disappointed her in the worst possible way and was forced, six months after we got married, to ask me for a divorce. But that all happened much later. It was only when I found out for myself what it is to love hopelessly, that I knew just how much despair I'd caused Lou.

And it was when we hit the jackpot with the Roberts and Kraft affair that John met Irish Maggie, the lawyer defending in a case of industrial espionage: five high-ranking figures working on the inside, who had nearly destroyed the company by giving away vital marketing and production information to their competitors. The morning he missed our meeting, John had gone to the trial as a witness for the prosecution. He stayed until the end because he was entranced by the defence tactics of the beautiful lawyer, who tried unsuccessfully to soften the blow for her client.

Two months after that morning at the courthouse, John asked Maggie to marry him. John naturally wanted Maggie and me to be friends, but the better Maggie got to know me, the more she disliked me, extreme feminist that she is. She'd decided that Lou was a victim. 'How can you stand the bastard?' she asked her at every opportunity. Lou felt so awkward that often she deliberately avoided her. Yet, despite our differences, I was pleased for John. Their devotion to one another reminded me of the love between my parents and I knew how rare that is in a couple.

I told Maggie the old story about a traveller in the Mani before the war who saw a Maniot on a donkey and some distance behind him a *Maniátissa* loaded down with wood. We all laughed except for Maggie, who was so livid that we all burst out laughing again.

'I'm just teasing you,' I said.

'I feel sorry for the women where you come from, that's all I can say.'

'The women where I come from can do anything they like with us, they even drive us to murder, so don't feel sorry for them,' I suddenly turned serious. A joke is one thing but it's quite another to say to my face that my mother was pitiable, and this coming from a little girl whose daddy did everything for her, who never had to sweat for anything, and who wasn't worth the tip of my mother's little finger.

'Poor things,' said Maggie sarcastically.

'Like you said! *Poor* things!'

I nodded for emphasis and Maggie sensed that she had lost the argument. But she couldn't resist having the last word.

'I hope you meet a woman and love her so much that she really makes you hurt. So that you finally get what you deserve.'

I laughed. Wholeheartedly. But the time came when Maggie felt so sorry for me that she wished she'd never said it.

# Pitta with *Synclino*

EVERY AFTERNOON, while I'm still covered in salt and my body feels damp from my bathing costume, I like to stop in the main square in Areopolis and buy two slices of pitta with *synclino*. I eat it standing there, with other kids and tourists, a stranger among strangers, and then I go up to the village ready to face my problems. I know that Maria will have sent some food over, she's thinking of us, despite being busy with work and all the cares of her household. I told her not to go to all that trouble, but she won't listen. 'It's no trouble, it's just a plate of food.' A covered plate of food waiting for you in the kitchen – a simple gesture, really, and though I've barely realised, it's the kind of thing I've missed most during all these years abroad. It reminds me of my mother and Aunt Aretí.

And yet not all problems can be solved by a plate of food. You need much more. I had hardly hoped that Uncle Nikifóros would agree to come back to Boston with me, but his refusal when it came was definite and final: 'I want to die here and be buried next to Aretí, tomorrow if possible.' It delayed my return because there were other practical matters that had to be settled. Who would look after him, for example, from the moment I stepped on to the airplane? The old lady, although she was ill, had taken care of him until the moment she had collapsed on to her bed. He hated the thought of anyone else looking after him, he felt as if he'd be betraying her. I tried to make a joke of it, 'We won't have Potítsa, we'll choose the ugliest woman we can find,' and he burst into tears, his head in his wrinkled hands. 'I don't want anyone under my feet,' he said.

I did in fact find a widow from Areopolis who has a car and can come up to the village at any time of day. Voúla had known my aunt, which counted in her favour, so we left her in the house and went to the *kafeneío*. We came home and the place was clean as a new pin, but what my uncle valued most was that she made sure to be gone by the time we got back. A smart woman, she understood exactly what needed to be done. Luckily I have Yiánnis to be my eyes and ears, and I'll leave him a large sum to cover emergencies. Not that I have any reason to doubt Voúla, I've checked her out, but life has taught me not to trust anyone. Surprises always come from where you least expect them.

Every day that passes brings me closer to my old home, the memories awaken and my senses acclimatise. I've started a long and painful journey back – both to the things I loved and to the things that made me stay away. Very often I have the feeling that I'm a complete foreigner: in the *kafeneío* I'm the centre of attention, in Areopolis likewise, and everyone looks at me, except for one person who seems not to notice I exist. Every Friday evening I see Marina Haritákou's little blue Opel parked outside her house. One Saturday I saw her in a fish taverna in Neo Oitylo, with a man I gathered is a lawyer in Kalamata, and has the impressive name of Aristomenis, but they call him Ari. She was wearing white, as she used to of old, trousers and a blouse that left one shoulder bare, her hair tied back so that it fell down to the right and in her left ear a long silver earring. Light, discreet make-up. She was incredibly lovely and Ari couldn't take his eyes off her. He was attractive and exceptionally attentive. He whispered something to her and she smiled. Her rippling laugh revealed her pearly teeth and that deceptively innocent little dimple on her cheek.

One day at midday, on my way back home, I saw Alexis waiting for the bus back to the village, sweating in the boiling heat. I rolled down the window and signalled to him.

'Hop in.'

He looked at me witheringly, raising his eyebrow. He reminded me so much of his mother that I almost put down the accelerator and drove on.

'Why?'

God give me patience!

'Because it's hot and I have air conditioning.'

'And you don't want me to get too hot?'

'Why should I want that? Come on, you're letting the heat in.'

He favoured me with a sneer, opened the door and got in. He made himself comfortable in silence, put on the seat belt. The boy is as stubborn as a mule. He looks at me with such fury at times, and then suddenly with such compassion, as if he can see into my very soul.

'I'm sorry I drove off and left you the other day,' I said, as sincerely as I could, 'but you overdid it. People don't speak like that.'

He didn't say a word and I made another attempt, trying not to overdo it.

'If you like, I could take you down in the mornings for your training.'

'Why?' he asked again and now he had turned round and was looking at me so intently that I felt awkward.

'Let's say so that we can get over the past once and for all,' I replied, and this time I meant it. Whatever the boy knew about my past, it was nothing to me now, I just wanted to bury it for ever, all of it. The problem was that there were some things I couldn't bury, however much I wanted to.

'There are things that can't be buried,' said the boy as if he had read my thoughts. 'So don't let's pretend. You want me to leave your friend Yiannis's daughter in peace. And my mother wants the same thing. If I won't do it for her, why should I do it for you?'

This time I kept my cool and it required a big effort. I spoke as calmly as I could.

'It isn't for me or for your mother. Do it for Effie and for yourself. She's young. You'll only end up hurting her. Her father will find out and she'll get into trouble. And you, I've told you before, you need to find an older girl, who knows what she wants, and who can teach you.'

We were coming into the village by now and I stopped in front of his house. He turned and looked at me curiously, biting his lip.

'I'm sorry,' he said, although he didn't seem sorry at all. 'I can't. I'm a human being, I have feelings and I'm in love with Effie. Do what you like. Tell her father.'

'I'm trying to tell you that actions have consequences.'

'I'm not afraid of the consequences,' he said pointedly, 'and nor do I shirk my responsibilities. Let Mitsikoyiánnis come and hang me, like you said, from the bell tower. I'm not leaving Effie. A real man doesn't leave the woman he loves. Good afternoon to you, Mr Anastasáko.'

He left me with his 'Mr Anastasáko' ringing in my ears, and the bizarre notion that he wasn't talking about his little girlfriend at all but about something else. I felt certain he was referring to the fact that I'd run away to avoid the consequences of a murder. I went back home with a bitter taste in my mouth, so bitter that the pitta with *synclino* had no taste at all.

# The Olympians

ONE RAINY MORNING in the early spring of 1993, I arrived at work, asked for coffee, complained about the eternal cold, turned up the heating – Lou had opened the windows to get rid of the cigarette smoke from the previous day – and switched on the computer. She put her head round the door.

'Don't forget the Joneses at eleven.'

Not likely. If we signed the deal we would pluck them good and proper, like my mother used to pluck the cockerels before she put them in the pot and cooked them up with macaroni, and there was plenty of fine down for the plucking. We had been preparing for the meeting for days. I had taken it on and was feeling optimistic but we still had a lot of work to do. I lit a cigarette on the stub of the last one, which was still burning in the ashtray. I had hardly opened the file on the computer when the internal phone rang. Someone had turned up without an appointment. It was Stefanos Olympios.

We hadn't seen him for nearly five years, but he looked the same as ever, except for the five or six kilos he'd gained. However he had lost his old cheerfulness. We asked for fresh coffees and sat down to catch up. He noticed the luxurious surroundings, a sign of how well things had gone for us these last five years since, and he commented somewhat caustically: 'Don't you Maniots claim to be of Spartan descent? I would take you for descendants of Croesus, more like.'

'When one has to deal with rich kids like your lordship,' I replied, 'there's no other way of being taken seriously.'

On first hearing, Stefanos's news seemed exceptionally good. He had taken over his father's business together with his big brother, Haris. Their father had retired and handed everything over to them.

But despite his good fortune, Olympios didn't seem particularly happy. The old conflict with his brother had been reignited the moment he set foot back in his homeland. He had no hope of competing with his brother, and when I finally met Haris I could see why.

We arranged to meet after work, to reminisce about our student days. Meanwhile Stefanos went to his hotel to rest, and John and I had our meeting with the Joneses. There were only two of them in the end: a tall, freckly man whose name I can't remember and April Donahue, a very beautiful black woman, whom I remember very well. Beneath her sober suit you could imagine her perfect, feline body and she had her hair cut very short, like a man. She was stunning: the way she sat and crossed her legs, the way she stretched out her hand to pick the pencil off the table, the way she sipped her coffee. She had the grace of a large African tiger looking for her prey. I wanted to be that prey. I couldn't resist it.

The meeting lasted for an hour and a half and finished satisfactorily, the freckled man said that they would telephone later that day, but I was far more concerned about April. I was sure about closing the deal, but she was as enigmatic as a Sphinx. I shut myself away in my office in desperate need of a cigarette. I hadn't smoked at the meeting as I never smoke in front of a client. Lou brought me some coffee looking troubled, but I barely saw her, my mind was elsewhere. She smiled at me, the good angel in my life, despite her pain and her sorrow, and I hardly noticed. I should be sent to hell just for that, never mind my other misdemeanours!

The day rolled by with its usual routine, until the evening when Maggie came to take John to the meeting with the wedding planner. They had set their wedding date for the end of October. She knew us well enough to bring food – we were always forgetting to eat – and the four of us sat in John's office. Lou had that sweet, sad look of hers, which Maggie knew well, and she asked me directly: 'What's up with you, pretty boy?'

I answered vaguely, as if nothing was up. What a creep!

John was very worried about the meeting with the wedding planner. It wasn't the first they'd had, and he knew what the outcome would be: an enormous estimate. He already had a headache, I could tell by the way he half closed his eyes, but he didn't want to spoil Maggie's fun. He wanted to give his fiancée her dream wedding. They left and when April phoned, Lou put her through to me.

I remember it as the day we closed on one of our most lucrative deals. As the day when the Sphinx laid her cards on the table and agreed with pleasure to go out with me the next evening, a dinner which was anything but professional and we both knew that from the start. As the day when Lou left for home in tears.

I worked till late, trying not to think about Lou and my appalling behaviour, and later I met up with the others in an expensive Chinese restaurant where I had promised to buy them dinner.

'Your tastes have changed,' commented Stefanos. 'In the old days you only ever ate in Greek restaurants!'

'Because they were the only places I could eat for free!'

John had taken two painkillers for his headache. The wedding planner they had seen that afternoon was the most expensive so far, and worst of all he had won Maggie's confidence and she was anxious to sign a contract in case they missed out on the deal he was offering. John could see them blowing all his careful savings on one wedding party and was feeling frail. I, on the other hand, was in terrific form. We had completed a deal, and I was looking forward to dinner with April. John was also unhappy about my upsetting Lou.

'She's a great girl, Odysséa. It's not for me to say it, but couldn't you at least play by the rules while you're at work?'

I was forced to admit that he was right and I promised to be careful. I didn't like upsetting him, and April was only a passing fancy after all. When we told Olympios about Lou he couldn't believe it. A willing lay at work, whenever I felt like it, and what a lay! We talked as if we were still students, as if we'd never grown up at all.

After dinner we went on to Pink's nightclub, our old favourite, for the first time in five years, and certainly nothing had changed there, except for the girls and the faces of the clientele. Olympios had made us a proposal to go to Greece for work. He needed a management consultant and we had been recommended to his father by a businessman friend of his in America. When Olympios told him we were his best friends from university, the old man had said: 'Well what are you waiting for? Bring them over,' and Haris had to agree.

My immediate instinct was to say no. I couldn't go back to Greece. It would be like entering the gates to Hades. There was silence from John, and for the first time ever in our relationship he had a go at me for something that wasn't to do with smoking.

'I'm fed up with this secrecy of yours about Greece, after all our years of friendship.'

He had dragged me away from our party at the club. The drinks had given him the courage to overstep the tacit limits I had laid down in our friendship at the very beginning. But he was right. If a friend who always respects your limits can't bypass them when they think it's essential, then who can? I felt trapped.

'How can I tell you about it, John? With your home that's like a Cornflakes ad? And what does Stefanos know, with his purse stuffed full of Daddy's money?'

'To hell with Olympios's money and the job, I couldn't care less and you know it,' he said. 'Something's eating you and it's over there, and if you don't sort it out it'll destroy you. Go and clear it up. So many years have passed. What could possibly matter so much after all this time?'

I remember my friend's eyes, clear as a cloudless sky, full of concern. It was too much for me. My anger evaporated. I looked down at the floor.

'I'm a murderer and a coward, John.' I said it that simply, the secret I'd been hiding all those years.

'You are neither one nor the other, I'm sure of it.'

He said it without hesitating for one second. And he believed it completely. As he smiled at me, pushing back that lick of hair that fell over his forehead, I saw how sure he was about me. Me, the son of a farmer, from the Mani, who had an accident with a gun, bringing death to two families. Those were the facts and that was how I must try to see them. I couldn't undo the crime. But I could stop being a coward.

'Don't let's talk about it any more tonight,' said John. 'Let's speak in the morning.'

'Can you take it? I'll need a whole packet of cigarettes before I can talk about it.'

'There's no getting out of it. Make up your mind. Now let's go and drink.'

He winked at me over his shoulder when we left in our pairs. I didn't want to go home, I couldn't bear the nagging of my guilt that evening. I wasn't so vile as to phone Lou after the April faux pas, even though I needed her warmth. It would only give her hope that I was bound to dash before the night was out, and so I went home with Kelly, a tall blond model I'd met before, whom I'd spotted at the other end of the bar. I couldn't bear to be alone.

I was afraid of going back. I was haunted by my mother's *moiroloy,* and that of Yiorgís's mother:

*My star, it was too early*
*for you to set so soon*
*our house still waits for you*
*and the streets where you played …*

It was the distraught face of Haritákaina that tormented me most. What had happened to Aunt Katerina, how had she coped? And charismatic Sotíris, the king in our games? And Haritákos in prison? And their little daughter? I don't know if anyone else in my position would have been able to forget, to say that it had been a tragic mistake, to write it off with a stroke of the pen. To enjoy the fruits of his labours and the joys that life offered to a man in the prime of his life, successful, fairly presentable, free of the insecurities of his first youth and the anxieties of survival. For me it proved impossible. I had to take this chance to go back, admit the truth about my father's sacrifice, and pay whatever price was demanded of me by the people I had unwillingly harmed. 'The debt has been more than paid,' my mother had said. But no debt is really paid if it isn't accepted by the person you owe.

The following morning, for the first time in all our years of friendship, I told all this to John, and at last he had an explanation for my chasing after women, my sleepless nights, my nightmares. Even my pitiful attitude to Lou made more sense. My need to forget my pain. My love of syrupy cakes.

'You are not a murderer,' my friend insisted. 'It was an accident. The other man is a murderer, the idiot who killed your father.' He could say all this because he's Dutch. If he had been a Maniot, he would have known that the 'idiot' didn't have much choice.

I left for Greece ten days later. John couldn't come, there was too much going on at work, and he had the preparations for the wedding to see to. I gave my fee for the contract with the Joneses to Lou, so she could pay for her sister's operation. If I had ever cared for a woman, that woman was Lou, and I wanted her to know it. Tearfully she accepted the money as a loan. But I had to come clean with her – she needed someone who really loved her, and it wasn't me.

'I'm sorry, I know I'm a fool, but I can't do anything about it. I'm just not made for a permanent relationship.'

'I know,' said my angel, 'and I'm made as I am, and I can't do anything about it either. I want you to feel free. I don't want you to feel guilty.'

I had felt free, more than free! Why else would I have gone straight from her arms into April's arms and then into Kelly's without caring about either woman?

The last thing I had to do before leaving was to settle the question of Maggie and her wedding plans. I couldn't leave John to deal with this fiasco alone. So for the first time Maggie and I had a proper talk and took a step closer, a real step closer to each other, and not just for the sake of appearances. She came to the office one day while John was at a meeting.

'Don't you think you should ease up a bit on the wedding?' I said to her. 'Why are you making John spend so much money? Can't you see how worried he is?'

She looked at me in such amazement that it was clear the problem hadn't even occurred to her. She had noticed how dispirited John seemed every time they met a wedding planner, but she thought perhaps he wasn't ready to get married, that maybe they had moved too fast and he was regretting it.

'I didn't know …' she stammered. 'We can share the cost, we can ask Daddy …'

'If you think that your husband is going to accept any such thing, you don't know him at all. Don't you think it's more important to make the man you love happy, than to impress your girlfriends? Grand parties don't make happy marriages, Maggie. Caring about each other does. John cares about you. Do you really care about him?'

We didn't have time to say any more – John came back – but I'd said enough.

***

I landed at Elliniko airport at the beginning of April, a bright, spring morning. The warm sun greeted me as I got out of the airplane, as if in welcome and comfort after my long absence. Stefanos was there to meet me in a silver Mercedes with a driver, a hefty young man with broad shoulders. I mouthed at Olympios, 'Is he carrying a gun?'

'No, he's knitting, what do you think?'

It struck me as strange. No member of his family had ever had a bodyguard before. He had always boasted about how relaxed it is in Greece, and how you never feel at risk from anyone or anything.

'It's those assassins, posing as idealists,' he explained. 'First they kill you and then they send an announcement to the newspaper to explain why. A hit list with their targets was found, and we're on it, as enemies of the people. Can you believe it?'

I had read about this so-called 'political' organisation that began by killing old colleagues of the Greek dictators and employees at the American embassy. It had gone on to murder journalists and Greek businessmen in cold blood, but I really hadn't paid it much attention. My friend told me they had been forced to take it seriously. None of the family went out alone any more, even his mother, a socialite who spent her time shopping and playing cards, and had nothing to do with their business activities. But, very likely, she was an enemy of the people too, setting a bad example. Who can tell?

We took the road along the sea front, which was busy with traffic. The last time I had visited Athens was when the doctor at the hospital told my mother that after losing five babies she couldn't have any more children, and she was inconsolable. 'We have Odysséas, Fotiní. May we be well!' my father had said, trying to comfort her. The three of us were squashed into the back seat of a taxi on the way to the bus station. The taxi driver was taking a double fare and there was an old man sitting next to him whom we dropped off on the way. I didn't really understand much, only that the doctor had said something that made my mother cry. I thought she was ill and I was numb with fear. 'Don't be afraid,' my father said, 'it's going to be all right.' And suddenly I was certain that it would be all right, because he had promised. And my mother was not a person to pine after what's lost and gone. She carried on with what she had – me and my father, who would have moved heaven and earth for her. It wasn't so very little.

All I remembered of Athens from that visit was the noise, car horns and grey blocks of flats, and as far as all that was concerned nothing had changed, except perhaps for the worse. But not the area where Stefanos lived. On the slope of a fir-clad hill, Ekáli. The house was on three stories, surrounded by a tall stone wall. There was a plainclothes security guard at the entrance. We were met by a Filipino couple and shown into a huge drawing room with large French windows through which we had a wonderful view of the garden and the swimming pool. A woman was sunning herself topless on a chaise longue, although it was so early in the year. I had no difficulty at all in recognising Máchi, who looked at me through her dark glasses and waved. The Filipinos were standing about waiting for orders, and I asked for a glass of cold water.

I found myself searching absently in my pocket for my cigarettes, forgetting that I'd thrown them away before I boarded the plane. I had been smoking up to three packets a day, and I knew that as soon as I arrived in Greece I'd be smoking twice as many. Anyway, cigarettes were a comfort, and I hadn't come back to my country to be comforted. I didn't deserve it. I had come back to pay my old debts and to leave the past behind me, whatever that meant. I couldn't bear any more hidden truths. I wanted to look ahead and not be tormented by shadows, to stop being a coward, to shut my eyes at last and go to sleep.

Outside by the pool, Máchi turned her back on me nonchalantly to get dressed, and then came and welcomed me with a kiss on the mouth. She looked good, her body had filled out and she was more feminine than ever.

'Shall we go for a week's holiday before they put you to work?' she suggested.

It seemed like an unnecessary delay to me, but this was Greece, Easter was coming up and their brother Haris was away. Nothing happened unless he was there.

'Why don't you go?' said Stefanos. 'You need to relax a little.'

Máchi wrapped herself in a long yellow burnous. She let down her hair and swung it loose. 'Come on, Odysséa, you choose. Where would you like to go?'

'Wherever you like. I don't know Greece at all,' I admitted, and it was true. I had rarely been beyond the boundaries of the Mani.

'You mean you're letting me choose?'

'Always.'

'Liar!'

She went off with her lilting walk to get dressed, unfortunately for me. I watched her going up the wooden spiral staircase and for a moment I had the sense that I was fifteen years old, awestruck, watching Potítsa's ravishing legs as she climbed the ladder in the tower house. What could the socialite Andromache Olympiou possibly have in common with the *Maniátissa*? Nothing, except an absolute awareness of her power over men.

I stayed with Stefanos for three days, together with Máchi, *Yero* Olympios and *Kyria* Dia, his father and mother, and her little dog Roxi, most unattractive of all canines. True to his every promise, my friend offered to cover the expenses of my stay in Greece. It was clear that I needed my own space, so they rented me a little two-storey villa with a pool in Saronida. From the top-floor balcony there was a view of the sea. A tall concrete wall shielded you from inquisitive onlookers. The house was owned by a Greek American who had been away for two years, so while the villa was being prepared I went away with Máchi to Santorini.

Máchi adored the island, and with good reason! A black rock swimming in the light! A jewel, a precious stone! We landed on the Monday before Easter. The tourists hadn't yet started to arrive so it was yet more magical. We stayed at Oia with its famous sunsets, in two separate suites. Máchi was absolutely straight with me. 'You should never go to an island as a couple, so says a psychologist I'm reading. It would be like going to a dinner party and taking your sandwich along in a Tupperware box.'

We explored the island together in a rented jeep. By day we swam in the warm waters of the volcano, and toured the beaches and villages. But in the evenings we went out separately, and ended up in bed with different partners every night. For the first time in my life I understood the meaning of rest and recuperation. Due to lack of money, or later due to pressure of work, I had never allowed myself to enjoy a real holiday. Early in the morning we would extract ourselves from our stranger's bed, and we'd meet to finish the night in her room or mine to swap experiences. On Good Friday Máchi took me to Pyrgo, a medieval village on the south of the island. We lit a candle in church and then followed the procession behind the Epitafio, walking devoutly along the narrow alleyways among Greek worshippers and tourists. There were tins along the tops of the walls with lighted rags in them, so that the village looked as if it was on fire. On the night of the Resurrection, fireworks lit up the sky as if it were day. Easter at home after all these years! I thought of my mother, who always kept a strict Lenten fast, especially on Good Friday, to keep the body in check as well as the soul; *mayirítsa,* the soup of sheep's innards eaten at midnight, after the Resurrection, eggs dyed red and the kid roasting on a spit on Easter Sunday. How delicious everything smelled: the house, the garden, the girls, the flower-covered rocks, the sea! What my mother would have said if she'd seen me eating fillet steak on Good Friday, and lamb chops grilled on charcoal, I hardly dared to think. I promised myself, when this was all over, that I would spend an Easter in the Mani, and keep a proper Lent like the old days, with bread and olives, for her sake.

I thought I was content during those few days. I had found the happiness of an amoeba, without any cares at all. Free of feelings that lift you up to heaven one minute and throw you down to hell the next. The happiest moments of my life always seemed to herald the most miserable. Like that evening in the Mani, walking home excited and overjoyed at capturing the 'king', just minutes before my world was devastated. My mother, waving me off smilingly, loading me with cheese pies. My father, leaving for the *kafeneíon,* on the eve of his name day, promising to be home early. And Yiorgákis, dancing about with that wretched gun in his hands, and seconds later lying dead on the ground like a hunted bird.

Early on Easter morning, slightly tipsy, I had telephoned John and told him that I was having a fantastic time. I had never felt so relaxed, not a thought in my head, I was bewitched by the place, and what's more I had a woman by my side with exactly the same needs as I had, and who understood me completely. She didn't want any ties – what I was able to give her was enough. An enjoyable fuck, nothing more, nothing less.

***

Delighted with ourselves and gloriously tanned, we went back to Athens ten days later. I settled down at Saronida and didn't see much of Máchi. My batteries were charged, I was full of energy and I threw myself into work.

Asprópirgo, in the industrial belt, was where the Olympians had their aluminium-processing factory. I was given a guided tour by Stefanos himself, first to the foundries, where the metal was heated up to melting point at thousands of degrees Celsius, and then to the various sections where the metal was set in purpose-built moulds, or turned into sheets of various thickness. My job was of course nothing to do with production, but I wasn't entirely ignorant, having worked on a similar factory in America. I was more interested in the marketing, sales and finance departments. I attended the managers' meeting, where I listened carefully to their assessment of the situation in their various sections. And finally, Stefanos introduced me to his older brother Haris, who had taken over from his father at the helm of the company.

Haris was a shark, nothing like Stefanos, and his father was right to make him first fiddle. He greeted me as if to say, 'Let's see if you're worth the money,' and he didn't seem particularly convinced by me. I was used to that. I liked this bright, unhesitating guy. He was the type who would follow my advice to the letter. What I couldn't abide was sentimentality, so useless and harmful in the world of business. He was married to an architect, Irene, the daughter of a well-known building contractor in Athens called Christofídis, with plenty of money, who, if somewhat uncouth, was in on all the public works. Wherever you picked up a stone you'd find him under there somewhere. Haris's parents had disapproved of the bride's family, but he put his foot down and insisted. 'Governments may fall, but Christofídis stays,' so people said. He had secured government 'loans' for the Olympioi at very favourable rates – 'handouts' would be more accurate. Ten years after his son's wedding, the old man had to admit that the 'builder' was as sharp as a razor, and his business highly profitable. He watched as Irene rose to the challenge and turned into a fine lady, and, as he put it, those stuck-up aristocrat girls weren't worth her little finger.

The couple had three children. A seventeen-year-old girl, Sofia, and a pair of hectic twin boys, aged fourteen, called Nikos and Savvas. I met them all one evening when they invited me for dinner. Irene was beautiful, busy and dynamic, Sophia melancholy, and the boys, after playing boisterously in the garden, went out banging the doors to meet up with their friends. Haris was pretty negative at the beginning and couldn't understand why his father had been persuaded by Stefanos to take me on. I made it clear to him that his family affairs left me completely indifferent. Our success would depend on how well we collaborated, and if he didn't want to throw away his money and waste his time, he would do well to forget about his quarrel with his brother and his aversion to me, and give me some support.

I worked a sixteen-hour day, so the house I had rented by the sea was an unnecessary expense. I hardly had time to look at the sea, much less to swim in it. In the evenings I went out with Stefanos. His friends were the cream of Athens society, rich girls, starlets, models, all the inanity of the city gathered together, and a perfect tonic after a hard day's work. Sometimes on my way back and forth by car I would watch people crowding round the bus stops, ordinary girls in jeans and T-shirts, and I longed for the city, to get out of my wretched car and walk in it, smell it, taste it. I confessed as much to Stefanos, who didn't understand. 'Go and mix with the plebs? Is that what you want? I despair at your taste.' He had forgotten that I was only the son of a farmer, the kind of person he generally avoided because they 'stank'.

After a while of being driven about in Stefanos's Mercedes by his driver, I rented at my own expense a white sports BMW, two-seater, a real dream. I arrived in it to work, to the delight of the ladies and a wry smile from Haris, who regarded it as the height of vulgarity. One evening I gave a lift to Stefanos's driver, who was waiting for a taxi at the factory gate. Dark, stocky, with a moustache. I could tell he was Cretan by his name, Sifis Kapetanakis, and the way he pronounced certain letters. I was surprised to hear that he was a graduate of the Sports Academy and a former teenage champion at the discus. He was waiting to be assigned as a PE teacher to a secondary school but it took ages to get down 'the list', he said, and in the meantime he was working as a driver-cum-bodyguard. 'For the time being,' he said pointedly. I looked at him, perplexed.

'What list is that?'

It was the list of trained teachers who hadn't yet been appointed, he explained. People who had finished university and hoped to work in education registered on the list and waited their turn. Prospective teachers were ranked according to their marks and when they graduated. If you graduated in 1985 with a low grade, you got a job before an A grader from 1986. I found it exceptionally unfair, but Sifis defended the system with enthusiasm.

'It's not meritocratic, I know,' he said, 'but it is objective. There is no other objective system of appointing jobs in the state sector. The only other way is if you have an uncle in the ministry.'

By the time we reached Sifis's house we had become such friends that we went to get some *souvlákia* in the square. I liked this guy, he reminded me of the lads from back home. We had a few beers and by the fourth beer he gestured to two girls at the table opposite. One was a short-haired brunette with blue eyes, the other had long black hair and brown eyes.

'Which do you prefer, don't let's quarrel.'

'You choose first.'

He chose blue eyes and short hair and sent over some beers. We joined them for a drink and left arm in arm. I had somewhere to go, but the same was not true for Sifis, who lived with his mother. He really liked the girl, but he was a proud Cretan and he didn't want to take her to some old fleapit where you pay by the hour. So he had no choice but to put it off and wait. Then in a moment of inspiration I took him aside and shoved the keys of my house into his hand. He knew where I lived, he had taken me there often enough. He looked at me gratefully.

'What about you?'

'I'll get the boss to pay for a hotel,' I said, and winked at him.

Naturally I wasn't intending to charge the hotel to my work, but the Cretan would never have accepted otherwise. Anyway, things went swimmingly for Sifis and Vassoula, but they ended ignobly for me and her friend. She was nineteen years old and a virgin, she confessed. I didn't have the heart to go on. She looked at me with her huge eyes. I stroked her cheek gently and barely touched her lips with mine. I took her home and went off on my own to find a hotel. 'Why?' she asked me sadly. I wouldn't be seeing her again, that was why. I wasn't interested in sensitive, romantic virgins. I was looking for a woman.

Sifis, who heard about it all the next morning, thanked me for lending me his house, and told me I was a wanker. We were friends from then on. I often had supper at his house, his mother bent over backwards to look after me. I got to know his sister, his brother-in-law, his nephews. They invited me to their village in Crete. He became my personal guide to the life of the city, the real city, not the bell jar I had so far got to know. He tried to infect me with the virus of politics, unsuccessfully of course. I wasn't interested. I had met plenty of political families in Boston, and knew not to expect anything good from them. Sifis was a fanatical PASOK supporter, like many Cretans, whereas I came from a right-wing family, like most Maniots, but I couldn't remember anyone at home being fanatical about it. 'If you don't work, you won't eat,' my father would say. 'Everything else is rubbish.'

Sifis told me all the gossip about the Olympians. Haris, the first fiddle, was in a permanent adulterous relationship with a very well-known and talented actress, and had numerous flings on the side. The builder's beautiful daughter, Irene, knew all about it and played dumb, according to the Cretan, for the good of the family and her pocket. My friend Stefanos, or the kid, as Sifis called him, preferred high-class tarts, of every colour and race. Now and again he would remember his old habits at university and sniff some coke. As for Máchi, her father dug his hands very deep into his pockets to keep her erotic exploits out of the gossip columns. Her last affair was with a married man and it cost her father a fortune. The guy fell in love with her and couldn't understand that there was no satisfying her. When he found out she was cheating on him he paid a guy to teach her a lesson, but Sifis had appeared by chance and intervened. The guy had a knife and was planning to disfigure the face of the pretty heiress. 'What are you doing in that madhouse, tell me?' Sifis used to say to me. 'What do you have in common with them, I don't understand?' I never told Stefanos I'd been hanging out with Sifis the pleb. He wouldn't understand that, either.

My friendship with Stefanos, as it had been at university, no longer existed. Meanwhile the company had financial problems because the market they were servicing had shrunk hopelessly after a series of faulty deliveries. They had solved the problem, but the damage was already done. Their equipment was way out of date and they needed to modernise. Companies in the Balkan countries paid starvation wages to their workers and it was impossible to compete. Finally, a virulent trade union had popped up out of nowhere and was making their life hell. The trade unionists were naturally wary of me, the boss's American buddy come to make him more money at their expense. Why should they like me? I didn't care, I wasn't being paid to be nice. I was paid to get results. And they were right: nothing I was considering was in their interest. I could see no other solution than the transfer of some of the factories to neighbouring Bulgaria, a change that would reduce considerably the cost of production.

I had never felt guilty about what I do. I had changed a great deal since the afternoon my teacher threw me out of the classroom and I'd sat at the bus stop thinking about the ants. I knew that in reality the fate of ants had much in common with the fate of humans, and no one really cared if they got crushed or not. People had tried to crush me, starting with Uncle Sarándos, a member of my own family, but I turned out to be a little tougher than expected. No, I didn't feel any guilt if, thanks to my advice, human ants were to be crushed. I never took the decisions. I only proffered solutions. I found it amusing to watch people suddenly lose every moral inhibition once you dangled a profit in front of their noses. As far as I was concerned, the people who worked for the Olympians didn't have names or personal histories. I thought of them as two words: labour costs. And the cost in this particular instance was far too great and had to be minimised, but first of all we had to weaken the unions. That was my job.

Until my own world turned upside down.

# Melénia

MY GRANDMOTHER ANASTASÁKAINA, long since dead, had warned me to beware of nereids. They lie in wait just where you least expect them and rob you of your speech, your mind, your sight. You long for them and for their beauty, beyond human comprehension, and you can have them for a little while if you are clever and well prepared, but you can never own them. They are ethereal. They are spirits from the blackest hell! You think they are devoted to you, but all they want is to toy with you for a while and then go back to wherever they come from. And you are left searching for them everywhere, half crazed, for as long as you live and breathe. Watch out for them when you're thirsty, my grandmother said. They wait beside streams, wells and springs, knowing very well how to trap you. They dance provocatively, they sing with the voices of angels, but they are creatures of the darkness and if you have any sense you should get away as fast as you possibly can and don't look back.

The first time I saw her, bending studiously over the heads of the twins, I should have realised and turned away my face, to escape the snare, to save myself. Instead I stood staring at her like an idiot. Her name was Aphrodite and I wasn't at all surprised.

The twins were a handful. Their last teacher had left, claiming she had spent all her wages on tranquillisers. The children had locked her up in the underground garage and left her there for three hours in the dark until their mother got back. Aphrodite was her replacement, and despite her youth – she was only twenty-five – she had the measure of them. They gazed into her eyes as if she was a goddess, and I would have done the same.

It was Haris's idea for the three of us to meet in the afternoons at his house. None of us could help but be distracted by the charming teacher sitting out on the stone terrace with the boys. 'That stone terrace means everything to me …' said Stefanos. '*Axion estí to pétrino pezoúli*. I've always wondered what Elytis meant by that.'

It was the month of May, the scent of flowers everywhere. And work was too tedious to hold our concentration. Whereas floral Aphrodite … She appeared not to notice us at all. We watched her from the half-open French windows in the office, with the twins obediently bent over their books and not once, not even once, looking up. There are times when I think I might still have escaped, she hadn't turned to look at me yet, I hadn't seen her eyes and that smile … But looking back I see that I was already lost, when in one movement she pulled the elastic from her hair and let it fall over her shoulders and her neck, as if it was alive. Then she combed it roughly through her fingers, and tied it back up again, more tightly, so it wouldn't fall into her eyes. When she got up to take a break and stretch her legs, I noticed that she was wearing jeans, a white T-shirt and tennis shoes, a simple outfit, but she was beautiful! Unbelievably beautiful! She reminded my of my mother's honeyed *koutalídes me méli*. '*Méli glykítato*, sweetest honey!' I mused, and I could almost taste them. Entire afternoons passed in this way, with us keeping an eye on her as we worked at the computer. And while we were comparing investment estimates and labour costs, one or other of us would comment:

'How tall d'you think she is?'

'Not more than one metre seventy, I should imagine.'

'Much shorter than your Kelly.' Stefanos was thinking of the model in Boston.

'How can you compare them? Beside her, Kelly is no more than a glorified clothes hanger!'

And it was true, there was no comparison. Aphrodite might not have been tall enough to make it on to the catwalk, but Kelly wasn't a patch on her. It wasn't just her beauty, it was something more than that. The fact that she ignored us – three grown men ogling her like schoolboys. She enjoyed her work and was completely absorbed in it. You could tell by the way she bent over the twins, talking and gesturing enthusiastically. Even her ponytail bouncing back and forth cheerily bore witness to the fact that however unlikely it seemed, the girl enjoyed teaching Ancient Greek to two boys who had no desire to learn it. Haris was delighted to have at last got some peace. So long as she was in the house the boys behaved like angels: he could even hear them earnestly trying to decline their perfects and pluperfects. She had bewitched us all!

She hardly spoke to us adults in the house. But she always said hello to the Filipino servants, the Ukrainian cleaner, the gardener from Georgia. She was especially friendly to Sifis, regarding him, as he explained to me, as a colleague, since she was also on that famous teacher's list waiting for a job. But she kept well away from her employers. When Haris called her into the office for a progress report on the children, she was formal to the point of rudeness, answering his questions and leaving as soon as she possibly could.

'What the hell? I wasn't going to eat her!' said Haris.

She had her background information on the family and was keeping a safe distance, Sifis told me. She wanted to keep her job. But Haris wasn't going to give up that easily, and he offered her a large sum of money as a gesture of gratitude for the good work she was doing with his sons. His childhood rivalry with Stefanos had found a new form of expression. The older brother had to be careful, since he was married, but the younger had no such reservations. After finding out where she lived, Stefanos sent her flowers every day and asked her out to dinner. As politely as she could, the lovely Aphrodite refused Haris's money and declined Stefanos's invitation. Sifis told me she had lost her parents when she was little, and wasn't particularly well off. Her foster parents, whose name she used, were 'very good people', and loved her as if she were their own child, but she didn't want to be a burden to them. I was beginning truly to admire her, but she didn't appear to notice me at all. One day we happened to leave the house together and the Cretan introduced us. Then for the first time she looked at me with those sweet brown eyes, and I formally shook her hand.

'Odysséas Anastasákos.'

'Aphrodite Yalanoú, pleased to meet you.'

Nothing earth-shattering happened, she just looked at me. Except that in her eyes something gleamed, some emotion, and her eyes flashed golden. The next moment whatever it was that had startled her vanished, she said goodnight to us and left. I stood there in astonishment as she climbed on to her motorbike, an old Yamaha 250. She wasn't wearing a helmet; it was slung over her arm like a basket. I never understood why people did that – the police always stopped them at roadblocks anyway and they rarely had time to put them on.

There followed many more afternoons during which I learned to guess her moods by studying the way she moved. The way she bent over the book and over the boys' shoulders, tenderly or a little firm, sometimes a touch irritated. Then I would know that the twins were playing up – I knew them well by now – and I wondered at her patient persistence. She was clearly a substantial person, but she also needed the work.

Then one afternoon we had a meeting that dragged on for longer than usual. There had already been trouble with the unions, which were rejecting the employers' latest pay offer. That morning the bus taking workers from Athens to Aspropyrgo had come off the road, and though no one was seriously wounded, tempers were frayed. The workers wanted to have a vehicle inspection before someone got injured. There was a row, Haris handled things badly, tempers blazed and the president of the union, who was looking out of the office window, gave a signal to the workers on the factory floor to strike. Instantly the machines stopped and the unionists left in a silence more deafening than the din of the machinery when it was working at full tilt. It was a disaster! The orders had to be completed, deadlines loomed. It was a conflict without logic or reason; when you talk to workers you have to negotiate and you have to respect their representatives. You can fire them if they make your life difficult and you can find a good excuse, or even better, you can bribe them to work for you. But you can't write them off just like that.

'You've made a mess of it,' I told Haris. 'From now on leave negotiations with the unions to your brother. You deal with your clients and your competitors.'

While we were talking, the lesson on the stone terrace had finished. The beautiful teacher put her books into her bag and stood up. She didn't do anything provocative, she simply patted her bottom to get the dust off her trousers, but we were transfixed. Our imaginations ran riot, we forgot all about production and unionists and wage increases. And then suddenly she gave us all a look, full of irony and contempt. It moved across all three of our faces to rest on mine. I felt as if she could see right through me, and realised that all this time we had been looking at her, thinking that she noticed nothing, the girl knew very well what was going on and that the laugh was on us. I was embarrassed and felt foolish. Never mind Haris Olympios, married for over twenty years and with a mistress more permanent than a wife, or Stefanos who paid far more attention to women than they deserved. Her scorn was directed at me! She narrowed her eyes, like a tigress, and I swore never to look at her again.

It wasn't difficult. The next afternoon the stone terrace stayed empty. It was the first place I looked when I went into the Olympiáiko, but out of an idiotic sense of pride I didn't mention it and pretended not to notice, not so much to deceive the others as myself. I couldn't concentrate on work, I barely managed to listen to what they were saying to me. I left early with the excuse that I was very tired. 'Go home and get some sleep,' the shark advised. 'Your schedule is insane, I can't stand the sight of you.' I went back to Saronida but the house was suffocating, I couldn't breathe. I put on my bathing costume, threw a towel into the car and went down to the beach. I dived into the sea, lights shimmered on its dark surface but I couldn't see what was under my feet or where I was swimming. High up the stars were glimmering and an orange half moon shone like a slice of melon. I threw all my strength into swimming out until I could go no further, turned on to my back and closed my eyes. All of a sudden I was overwhelmed by the image of a girlish figure sitting on a terrace, a cheeky ponytail, and eyes more golden than the stars winking at me overhead. *Méli glykítato* … What if she had gone, what if she never set foot in Haris's house again, how would I find her? The thought pierced my heart like ice.

After some time I got out, shivering, and wrapped myself in my towel. I lay down on the sand, closed my eyes, and thought about that ponytail. I decided that I would find her no matter where she had gone. Sifis would help me, they were mates, and he was sure to know where she lived. I would definitely sleep with her, and Stefanos and Haris would just have to survive. The thought lulled me to sleep! *Méli glykítato* …

For three afternoons in a row Aphrodite hadn't reappeared on the terrace, and what with the strike at the factory and the muddle with the union, I didn't have a chance to see Sifis. Eventually I asked Stefanos, who after dealing brilliantly with the unionists, took me out to celebrate in a club by the sea.

'What's become of the lovely governess. I never see her on the terrace.'

'She's giving her lessons in Nikolas's room.'

For the first time Stefanos, in dealing with the unions, had discovered that he was better at something than Haris. And yet he looked miserable. I had urged him not to be jealous of his brother, and not to fall into the trap of competing with him. The brothers' relationship had been a lost cause ever since their mother had failed to do what the most uneducated mother in the country would have done out of pure instinct when her second son was born. Instead of making Haris feel secure by taking him in her arms, cuddling him and talking to him, she tried to manage his very natural jealousy by bribing him with little presents and money, and the boys' rivalry was inevitable.

Stefanos was lovelorn. He had tried again to approach Aphrodite but she wanted nothing to do with him and she made it absolutely clear, once and for all. If he insisted, they had better replace her now, she told him directly, and left him standing stunned and humiliated on the doorstep while she got on to her motorbike and vanished.

'So why are you wasting time with a pleb?' I couldn't resist saying, not without a touch of hostility.

'I want her, Odysséa,' he whispered, and something in the tone of his voice made me shudder. I made a sign to the waiter to bring another drink and knocked back what was left in my glass. My throat burned and I bit my lip frantically. I would never be able to get near her now. Not without risking a friendship, and that wasn't my style. Friendship had always meant more to me than girls.

But she had guts, and she had dignity. Not many would have said no to Stefano, and especially not in her financial situation. And yet it wasn't just money that made Stefanos attractive to women. He had a cosmopolitan air, always polite and attentive, with one hand in his pocket too, of course, ready to bring out the cash. It scared me that he might eventually have his way, and I couldn't bear to think about her in the arms of Stefanos, his fat hands gradually moving over her body. It was the first time I had ever cared whose hands apart from mine touched the body of a woman I fancied. In any other situation I would simply have waited my turn. And how long would the rich kid go on wanting her once he had had her? I couldn't bear it …

An appalling week went by when I didn't see her once and I took care not to spend a single night without a woman to keep me company. I worked so hard that I didn't think about her at all and I pretended that nothing was wrong. I missed John. You can't talk about that kind of thing over the telephone. 'I miss you, you wanker, I even miss the smoke,' he yelled at me from the other side of the world. The smoke! I hadn't smoked since the moment I got on to the plane and the lack of nicotine at times drove me wild. I would search absent-mindedly in my shirt and trousers for the familiar packet, and then remember I didn't have any, and I didn't know what to do with my hands. I carried on suffering in silence. How long does an addiction to nicotine last? It's not heroin after all, I said to myself. But it does last, damn it, it lasts a long time.

\*\*\*

At the beginning of June, Haris introduced me to a shipping magnate called Kastrinós, just over from London, where he lived and had his offices. He spent the summer months in Greece, not in his villa at Old Psychiko but on his boat, a large yacht he kept moored in the marina at Faliro, from where he made trips to the islands. Haris thought Kastrinós might be useful if ever I decided to bring my business out to Greece. So one Saturday afternoon I went with him and his friends on a short cruise around the Argo-Saronic Gulf. He was a very agreeable host, cheerful, smart and never boring. He wandered tirelessly around the deck in his bathing trunks and a white T-shirt making sure we all had a good time. He was a bit short, but in excellent shape. Like a bronze statue of an athlete, you could see every muscle.

We talked about various things. He appeared interested in my situation, having heard about me from Haris. We sat in deckchairs in the shade of the awning, nibbling at fruit and discussing the effect on the Greek economy if we managed to secure the magical Olympic Games. The shipping magnate was enthusiastic, I less so. Huge amounts of capital were necessary for that kind of organisation and 'silk underwear requires a classy bum,' as my father would have crudely put it.

Kastrinós drank ouzo and lit a cigarette, but left it in the ashtray as if on purpose, so that the smoke kept blowing into my face. He stretched out his sinewy legs and on his left thigh I spotted two deep scars, scored by a knife blade. He saw me looking. 'A woman,' he remarked without my asking him. 'Of the very dangerous kind, but worth the risk.' I apologised for my indiscretion. 'There's no need,' he said, looking far out to sea as though he was remembering the deed. What kind of womanising could a person like Kastrinós have got involved in to take two cuts like that on his thigh. He looked as if he wouldn't hurt a flea. What jealous lover had he driven so far to the edge? I didn't feel relaxed enough with him to ask, and he clearly wasn't going to tell.

Kastrinós invited me to what would be his third wedding. I had all the gossip from Neféli, stunning, dyed-blonde, the daughter of an industrialist and a friend of Stefanos. Plans for the wedding were the talk of the town.

'Why do they need to spend so much money? They'll be divorced within the year,' said Neféli.

I didn't want to be alone that night and so I'd called Nefeli, and we were driving home along the road to Saronida. I had the roof down and her hair was blowing out behind. For some reason, she said, women could never stand Kastrinós for long, and sooner or later they all left. Rumours abounded. Some said he was gay and was having a relationship with his bodyguard, since he never went anywhere without him. Others said he had weird sexual preferences that women didn't like. I listened to her chattering but my mind was elsewhere. I couldn't care less about Kastrinos's sexual proclivities. I watched the curves of the road by the sea and thought of Aphrodite's dark hair caught up with that little hair tie. However much I tried to stop thinking about her I couldn't, even at work. I wanted her but my friend had first call, and she had frozen Stefanos right out and left him to stew in his own juice. The pleb had her revenge and no mistake.

It was after that night with Neféli that Stefanos began ringing my doorbell early in the morning to tell me his woes. I didn't pay much attention to it at first, but when he turned up with his pupils dilated – he had been sniffing coke and was barely lucid – I became seriously concerned. I spoke gently to him, suggesting that we go out together, so that he could see with his own eyes that Aphrodite was not the only woman in the world. 'Forget it,' he said, 'I'll call the world to come over here.' He punched a number on to his mobile and half an hour later the doorbell rang. A tall Serbian and a petite Greek girl, who introduced themselves as Vinka and Mary, appeared on the doorstep. He chose Mary, probably because she was more like Aphrodite, and they shut themselves away in the bedroom. I sat looking at Vinka, all two metres of her, and didn't know what to do with her. I paid her on the spot, sent her away and went off to bed. I was too overwrought to sleep. I couldn't stand the fact that I was unable to get my hands on the governess and find some peace. And I had a very bad feeling about my friend, who had completely lost control. The next morning Stefanos, as is usual after the passing of a typhoon, was a complete wreck. Mary had already left. I made coffee and we drank it on the balcony looking out over the sea.

'I want you to wish me good luck,' he said. 'I'm going to need it to face my parents and Haris. I've decided to marry Aphrodite.'

I froze. Not because it was likely to happen – no way would the Olympians allow a pleb to enter their palace and no way would Stefanos ever have the spunk to go against them – but because it showed how seriously he felt about her. Now I had no chance with her. It was out of the question.

\*\*\*

I went to Kastrinos's wedding with Máchi, as her official escort. We were besieged by journalists both at the church and at Kastrinós's house at Old Psychiko, where the reception was held. The cameras flashed as I went into the villa holding hands with Máchi and I heard someone shouting behind me: 'Who's the guy humping Olympios's daughter tonight?'

That would be me. I turned round to give him a piece of my mind, but he saw my look and disappeared into the crowd. The same question was all over the gossip columns on the following day, along with my photograph. Seventeen years earlier, there had been another photograph of me in the newspapers, in my house in the Mani. The headline read: 'Double murder at a village in the Inner Mani. Revival of old vendetta or unlucky accident?' During that era there was no concern about printing personal details or protecting underage children from appearing in the newspapers. How likely was it that anyone had seen both photographs, with an interval of seventeen years, and realised that they were the same person. Someone might. And the Haritakaíoi, who had lost all trace of me for years, would know exactly where to find me. Not that I was frightened, anything but. Let them come if they liked. It would save me the trouble of looking for them. Time was marching on, work was shaping up, and soon I would be free of my obligations to the Olympians. I yearned to go home, really home, to the Mani.

The evening of the reception, vapid as all the others I'd had to attend in Athens, ended with my breaking finally with Máchi, even if the newspapers did see romance in the air. I had wandered about for a while with a glass in my hand chatting to people in the beauti- fully lit garden. I sampled the delicious food served at the buffet and watched as Máchi went wild on the dance floor. Then, when I had stayed there long enough to feel I'd done my duty, I got ready to leave. At that moment Máchi grabbed me by the arm.

'You're not going to leave without me!'

'There's no need to spoil your evening …' I tried to get away.

'Are you as bored as you look?'

'Much more, but you stay if you want to.'

She sniffed and cast a look around the room at the other guests.

'You're right, it's getting boring. Where will you take me?'

'To my house, if you like …'

'Okay, we're out of here!'

We flew through the empty streets. I felt I deserved to have a relaxing evening and there was no better company than Máchi for that kind of thing. I couldn't have known how it would end. I undressed her, threw off my clothes and pulled her with me into the pool. She screamed as she hit the cold water. We swam naked and then got out and ran inside, dripping and shivering. We dived into bed until gradually our bodies warmed up and took fire. We had a good time, as we always did, until she lit a cigarette in the bedroom and spoilt it all. I got up and opened the balcony door to let out the smoke. Outside the night was a dark, mauve colour and you could barely distinguish the sea. She looked at me so intently, with such a strange expression in her eyes, that I felt awkward.

'Did you know that Stefanos wants to marry the little teacher?' she said out of the blue.

I shrugged my shoulders.

'There was a big row yesterday with Daddy,' she went on. 'Haris is against it too, the hypocrite. But at least Irene had money, this one doesn't have a bean. I saw through her the first time I met her, the little slut. I can't imagine what you all see in her and don't tell me you don't fancy her. I've seen the way you look at her.'

I shrugged my shoulders again.

'Admit that you fancy her,' she went on, blowing smoke in my direction.

'She's a beautiful woman, hard not to notice. So what?'

'What about me?'

I couldn't understand what she was driving at.

'What about you, Máchi?'

'What am I to you, that's what I'm asking.'

I shrugged my shoulders for a third time.

'We sleep together, Máchi, for as long as it suits us. We sleep with others as well, and I hope you're careful. I always am.'

She had never suggested wanting more from me, it was she who had laid down the rules and they happened to suit me. She told me

I was the most cynical shit she had ever met. I said I wasn't cynical, just honest. Then she went outside, naked as she was, to pick up her clothes from the pool. I sighed with relief and lay down, stretching out my tired body to take up all the space on the bed. I wasn't worried about Máchi. She would take my car and go back to her house – it wasn't the first time she had left so late. That night I had no trouble at all in sleeping. I didn't even wait to hear the car start up.

In the morning the car was still in the garage. I started phoning around. She didn't answer her mobile and I didn't want to call on the landline and worry her family unduly. But I was concerned, she had behaved a little strangely that evening. So I decided to go by her house on my way to work. I shoved a wad of banknotes into my pocket along with my keys, picked up my mobile and threw it on to the passenger seat along with my briefcase. There was traffic along the road by the sea and Kifissias was jam-packed. I phoned her again five times on the way and she didn't answer. I left the car in front of the heavy iron gate and the guard let me in.

'*Kyrios* Olympios?'

'*Kyrios* Nikos is inside. *Kyrios* Stefanos left early.'

'The young lady?'

'Inside …'

Goddamn you, Máchi, I thought, and relief flooded through me. I went on into the garden. There wasn't a soul anywhere. I walked across the immaculate lawn, went into the house by the open French window and called her. Not a soul … I remembered an early morning seventeen years ago at the tower house, when I had gone through another open front door and called out to my mother … and shuddered involuntarily with the same, suffocating presentiment. By the pool, I thought, and went back out into the garden to go round the house. They were there, the old man and Máchi … she floating lifeless with her arms spread out and he, in his dressing gown, struggling to hold her head up out of the water and calling for help. The guard at the gate, and the Filipino couple, so ever present as a rule, were nowhere to be seen. For an instant I was paralysed by the sense that I was reliving the death of Yiorgís. And then I thought about time. Time that never turns back. I dived in as I was, in my clothes. Old Olympios had lost his glasses in the water and was squinting to see who had come to help. I took Máchi out of his arms and carefully holding up her head, I pulled her over to the steps. She didn't react, she was lifeless and pale as death. I dragged her out and tried to tell if she was breathing. While I was resuscitating her, the Filipino maid finally arrived and the old man phoned an ambulance. Máchi wasn't responding.

The ambulance arrived in under ten minutes. She had a pulse, the paramedics said, but a very weak one. Her father was soaking wet, so I gave him my word that I wouldn't leave her for an instant until he changed and joined us at the hospital. As I sat next to her with pools of water forming at my feet, I thought of what she had said the night before. Was this my fault? She had always been so bright and vivacious, now so tragically helpless and alone. I looked at my watch. The dials had stopped.

The driver turned on the siren to open the way through the impenetrable traffic. Move over, I wanted to yell at them. We have to get there. Máchi doesn't deserve this, she's a spoilt kid, but she doesn't deserve to die! And I don't deserve to be saddled with another crime …

At the hospital, while the doctors took care of Máchi, I sat in a dreary waiting room with her father, both of us plunged in guilt, each for our own reasons. The old man with pursed lips, stifled by grief, huddled on the edge of the sofa, on the point of collapse. I with my shirt and jeans sticking to my body and my feet leaving pools of water everywhere. We didn't talk at all, until finally the doctor appeared, a heavy, white-haired guy, his large stomach visible under his flapping white coat. We leapt up. She would be all right, he assured us. Máchi had taken tranquillisers and they had pumped out her stomach. She had come round and we would soon be able to see her. It would be a good idea for her to see a psychologist, he advised her father, because she had escaped this time, but …

Nikolaos Olympios waited for the doctor to leave and then turned to me. He was looking for answers and he wanted them from me. He asked if I had been with her the night before and if anything had happened. I couldn't bear to look in his eyes, so full of helplessness and grief.

'She did seem a little odd,' I confessed, 'and she was upset when she left. I didn't stop her going. She usually takes the car, but when I saw it there in the morning, I tried to phone her and she didn't answer, so I came …'

He rubbed his temples with his fingers, closed his eyes for a second and then suddenly he asked me: 'Is your father alive?'

I shook my head.

'There is nothing worse than to fail as a parent. And I have failed with Máchi …'

He seemed to crumple before my eyes. Nikólaos Olympios, who had built a small kingdom out of nothing. I longed to say that if his daughter had been forced to get up at dawn every morning to look after a child or two, and go to work to put bread on the table, she would never have risked her life in such an idiotic way. Because she would have known that life was precious. The only thing of any value or worth to his daughter was her Louis Vuitton handbag. That was what really weighed on him, his failure to teach her the value of life.

As he was thanking me a nurse appeared and told him that his daughter wanted to see him. He got up and staggered down the long passage, while I sat there wondering whether I was at fault. I'd been carrying the burden of two murders ever since I was fifteen, I'd made that bed and had to lie in it, but to be saddled with Máchi's suicide attempt was taking it too far. My damp jeans, my half-dry shirt and soaking-wet shoes were making me irritable. I got up and started pacing up and down the passage, until her father came back to tell me that his daughter was okay, but she refused to see me.

'Don't fret over her, my boy. You go home and change. Take a taxi from here and I'll send your car round later.'

I found a taxi, but it didn't occur to me to think how I would pay. The banknotes I'd put in my pocket in the morning were wet. We got stuck at Kifissias. The taxi driver was tapping his fingers nervously on the steering wheel. It was hot and he wanted to talk.

'They say you have to die to go to hell, but this is hell, my friend. This furnace they call a city. Can you imagine anything worse than this?'

And in fact I could. To hold in your hand the gun of your dreams one minute and the next to wake up in a nightmare having killed a child. To be the cause of your father's death. To work in an illegal factory in America and sleep under bridges or in a homeless shelter. To be the 'guest' of your American aunt who regards you as an annoying parasite. To scrub greasy oven trays and saucepans at the Mythos. Yes, I could imagine many much worse types of hell than driving a taxi in Athens, but I gave him the first example that came into my head, even though it wasn't my own personal experience.

'To be a factory worker in an aluminium foundry. To feed those huge ovens with metal and have to stand right over them.'

'I didn't take you for that kind of worker, my friend,' he said and stared at me in the mirror.

I looked back at him. Short, fifty, balding, with a paunch. The kind who not only transports passengers but psychoanalyses them as well, and tells them all their sorrows.

'It's a stressful job, ours,' he went on undaunted, 'but it has its perks. If I told you what happened yesterday evening, you'd think I was lying. I had to pinch myself, I thought I was dreaming.'

The last thing I needed just then was to hear about the perks of being a taxi driver. What I wanted was for the road to free up so that I could get home, have a bath and change my clothes. But Anéstis, as the taxi driver told me he was called, was well used to bottlenecks and made sure to kill the time as well as he could. He therefore related to me what had happened the previous night on the sea road. He had taken some drunk tourists to their hotel, and on the way back a woman had waved him down, at around three in the morning. He stopped. She was around thirty, very beautiful and expensively dressed. She gave him an address in Ekáli and slumped down in the back seat. He looked at her curiously in the mirror. What could such a beautiful woman be doing in the middle of nowhere at that hour? Then he heard stifled sobs and realised that she was crying. He asked her whether he could help in any way, but didn't get an answer – she just blew her nose. He didn't speak to her again. Coming up to Glyfada, the woman asked him: 'What's your name?'

'Anéstis. Yours?'

'Máchi. How much do you make if you work all night?'

'It depends on the fares.'

'I'll pay you double. Take me to the nearest hotel.'

None of his colleagues believed him in the morning. On the contrary they jeered at him remorselessly. And why should they believe that a beauty with a fat wallet paid him to fuck her, and roughly what's more? Even Mitso, his buddy, his best friend, said to him nastily: 'Give it a rest, Anésti, we don't want to hear about your blow jobs first thing in the morning.'

But Anéstis is not a joker or a bragger. He took a handful of 5,000-drachma notes out of his pocket and shoved them under their noses till they could smell them. The scumbags! He even promised them to spend every last penny of it at Sfakianáki's! Because Anéstis is a gent. Not some wanky loner like other people one could mention.

How could I have imagined that the explanation for Máchi's despair was waiting for me right outside the hospital where she was being cared for! I felt a weight fall from my shoulders. Suddenly I was sure that whatever drove Olympios's daughter to take an overdose and dive into the pool, it had nothing to do with me. She had been angry with me, sure, but I wasn't the one who drove her to it. I felt so relieved. I was thirty-two and brimming with health. Outside, the brilliant sunshine was toasting the car, the rain and damp of

Boston were far away. I relaxed, and suddenly, freed from guilt, I didn't care that I was still wet and my clothes were glued to me. Máchi was going to be fine, and whatever problem she had with me, we would sort it out. I, at any rate, had every intention of doing so. I would tell her gently that she was the most desirable woman I have ever known, but there was no hope of anything more. I just wasn't at that 'stage' yet, as Sifis would say. And then I would take care to keep my distance from the little punk. Death was just another game for people like her, popping pills and sniffing coke. But death is no game, nor are the fateful Erinyes who fuck up your life. Life, on the other hand, is a gift – a desirable woman, pulling at the sleeve of my crumpled shirt and winking at me from behind the stationary cars. All I wanted to do was to give myself up to it!

Half an hour later, still on Kifissias, we had barely covered two kilometres stopping and starting. It wasn't ideal, given that I was soaked to the skin. But I didn't care. Anéstis was swearing on all the saints and didn't mind that I wasn't listening; we were best buddies by now. The other drivers were equally infuriated, opening their windows ready for a fight, honking and gesticulating rudely. But in that river of motionless steel, motorbikes and scooters passed by in a flash and were gone. A motorcycle drew up beside us and the driver gestured to Anéstis to move over. He did so and let out a whistle. Then the rider tucked in to our right to pass us and her firm thigh, in tight jeans, was at about eye level. No helmet, her hair tied back in that little band. A few wild ringlets had escaped around her forehead. She was wearing sunglasses and frowning slightly. She moved off and all I could see was her white shirt billowing out in the wind. The river of cars moved again and Anéstis drew over into the right-hand lane where there was a gap. Then just around the corner I saw that the cops had stopped her for not wearing a helmet. The girl had got off her bike and was saying something intently to the policeman. Sometimes you don't have time to think about things, you just react. On a sudden impulse I told Anéstis to pull over.

'You don't waste time, my friend,' he remarked.

I got out of the taxi, intending to play the knight in shining armour, but when I put my hand in my pocket to get out some money, I pulled out the mess of sodden banknotes which had disintegrated into my jeans. My confidence evaporated. By now I had attracted her attention and she was looking at me with interest. The cop, too. She handed him her papers and then approached me. Then she drew off her sunglasses and placed them on her head.

'Is anything the matter?'

Dazzled by the golden glints in her sweet, brown eyes, I remembered my grandmother and the nereids. 'Watch out for their eyes, my chick, don't look into their eyes, just walk straight on by or they'll drive you crazy,' she'd told me, and there I was, gibbering like an idiot about an accident and falling in the water, clutching my wad of sodden paper. A really excellent impression I made, standing there like a drowned rat. She leant over to the window of the taxi.

'How much is it?'

'Eight hundred and fifty,' muttered Anéstis, equally stunned.

She took a few banknotes out of her pocket and paid.

'There you are,' she said earnestly. 'Problem solved.'

There wasn't a trace of irony, but I was sure that she was teasing me. We looked at each other for a few endless seconds, I can't possibly calculate how many. Then the cop called her.

'Miss …' and he handed her a piece of paper. 'Penalty!'

It was idiotic of me to have imagined that she needed help. It wasn't the first time she'd been stopped by that particular policeman, I realised. It was the third time he'd fined her for not wearing a helmet. It was impressive to see how determined they both were, he to fine her and she to insist on not complying.

'Aren't you embarrassed, picking on me just to prove your authority? It's my choice not to wear a helmet, and I'll pay for it if something happens. I haven't gone through a red light or killed anyone. Why don't you catch a criminal who's destroying people's lives, and do something useful for a change.'

'Are you not wearing it just to provoke me?' asked the policeman.

'Please speak to me in the plural, like I do. We aren't buddies. And secondly I don't like your clan. You make a mockery of society,' was her tart reply.

'We have a job like everyone else.'

'Well I hope you enjoy it, it's all you deserve.'

If that kind of outburst had happened in Boston, the policeman would have nicked her on the spot. He just stood and waited, holding the penalty ticket.

'I'll tear this up,' he went on in the singular, 'if you promise me you won't ride your bike again without your helmet. Do you not have parents who worry about you?'

'It's none of your business!'

He waved the paper in front of her face.

'Speak up. What shall I do?'

She looked at him nonplussed for a moment. Medium build, a little rotund, chubby cheeks, a deep furrow across his forehead. But only for a moment. Stubbornly she grabbed her papers and climbed on her motorbike.

'Nothing doing!' she shouted at him. 'I don't want any favours from you!'

She started the motor and turned to me: 'What are you waiting for? Climb on.'

I thought she'd forgotten about me. I got on to the scooter and just had time to catch the look of disapproval on the policeman's face before we whizzed off, weaving in and out of cars that were still at a virtual standstill. How we got to the crossroads with Mesogeion, I scarcely know.

'Where are you going?'

She was speaking to me in the plural again, having abandoned it earlier. I told her to leave me somewhere to get another taxi.

'And how will you pay for it? Tell me where you live, I'll take you.'

Her ponytail was tickling my nose, her warm, young body leaning against me, and I breathed in her scent. I felt like I did when I was a child, knowing what was right, but unable to resist doing wrong. Besotted, I gave her my address in Saronida. She went down Syngrou Avenue and came out on the sea road in record time. She moved deftly in and out of the cars and with great care, despite the lack of a helmet. I relaxed. The sea glittered in the sunlight, old women sunning themselves, children paddling in the water, and as we raced on I felt the cooling breeze and the caress of her hair. My jeans were almost dry, along with my crumpled pride. I wanted very much to move closer to her, but I didn't dare. I was thinking of Stefanos. Our friendship at college in Boston, late nights, parties, jokes. Of the numerous times he had picked up the tab for us, when John and I were penniless and his wallet was stuffed with banknotes. His desperate, dilated pupils and ceaseless talk. He had confided his feelings to me and I couldn't bring myself to betray him. I desperately desired to do what was wrong, but I must do what was right. Sure, I wanted the girl. I had never wanted anyone so much. But friendship is above everything …

She turned off the engine in front of my house. I invited her in for a coffee, a drink, anything, to thank her, and to give her the money I owed her. She refused. She didn't have time, she was in a hurry, and as for the money it wasn't an issue. I wanted to say something clever to impress her, but I had lost my tongue. She didn't smile, she just looked at me and I felt flooded with a sense of shame so intense that it loosened my tongue.

'Apart from the money, I owe you something else. An apology. I'm sorry for forcing you off the terrace. I'm sorry that I made you feel so awkward that you had to go inside … but you were such a lovely sight there, much more so than Stefanos or Haris. You saw me looking at you, and I felt ashamed, and whenever I feel ashamed I behave like a wanker. I'm sorry, Aphrodite …'

She nodded and put her glasses back on. She turned on the engine.

'Okay,' she murmured. 'It wasn't such a big deal. Forget it.'

'If you'll forget it as well.'

'I already have …'

She smiled at me and then with a wave of the hand she turned and was lost around the bend in the road. As for me, it took me some time to recover. *Meli glykítato* … And right there, in the heat of the afternoon, Aphrodite became my *Melénia*. My honey child. From the honey *koutalídes* my mother made, that I could still taste on my tongue. The most irresistible sweet of them all, the image of a vanishing girl. Hidden away in the drawer of my soul. My hopeless love. My wounded heart. My dream betrayed. My crushed pride. And that wretched sense of honour … 'You should have realised,' John said to me afterwards, 'that she wasn't like the others, for you at any rate. You never remember women's names, except for Lou, and you married her. And then Melénia turns up, and not only does she have a name, she has a name you've chosen for her, taken from one of the most precious memories of your mother.'

I went inside with a deep sense of loss. Then I smiled into my mirror. What I did know for sure was that I liked her, I liked her very much.

Sifis brought the car round for me and found me in the middle of lunch. I had cold chicken and tomato salad, but because I'd forgotten to buy any bread, I was dipping rusks into the olive oil. He wrinkled his nose in disgust.

'I told you to come over to our house for meals, but you never listen.'

I opened a beer and pushed the plate across to him to have a snack. He refused and invited me over to his house for dinner instead. His mother had made stuffed tomatoes.

'You're the hero at the Olympians' today.'

Sifis told me there had been a huge row, Stefanos had banged his fist on the table and demanded the right to marry Aphrodite. I emptied my food into the dustbin where it belonged. All of a sudden I felt a knot in my stomach.

'What's up?' The Cretan winked at me. 'She'll tell him no, I'll lay a bet on it.'

I wasn't so sure. It was one thing for the kid to offer her dinner, quite another to offer her a church wedding, with all the honour and glory. She had lucked out. I caught myself searching for a cigarette.

# The Clever Bird

WHEN MÁCHI CAME OUT of the hospital I went to see her. She was sitting up in bed, a nightdress barely covering her gorgeous body, and looked pale and exhausted. I went to kiss her on the cheek, but she put up a hand to stop me. I sat next to her and for a while we said nothing. The room smelt powerfully of smoke, an ashtray full of cigarette ends was on the bedside table. I asked her straight out.

'Is it my fault?'

If she had wanted to punish me, a 'yes' would have done it, but Máchi wasn't a bad person, anything but. Just spoilt. She put her hand out thoughtfully for the cigarettes.

'Of course not. You just said the wrong things at the wrong time. You should learn to tell the odd lie now and again, you're not stupid. Just out of courtesy. We all need that.'

When I had told her, so cynically, that I slept with other women – which she knew anyway – I was depriving her of what she so badly needed: someone's full attention. I asked her to forgive me, I told her she was the only woman whose company I enjoyed so much, but I wasn't used to saying things just out of courtesy, and raising people's expectations. I couldn't be with only one woman, just as she could never be monogamous. I wished I had been like my father, who lived with my mother his whole life and for seventeen years never looked at anyone else, not even Potítsa when she offered herself to him on a plate. She smiled and reassured me.

'I saw you looking at that kid though, like a besotted fool, and I was jealous. Nobody will ever look at me like that, I thought ...'

'Are you blind? People never stop looking at you!'

She granted me a tired smile. She knew that we were over, that she had overstepped the limits, and I no longer found her fun to be with. She stretched out her hand and stroked my cheek indifferently, as you might pat a child you don't much care for.

'Why don't you ask her out? The little teacher, I mean,' she surprised me by saying. 'I'm very curious to see what will happen the moment she gets difficult. Because she will be difficult, for certain. Don't let my brother put you off, he doesn't have a hope with her. Unless he's serious about the marriage …'

I stroked her hair, equally indifferently. What did she think would happen? That I'd make a fool of myself like Stefanos? That I'd be driven to drink and coke, that I'd take up smoking again out of frustrated love? I wasn't the type, I had more serious problems to deal with than whether a woman fancied me or not, I told her. She gave me a pitying look.

'You don't know what's happening to you,' she murmured as I left.

On the way to the factory I thought over what she'd said. If Stefanos hadn't been in the way, if my hands hadn't been tied, there was no way I'd have trouble with the girl. No chance in a million. I saw it in her eyes. 'You see? Problem solved,' she had said, giving Anéstis the money. Her eyes! Chestnut, common chestnut-coloured eyes like most Greeks. And yet I had never seen such sweet eyes. They glinted like gold. You could just sun yourself in their warmth, let your soul sweeten and melt like butter.

I wouldn't go any further unless Stefanos made a hash of things, but he did seem to be losing control. There are people and people, and it has nothing necessarily to do with social class. I had known rich girls who behaved worse than the cheapest tarts, and prostitutes who did whatever they did with dignity. It has nothing to do either with education or the size of your pocket. It is something else that comes from within you, your quality as a human being, what remains of the fruit once you have removed the rind. In the case of the beautiful governess, Stefanos showed me a self I simply didn't recognise, although we'd been through so much together. I suspect that he didn't recognise himself. Pushed on to a downhill slope by his wilful stubbornness, an ever more frequent flirtation with drugs and drink, his deeply wounded pride and broken heart, he had become another person. This wasn't the friend I knew. And I didn't owe him a thing.

Things finally fell apart for Stefanos at a party, the twentieth anniversary of Haris's wedding at his house. I was naturally invited, for yet another dull evening among indifferent people, and useful only for networking. But then I saw her. She was dancing with Kastrinós, the shipping magnate. He looked besotted, his gaunt cheek nervously twitching. She was wearing white – a short white dress and high heels. Lightly made up and looking strangely pale, her body stiff, as if she couldn't hear the music. I watched them from afar as I sipped my gin, and saw Stefanos ask Kastrinós if he could dance with her. Aphrodite changed partners, the shipowner went to find his wife, and I couldn't bear to look. I found Sifis in a dark corner of the garden and we gossiped about the guests. The Cretan knew them and their goings-on, since he went everywhere with Stefanos. Irene Olympiou came to ask if I was having fun and we danced a slow number together. I avoided dancing with Máchi and could tell that she was avoiding me, too. I danced with Nefeli, her friend, and with a very beautiful actress, apparently in line to be Haris's next mistress. You couldn't blame him. I looked for Aphrodite among the couples dancing. I couldn't see either her or Stefanos. Why had the Olympians invited their classics teacher to a family gathering? 'To keep an eye on the twins, why else?' Sifis had told me. 'And don't imagine she wanted to come. She'll be off soon, I'm afraid, the way your friend is hounding her.' Anyway for the time being neither she nor my friend were anywhere to be seen, and I wondered whether they were off hounding one another.

I emptied my glass and decided to leave. My car was in the underground car park. I said goodbye to the others and went down in the lift. As I opened the door and stepped out, a vast spotlight that worked on a sensor lit up the darkness like daylight. Then I saw them! Horrified, I recognised Stefanos's heavy bulk and Aphrodite's white dress beneath him. Andrei the gardener was holding the girl still on the bonnet of Irene's Peugeot, with his hand over her mouth. My mind didn't want to take in what was happening, but then he punched her in the face as she tried to struggle, and Aphrodite's head jerked back and was still. As if in a dream, I saw Andrei rip her dress at the bust and Stefanos undoing his trousers. I didn't have time to think, I only remember the anger, the fury, stifling me. I think I hit Stefanos first. The next minute I was rolling on the floor with Andrei among the cars. I only came to my senses at the sound of the Georgian's head repeatedly knocking against the panel of the Mercedes. How many times, I can't remember. I could have killed him. I let him go and his body slumped heavily to the floor. Stefanos was groaning and rubbing his wounded chin. He looked at me bleary-eyed. Taking deep breaths I held back my fist and tried to focus. I looked at the battered girl. Still motionless on the bonnet, bare-breasted, with her dress pulled up, underclothes in full view, legs parted. The sight made the blood race back to my head.

'Odysséa …' stammered my friend.

'Go fuck yourself!'

She opened her eyes with difficulty and her eyelids fluttered as I took her hands and pulled her up. She saw Stefanos lying on the floor, Andrei unconscious. She looked at me in anguish as I lifted her into the car.

'What happened?'

'Nothing. Let's get out of here.'

By the time I had walked round to the driver's seat the girl had realised that her dress was torn and her breasts exposed – which despite my fury was the first thing I had noticed. Bad habits die hard. She tried to cover herself, trembling, her teeth chattering. I gave her my jacket and she whispered a thank you as I revved hard and drove away from the house. As we left I saw Kastrinós and his unsuspecting wife looking nonplussed at the car. On Kifissias, at the first red traffic light, I realised I was in a state of shock myself. The girl next to me was still trembling. I could see the tears in her eyes as she hugged my jacket around her.

'Put on your seat belt,' I said abruptly. How could she put herself at risk like that? She didn't wear a helmet, she didn't wear a seat belt, she went off alone with Stefanos into the garage. Did she have no idea at all?

But she had taken enough aggression for one night. She threw my jacket down on the seat and grabbed the door handle.

'Stop on the right and let me out,' she shouted at me. 'Or I'll open the door.'

She had stopped crying and I didn't doubt for a moment she would do what she said. My anger evaporated and I sat there, feeling empty and unbelievably tired.

'Where will you go with a ripped dress?'

'Home.'

'How?'

'On foot!'

She raised her eyebrows proudly and stubbornly stuck out her chin. I gently pressed down the brake and pulled over, turning on the hazard lights. She grabbed the handle, but I'd locked it.

'Let me out,' she shouted at me like a wounded animal.

'Listen to me first and then I'll let you out. You're alone, it's late, you have a ripped dress, and no money. You're hurt. I'll take you home. You have nothing to be afraid of from me. I don't rape women, believe me. If I'd wanted to, I had my chance earlier. Calm down and don't act like a child. I can't leave you here in the middle of the night. I owe it to you. Let me take you home and then I'll go.'

She bowed her head in defeat.

'I live in the Plaka,' she whispered.

I rejoined the traffic and she wrapped herself in my jacket. We didn't speak again, except for directions. I asked, she answered.

'Turn into the side street.'

'On the right?'

'Yes. Stop here, it's pedestrian.'

I left the car any old how. I, who cursed my compatriots for parking wherever they felt like it. I walked with her along the pedestrian street and took her to a low green door covered in jasmine. She walked with hurried, firm steps. The traffic hummed in the distance. She asked me to come in – I desperately needed something to drink and I told her so. My chin was aching, Andrei had whacked me with his fist. We went into the tiny yard full of flowers and I remember an intense scent of nightflowers. I felt dizzied by the sense that I wasn't just going into a house, her house, but into a mysterious world that I knew well. I had tucked it away in the secret drawer of my memory and now she, like another Pandora, was opening that drawer. I couldn't stop it all spilling out from within me. Memories, feelings, fears. I collapsed on to the chair beside the small square table under the vine.

'I'll wait for you here,' I whispered.

She unlocked the door and went in. I closed my eyes and breathed in the nightflowers, which my mother had so loved. How long was I there?

'I only have ouzo.' Her voice startled me. 'My brother sometimes drinks it.'

'Do you live with your brother?'

She shook her head. She had put a tray on the table with a bottle, two glasses, and a jug of water. She brought some iodine and cotton wool. Her hair was wet; she had had a bath and was wearing jeans and a thin, long-sleeved blouse. She was still shivering. She poured ouzo into the glasses, and put plenty of water into her own.

'Do you want some?'

I shook my head and knocked back the glass. It burnt my throat. Better that way. Her lips were swollen and beginning to bruise. I put some iodine on a piece of cotton wool and signalled to her to sit down opposite me. She obeyed and I touched the cotton wool to her lips. She grimaced in pain but didn't say a word. 'Maybe it needs some ice,' I murmured. We were very close, we could feel one another's breath. Maybe that was why she hurriedly got up to bring me two freezer bags of ice cubes and two towels. She wrapped each bag in a towel and pressed one of them to my chin. With the other she covered her lips.

'Does it hurt?' she asked.

'Not much,' I lied. 'You?'

She shook her head. No, she replied, it didn't hurt, only a little … More lies. She sat back opposite me and took a few sips from her glass. She refilled mine.

'Thank you,' she said softly. 'I can't find the words …'

Her voice broke, her eyes filled with tears. She wiped them hurriedly with her hand. 'I'm sorry,' she stammered and looked away. I wanted so much to stretch out my hand and stroke her hair. I didn't dare, after all that had happened to her. So I sat there in silence. She put her knees up to her chin and sat huddled in the chair like a foetus. She looked defenceless. I still couldn't take in what I had witnessed. I needed another glass to find the courage to ask her what exactly had happened. And she took another sip before she could tell me. It seemed that Niko, one of the twins, had told her that his mother wanted to speak to her in the garage. She thought it odd, but had no reason not to go. However, Stefanos was waiting for her there, completely unlike himself, talking very quickly and looking strangely agitated. He had none of his usual good manners and seemed deranged. She knew as soon as she saw him that he'd been sniffing coke. At first she wasn't worried when he made the usual advances. But as soon as he realised that he had no chance with her, he grew angry. She tried to keep her cool but then he pushed her down on to the Peugeot, she struggled away from him and ran to the elevator. It was occupied. Someone was coming down. She felt her breath returning: whoever it was would help her and Stefanos would be found out. But it was Andrei.

Aphrodite wiped away her tears.

'Will you do me a favour? Could you ask someone to bring me my handbag? I have all my papers in it.'

'You mean you won't go back?'

'I should never have gone in the first place. And then, when I saw you all looking at me in the garden, I should have handed in my notice. But I hoped …'

I understood. A young girl who needed the work, who had the misfortune of being too attractive and had to endure three pairs of eyes on her, literally gobbling her up, playing with her suffering. As for the other two, it was no surprise, but what about me? Shame flooded through me, but there was something else that called to my conscience. I really didn't know many women who would have said no to Stefanos's wallet, I had seen it often enough in Boston. He had his way with women and he almost always got lucky.

'I want to ask you something,' I said hesitantly, leaning towards her. I knew more or less what her answer would be, but I needed to hear it from her. 'Why did you say no? To Stefanos, I mean. Did you know that he quarrelled with his father over you? He's head over heels. He will marry you, if you handle it right.'

'Mr Anastasákos, I teach Ancient Greek. That is my job. What you are talking about is a different profession.' She had remembered to use the plural again.

She looked at me and her eyes were dry now, they showered me with their light like the Maniot sun at midday. I drew back to avoid being burnt. She had a wild pride, a dignity that perplexed me. I asked her if she would be going to the police. I said I would support her if she decided to report him, she could count on me.

'Would you really fall out with your friend over me?' she asked. 'You even work for the Olympians. Wouldn't you have a problem with that?'

'I was there when it happened. I can't not tell the truth.'

I drank the last mouthful of ouzo and got up to go. I didn't want to, but I had to sooner or later. She assured me that she didn't need anything and thanked me again. I asked her hesitantly whether she needed any money. I could help her out until she found another job … It would be a loan, in any case. Her refusal didn't surprise me at all and I didn't insist. I would be seeing her again, I would make sure to take her handbag to her in person. She walked with me to the gate. Her lips were swollen; nevertheless I felt a strong desire to kiss her. How could I? After Stefanos's grossness, God only knew how she would react.

But I stretched out my hand and stroked her cheek to say goodnight. I don't know how, my finger got caught in a dark brown curl and to free it I gently touched her neck. Her shudder passed through me like a current and inadvertently my thumb travelled from her chin to the hollow at the base of her neck. How soft her neck was, like the stalk of a flower, my hand could have completely encircled it! It was only a caress, completely innocent, or so it started. But it was enough for us both to be aware of where it was leading us. My blood was racing, I felt the tingling of desire in every atom of my body. I wanted her! Unimaginably! And I had to leave before I did something I would later regret. I pulled my hand away suddenly and went out into the road, still feeling dazed. I had barely reached the car when I realised that I was still holding the towel with the ice cubes to my face. Not against my chin, which hurt, but against my nose, to breathe in her scent.

\*\*\*

The next morning there were a number of missed calls to my mobile, all from Stefanos's house, and a message on the answerphone from Olympios senior. 'Mr Anastasáko, please get in touch with me urgently.' I wasn't at all in a hurry to phone them, and I preferred to go there myself. I made some toast, filled the cafetière and while the coffee was brewing I jumped into the pool. What a fantastic sensation water gives you when you're young and healthy! I felt alive in every muscle. I got out feeling refreshed and ready for the hunt, like a carnivore stalking its prey. Aphrodite! I smiled at my reflection in the bathroom mirror, as I smeared myself with shaving foam. I whistled! I no longer cared about threatening my friendship with Stefanos. How could I turn a blind eye to what he'd done? Spoilt rich kid! I laid my plans as I drank my coffee and munched my toast. I had a reason to see her – the lost handbag – but I had to be careful. It would be crass to make a straight play for her. I would have to take her somewhere where she felt safe, but where? I pondered about it all the way to Ekáli and when I found the solution, I hooted triumphantly at a poor man who dared to put on his indicator to change lanes in front of me. I laughed to myself and started softly singing along in a high voice to Bithikótsi on the radio. *Love was made for two and three don't fit into two.*

I found Máchi with her father in the garden drinking coffee, the newspapers open on the table. The old man looked anxious, his daughter anything but, as if she wasn't in the least concerned by what had happened the previous night. They offered me coffee and some little croissants which smelled good, and they barely said good morning before starting on me. They'd been trying to get hold of me all night. What did I mean by putting my friend – to whom, by the way, I owed my job – in such a difficult position. Olympios seemed to have forgotten I was the hero of the house, the man who had saved his only daughter's life! I wasn't some naive child he could wag his finger at.

'What d'you think I should have done to help my friend? Take my turn in fucking her?'

Máchi giggled stupidly and lit a cigarette.

'You managed just fine,' she said ambiguously.

I looked at her angrily and asked after Stefanos. He was in his room, inconsolable, in black despair. I got up to go and see him.

'Do you know if she'll go to the police?' asked his father.

Imagine, his son gets himself blitzed and tries to rape a woman and that was all he cared about. I shrugged my shoulders, I didn't deign to answer. What could I say? No, I didn't believe that Aphrodite would go to the police, what would be the point? To see her photograph and the whole story spread over the newspapers? So what if I had witnessed everything and backed up her story? They'd find plenty of people to say that the girl had brought it on herself, that she was after their money and was blackmailing a respectable family. You try getting a fair trial when there's a rustle of banknotes. Only in the cinema.

In his room, Stefanos broke down and poured out his anguish. The cocaine had worn off and he was full of remorse. 'What have I done? What have I done …?' he kept saying. For a moment I felt sorry for him. My whole life I've been saying: 'What have I done, what have I done …' but there was a difference. It's one thing to unwittingly destroy and be destroyed, and quite another to do it out of choice. And Stefanos had a choice. To accept the obvious, to respect Aphrodite's refusal and leave her alone. I only had to remind myself of what I'd seen with my own eyes and the anger rose up again.

'How is she?' he wailed.

'How should she be?'

'She'll never want to see me again.'

'As for that …'

His chin, where I had hit him, had turned a yellowy black.

'There's something I need to tell you,' I said firmly. 'I like Aphrodite. Very much. All this time when you were trying to have a relationship with her, I stood aside. But now it's different. You don't have a hope. You've made a mess of it and so I'm going to make a move. It's your turn to stand aside.'

He started to laugh. Loud, ringing, almost hysterical laughter. It was the one thing I didn't expect.

'Why are you laughing?'

'I'm laughing because you're an idiot,' he managed to splutter. 'You go on then! You make a move! I'll stand by and watch you make another balls-up.'

'I don't intend to rape her ...'

'No, of course not. You'll find some other way to fuck it up, like you always do. And she won't take it any better, believe me. You're kidding yourself if you think you can just make use of her in your usual way. She's not like your *Japonéza*, not this one ...'

He started to laugh again, so much that his eyes were streaming with tears. I got up to go. I'd had all the craziness I could take from this family.

'I didn't want to hit you,' was the last thing I said to him.

'And yet ... that's exactly what you wanted to do from the start,' he said cuttingly through his laughter, and I knew he was right. I could still hear him laughing all the way down the stairs.

Before I left, the old man asked me to intercede and ensure Aphrodite's silence with a little present. I refused. Then he mentioned Kastrinós. He was a trusted friend, surely he would do them that favour. The man had known Aphrodite, apparently, years before, when her mother worked as a maid in his house in Palaio Psychiko. That was why he had danced with her the previous evening. Kastrinós was very persuasive. He would persuade the girl there was no way she would get money by blackmailing them.

I didn't want to hear any more, I left in disgust. I was anxious to find Sifis. I had phoned him already that morning about the handbag. The housekeeper found it thrown behind the Peugeot. The Cretan had it with him, and after one or two gritty remarks about the latest events, he gave it to me.

'Do you want me to take it to her?' he asked eagerly.

'No way!' I said, and gave him a wink.

# Internet Explorer

I'M NOT A BIG FAN of the internet. Marina had limited the time I spent on the computer ever since I was a kid – some of her students are so obsessed with it they have no contact with reality. *Pappoú* thinks it's a satanic plot by 'plutocrats' to bring people into line and lead the young astray. Therefore I owe it to myself not to be tempted by that kind of thing, and if I must be addicted to the internet, I have his blessing, so long as I become a hacker and make it my duty to blow all American nuclear testing sky high, and infiltrate and sabotage the State Department in an elaborate way. Sadly I don't have the skills for that kind of thing. However, recently, I have been dedicating a lot of time to the computer, to hack my way into Mitsikoyiánnis's house, which is no less dangerous, believe me. If ever he gets wind of what I've been up to with his daughter, I'll be hanging from the belfry, as that creep Anastasákos so vividly put it.

Effie and I Skype at night when the others are asleep. It's a major blow after having your girl in your arms to suddenly be reduced to seeing her on screen. But since Anastasákos appeared on the scene, we have to count ourselves lucky. I tell her to be patient. He'll have to shove off eventually, how long can he possibly stay? The summer is rolling by, the holidays'll be over, and in September I have to go back to Athens. I have no intention of going back a virgin. I'm trying to be cool about it, I don't want to upset Effie. The American has her in the palm of his hand, he poisons her mind at every opportunity. He says she's far too young, what about the consequences, I'm not thinking about her, all I want is to fuck her because it's natural at my age. He tries to play the therapist. He thinks everyone else is like him, the wanker! Don't listen to them, my darling, don't let them shut our life into a trap, just look at me! Look at me and feel yourself flow through me, giving your rhythm to the beating of my heart. Anastasákos can't understand it, you have to feel a thing like this to understand it. What can he possibly feel?

He always stops when he sees me waiting for the bus and gives me a lift. We barely talk at all on the way, there is nothing to say; there's a lot to divide and almost nothing to unite us. At first he tried to make conversation, stupid things like: 'And how is school going?' or 'What are you thinking of studying?' Stuff like that, but I cut him short. I don't want to talk to him and if I get in his car it's so he doesn't have the illusion that I'm afraid of him. I want him to know his place and watch out. We'll manage fine, so long as he doesn't make the mistake of underestimating me.

My mum and I bumped into him one evening at the supermarket. He was with Evangelía, Pavlákos's daughter. Ever since Anastasákos came I don't like Marina going about too much on her own. Just the thought that he might see her and say something or other makes me mad. And blow me if we didn't bump into him by the washing powders, with Evangelía smooching up to him as usual. Our shopping trolleys got entangled and I was riveted to the spot. I have to admit he looked a million dollars. Like a Swedish athlete! She was wearing a mini skirt up to her navel and a tits-out shirt, as if she was on a day outing from a brothel. He was wearing bermuda shorts and sandals and a polo shirt. We said hello as if it was all perfectly normal. Evangelía looked down her nose at my mother, and he looked completely indifferent, but why should Marina care? She chose her fabric conditioner and water softener as if to say 'who gives a shit', studied her list and said: 'We've forgotten the cheese.' She didn't have her reading glasses with her, they spoil her image, so she couldn't read a thing but she played it totally naturally. They arrived at the end of our queue while we were at the checkout. Anastasákos was pushing the trolley, Evangelía beside him twittering like a goldfinch. He saw that we were looking at him and I don't think he was happy about it, embarrassed more like, and I said so to Marina when we got back to the car.

'She's pathetic,' said my mum.

'Pathetic,' said I, 'but she has him by the nose …'

'Do you think so?' she asked me, keeping her eyes on the road. 'Do you like Evangelía? I want your opinion, objectively.'

Objectivity does have its problems. She isn't a bad looker, what can I say? Pert breasts, a bum to die for …?

'She's not my style,' I said. 'But how should I know what his style might be?'

'She's not his style either and she knows it, I think, but she's too dumb to accept it. He just puts up with her. Because she's his friend's daughter.'

'Is that why he gives her the leg-over?' I couldn't hold my tongue and I don't like talking to my mother like that.

'He doesn't give her the leg-over,' she answered back. 'He won't do anything, not even if she kneels down and begs him to. Because she's Pavlákos's daughter.'

That evening I texted Effie and asked her. No way, she said, Anastasákos came to their house every evening as soon as his uncle went to bed. Old men go to sleep after they've shut up the chickens, as everyone knows. If anything had been going on with Evangelía she'd have sussed it from what was said at home, and anyway Evangelía was hardly the type to keep a secret.

Effie suspects there's something up, because I keep asking her about the creep. I don't mean to but we talk every day and see each other so rarely – we're like old-fashioned lovers exchanging frantic letters and falling in love by post. We say things to each other we never thought we'd say, and if Mitsikoyiánnis ever catches a look at his daughter's computer screen, we only have one hope – that he can't read Gringlish.

The internet is a big deal, whatever Grandad says. You press a button and you have the information in front of your eyes. Masses of information, as much as you want. The blue glaciers of Argentina and Chile, penguins and seals, offers for hotels and houses, historical information, the customs and morals of savage people who didn't wear clothes. At one point I became obsessed with Tierra del Fuego. Apparently they didn't have huts to shelter their naked bodies, so they kept fires burning night and day so as not to die of the inconceivable cold, and that was why their country was called that, Tierra del Fuego – land of fire.

There is nothing more exotic for a Greek person than an iceberg! Our minds cannot comprehend such unbelievable temperatures. And yet, I'm certain, even in conditions to us incomprehensible, there are some Greek people living there. People who've been bewitched by another, unknown world, forced by God knows what circumstances to live there. Maybe they haven't been driven away by an unintentional murder, like Anastasákos, but something's bothering them. Their own selves, perhaps.

On the internet I found the phrase: 'In winter the city of Boston is transformed into a vast ice rink.' I imagine a city immersed in endless cloud, blue, like an iceberg, the people wrapped up in thick coats, hats on their heads, hurrying inside and shutting the doors behind them. Safe inside his four walls, giving orders, Anastasákos struggles to forget that he was once a carefree child who liked to play with guns. He thinks of his tragedy as he lies awake at night. He so desperately wants to escape it that he has forgotten the only people in the world who really care for him. Poor old Dimákos, his aunt, so near death. And maybe that is his punishment. His *tísis*, as my mother would say, like in the ancient tragedies. I get on to Google and type 'Boston weather'. I read the weather forecast in that faraway city where the enemy has his home. Like him, I breathe in the delayed spring, and raise the collar of my raincoat. It is a lacklustre summer and I open my umbrella to the drizzle. The autumn is wild and I stride hurriedly through the fallen leaves, the winter is merciless, and I dig my hands into the pockets of my coat and wrap a scarf round my ears. Like him. And I wait. I no longer know what for. As if in a dream I remember a place full of light, a dot on the map which once was my homeland. Where my parents are buried and my house lies abandoned, where a woman is waiting for me, who has her own cross to bear. I don't care about her, I no longer even remember her. Her face is lost among all the others who have passed through my life. Anyway I am married. I have no children, but there is of course the famous 'niece'. White as a lily, with a violin in her hand. She has taught me a different music, happier, I can no longer stand the sad *moiroloy* of the guilty. And I am not likely to go back. Ever.

# Ethnikí Elládos

I TOOK THE WHITE, summer handbag and checked to see if her papers were inside. There was just a tax slip in the name of Evángelos Yalanós, and a statement from the tax office. In her purse there was nothing except two thousand drachmas, a hundred-drachma note and a few coins. No photographs. Not even her identity card, which most people keep in the transparent compartment of their wallets. Nothing to tell me her birth date, where she was born, or the names of her parents.

I decided to go and see her that evening without phoning. For the moment I was expected at work. The quicker I could finish the job I was being paid for, the quicker I could get away from the Olympians and their crazy world, and concentrate on the reason for my return: Getting back to the Mani.

I arrived at the factory inevitably late. And a good day, as they say, begins early. Instead I had a heated discussion with the maintenance engineers and an unfortunate conversation with the technical director. They had spent millions of drachmas on machinery, which due to repeated and unexplained breakdown had been a complete waste of money. It was a second-hand machine for metal sheeting, chosen out of four that had been on sale in four different parts of the globe. Efthimios, the technical director, had made the decision to buy this one from America. He was a tall fifty-five-year-old, and he wasn't fond of me. He put up with me simply because he didn't have a choice.

I went to see him in his office. The air-conditioning unit was on full blast, as well as the ceiling fan. He was holding a sharpened pencil, and looked at me as if he was fully aware of what I was going to say. I suspected him of having taken a hefty bribe to choose the faulty machine, he might even have shared it around with some of the subordinates who signed the deal with him. Stefanos had tipped me the wink, he didn't like Efthimios because he had a special relationship with his father and had ideas above his station, meaning he didn't hesitate to disagree with the sons as and when he saw fit. He looked at me and I knew that Stefanos was talking nonsense. I have always trusted my instinct, but I needed to check things out. So I asked to see all the offers they'd received for the extortionately expensive sheeting machine and he made no objection. He called in his secretary who handed me two thick folders. I had a problem with the valuation of the technical features, but I could send a fax to John with the main points and he would find a way of checking them out.

I couldn't avoid making it obvious that Efthimios was under suspicion, and he wasn't the kind of man who takes it lightly when you insult him. He offered me his office to work in and I declined. I never feel guilty about my behaviour towards the various executives of the companies I investigate – most of them have something to hide. But as I was leaving I felt the need to say something to him. I already knew that he spent endless hours in the factory, he loved his job, he cared about it. He had worked for the senior Olympios longer than anyone else, ever since he was a lad. He didn't always agree with the sons, and they didn't like him. Perhaps that was why he didn't like me. The sons of bitches turn up, they bring their buddy with them and try and teach us how to do our jobs, he was sure to be thinking, and he wasn't the only one. He was the kind of person who never betrays trust, but is devastated by ingratitude. He reminded me of my father, who would have been about that age had he lived. I felt I had to apologise. I had nothing personal against him, I said, on the contrary, I respected him greatly and was sorry, but I had to do my job.

'There is no reason for you to be sorry, Mr Anastasáko. On the contrary, I am sorry. And I am very happy not to be in your shoes. Because I would never be able to do your job.'

I closed the door behind me feeling ashamed. I knew why this man reminded me of my father even though he was no illiterate peasant, and had absolutely nothing to do with the Mani. The two of them had the same system of values. I didn't bother to check the files with the offers. Time is money and I wouldn't find anything in them. I was certain he had chosen the best machine for the job.

I got a cup of coffee from the machine in the corridor, and hid myself away in Stefanos's office. I was alone. My friend, deep in his own misery, hadn't arrived yet. There was a lot to be done, but I couldn't concentrate. Efthimios, Stefanos, Aphrodite … I needed to talk to one of my own people and I had no one else but John, thousands of miles away. It was two in the afternoon, seven in the morning in Boston. I telephoned him from my mobile and woke him up.

'Are you all right?' was the first thing he asked me.

'I'm fine,' I reassured him. 'I'm missing you. I've stopped smoking and there's no one to complain about the smoke, no one calls me "pretty boy", there's no one to tidy up after me. Total nightmare …'

I heard him laughing at the other end of the line. We spoke for a little while longer. The preparations for the wedding were well under way and I would be sure to be back in time. I was his best man, damn it all. His *koumbáros*, in a manner of speaking. He wanted me back as soon as possible, things at the office were frantic, he was barely seeing Maggie. I didn't say anything of what I'd wanted to say. I didn't mention Aphrodite, or the journey I was planning in the Mani, which was drawing near, or about quarrelling with Stefanos. But I felt much better when I put down the phone. So much better that I organised a rendezvous with Dimitra, a girl who worked in the accounts department. For later. After I'd seen Aphrodite, whom in no way would I be putting under any pressure just now.

I left the car in a car park and walked to Aphrodite's house in the Plaka. She had rubber gloves on and was obviously doing the house-work. I apologised for turning up unannounced, saying that I was on my way back from work where things were busy and I'd forgotten to call. Lies, naturally. I'd been thinking about her all day.

We sat down at the little table in the yard. She brought me a coffee and a kind of sweet I'd never seen before. 'Try it,' she said, 'I made it for my brother.' Everything was tidy and clean like last time, but now it was obvious she was expecting someone. The trunks of the lemon tree and the vine had been freshly whitewashed, the flower pots carefully weeded, a basil plant on the little table was giving off its scent. I was afraid that I really had come at an inconvenient time and I told her so. No, she answered, on the contrary. She was expecting her brother the following morning. His name was Vangélis and the tax slip and statement that I'd found were his. They didn't live together, he worked somewhere in Patra, he was training to be an officer in the Air Force. She was proud of him, I could tell. I gave her the bag, which I'd been holding all this time. She thanked me. I picked up my cup and my yearning for a cigarette was so intense that she noticed me, yet again, unconsciously searching in the pockets of my jeans.

'Have you run out of cigarettes? There's a packet Vangélis left somewhere …'

'I'm trying to give up, don't tempt me. I smoked so much in Boston that my colleague wanted to get rid of me …'

I talked to her about John. I don't know why. How he forced me to smoke outside our bedroom when we were students. I didn't obviously mention the other side of the deal, whereby I locked him out of our room if I had a girl in there. I told her about Maggie. That they were getting married in October and I was best man. I remarked how much I liked her house, a small oasis amidst the noise, dust and dirt of the big city. She smiled, showing a row of pearly teeth and a playful dimple on her cheek. No, this house wasn't hers. It was her foster mother's, the woman who had brought her up.

'What about your own parents?' I asked her, not caring how tactless I was being.

'They're gone,' she replied.

Was that why I felt bound to her from the start by some strange relationship? I started telling her about my planned return to the Mani, vague things, that my parents were buried there and I hadn't been back since their death. That I had been away seventeen years. I heard myself talking to a woman I hardly knew about things I never spoke about to anyone, least of all the women I wanted in my bed.

She was sitting on the deckchair with her knees tucked up to her chest, like the last time. She didn't speak, she just listened, and when I stopped, she handed me the little plate with the sweet.

'When I am very, very miserable,' she told me, 'I sweeten my mouth and my stomach. Somehow, your soul gets sweetened that way too ...'

I looked at her sitting there opposite me, a delicious honey *koutalída*, the best, and I made my move.

'I have two tickets for the football match tomorrow evening. Ethnikí Elládos are playing. I was going to go with Stefanos, but that's out of the question. What d'you say?'

'And you have no other friends, naturally ...' she said, ambivalently.

'None as good as you. What d'you say?'

She considered me and I looked straight at her, so as to leave no doubt as to the honour of my intentions. Then I remembered that she was expecting her brother and I realised in shock that she couldn't come even if she had wanted to.

'Okay.' She surprised me.

I had got what I wanted, so I had no reason to stand Dimitra up and I had to go home to change. When I got to the door I reminded her yet again that she could phone me any time she wanted if she needed anything, but I didn't attempt any innocent caresses because who knew where they might lead. I knew I had to wait for her. She was not the kind of girl to sleep with anyone who comes along. Anyway she was worth waiting for, you only had to look at her to see that.

I can't remember much about dinner with Dimitra and the

night that followed. One night like so many others in my life, with women who didn't matter, conversations that didn't matter, feelings that didn't matter. The following afternoon, however, is etched in my memory second by second, sentence by sentence, heartbeat by heartbeat.

\*\*\*

She arrived at the stadium five minutes late. The first thing I noticed was that she wore a helmet. I asked her if the fine had been a big one. 'It wasn't the fine that persuaded me,' she said. 'It was the cop, he persuaded me. He tore up my fine.' She had met him again at the same spot in Kifissias and stopped to thank him.

'What have you got against cops?'

'I can't stand them,' she replied, shrugging her shoulders.

I took her hand so we wouldn't lose one another in the crowd. Its warmth passed through into mine.

The crowd went wild as the players entered the stadium and during the match, but although I'd been so keen to watch the match, all I can remember is Aphrodite's profile, her classic nose, and forehead of an ancient *kore*. Ethnikí won 2–1, I think, against some Eastern European team.

Afterwards we bought a couple of hot dogs and some beers and sat down on a cement wall. Once again I felt strangely comfortable with her, weirdly relaxed talking about things I never usually spoke about. The moon was looking down on us and we sat eating and watching the motley crowd as they slowly streamed out of the stadium. Young kids with their parents, couples, groups of teenagers, older people with their grandchildren.

'So, how are you?'

It was the first time we'd mentioned the incident in the garage ever since that night.

'Fine, as you see, thanks to you.'

'Won't your myriad admirers have something to say about me stealing you away tonight.'

'Serves them right, since none of them bothered to get tickets for the match.'

We both laughed, and from a distance we looked like any ordinary couple. I was hoping I could persuade her to come for a drink, and so I asked her: 'What are you doing now?'

'I'm going to bed,' she said. 'I'm trying to qualify as a tour guide and I have exams. We're not all as brilliant as you are. That way I can at least get some studying done tomorrow.'

I wiped the mustard that I sensed on the side of my mouth. Was she fooling with me?

'Do I look brilliant?'

'That's what everyone is saying,' she said, shrugging her shoulders, 'even though it's hard to believe it when your chin is covered in mustard. You came, they say, to rescue the Olympian's business, which instead of making a 200 per cent profit this year, is only making 100 per cent. It's at risk, in other words. Don't worry. They'll let a few people go, move a factory to where people work for nothing, grab an unrepayable loan or two. They'll survive.

I nervously wiped my chin with a paper napkin. In three sentences she'd described my entire plan for the Olympian's business! Minimise the workforce, move units to where labour is cheaper, creatively use the law to fiddle a loan from the state. She went up a lot in my estimation, not for what she said, but for having the courage to say it to me.

'You don't have a very high regard for my work, do you?'

She took out a tissue from her bag and cleaned my chin with it. My nostrils filled with her scent. How could I get so messy without realising it? Then, perhaps because we were so close, she looked a bit embarrassed.

'You helped me, and all I do is give you a hard time.'

'You've got a tongue like a lash. Tell me though, I'm interested in how you see things.'

'Well, I heard a few things said about you at the Olympians. How you started with nothing and made a name and money in the wicked world of business, thanks to your hard work and talent. But I'm just wondering. Why do you waste your talent in helping people like the Olympians? What do you have in common with them? Haris was definitely a hangman in an earlier incarnation, and Stefanos, if he doesn't get the toy he wants, he breaks it. There must be more useful things you can do. For others, I mean. Unless your purpose is to make money, so you can be like them one day. In which case, go right ahead.'

It took a few seconds for me to realise that I was searching about my person for something that I was never going to find. My cigarettes.

'How can I answer your criticisms without a cigarette? And I've quit smoking, damn it!'

She shifted about awkwardly, about to apologise again, but I stopped her. She reminded me of Maggie – who always said exactly what she thought. Except that her remarks had nothing to do with feminist theory. Aphrodite held a deeply rooted belief that whatever we do, whatever we achieve in life: it must above all serve the whole, it must serve others. And if it happens to be profitable, then so much the better. Haris did well to find such a teacher for his children, but I don't think he would respect her views. Man is rapacious and he is motivated by one impetus alone, that of gain. That is his nature and you can't argue with nature – at least there's an innocence about it. Capitalism has a hundred heads, just because it's a system that suits human nature. Anything else, however lovely it sounds, is missionary zeal and belongs in the sphere of fantasy. Haris wouldn't hesitate to destroy anyone, so long as he made a profit. He was the kind of person who crushes ants. Whereas Aphrodite was more likely to trip up than step on one.

'I like my work, it excites me,' I said, trying to explain. 'It's like a bet that I need to win every time. I love discovering the different tricks people use to make money. What do you think makes a business go down the pan, usually? Either someone's been a fool or someone's put their hand in the till. There is no such thing as sentiment where capital is concerned, it's true. But when a business is going well, that's good for everyone. It puts people in work. Businesses shouldn't fold, that isn't good for anyone. It isn't about the money or about the kind of power people like Olympios have. I enjoy it, just like you enjoy your work, even though it's so difficult to progress in it.'

She looked at me intently, but it was dusk and I couldn't properly assess the amber glint in her eyes.

'Can I ask you just one more thing?' she said with some hesitation, and I nodded for her to go on. 'The other day you asked me why I said no to Olympios and I told you. So, why do you sleep with his sister? Is that for the money?'

She was looking at me right in the eyes as if she was searching for the truth, which I couldn't have hidden from her if I wanted to.

'No.'

'Do you love her?'

'No.'

'Then why?'

'I have fun, or to be exact, I did have fun. It isn't the same any more, and so ...'

'Thank you,' she said and nodded.

I don't know what she was thinking. I had the sense that I was being put through some kind of test, with no idea how I was doing.

'Shall we go?' she said and jumped up.

We walked together side by side, through the crowd that was gradually thinning. We reached the car park in silence. Once again I felt wary about getting too close to her. I didn't want to frighten her away. I risked an affectionate look.

'Thank you, *Melénia mou*, for a lovely evening.'

She started slightly.

'What did you call me?'

I gave her my most charming smile. I wasn't going to touch her, but there was no reason to hide my intentions.

'Melénia. It's from *mélissa mélissa, méli glykítato* – a children's game from the Mani – and after my mother's honey *koutalídes*. Does it bother you?'

She shook her head and gave me an odd look. She tried to smile.

'I like it, I think.'

She got on to her motorbike, forcing a smile, and slung on her helmet. I didn't want her to leave before I knew when I would see her again.

'Would you like to go swimming tomorrow?'

'I'm supposed to be studying.'

I'd forgotten and I shrugged my shoulders sadly.

'The day after then? Am I being too keen? I'm sorry.' I hardly knew what I was saying.

'Phone me,' she said. 'In the afternoon though.'

She waved her hand, started the engine and set off. I got into the car and drove away. The radio station I'd been listening to earlier was playing *rembétika*.

*It's me whistling on the stairs*
*άνοιξε μέσα για να μπω*
*και στρώσε μου να κοιμηθώ.*

At home I opened the balcony door and lay down on a deckchair, looking out over the sea. I breathed in the smell of summer approaching in all its glory.

What was she doing right now? Was she asleep, with her hair spilling over the pillow? In her bedroom, nothing but the sound of her breathing, her breasts rising desirably as she breathed. Her breasts, as beautiful as Aunt Potítsa's when she came into the house wearing her tight shirt with the buttons undone.

'If you keep letting that devil in here you'll close up your house.'

But it wasn't because of Potítsa that our house closed. It closed because of me … I leant back in the deckchair and shut my eyes, letting it all pass before me. As if it was yesterday! How had the image of Melénia become so entangled with the images of my old life! My father's house, the figures of my parents, the stories of my grandmother sitting by the fire. My friend Yiánnis, always by my side in every scrape. That cursed rifle with its gold engraving on the handle. Yiorgákis. The tragedy, my cowardice, my escape. It was time for everything to be put in its place. There were truths that needed to be told, truths that hurt us all. It was nearly dawn by the time I went to bed with my clothes on, with one solitary thought by way of consolation. A girl, sweet as honey, warm, tough, tender, unbelievable … Where had she been all my life? I had one and a half weeks to go before the journey home!

*\*\**

We met to go swimming two days later. She arrived at Saronida by bike, wearing a turquoise halter-neck shirt and denim shorts, not very short – but short enough to show off her beautiful legs.

'Do you want to drive?' she offered.

Of course I did. I had belatedly realised that this town belongs to small, flexible vehicles, not to expensive cars. It was hot, but on the bike it was heaven, cooled by the breeze coming off the sea. I had no experience with bikes, I preferred cars, but this trip made me change my mind.

'Don't be nervous, step on it,' she shouted to be heard through the helmet and above the noise of the engine. 'I'll tell you where it's dangerous.'

The sea shimmered under a golden sun and the feel of her body behind me made me dizzy. For a while I became that unruly child, with his hands covered in prickly pear spikes, playing catch on the rocky, windswept slopes of his homeland, afraid of nothing and no one. Happy and free. The man I would have become if my life had turned out differently.

She took me to a sandy beach near Sounion. I tried not to stare at her when she took off her clothes, folded them carefully and put them in her beach bag. It wasn't easy. In her sky-blue bathing suit with her dark hair loose she looked like a mermaid. We dived in almost immediately and she swam well, with long dives and strong strokes. I told her so.

'My brother taught me, I mean the son of my adoptive mother,' she explained.

I asked her about her exams, partly to distract myself from desiring her, and partly because I felt that everything about her life was in a strange way my concern.

'And what are you thinking of doing if you pass?'

'To do officially what I'm doing unofficially at the moment,' she explained. It was only seasonal work. Guided tours to archaeological sites and museums, but it would keep her going until she got a job in a school. She wanted to avoid tutoring in people's houses from now on. And she didn't have much hope of getting locum work, even at schools in the middle of nowhere. I couldn't resist asking her why she'd chosen such a difficult way of earning a living.

'It's what you said before. I enjoy it. And I don't mind how much trouble it takes, if I can do something I like.'

'Well, I know you don't mind trouble,' I said feeling strangely moved. 'You actually like the twins. I can't look at them without wondering where Herod was when they were babies.'

She threw back her head and laughed. Have you watched as the rising sun spills glittering fragments of gold over the sea? That was her laughter. Her eyes shone and the dimple appeared on her cheek. I was wrong, she said. The twins were very sensitive boys. They just needed a little attention, like all children with busy parents. I disagreed. It was one of the boys who had sent her to the garage, after all. But she wasn't having any of it. The boys loved her, they would never have harmed her, they had been tricked, just as she had been, she was absolutely certain.

We stayed there until dusk, the sea turned mauve, and people began to trickle away. I told her about the journey I was planning to make in almost a week. It was always on my mind and bizarrely this unknown woman was the only person I'd talked to about it. I couldn't discuss it even with John. She told me about the dreadful loneliness she had gone through after her mother's death. 'The earth fell away from under my feet,' she said. And about the year she spent in an orphanage. And about Myrtó Yalanoú, her foster mother who was so full of love and shared it equally between the children. About her foster father, crippled for years, confined to a wheelchair, lost in the world of his books and his imagination, a distant and inaccessible figure even to his natural son. They could no longer cope with the bustle of Athens and had moved to their country house in Loutsa, where she visited them at weekends. She was sitting up on her beach mat now, with her knees to her chin. I couldn't see her eyes any more, but I guessed that tears were on the way and she was finding it hard to hold them back.

'Don't you have any brothers and sisters,' I asked her. 'Natural ones, I mean.'

'I had two brothers. They died years ago, and it was her grief at losing them that killed my mother.'

She turned towards the vanishing horizon. It was obvious that the memories of her old life only brought her pain and if anyone could understand that it was me. Maybe that was why I had felt such a strange spiritual kinship with this woman. We had a lot in common. The loss of our parents, the struggle to make a living, a past that pained us. And that was why when I was with her I seemed to drop all my habitual defence mechanisms. I had no plan, no tactics. I gave myself up to the pleasure of her company, a clever woman, sensitive, perceptive, proud and unbelievably beautiful, unaffected, unpretentious. I let the moment guide me, I didn't dare stretch out my hand for an innocent touch. My feelings weren't innocent at all and I was convinced she could read my mind.

I suggested we find a place to eat nearby and she agreed.

We sat in a little taverna serving seafood of the cheaper variety – squid, octopus, whitebait – and ordered a little of everything. She ate unaffectedly, nothing like the women in the Olympian milieu. We had that in common, too. She was a pleb like me, she didn't wrinkle her nose in disgust when we shared the salad from a plate in the middle, nor was she shocked when I dipped my bread in the olive oil, 'like Christ with his disciples,' as my mother used to say. She did the same.

'I was sure you'd be a "dipper",' she remarked. 'You can't have been completely spoilt by hobnobbing with the Olympians.'

She had humour and she teased me, she wasn't afraid of words. Afterwards she thanked me for dinner, but I didn't want us to part before making sure we'd meet again.

'Do you cook?' I asked her. She nodded, somewhat baffled.

'If you really want to thank me, cook for me. I rarely eat home-cooked food.'

'With pleasure! Do you have a favourite dish?'

We made a date for the day after the next and I let out a sigh of relief. Supper, at her house. I had nearly two days to plan my next move. In the usual course of events I would have known what to expect and where it would lead – I had only one goal, after all. But with her I had no idea at all. It was the first time in my life, the first and the last, that a woman had made me feel that way, but in my confusion I still had the arrogance of the hunter. Maybe I didn't want to accept that I was already naked, powerless, at her mercy.

Back at home I had a swim and turned on my computer. Work first. As soon as that was dealt with I'd be able to go back to the village. To face up to the thing I'd spent my life fighting to avoid. An idiotic finger on the trigger, a dead boy, a silent guilt, an ignomini-ous flight. I had no plan, even for that. Sotíris Haritákos would be a man by now, like me, and it was time for us to settle our scores. I was guilty, so I would admit my guilt to him, and he could do what he liked. It was wrong for the charge of murder to hang over my father's grave. And if there was a law that made a person pay, seventeen years later, for a crime he committed when he was a child, then I was happy to confess and be punished, if Haritákos wanted it. Maybe then I would at last be able to sleep. And if he wanted to settle it another way, so be it. I don't know why, I always saw my punisher as Sotíris rather than the old man. Maybe because the old man 'got his blood back' when he killed my father. 'We gave our blood for the blood we spilt,' my mother had said. 'The debt has been paid.' And she was right to a certain extent. Would Sotíris prefer, instead of involving the law, for us to settle our differences in the old, traditional Maniot way? I didn't want us to get to that point; it would either mean my going like a lamb to the slaughter or potentially harming him. I had come back to get rid of my guilt, not triple it.

It was almost dawn when I went to bed, and even then I couldn't sleep unless I focused on a single image. A girl with the scent of nightflowers, who has upon her all the gold of the sun, washing me with her pearly smile. She looks at me thoughtfully, and asks: 'Are you sleeping with Olympios's sister for the money?' Ah girl! Do you care even a tiny bit? Because if you do care, if what you feel is not out of obligation, or pity, I'll do anything. To hell with the Olympians, and their sister, and their money. Tell me that you care, because in a few days I have to go down to hell and I want something to hold on to. And that smile of yours looks like a sturdy branch to me.

\*\*\*

I got ready early. Bath, close shave, aftershave. I wore jeans and a T-shirt that Lou liked. I debated whether I should buy Aphrodite sweets or flowers and decided on the former. I didn't want my visit to remind her of Stefanos's bouquets and what had happened with him. 'When you sweeten the stomach, you sweeten the soul,' she had said. I arrived too early and waited a bit, and finally rang the bell at twenty-five to nine, certain that I was late.

She greeted me wearing a plain mauve sleeveless dress just above the knee and flat sandals. Little make-up, her hair down, with a few unruly wisps tied back. She was smiling. Aphrodite. By name and by nature. She had laid the garden table with a white tablecloth, and there was a mouth-watering smell coming from inside. Roast kid with roast potatoes and warm cheese pie. Salad, roast peppers and tomatoes stuffed with feta, aubergines with *graviera* cheese, and chilled red wine. All out of this world. The wine was good, we relaxed a bit and I began to feel more like myself. We talked, we laughed, she told me a couple of good stories she'd heard from her students, and I reminisced about things that had happened at college. I had never had a better time with a woman, and I hadn't even slept with her.

We breathed in the scent of the nightflower and watched the moths drawn to the light.

We cleared the table together, and as we were putting the plates into the sink I could feel her holding her breath. I could have taken her in my arms then, but I didn't. Our intimacy, our companionship had been so perfect, I didn't want to make a mistake and spoil everything. I didn't want to prove Stefanos right. And then, as we stood by the front door saying goodbye, I felt incredibly shy. I couldn't find the right words to thank her for the delicious food and good company. I could so easily have kissed her, but I didn't dare. All the way back home I first congratulated myself for my self-control and then kicked myself for being such a fool.

We didn't meet the week before my journey back. But I phoned her.

'I wanted to see how you are, how work is going, whether you need anything.' And a few days later she phoned me.

'I wanted to see if you were ready for your trip, when you're leaving and if you're okay.'

When I called her she was about to take a group of French people up to the Acropolis, so she couldn't talk for long. When she called me I was with Thália, one of Máchi's friends, swimming naked in the pool at Saronida. I couldn't talk much either, but the phone call acted on me like an aphrodisiac and it was the first time I'd made love to a woman while thinking of another. When I was done, I felt emptier than ever. Why on earth? I thought it might be my usual boredom after scoring. But it wasn't that. Quite unconsciously, I had crossed the notional boundary that separates a carefree man from a man deeply in love. That same notional boundary that my father once crossed and from then on never looked at another woman. He knew what was happening to him. Whereas I, a seasoned egotist, accustomed to easy pleasures, how could I know it? *Σέρνει καράβι*, the ship's in tow, as they used to say in the Mani but I didn't believe a woman existed who could keep me in tow the way the old saying suggests. But sayings are wise. They are the distilled wisdom of centuries. And if you never suffer, you never learn.

# Mani

ON MONDAY I GOT UP EARLY, having hardly slept at all, and set off on the Athens-Corinth road, returning the way I'd left when I was fifteen years old, alone in the world, my only belongings the clothes I stood up in, a change of clothes and an airline ticket. I hadn't spoken to Aphrodite for four days. I hadn't stopped thinking about her, but I resisted the urge to phone her again. I needed to keep my head clear and my mind alert for the journey home.

On the way I stopped to look at the Corinth canal and thought of my father and smiled. 'We're beyond the ditch,' he would say, alluding to our superior race. 'No Turk ever set foot in the Mani! We Maniots began the revolution, you know, on the seventeenth of March …'

It was still early, the heat yet hadn't begun to make itself felt. Tourists and parents with little children stood beside me looking down at the canal. I wanted a cigarette badly so I went back to the car rather than give in to the temptation of going to the kiosk. I followed the signs to the new National Road, which wasn't as narrow as I remembered – they'd widened it and the road works were still ongoing. To the left, the Saronic gulf shimmered in the morning light and the traffic was building up. Gone was the old road that took you through Argos, climbed up Kolosourti and ended in Tripoli. The new road, with two lanes in each direction, crossed the mountains, cut through a tunnel and got you to Tripoli in under an hour if you put your foot down.

I followed the signs and turned off for Sparta. The sun had risen high, but it still wasn't very hot and I put down the car roof. I passed the outskirts of Lakonia and breathed deeply the comforting smells of my homeland! I passed Sparta, and on to the mountain range of

Taygetus, bare under the sun. Here and there towers sprouted out of its naked slopes competing for height with sporadic trees in among the rocks. At one turn-off someone had written in capital letters on the rock: 'THE MANI IS ONE AND INDIVISIBLE. UNION NOW.' It was an old slogan, from the time when the region was divided in half for administrative purposes, because my compatriots, so they said, were as unruly and combative as ever, and refused to subordinate themselves to the central authorities. It smelled of thyme and cistus and the heat made the air so dense you could cut it with a knife.

I arrived in the village at lunchtime and there wasn't a soul about. The three-storied tower of the Haritakaíoi greeted me and I saw in passing that it was choked with dry grass nearly as high as the wall and looked entirely deserted, as if no one had been there for years.

The cemetery was on the edge of the village in a small garden with cypress trees. I parked at the entrance and looked for my parents' and grandparents' graves. I found them tended and clean, with their lamps lit. Someone remembered. Aunt Aretí? Potítsa? Yiánnis's mother? I felt the hot salt tears on my cheeks. It was so long since I had cried, I could scarcely remember. There was a faded photograph on my parents' grave, a man and a woman smiling at each other. I searched for some candles in the little church of Ayia Paraskeví, and lit them in the special alcove at the grave.

My mother, with her hair loose, scratching at her cheeks and her breast in lament. I shivered in the midday heat of summer, as if the cold hand of death had touched me. Not far away, I found Yiorgís's gravestone. The little lamp was lit and recently someone had made an attempt to weed it. I wondered who. Aunt Katerina? The boy in the photograph was laughing, gap-toothed, a dimple in his cheek. It reminded me of something, but I couldn't think what. I pulled a few more weeds and wiped my eyes. It was time to go home. I drove towards my house with the sense that the years had been no more than a passing breath.

She was sitting on the low wall right next to the old wooden door, trying to stay in the meagre shade. There was a small holdall beside her and on it a tiny handbag. She wore, as she usually did, jeans, a cotton blouse and canvas sneakers. The last person I expected to see. Aphrodite! Melénia ...

I got out of the car. My voice sounded coarse and angry despite myself.

'How did you get here?'

She took off her sunglasses and stood up.

'It's wrong to revisit difficult memories alone, and I thought I'd keep you company,' she said, and a shadow of compassion passed across her face. I felt the blood rush to my cheeks.

'Well you chose the wrong day to act like Mother Teresa, I don't like to be pitied.'

She blushed at my rudeness, but didn't seem in the least intimidated.

'Aren't you going in?' she asked, pointing at the door.

Biting my lip to hold back my annoyance, I unlocked the outer door and went through into the overgrown yard. The door to the tower house was almost completely hidden behind tall, dry grass, just like the Haritákos's tower. Above us a shutter swung off its hinge. A large cactus had grown up beside the old stable and there was ivy on the wall. Where had it found water? The vine lay withered on the ground. My anger had evaporated and my heart was beating so loudly I could hear it. There, for certain, next to the wall, buried in the grass, was the big millstone I used to climb on when I was little. The place where my parents used to drink their coffee in the evening. My mother, standing waiting at the door. The place where I'd seen my father lying dead that morning. A few more steps and I could touch it. My feet were rooted to the spot, and then I felt Aphrodite's warm hand in mine. I squeezed it gratefully. My eyes were burning again and I turned to look at her. There was no one in the world I would rather have had beside me at that moment, nothing I could have wanted more. Just let it not be out of pity.

'I'm sorry, *Melénia mou*, I'm a lout sometimes, I know it.'

She looked at me steadily.

'Go in.'

The kitchen door yielded to a shuddering creak and a pair of pigeons fluttered up.

'The roof must have a hole in it,' she whispered.

Where was her hand? I took it and we went inside. Everything was exactly as I had left it seventeen years before. The kitchen table, the plates on the rack, even my mother's knitted jacket forgotten on the back of a chair. I picked it up, but it only smelled of mould and dust. I touched the plates and the old table. I stroked the back of the chair.

'Come on,' I whispered to her.

The ladder leading to the upper floor looked steady. I climbed it and pushed away the trapdoor. I had almost got up on to the first floor, with Aphrodite behind me on the ladder, when we heard a gunshot crack out like thunder through the empty house.

'Get down, you devils, and come out here with your hands up! Have you no respect?'

The owner of the voice was evidently waiting for us to come out, keeping his aim on the door. I signalled to Aphrodite to come down and we saw the man jump down from the wall, admirably nimbly, considering his age, and stand in the doorway. He had us in range with his hunting rifle. I could barely speak for the lump in my throat.

'Uncle Nikifóro!'

He studied me for a moment in confusion. And then let out a sob.

'Come out here, curse you. I can't see in the dark.'

He dragged me outside and the rifle fell on to the grass. And then he took me into his arms, as warmly as when I was a boy running from a scolding, and held me tight.

'You've come, my son,' he stammered through his sobs. 'Aren't you ashamed, you wretched boy, not one single letter!'

'Aunt Aretí?' I asked by way of an answer.

'Yes, devil take you! She's next door, she's waiting for you. All these years she's been waiting for you.'

I needed to look into his eyes, to make him understand.

'I couldn't,' I managed to mutter, 'forgive me, but I couldn't …'

He hugged me again.

'I know, my son,' he whispered. 'Don't listen to an old fool. You've come now! And you're well … Look at you! And you've brought this lovely girl!'

He was smiling, his eyes streaming with tears. In all the emotion I'd forgotten about Aphrodite who was standing, looking awkward and tearful, on the doorstep. I took her by the hand to introduce her.

'This is my friend Aphrodite. And this, *Melénia mou*, is my Uncle Nikifóros.'

My uncle hugged her, clearly racing to the wrong conclusion.

'When did you arrive, *koróna mou?*'

'In Greece? Some time ago.' I bowed my head. For seventeen years I hadn't once stopped thinking about them. And yet for all those years I was so obsessed with my own guilt that I hadn't once gone to the trouble of finding out how they were.

He picked up the rifle from the overgrown grass where he had thrown it.

'I'll go next door to prepare Aretí a little. It's best if she doesn't see you too suddenly – her heart, you know. You take your time and look around, and then come over.' He turned back at the gate. 'You've grown into a fine man, my boy. Your parents would be proud of you. She's a lovely girl!'

We stood there awkwardly as the old man walked away.

'I'm sorry,' I said. 'When we go next door I'll explain …'

'I can't come next door, Odysséa,' she said shyly. 'I have to be in Kalamata this evening and I need to catch the bus. I work for a tourist company now. I'm scheduled to meet a group of Germans at their hotel to take them out to supper. We're going to Pylos tomorrow.'

The sadness in her eyes seemed to fill her face with shadows. She avoided looking at me. It was my fault, me and my loutish manners.

She had been generous, and all I'd done was quibble and be difficult. I couldn't let her go now. I put my hands on her shoulders.

'Please, *Melénia mou*,' I said as sweetly as I could, 'you'll be on time this evening, I promise you. I'll take you there myself.'

'But I can't allow you to drive all that way at night on that dreadful road,' she murmured.

'Yes, you can,' I insisted, looking at her tenderly. 'If you don't stay, I'll think you're still angry with me for behaving like an oaf. I'm sorry. I was surprised, that's all. And … I don't like people to see me crying …'

'I should apologise for appearing here out of the blue. You have every right to want to be alone at a time like this. I understand, and that's why it's best if I go.'

'But didn't you see how pleased my uncle was that I came here with a woman? Do you want me to disappoint him?' I said. 'Don't leave me alone with the past, Aphrodite. Hold my hand while I pass over this threshold again. Isn't that why you came?' She looked at the ground.

'Okay.'

My hands were still on her shoulders, and I felt more than ever the need to kiss her. But I didn't dare. I was afraid she might change her mind and slip through my fingers like the wind. All my anger had vanished and I just wanted her with me.

'Shall we go up again?' she said, breaking the silence.

'Follow me and be careful on the ladder,'

As we went up through the narrow opening, a beam of light falling through the dilapidated shutters lit up my small iron bedstead, the one I had shared with Potítsa. Beside the wooden cupboard, still untouched, lay my leather football, the one my father had bought in Sparta during my last autumn at home, and on the old wooden table where I had left them, my books covered in dust.

'Your bed?' she asked me, touching the iron bedstead. I nodded. The room had originally been my grandmother's and after her death it became mine. When she was alive I slept downstairs next to the kitchen. It was the only room with heating in it and they didn't want me to have to climb up the ladder.

She leafed through the books. Maths and Ancient Greek from the third form. Underneath, a Bic biro without a top, its end chewed, and an ink rubber. I had the strange sensation that she was touching my old things as if to comfort them for being left, unwanted, all these years. Her face in the shadowy abandoned room looked ghostly. Like an ancient goddess of youth, exorcising time's decay. We climbed the stairs to the upper floor. Here the shutter was in place and it took our eyes a few seconds to get used to the dark. I felt my way over to the window and opened it. The house seemed to let out a pained groan. There was dust everywhere. It danced in the sunlight that lit up my parents' iron bedstead and the one and only dressing table beside it. I touched the bedstead and stroked the old pillowcase, worn and covered in dust. It was having her beside me, this lovely, sassy woman in an empty abandoned house, that made me decide I would do it up, whatever happened.

'It's a very lovely house,' she said as if she was reading my mind. 'It's as if time has stood still here.'

'It's an abandoned house. But I'll fix it, and then I'll invite you to come and see it. And as for time, it's time it went forward.'

As she stood there next to the tiny window, the sunlight glinting in her eyes, I wondered what it would be like to share this room with her until death and to fill the tower house with children. My father would have wanted it, for sure. She turned to the dressing table to look at my parents' wedding picture, and a picture of me in traditional dress. The Maniot *vraka*, black waistcoat with gold piping, white full-sleeved blouse with the double-headed phoenix embroidered on the sleeve and on the black headscarf. I wore it like a pirate, and tucked into my red belt were two pistols and a sword bigger than myself.

'It was for the parade of the seventeenth of March,' I said and I pulled her upstairs to show her the *zematístra* on the top floor, where they poured down boiling oil on to the enemy. I told her the story of our long feud with the Haritakaíoi, pointing out their tower guarding the pass, and about the pact the two families had made when it looked as though there would be no heirs left to carry on the family name. 'After that the Haritakaíoi did better, they gave birth to plenty of sons. But for my family the pact was a godsend. My grandfather, who died young, only managed to have one son, my father. And he only had me.'

We laughed and Aphrodite pushed away a couple of unruly curls. I was bewitched by her smile, as if the past and the pain of it had no meaning any more. We walked up the path by the millstone, the shortcut to my uncle's house, and stood side by side looking out over bare, precipitous cliffs towards the horizon. Thin olive trees, cactuses and here and there a cypress tree, pointing like a raised finger to the immensity of the sky. Small stone houses, tower houses, and opposite us the deserted tower of the enemy, where I had watched the cuckoo settle all those years ago.

There were footholds in the wall to climb down. I held out my arms and she jumped into them. I felt strangely shy, less like the man from Boston than the bashful fifteen-year-old boy finding out for the first time what it meant to know a woman. Only then it was my body, now it was my soul, shuddering and letting go. She hid her face in a cascade of hair and avoided my eyes. We couldn't bear to look at each other. So I put her hand gently to my lips, like a knight from another era.

'I don't know why you came,' I whispered, 'whether it was out of pity or out of duty. But if you weren't here, this day would have been unbearable. And I'm sorry that …'

'I'm sorry,' she said in the same tone. 'And it's not about pity or about duty. Call it solidarity. Towards you, who stood by me when I needed it. Why did you do that? Out of pity?'

The sound of my Aunt Aretí calling us stopped me from answering her, and later I was grateful. I had lost control and didn't know what I was saying. It was that somehow she was different, she was difficult, she reminded me of the girls of my homeland. I saw my aunt, dressed in black, coming out of her garden with her arms open to greet me. She was singing her lament as she approached. Her *moiroloy* to me, her lost boy, to my dead parents, and to her own son who had died. I ran to her sobbing, hardly able to breathe, as if she were my mother. I kissed her hands! And wept.

Aretí had already managed to make *kayianás,* and had set the table with bread baked in her oven, fried potatoes, tomato salad and red wine. As a boy, whenever I passed by she would fill me up with anything delicious she happened to be cooking. I was always hungry then and I was hungry now. As we sat down at the table I realised that I had been hungry for seventeen years and that I would never stop being hungry unless I tasted her *kayianás.*

'What do you eat, *koróna mou,* out there in the *xenitiá?'*

'Nothing to compare with your cooking. This is ambrosia, food of the gods. Ask Aphrodite, she's an expert on the ancients.'

The questions rained down. I told them all there was to tell. About my Uncle Sarándos who was frightened of his wife, about my studies, my work, about missing home so much sometimes I couldn't breathe.

'And what will you do now, will you go back again?'

I told them I would do up the house and come down at weekends, that I had to go back to America in October for John's wedding. 'After that, I don't know. I can't go on living so far away. Maybe it's time to think about coming back.'

My uncle wiped the tears from his eyes and refilled our glasses for a celebratory toast. When he got to mine I put a hand over my glass.

'I'm driving Aphrodite to Kalamata tonight.'

All this time Aphrodite had been listening to us in silence, with evident emotion. My aunt had warmed to her at once. She was tactful and respectful, and stopped my aunt from getting up after supper, instead clearing the table and washing the dishes herself so that my aunt could spend this precious time with me. At every moment she knew the right thing to say, and it felt so natural for her to be with us, as if she'd known us for years. The old man smiled and stroked his moustache.

We phoned Yiánnis and he promised to come over the following morning.

'He's the man for your house,' my uncle said. 'He's a surveyor, he knows about tower houses and he does good work. He has an office in Areopolis with Maria, his wife. You know her, Pantelis Leoúsis's sister.'

'The *kolaoúzo*? He married the limpet?' It seemed incredible.

'Yes, last year, at Easter. You should see how they've done up their house, you'll be amazed.'

I asked about Potítsa. She was living in Athens with her eldest son. The second son had left for Germany and the youngest, Haralambis, was working in the merchant navy as a third mechanic. While Aphrodite was in the kitchen, I asked about the Haritakaíoi. Uncle Nikifóros looked at me uneasily and his face clouded over.

'Michális is still in prison,' he said. 'We hear their news from Potítsa,' he said. 'She used to see Katerina in Athens before she died.'

'Did Haritákaina die?'

'Sotíris was killed. Three years after you left. He was hit by a car. Katerina couldn't bear it, she fell ill within the year. Cancer. She fought it for two or three years, but in the end the evil defeated her.'

'But what about the girl? Didn't they have a girl?'

'I have no idea. Potítsa didn't know.'

'Well, somebody had weeded Yiorgákis's grave today. And the lamp was burning,' I remembered.

'Did you go to the cemetery?' my aunt murmured, clasping my hand.

'Is it you who looks after my loved ones, aunt?' I asked.

'We mustn't forget those who have gone, my boy. You can rest easy, though. I am here and I won't let their lamp go out.'

At around seven I left my bag in the room by the kitchen and my aunt waved us off.

'Come back whatever time you like, the door won't be locked,' she said. Before I had a chance to reply, her old man said, chuckling beneath his moustache: 'Don't expect him back tonight. Expect him in the morning. Or more likely for lunch.'

'Why?' asked my aunt anxiously and a little confused.

Uncle Nikifóros nodded towards Aphrodite, who was already in the car waiting for me.

'*Cherchez la femme,*' he threw out in French, and I laughed as I got into the car.

She was so close to me now. It was such a small space that her presence filled it completely and I found it hard to be casual.

'I feel bad,' she confessed. 'I pop up out of nowhere and muck up your plans, and now you're going to be driving all night when you could have been with your people and had some rest.'

I concentrated on the road, more because it suited me and less because I ought to.

I asked her whether she had been to the Mani before, and she answered vaguely that she had come when she was a child and had adored it. She completely understood why I wanted to come back for good.

'I always knew, when I breathed this air again, that I would never want to leave,' I said. 'I would never have left home if I'd had the choice. And I want to thank you.'

'What for?' she murmured.

'For coming. And for being so sweet to my family ...'

She shrugged her shoulders.

'I'm glad I came. They're wonderful people ...'

We stopped talking. I heard her regular breathing and saw that she had fallen asleep. Who knew what time she had woken up that morning to be in the Mani before me? I sneaked a look at her, her hair spread over the headrest, her long, thick eyelashes, her beautiful mouth. Her head slipped down till it was right beside me and I could smell the scent of her hair. I concentrated on the curves in the road, feeling strangely calm.

In Kalamata I found the hotel and stopped under a large pink bougainvillea in the car park. I switched off the engine. She was still fast asleep.

'*Melénia mou*,' I whispered.

She didn't respond.

'Aphrodite,' I shouted louder and she looked at me sleepily.

I bent down and touched her lips gently. She didn't react and I kissed her again, until I felt her mouth eager beneath mine. Then I left a dozen little kisses on the circumference of her face and on her neck, tender as the stem of a flower, while she stroked my hair. My mobile rang suddenly and we pulled apart. I found my phone with trembling fingers and turned it off without looking to see who it was. We looked at each other, inexplicably shy.

'Thank you for bringing me,' she whispered, and looked down. 'I'm sorry you have to drive back all that way! I must go. Goodnight.'

I sat and watched her go, feeling like a fool. I punched the steering wheel. 'Damn!' I looked at my hands and they were still trembling. What was the matter with me? All I did was kiss a girl … This had never happened to me before, not even in the days of Potítsa.

I don't know how long I sat in the car, swearing at myself for letting her go like that. I couldn't leave now. A fire has to be put out when all it takes is a handful of water. God help you if you leave it. But there are fires that become forest fires before you've even caught sight of a flame. They blaze silently inside you. And when you feel the first red flames, it's already too late. You have no choice but to sit there and roast.

*** 

I went into the lobby just as Aphrodite was heading towards the bar with a tall, blond German man. She didn't see me, but I caught sight of the foreigner's eyes devouring her whole, and despite the niggling envy, I couldn't blame him.

I went to the dining room on the terrace of the hotel. I wasn't hungry, but I had to pass the time somehow. I ordered a chop, salad and a beer. My order hadn't yet arrived when I saw her come in with a group of forty Germans. She was wearing high heels and a white dress – she knew how well it suited her tanned skin and dark brown hair. I was hidden from view. She sat down at the row of tables reserved for them, next to the blond guy with the nondescript eyes.

From the terrace you could see the whole of the Messenian gulf and over on the horizon the lights of the Mani. It smelled strongly of nightflowers again, the first stars had appeared in the sky and the moon was rising like a large orange ball. I ate slowly, looking more at Melénia and the party of Germans than at the superb view. She was saying something to the blond guy and gesturing. He seemed to hang on her every word, as did the others sitting around her, all of them men. 'She's got the ship in tow,' I thought to myself. She had the tourists in tow, and she had me in tow, two hours' drive from my house and from the people I hadn't seen for seventeen years, sitting in an indifferent restaurant and waiting for I didn't know what. I felt foolish but I couldn't leave.

I finished my food and signalled to the waiter for another beer. By the time he brought it, the first foreigners had got up from the table. But the blond guy and the others sitting near her stayed for another hour. I had resorted to whisky and had drunk two, trying to think rationally and to control the wave of jealousy that was suffocating me. It was her job to smile at them, what was she supposed to do?

At half past twelve the blond guy decided to leave her in peace. He was clearly biding his time, because from the way he spoke to her and said goodnight it was obvious he would be back on the attack again tomorrow.

'Pigs might fly!' I felt like shouting at him.

I had drunk another whisky. I wasn't drunk, but my desire was more intense than ever and the waiting was getting on my nerves. My time had come and I knew it. I let her go upstairs to her room and gave her five minutes. Then I went to reception and asked them to phone her. She answered almost at once.

'*Melénia mou …*'

'Did you get back okay?' she asked, sounding surprised.

'No, I didn't go at all, I'm downstairs. I need to see you.' I hesitated a little, but it was now or never. 'Do you want to come down or shall I come up?' I held my breath.

There was almost a minute's silence, like on national remembrance days. She was weighing up her options. We both knew it. A 'no' simply meant delaying, but a 'yes' meant a great deal more than an enjoyable night. For me a night had always been a night and nothing more. There are always women to share it with. I closed my ears to all the other voices and listened only to my desire.

'Room 43. Come up.'

I didn't stop to think, I leapt into the lift and went up to the fourth floor. She opened the door barefoot but dressed. She looked a scrap of a thing without her heels on. I closed the door.

'I thought that guy was never going to go to bed,' I whispered.

We stood there and just looked at one another. She was so beautiful! Sweet, warm, unbelievably sexy with that engaging modesty of hers! The intoxicating scent of her hair overwhelmed me.

'*Melénia mou …*'

First I touched her cheek lightly and let my fingers pass behind her hair so I could caress her neck. She held her breath.

'I look at you and feel like a moth to a flame,' I murmured.

I curled my hand round her tender neck, fragile, like the stalk of a flower. Narcissus, anemone, cyclamen. And while with my fingers I stroked her throat, my thumb travelled from her chin down to the hollow at the base of her neck and then up again.

'From the moment I saw you on the stone terrace I've wanted to touch you. You too?'

'Me too.' She shuddered at my touch. 'I look at you and it's as if I'm waiting under a tower for the boiling oil to fall.'

I laughed softly.

'Let's get burned then. There's no one to stop us.'

# Boiling Oil

I SLEPT WITH THE SENSATION that I was lying face down on a meadow covered in flowers and surrounded by rocks. I opened my eyes to look for her, but she had gone.

I sat up on the bed naked, and stretched like a drowsily contented cat. All her things were gone. The group's itinerary included staying overnight in Pylos, a visit the following day to Nestor's palace and then returning to Athens along the western finger of the Peloponnese. I looked at my watch again and checked my mobile for a missed call, but there was nothing. I buried my nose in the pillow. It still smelled of her. *Méli glykítato* ... Afterwards she had held my hand tightly and kissed all my fingers one by one. 'Thank you,' she had said, inexplicably, her eyes welling with tears. I had kissed her closed moist eyelids, and felt her heartbeat against my chest, rapid, irregular, trying to find a rhythm, like my own. Neither of us spoke. She just held me tightly until I fell asleep.

I dived into the bathroom, washed and gave my naked body a self-satisfied grin in the mirror. I had, at last, made love to the goddess Stefanos wanted so badly, Haris lusted after, and the German stranger dreamed about. But only I had her! I looked at my watch again. Half past eleven. She still hadn't phoned me because she didn't use a mobile. Wherever she was, she would definitely phone at the first opportunity. They always do.

I went down for breakfast hungry as a lion. I ate slowly, keeping an eye now on my mobile, now on the view of the sea, and making a bet with myself as to how long it would take her to get in touch. I gave her till lunchtime, one minute after the group stopped for lunch. I decided not to phone her. I was so sure that she would phone me. I was out of my comfort zone and trying helplessly to stay in control. I finished my food, paid and left for the Mani.

\*\*\*

Yiánnis and I looked over the tower house together and discussed how we could give it all the modern comforts I felt to be essential, without losing its character and still respecting its history. Maria, the limpet, was to design the interiors. She was a beautiful *Maniátissa* now. I reminded her how she used to tag along after her poor old brother, Pantelis.

'The fact is I wasn't tagging along after my brother – it was Yiánnis I was following, like a little dog.'

A whole week later and there was no sight or sound of Aphrodite. Not so predictable, after all! I was so put out that I didn't pick up the phone to call her. I wasn't going to plead with her. It didn't cross my mind that she might be waiting for me to call and feeling hurt by my silence. I stayed in the Mani for ten days and on the eleventh I left for Athens. I entrusted work on the tower house to the capable hands of Yiánnis and gave the old man my word that I would come back at the weekends.

When I reached Athens, there was a call on my mobile, but it wasn't Melénia. It was Kelly, the model from Boston. She was being photographed on the Acropolis for a fashion magazine, heard I was in Athens and wanted to meet up. To prove to myself that I could sleep with anyone I liked, that everything was fine and nothing had changed, I picked her up from her hotel, took her out for dinner and then to a club down on the sea front. We went back to her hotel and had sex but afterwards, as usual, I couldn't sleep, there wasn't room, I couldn't breathe. And I felt miserable.

The next morning we were both in a hurry, there wasn't time for breakfast. I had to get to work and she was expected for her first photo shoot. The entrance of the hotel was blocked by a group of

Germans and among them, too late, I recognised the blond guy from the party in Pylos. I had no time to react, Kelly was standing right next to me as we came face to face with Melénia! I flinched, as if I'd had a pail of boiling oil flung down on my head. I knew at once that I'd messed up, just as Stefanos predicted I would, and messed up badly … I would never have another chance with her, ever. Because on that score Melénia was entirely predictable. I would never have expected those sweet, chestnut eyes to turn to pure cold ice.

I felt a sharp pain, almost physical. Ignoring Kelly and the tour group, who were looking at me oddly, I grabbed Melénia by the hand.

'I have to see you. Tell me when and where. I can explain …'

I almost said, 'It isn't what you think it is.' She looked at me scornfully, raised an eyebrow and spat two words into my face.

'You're pathetic.'

I flinched again and watched as she ushered the tour group into the Pullman without granting me a second glance. The blond guy looked at me triumphantly through the window and the bus was lost in the traffic. I became aware of Kelly's annoyance and the ironic gazes of the people around. I had become a spectacle and it didn't suit my character. I couldn't care less if I made a fool of myself. And I couldn't give a damn about Kelly.

I apologised and left in a hurry for work. The whole of the next week was excruciating. I woke up, worked like a lunatic, forgot to eat or hardly ate and slept very little or not at all.

'You're pathetic.'

She had told me I was worthless. And the worst thing was I felt worthless. I phoned her many times. Generally she didn't lift the receiver and when she did she hung up without giving me a chance to say a word. Even the worst criminal has a right to apologise for his actions, what the hell? Except for the people I was working with I didn't see anyone that whole week. Not Sifis, nor Stefanos, nor a single woman. Kelly phoned me a couple of times – wanting an explanation as to why I had vanished. I apologised and said I couldn't see her again. I tried to concentrate on work, and to some degree I managed it, but something or other kept reminding me of Melénia. The pink bougainvillea in the garden, like the one in the hotel car park in Kalamata, the pot of basil on the balcony, like the one on the table in her garden in the Plaka, two swallows swooping in under the eaves. Thoughts of her kept returning persistently to torment me and I felt an enormous temptation to stop at the first kiosk and buy cigarettes. I didn't do it, not because I didn't want to fall back into a harmful habit, but because cigarettes were a comfort I didn't deserve. On the contrary, I deserved to suffer.

I couldn't think clearly. It was as if she had taken over my being. There was no reason to think myself worthless. I had never said anything to make her believe that the night we spent together meant anything particular to me, I hadn't promised her the slightest thing. After all, I hadn't even invited her to the Mani. She herself had turned up outside my family home to my evident annoyance at the time. Although afterwards … Anyway, I hadn't forced her in any way to do anything and I had said nothing in words. But I had said a great deal without them, and for a Laconian, unspoken things are more significant than what he says. And in that sense, yes, I was worthless.

In an attempt to keep up my spirits, but also because the time had finally come, I decided to busy myself with the real purpose of my return to Greece. I had gone to the Mani to meet Yiorgís's family, but his brother and mother were both dead, and the younger daughter had vanished without trace. The only Haritákos left was my father's murderer, *Bárba* Michális, serving seventeen years in Corydalos.

Michális had been sentenced to life imprisonment for first-degree murder, but the man wasn't a criminal in the usual sense, he had only acted *in extremis*. And so it wasn't a case of the usual Maniot vendetta. Using my contacts I had no problem in getting to see him, despite being the son of his victim. I might easily, according to the unwritten laws of my region, have come with the intention of killing him. But the authorities who gave me permission didn't know the Mani at all. And anyone could see I was a pampered technocrat, with absolutely no intention of continuing a murderous vendetta.

I saw him in prison one afternoon during visiting hours. He was stunned, at first, by my likeness to my father. But when I introduced myself he merely sat calmly opposite me and waited. He looked at me with admirable sangfroid, considering that he might have been facing certain death. But after seventeen years in prison he bore no resemblance to the person I remembered. He was a little old man, and if you saw him in the street you'd expect him to sell you a lottery ticket, not kill you.

'Good evening, *Barba* Micháli.'

'Good evening, my son,' he said softly.

My son! The man had killed my father! I asked him about his health, I offered my condolences for the death of his wife and son. He asked me how I was and where I lived. But I hadn't come for this. I had to speak.

I told *Bárba* Michális that I had come back to see him, to tell him that it was I who shot Yiorgís. I didn't mean to, God knows. I swore it on my father's grave. We were playing, he told me that the gun wasn't loaded. I asked him if I could see it. And then what happened happened. My father came and told me to go home. He told me to say nothing to anyone.

'And then it was too late, it was too late for everyone. But it's me you should kill,' I said. And then he said what I never expected to hear.

'I know. I realised it. Not at first, naturally, it took time. I'm not all that clever, as you probably know. If I was, why would I have done so much harm to my family? Sotíris might be alive now, and Katerina and my daughter wouldn't have been left all alone. Here in prison even the most dimwitted of us have plenty of time to think. Why would your father kill Yiorgákis? Our families had nothing left to fight over. He wouldn't have made a mistake with a gun. And why didn't he struggle? He was a head taller than me and he was strong. I would have had a hard time if he'd resisted me. But he didn't. He was protecting you,' he said shaking his head. 'That was why. He couldn't be protecting anyone but you. Only a child would have made that kind of mistake with a gun, and only for you would your father come to me, like a sheep to the slaughter.'

He was silent, tears in his eyes.

'I didn't come for you to forgive me, *Barba* Micháli, how could you? I will never forgive myself. I can't sleep at night. I only came to tell you so that you know. Do whatever you think is right. I can go to the police. I don't know if I can be prosecuted, but I'd prefer it to the guilt. I can find the best lawyer for you, to reopen the case so you can get out of prison. I can help you and your daughter. I'll do it willingly …'

'And what about your father? Do you think that I sleep at night? I loved your father, Odysséa. I don't want to get out before my time, I deserve to be inside. I worry about my daughter though, a girl alone, the kind of girl men flock to, but I'm not afraid for her. She's a *Maniatopoúla*. She comes to see me, she gives me courage and if it weren't for her, what reason would I have for living?'

He shook his head again sadly.

'I want you to think of me as a father, if you'll agree, in the place of the one I killed, like in the old feuds. I don't want you to be punished for anything – you were a child, and the only person who deserved to be punished is in prison and sitting here in front of you. That's all.'

He looked at me with eyes full of tears and I wiped away mine. I gave him my card.

'Whatever you need, you'll find me here,' I said to him. 'You can think of me as your son in the place of Yiorgís, like they did in the old days.'

He wouldn't accept anything from me, not money nor any other kind of help, it was enough that I forgave him. The meeting had gone much better than either of us had expected. I had come to Greece hoping that if I spoke out and admitted what I'd done, there would be nothing to stop me being happy with the new life I had made for myself in Boston. But it wasn't like that. I knew that I would never forget Yiorgákis and that cursed evening. It was a crime I would carry with me to the grave. The innocent blood of a child. But I might be better able to fight it. Is there anyone who doesn't have ghosts to burden him? Whatever happened, nothing would change the fact that Yiorgákis was dead, his father's forgiveness wouldn't bring him back, and neither would my guilt at what I'd done.

I went home. I thought of phoning John, but it was still too early. I tried Melénia's phone again. I had a presentiment that she would pick up this time. For two days I hadn't phoned her, thinking that if I gave her a little time to calm down maybe she would at least listen to me. I was right, she did pick up.

'Aphrodite …'

She put down the phone. Annoyed, I threw the mobile on to the sofa and bit my lip.

'I look at you and it's as if I'm about to have boiling oil flung on my head,' she had said.

Who had flung boiling oil on whom in the end? And now she was leaving me to fester. For how long? For ever? A dismal future, with everything except what mattered most. I grabbed my mobile and called her repeatedly, five times. In vain.

On Friday evening, as I had promised, I left for the Mani. Aunt Aretí was expecting me. The cockerel had been slain and was simmering on the stove. I felt a strange kinship with the cockerel. My uncle had been humming all day and couldn't sit still. 'The boy is coming!'

But when he saw me he knew immediately that something was wrong.

'What is it, *pouláki mou,* why do you look so downcast?' asked the old lady when she saw me fiddle absent-mindedly with the macaroni.

'Nothing, problems at work.'

When she got up to clear the plates, her old man, who all this time had been looking at me in silence, spoke up.

'How's the girl?'

I couldn't help smiling at his ability to read my mind. Ever since I was a small child he had always guessed when I was up to something before I even did it.

'She doesn't even want to see me, *bárba*, or hear from me.'

'Is it your fault?'

I nodded.

'Only mine. She knows I slept with another woman.'

'And do you want her?'

'More than anything, believe me. And don't ask me why I went with another woman. I have no answer. I'm just made like that.'

The old man threw back his head and laughed.

'That was before,' he commented. 'By the look of you, *koróna mou*, you are right in the bucket with the shit. Now she's going to pull the chain and you'll find yourself down in the earth closet. Have you been with another women since you quarrelled? What are you looking at?'

I was so astonished I could barely open my mouth. How could he know I had scarcely looked at a woman since?

'You see?' he went on. 'And even if you do, it will never be enough. There'll always be something missing. And you won't be able to manage without that something. Come on ... don't look so glum, we've all been through it. She'll forgive you ...'

I shook my head in despair.

'Not her, *bárba*. When she says no, she means it. She's a proud woman.'

'Do you think I couldn't see what type of girl she is, *koróna mou*? She's a peach ... she loves you and she'll get over it. But it's up to you. Have you spoken to her?'

'She hangs up on me, she doesn't want to talk to me.'

He thumped the table impatiently.

'Ach, this generation of yours with their telephones … Why don't you go and see her? Make her listen to you. I can't believe America's turned you into a total idiot.'

That night I slept in my old bed by the kitchen, in its scented sheets. I dreamt of Aphrodite with her hair loose, floating on her back in the pool at my house in Saronida. And then of my mother in the tower house, holding little Yiorgís in her arms. 'It's all right, *Odysséa mou*, he doesn't think ill of you …' I leapt up, soaked in sweat, and couldn't go back to sleep.

On Saturday Yiánnis and I looked over the work at the tower house, and he and Maria invited me to lunch. In the afternoon I went down to Limeni and swam until I was exhausted, and then sat on the rocks to dry. I took my time in going back to my uncle and aunt's. And then I lay down on the bed and phoned Aphrodite again. There was no answer.

\*\*\*

By Sunday morning I couldn't stand it any more and left as soon as the old people were up. My aunt pressed enough food on me to last the whole week, fussing and telling me to be sure to put it in the fridge, with all the loving concern of my own mother.

I said goodbye to my uncle and told him I was going to find Melénia, and he just chuckled.

'Off with you then, and let's hope it's all you have to worry about.'

I left the village and took the road for Athens, with the tower of the Haritakaíoi receding in my rear-view mirror. That tower had marked my destiny, but maybe this time I would have good luck on my side.

Apart from buying a souvláki in Sparta I didn't stop. I went straight to the Pláka and rang the doorbell. I felt the blood drain from my face. In the doorway stood a tall, impressive guy, the kind women adore. He had brown hair, blue eyes and broad shoulders. He looked at me inquiringly. I had come too late! Melénia, hurt and bitter, had found comfort in someone else's arms, and I deserved it. For the first time I understood my father's feelings that morning when he put on my mother's apron. So as not to lose everything he loved.

I said hello awkwardly and asked to see Aphrodite. The guy gave me a challenging look and asked my name. I gazed steadily back at him and introduced myself. No Anastasákos has ever left the field of battle to the foe.

'Vangélis Yalanós,' he replied suspiciously. 'Come inside.'

I felt the blood gradually draining back. It was her brother. The pilot.

He told me vaguely that his sister had mentioned me. I answered as if I knew all about him too.

'You're the foster brother, who taught her how to swim.'

'I'm her brother out of choice now, and I love her more than my own sister who died. So you'd better be careful!'

Right! He didn't mince his words.

'I don't know what your sister told you, but whatever she told you, she's right.'

He didn't seem put out; on the contrary, he smiled. At that moment she came in.

'You have a visitor,' he called out. 'I'll be over at Chará's. If you need anything …'

'Don't worry, I won't need anything,' she answered looking at me. They kissed each other on the cheek.

'I'm not going to say I was pleased to meet you,' the guy remarked as he was leaving. 'Time will tell.'

I started at the sound of the door slamming, but the silence was even more alarming.

'Well?' she said.

'Please, can I speak to you?'

'Okay. Speak.'

I didn't know where to start, and so I began with the most important thing.

'I love you. And whatever happened was because of that. I was afraid, I think, to admit it. That's what Maggie would say.'

'Is she the woman you were with?'

'No, she's the wife of my friend John in America.'

'Did you fuck her too?'

'For God's sake, Aphrodite.'

'I'm simply trying to understand. What exactly do you want, Odysséa?'

She was standing right in front of me with that icy look of hers. I was frightened and there was no doubt who the hunter was now. Her eyes, cold with fury, dripped poison. I couldn't be silent, I had to give it one more try.

'I love you,' I said again, as if that made everything all right. 'I made a hash of things, I know that. I hurt you and I didn't mean to. But you mustn't think about that any more. What you saw meant nothing.'

She smiled, but only with her lips.

'That's for sure,' she said. 'What I saw meant nothing and what happened between us meant nothing either. A bet with your friends. Did you tell them? You'll laugh a lot, the three of you, the gang at Ekáli. And did you tell them that I thanked you afterwards?'

It was the second time I'd felt as pale as a sheet.

'What are you talking about? What kind of person do you think I am? Why do you think I've been chasing you all this time, if you mean nothing to me? If it had been anyone else, I'd have forgotten her name by now.'

I had raised my voice without meaning to, but that wasn't going to get me anywhere.

'But this is you, *Melénia mou*, and I can't forget you. I love you. I've never said that before. It took me a little while, I know, to realise it, but …'

'It took you too long,' she said cuttingly. 'I want you to leave. Now. I want you to forget me and my name. And I never want to see you again. You're even worse than your friends the Olympians. They at least are honest.'

Distractedly I rubbed my throbbing temples. I couldn't take it in.

'You can't mean what you say,' I whispered in desperation as I paced distractedly across the tiny garden. 'You can't mean it. This isn't the girl I was with in the Mani.'

That was it! She was too proud to admit she still loved me, even after seeing me with Kelly. She wanted somehow to take it all back. I turned round and looked at her.

'Are you saying this to drive me mad?' I shouted at her.

'I'm saying it so that neither of us wastes any more time. The person *you* were in the Mani has no connection with the person who farts about with the Olympians discussing how many people need to lose their jobs so they can make more money, and how to fuck the Ancient Greek teacher. The man from the Mani was worth loving and sleeping with. The person I have before me now isn't worth spitting at,' she said scornfully.

I suddenly felt completely empty, defeated. I realised that what she had felt for me, if she had ever felt anything, was dead and gone, and it was nobody's fault but my own. I was nothing to her now but another nuisance, like Stefanos or Haris.

'I'm sorry,' I whispered, 'I thought that …'

I felt helpless and I would have preferred it if she'd hit me. If she had squashed me like an ant under her cheap cotton deck shoes. I rubbed my painful temples and my eyes, which felt strangely dim. And I saw that I had no hope.

'You're right,' I whispered. 'You're right about everything, except for one thing. I love you. And I'm sorry. I won't bother you again. Good afternoon.'

I didn't wait for an answer. I practically stumbled my way to the car.

On my way to Saronida I stopped at a kiosk and bought a lighter and two packets of cigarettes. I went into the house smoking and lay down fully clothed. I smoked five cigarettes in succession and I felt my stomach retching. I went to the bathroom to vomit. I had pains in my gut and didn't dare come out again. When I finally closed my eyes at around dawn, my sleep was full of nightmares. Little Yiorgís, jumping around his father's feet like a little goat and then the gunshot and the boy lying on the ground with his head hanging limp like a wounded bird. My father, with a hole in his chest, and a dark red stain on his white shirt, his finger on his lips. I sprang out of bed at the sound of another gunshot. But it was someone insistently ringing the bell. I dragged myself with difficulty to the door. It was Sifis, shocked to see me in such a state. He insisted on my seeing a doctor.

'You're burning hot. You've got a fever.'

It was true that I was shivering all over and there was nothing in the house except surgical spirit, not even an aspirin. Sifis went to the nearest chemist and bought some paracetamol, but I couldn't swallow the pills without being sick. Maybe it was the souvláki I had eaten in Sparta. He had to hold me up to get me into the car. He took me to the nearest accident and emergency and they kept me in, put me on a drip and did every kind of test. The only good thing was that I had lost my desire to smoke.

I stayed in hospital for four days and Sifis hardly left my side. It turned out I had salmonella poisoning, I lost five kilos and looked as pale as ashes. Stefanos came to see me and suggested I go and stay with them at Ekáli so they could look after me. I said no. Then Máchi came and finally *Kyra* Rinio, Sifis's mother, with a bowl of chicken soup.

'Come to us,' said Sifis, 'until you feel better.'

But I needed to be alone. I was behind with work, what with one thing and another, and time was passing. I needed to finish. It wasn't easy to concentrate. The meeting with Melénia went round and round in my head. Where was the sweet girl who had shuddered at my touch?

'The person in front of me now isn't worth spitting at …'

Christ! Nobody had ever spoken to me like that! Aphrodite wasn't the kind of woman who would let you use her, like Lou, or who would sleep with anyone for fun, like Máchi. She had been deeply hurt. And all I could think of was that I missed her unbearably!

The doorbell rang. Sifis, I thought. But it was my uncle and aunt, the two people I least expected, with a large sack and a cardboard box full of good things. The old lady immediately got to work in the kitchen to cook and prevent me eating the dreadful muck that was making me ill. My uncle kept me company with endless games of draughts and beat me every time, making no allowances for the fact that I was a sick man.

'Count yourself lucky that you caught me when I'm ill …'

'Not ill, just useless, *koróna mou* …'

They stayed with me for four days, spoiling me like a child, and then left by bus, the way they had come, refusing absolutely to take any money for a taxi. I offered to take them back to the Mani by car if they waited till the weekend, but they declined.

'You've had us round your neck for long enough,' said the old man. 'And anyway we can't stand Athens. And we've left Yiorgána in charge of our animals. Come as soon as you can, we'll be expecting you. You can take a look at the building work.'

My aunt had left everything spotless, with my clothes washed and ironed and four meals in the fridge. My uncle hadn't mentioned Aphrodite, he knew full well that nothing had gone as we'd hoped and he didn't want to upset me. The love of the old couple had strengthened me and soothed my wounded pride. I had more or less recovered, and went back to work determined to get over the dowsing administered to me by Aphrodite.

At the weekend I went down to the village in the knowledge, for the first time in so many years, that my people were expecting me there. The old folk needed me now, they were growing old. And maybe I needed them even more.

The work on the tower house had progressed and Yiánnis promised that in three weeks it would be habitable again. I asked him if he could take a look at my uncle's house while he was at it. It wasn't acceptable in this day and age for them not to have an indoor toilet, central heating and air conditioning. I didn't mention it to them, I thought I'd leave it until just before I left, to give them less time to object. On Sunday evening Aunt Aretí waved me off to Athens with the sign of the cross.

\*\*\*

On Monday afternoon Máchi phoned.

'What's up? I haven't seen you for ages. You keep running off to the Mani.' She suggested we meet up, but I pretended I wasn't well enough.

'There must be someone holding your hand.'

'Not a soul.'

'Don't tell me you've become a monk!'

'More or less!'

I saw Stefanos one day after work. He told me that Aphrodite had cut off all avenues and bridges of communication, she didn't want to have anything to do with either him or his family. She wouldn't accept the money they offered her to secure her silence, which didn't surprise me at all. 'Honour can't be bought,' as Sifis would say. Kastrinós had refused to mediate. So it was Máchi who had gone to meet her, curious as hell. Aphrodite welcomed her into the little yard with unaffected dignity. She listened in silence, gave nothing away, and then asked her to leave. What exactly was said between them my friend didn't know. But Máchi came back looking like thunder and wouldn't say a word. Stefanos hadn't got over her, he confessed, and he didn't know if he ever would.

'I don't know what to do!'

'Cut the coke,' I advised him, 'like I did with the cigarettes. I took it up again, but then I got salmonella and it finished me off.'

'And what about Aphrodite? Did you strike lucky?'

'It all happened like you said it would. I behaved like a wanker as I always do. And it's over.'

He didn't ask me anything further. I made it fairly clear I didn't want to talk, and we parted, both relieved that our relationship was back to normal.

I went out for dinner with Zina, head of accounts in Haris's company. Bright and beautiful. But I wasn't really in the mood and after dinner I drove her back home. My uncle was right. From now on there'd always be something missing. I hadn't seen Aphrodite again, I hadn't even phoned and I could still feel her parting words like a slap across my face.

Then one evening Iason Kastrinós phoned me, saying that he wanted to see me. It never hurts to network and especially since eventually I intended to base myself in Greece. I remembered old Olympios saying that Kastrinós had known Aphrodite when she was a child. I thought it a good opportunity to find out more.

We met in a fish taverna in Tourkolímano, where Kastrinós was a well-known customer. At first we talked about work, and he asked me to help him with his company, but I refused for the time being. I didn't have the time, I had to be back in Boston by the end of September. We agreed to talk about it again sometime in the future.

Towards the end of the meal he brought the conversation round to Aphrodite. He had seen her leaving with me on the evening of Haris's reception and of course he knew exactly what had happened. With his eyes fixed on mine, and a muscle twitching violently in his cheek, Kastrinós told me what a terrific woman she was, that he had known her as a child and that her mother had been his maid – her natural mother. I took the risk of telling him she meant a lot to me, in the hope of finding out more.

'Does she feel the same about you?' asked Kastrinós.

'I don't know. We went together to the Mani, but then I behaved like an idiot.'

'What do you mean?' he suddenly asked. 'Did you make love? Tell me, it's important.'

I nodded and then regretted it at once. He insisted I tell him what it was like, because it was, he said, important.

'Like with every normal woman,' I said abruptly. 'Why?'

Then Kastrinós told me, his voice trembling strangely and the nervous twitch disfiguring his face, what he had pieced together about the life of the woman I loved. He told me that Aphrodite had been raped when she was a child of eleven; somebody had taken advantage of her mother's illness to use her in the worst possible way.

I choked on my water.

'That's why I said it was important. Because after that experience, I doubt she has ever made love again.'

I sat there in shock, gradually putting together the pieces of the puzzle in my mind. Her hesitation, her tears, the two small burn marks on her breast and under her arm. Everything made sense now. That was why she couldn't forgive me when I betrayed her. She had felt used again. How could I have been such an idiot? That was why she hadn't phoned me afterwards and had waited for me to make the first move.

It's a question of whether you can avoid having your life buggered up before it's even begun, I thought as I drove away, and I knew what that meant. I couldn't get my mind off the image of Melénia, suffering in silence at the tender age of eleven. What must she have felt after my visit to her last Sunday? What must she have felt when she saw me coming out of the hotel with that floozy. I couldn't bear to think of it.

I looked at my watch. Half past eleven. Would she be asleep by now? I drove straight to the Plaka and parked in the usual place. I rang her bell impatiently, but no one answered. I sat on the low step. I didn't care, I would wait. I would wait for days. How I would love a cigarette right now! 'Don't leave me alone,' I would say to her. I would fall on my knees. 'Nothing has any value without you. Even my return home has lost all its beauty.'

She arrived on her motorbike. My watch said half past twelve. She took off her helmet, and if she was surprised to see me, she didn't let it show.

'What are you doing here?' she asked coldly.

'Please, can I talk to you?'

She looked at me curiously. I was still pale and thin after my stomach bug, with black rings round my eyes. She unlocked the door and began to push the bike into the yard. I helped her in silence and followed her inside.

'Do you know what time it is?'

'Not later than it was that night in Kalamata,' I reminded her. Her face froze.

'What do you want?'

I ignored her question and went inside.

'You haven't asked me where I've been all these days.'

'I want you to leave,' she said sharply.

'I was ill – in hospital,' I went on as if I was talking to myself. I must tell her what I wanted to say. 'The afternoon when you sent me away, I had salmonella.'

'I don't remember giving you anything here.'

'Except for a good dressing-down? No. But it seems that I took it badly.'

I smiled at her as if nothing was up and pointed to the chairs, as if she was the guest.

'Come and sit down,' I said, and settled into the chair while she stood staring at me with angrily pursed lips.

She eventually sat down because she didn't have any choice, but she made sure to keep the table between us. I realised I might be frightening her, bringing back memories that she wanted to forget, and my heart ached.

I spoke as gently as I could. 'The old folk came to look after me, you know. They cooked for me, my aunt did, I mean. Whoever heard of a Maniot cooking? He beat me at draughts. And I went to the village. Twice. I've started doing up the house. In twenty days it'll be habitable. I've missed you, but I've been hoping that in twenty days, when it's ready, you might come and see it.'

I just kept on talking, trying to persuade her before I lost my chance.

'You're very chatty this evening, for a Spartan,' she said sarcastically.

'And you are exceptionally silent, for an Athenian. Never mind, I'll speak for the two of us. That'll be safer for me. So,' I went on without paying any attention to her icy look, 'since you wouldn't talk to me and you sent me away, I made my own plans. I couldn't ask you, you see. We're going to the Mani together at the weekend. My uncle and aunt asked after you – I didn't tell my aunt what happened but I told my uncle everything. I had to tell someone. October isn't so far away and I have to go back to Boston for John's wedding. So you can come with me, and we'll stay there for six months or so, maybe more, till I've sorted things out and then we can leave. You can work there if you like, at the Greek school, I know them, or you could do a six-month stint at the university. We can research it together. Then we'll come back here and get married. Or we can get married before if you like, we have time, and I can beat John and get married first. I'd like us to live in the Mani, but it'll be difficult for me to work in the fields again full-time, I'm too spoilt. Besides I don't see you as a peasant woman, making cheese and milking goats and sheep. So we'll stay here. I might buy the house at Saronida or some other house, whatever you prefer. But we'll go to the village for saints' days and weekends and in the summer, and if we have a son, which we definitely will have, we'll call him Alexis – no question about that. My father's name. And if it's a girl, you can call her whatever you like – which is a big concession for a Maniot. I would like four children, two boys and two girls. Money will never be a problem, I earn plenty. So much that you don't need to work if you don't want to. But you enjoy it, I can see that, it makes you happy. And while we're on the subject of my work, I give you my word that I'll change my ways, I'll do things differently.'

I took a deep breath and looked at her directly, to show how hurt I had been.

'I don't want you to be ashamed of me, *Melénia mou*.'

She seemed confused.

'What are you saying? Did the salmonella get to your brain?'

'Salmonella, no. Love though, yes. I love you. I told you, but you didn't listen. I realised it in the Mani and it took me by surprise. And I slept with another woman, there's no denying it. I did it to convince myself that nothing was up. But everything's up in the air, and I can't reach it. I haven't had sex since then, I can't. It isn't the same since I've been with you. Come on, let's try again, don't let's spoil it all for something that isn't important and isn't likely to happen again. I swear on my parents' grave. If you don't want to sleep with me yet, I don't mind. But let me see you, give me a chance to help you trust me again.'

I stretched out my hand across the table and took hers. She didn't pull it away.

'There are some things, *agápe mou*, that I need to tell you. But I'm not ready yet. I could just keep them from you, I know, but I don't want any ghosts between us. If you don't find it difficult to hear what I have to tell you, and agree to spend your life with me after that, then yes, what I'm trying to say is, marry me then. Come on, *Melénia mou*, say yes!'

I stroked her hand gently with my fingers, I caressed her with my voice, with my eyes.

'I feel dizzy,' she whispered.

'Don't you love me a little? Say it.'

Like the moon dipping into the water, her eyes filled with tears, and I knew it was time to cross the gulf of my betrayal, her anger and the ghosts that haunted her. I got up and walked round the table that parted us. I opened my arms.

'Come here!'

She buried herself in my arms with a sob. I felt her shudder.

'You know, I have secrets too,' she whispered. 'And I don't dare to tell you …'

'Who doesn't have secrets, *kardoúla mou*? We'll tell each other everything in time. When you're ready. Would you like that?'

She pulled back and looked at me through her tears.

'Will you give me another night, Odysséa? Another magical night, like the one in Kalamata? Will you chase away my ghosts? And after that I don't care what happens …'

I felt a lump in my throat.

'What could possibly happen? I swear to you. We'll have so many magical evenings, that there won't be a single ghost left between us.'

She took me by the hand and unlocked the darkened house. We didn't turn on the light. In the bedroom there was only a small reading lamp burning. I could just see the single bed and a bookcase. I hugged her, but there was something missing, something I wanted to hear from her lips.

'Tell me that you love me a little,' I begged her.

'You know it! I'm crazy about you. And I hated you so much because of it …'

'That's over now, *Melénia mou*. Love me now.'

Even now, years later, when I think of that night, I know that however many women I sleep with, it will never be like that again. I tried to explain it to John. How I had wanted to exorcise the past, the pain, her fear and desolation. I could feel her entrust herself to me, losing herself among the hidden doorways of passion, following me to the mystery of ecstasy and I lost my mind. Love is very beautiful when you take. But it is glorious when you share. I gave generously, yes, but so did she. With her I learned the miracle of love, that it isn't only the body, it is the soul, it is your whole being that comes alight. Just before I fell asleep, I chuckled in her ear.

'What is it?' she whispered sleepily. 'What's the joke?'

'It's the first time I've slept with a woman in such a narrow bed. And it's the first time I've had enough room.'

# Intoxication

THE NEXT MORNING I went to the kitchen and made coffee and breakfast for both of us. Like my father had done on that morning long ago. She woke to the tempting smell of coffee. I knew that she took it *métrio* and I had made two double Greek coffees, fried some eggs, and made toast. I was naked from the waist up, barefoot. She came into the kitchen in a long T-shirt, looking perplexed.

'What are you doing?'

'Make the most of it,' I winked at her, 'we men from the Mani don't usually do this kind of thing. We like being fussed over. Here, take a seat.'

She took the cup of coffee and sipped at it while I tucked into the food.

'Why aren't you eating,' I said with my mouth full.

She said she couldn't eat anything first thing in the morning, her stomach was in a knot. I opened my arms and beckoned to her.

'Come here.' I sat her on my lap. 'Breakfast is the most important meal of the day. You mustn't look down on it. And anyway, I've made you my speciality. Fried eggs. *Oríste!*

I dipped a piece of bread into the yolk and put it in her mouth. She chewed it slowly.

'You see? Eating gives you an appetite, *Melénia mou*, and that isn't just for food,' I teased her.

'Why do I get the feeling that you're caressing me whenever you call me that?' she asked me as I fed her from my plate. 'From the very first you've made me feel strange.'

'I'm a traditionalist at heart, that's why. A name is a caress and where I come from you don't call your wife by her name in front of others. It's only for private moments. You won't have your name when you marry me, after all.'

'Well what am I going to have, a number?'

'You'll have *my* name. And when we're out I'll call you my little old lady,' I said and I tweaked her nose. 'And you'll only be Melénia when we're alone, or Aphrodite, my goddess of love.'

She threw back her head and laughed.

'Tell me something. Is there ever a moment when you forget that you're from the Mani?'

I shook my head emphatically.

'Never. Our home marks us all in one way or another. I think my life would have been different if I'd been born in Athens, I would have reacted differently to what happened to me.'

She smiled and dug her hand affectionately through my hair.

'You mean like last night?'

'Exactly! I felt like my pirate ancestors as they leapt aboard a ship!'

From that day onwards my Maniot origins became our little joke. She kept finding ways to tease me, which didn't bother me in the least because we always ended up in bed. Nothing overshadowed our days together. Even Yiorgís's murder seemed distant, a wound that had healed, although the scar was still there. But it didn't hurt any more. We slept, holding each other tightly, and woke up together. It didn't matter where. Whether in the narrow bed in the Plaka or in the huge bed at Saronida, we used exactly the same amount of space. The space you need when two bodies become one.

On the first weekend that we went down to the Mani as a couple, we stayed at Uncle Nikifóros's house. I suggested that we went to a hotel to be more comfortable, but she refused. 'We'll upset them, Odysséa, they'll think we're looking down on them. Me, I mean.' She was right. The old people tried to offer us their bed, and it took me some time to persuade my uncle that the single bed I had so often slept in was just fine. He only gave in when I took him aside, winked at him and said: 'When two people are in love they fit anywhere.'

We went for a swim at Stoupa, and then looked in on Yiánnis, who was at the tower house overseeing the work. News travels so fast where I come from that there wasn't a single person who didn't know that I was back and that I'd brought a *neráida* with me.

'I'll say one thing,' commented Yiánnis. 'Kosmás the *kafetzís* caught sight of you yesterday. By the evening they knew it at Prosiliakó, by dawn at Aposkiaderó, and by the afternoon, the whole of Sparta and Kalamáta. And he even says that he knows Aphrodite from somewhere, he says he's seen her before, the wretch. He's outrageous.'

We got back late on Sunday evening and two days later I handed in my report to the Olympian group. The workers were happy, because I had protected as many jobs as I could. I suggested moving excess staff to other posts where I knew they were essential. I persuaded Haris that moving the factory abroad would be likely to provoke an extreme reaction from the union and disapproval from the old man. A big strike would lead to certain disaster and Olympios senior, who was old school, would never agree to it. 'Wait,' I advised him. 'This isn't the right time.' I proposed a series of small expenditures, bringing relatively big returns. I had seen it done in America and John checked it out for me. I had to work hard to persuade him, but the 'shark' took it all on the chin. Even the old technical director, Mr Efthimios, came and pressed my hand.

'Mr Anastasákos, I owe you an apology. I wasn't expecting such results, to be honest. You frightened us a little.'

I really only did it because I thought Aphrodite would approve. She teased me endlessly about being an arrogant Maniot, and I teased her about her duties as a good *Maniátissa*. One morning when she had made my favourite *koutalídes* I pushed a piece of paper across the table with my list of the duties of a good Maniot bride:

1   Get up first and make breakfast.
2   Do the cooking.

3  Do the laundry.
4  Wash the dishes and scrub.
5  Never contradict your husband, his word is law.
6  Never take the initiative.
7  Don't tell him what to do.
8  When he itches you scratch him where it itches.
9  Don't bother him with routine jobs that you can do yourself, e.g. digging, carrying sacks, etc.
10  Listen and don't question.
11  Only speak when spoken to, chatter is the worst fault in a woman.
12  Always walk ten steps behind, we are not equal.
13  If you don't get a male child from the marriage, urge your husband to find another solution.
14  Don't spend your husband's money on frippery and fun.
15  Go to sleep last and don't nag him in bed.
16  Carry out your marital obligations wherever and whenever the master of the house dictates.
17

The seventeenth was blank, I hadn't thought of one yet and Aphrodite, after reading carefully, looked up enquiringly.

'There isn't a seventeenth rule?'

'I'm working on that one. Ah, I've got it! Write this down: *When he's too hot, fan him, like now!*'

Before I had a chance to finish, she grabbed the plate of *koutalídes* and locked herself in the bathroom.

'I'll eat every single one even if I burst, if you don't take them all back. Except for sixteen.'

'Please come out! I only wrote the others so you'd agree to number sixteen.'

Our fooling about always ended with us making love, more and more passionately. Melénia overcame her shyness, freed herself gradually of her ghosts and gave in to her body. At first, I led the way, but soon she surprised me pleasantly by taking initiatives I wouldn't have dreamt of. I could feel her changing into a magical, erotic being, and my heart was overflowing.

'Don't you think it's time for me to meet your foster mother and brother?' I asked her one day.

She gave me a thoughtful look.

'Not yet.'

I was dumbstruck. I hadn't expected her to say no.

'Are you afraid you might regret it, *Melénia mou*?'

I watched as the old familiar shadows travelled back to her face.

'I'm afraid you may regret it, Odysséa.'

I didn't press her. I had no reason to hurry. I believed that time was on my side. She was being careful and why wouldn't she? She had lived through a dreadful experience when she was a child and had learnt not to trust people. She would become surer of my love as each day went by. She would trust me, I was certain of it.

'I love you, Melénia. No one and nothing will change that, whatever happens.'

We were lying in that narrow bed in her little house in the Plaka, naked and entangled in the half-light, and I was fully conscious of the burden of my promise.

I had lost touch with the Olympians and their circle, which was a relief – it had never felt natural to be with them. I saw Sifis now and then. We went out as a foursome, with Vassoúla and Aphrodite.

We spent our second weekend together in Spetses. We wandered around the narrow alleys, visited Bouboulína's house and walked along the Old Harbour in the evening. I tried to get her to cancel her tour to Sounion on the Monday, but she was committed and couldn't let them down. What did we care? We had all the time in the world to go back again.

\*\*\*

Halfway through the following week Yiánnis phoned. The house was ready, we could go and stay in it whenever we wanted, and Maria had even filled the fridge with food. On Thursday evening Aphrodite came home announcing that she had managed to get the whole of Friday off. So we could leave first thing in the morning and gain a day. I've never forgotten that journey – bittersweet as the glacéed orange that Miltiades's father used to serve at Gytheio. The radio was playing rock ballads and the kilometres were endless. As I drove I stretched my hand across to take hers: touching, breathing in her scent, leaving little kisses on her hair that smelled sweet. I even caught myself humming along to some of the songs I knew and she laughed.

'You can't expect to have a beautiful voice, when God has given you such beautiful hands.'

I looked at my hands on the steering wheel.

'Beautiful hands? No one has ever told me that before.'

'And yet … the first thing I noticed about you was your hands, when you were holding those sodden banknotes, remember? And you looked so lost, as if without the money you felt you'd lost your gravitas. Before you ever touched me I knew that your caress would be magical, because of the tender way you kept hold of those banknotes.'

I took her hand in mine and squeezed it.

'Tell me,' I asked her, 'how did you find the courage to ignore my being angry when I found you waiting outside the tower house? Not even John would have borne it. You stood there as if you weren't frightened of me at all, and that's as frightening as I ever am. How did you manage it?'

She chuckled.

'I was terrified!'

'But you didn't leave! You took my hand and held it!'

'I loved you, Odysséa. What else could I do?'

'You loved me? Past tense?'

'I love you! Whatever happens, remember that,' she said, and there were tears in her eyes.

I put my arm around her with my eyes fixed on the curves in the road. She was mine and I belonged to her. I had never felt that before, ever, for anyone. I was happy. But I could smell her fear in the scented breeze and it pained me. She loved me, but she didn't trust me, I thought. Not yet.

'Nothing is going to happen, you'll see,' I reassured her. 'Everything will be fine, *Melénia mou.*'

She looked away. I couldn't see her tears but I could feel them flowing through me.

At one in the afternoon we drove past the Haritákos's tower and entered the village. The old folk had put the new key under a stone by the entrance. Because it was lunchtime, we didn't go to say hello. Uncle Nikifóros would want his afternoon nap.

The dry grass in the yard had gone, only the prickly pear was still in its place and beside the large millstone a table had been set up with four wooden chairs. The tower house rose up threateningly in its Doric stone surroundings, in the burning midday heat. We unlocked the door to the old kitchen and went in. Cool air caressed our faces. The place had been transformed.

It was nothing like the fancy houses I'd seen in America that tried to impress with blatant excess. Here all was simple and plain, as it should be in a Maniot tower, made of stone from the land, its noblest ambition being to defend that land. Even my mother's old oil lamps and the old-fashioned coal-fired iron had found a place in the smart new kitchen.

My friend had done an exceptional job! All the old buildings connected to one another – the old stable, the chicken house, the storerooms and the tower house. There were floor tiles in earthy colours to match the stone, and the nobility of the house was delicately enhanced, respecting its character and its history. Aphrodite was enchanted. I had spent almost my entire Olympian fee on it, but the result had surpassed all my expectations by a long way.

The bedrooms were on the first and second floor, as before. The wooden stairs that were still usable had been carefully rubbed down and polished. In both bedrooms white, handwoven curtains had been hung in the small window, to match the handwoven bedspreads Maria had chosen. The top floor, which had been a storage space in the old days, was now an office, with a computer, telephone, fax and a large bookcase.

On the bed in our new room – which had been my parents' and grandparents' before us – we lay down in each other's arms and looked up at the wooden ceiling. My parents smiled at us from their wedding photograph on one side, and the boy in his *vráka* grinned cheekily on the other. His expression, full of faith in the future, seemed at last to be justified. I had been forced to flee, yes, but I had come back, triumphant in my way. I had settled accounts with the past and rebuilt my house. I had Melénia beside me, and one day the tower house would come alive again with the voices of our children. Life would go on and my father's sacrifice would, at last, have been vindicated.

'I was happy in this house before everything fell apart,' I murmured. 'When I was a boy in New York, at the mercy of my American aunt, whenever things got really bad I would think about this house. I told myself I would come back here one day. If I could find the courage. But the trouble is that even though my enemies have forgiven me, I can't forget.'

She looked at me with her sweet, brown eyes.

'Forget what, Odysséa?'

'I'll tell you. Everything. Give me a little time. And if afterwards you still love me …'

She took my hand in her beautiful soft hands. She kissed my fingers one by one.

'I'm crazy about you,' she whispered, and there were tears in her eyes.

\*\*\*

I woke up in the afternoon and found her in the kitchen.

'Go next door and invite your uncle and aunt over for dinner,' she asked me. 'And phone Yiánnis. We're celebrating here tonight!'

Aphrodite cooked chops on the barbecue in the garden and we ate outside at the big millstone. Yiánnis and Maria were away in Sparta, but the old folk came. My uncle told us amusing stories from the past in our village and my aunt took Aphrodite's hand in hers.

'I can die in peace now. I'll be able to tell Fotiní that Odysséa is in good hands.'

'It is I who am in good hands, Aunt Aretí' replied Melénia. 'I've never felt so safe before.'

We stayed together until late. Aretí tried to help clear up but Aphrodite stopped her.

'Sit down, *thía*. I don't want you to do anything. Just rest for a change. Everything does itself in this kitchen. I'll just put the plates in the dishwasher and I'm coming.'

She brought out a plate of ice-cold watermelon and left us. The old man smiled beneath his whiskers.

'All's well then, my son. And better than well!' He beamed. 'Make sure you never give this girl cause to grieve,' he said, and wagged his finger at me. 'Because if you do I'll be on her side, you can be sure.'

Why would I hurt her? It would be like ripping my own flesh. Now I knew what priests meant when they said that Eve was fashioned out of the rib of Adam. We were one.

When the old folk left we sat at the big millstone for a long time, with our arms around each other, looking at the stars. I pointed them out to her by name, one by one, the way Uncle Nikifóros had taught me when I was a boy. The tall stone walls around us, which in earlier times had guarded my homeland from its enemies, now kept us from view. We threw off our clothes slowly and made love on the hard, cool stone. Time vanished, leaving only now. The magical, superb now of a Maniot evening, a story by the fireside, *koutalídes* with honey and *kayianás* with *synclino*. Of a child who had lived in paradise and been justly cast out for his appalling crime. Hubris to ask for paradise again. And the one and only punishment, to lose it a second time.

# Betrayal

ON SATURDAY WE DROVE TO GYTHEIO, and passed by Miltiades's *kafetéria* to say hello. I spotted an unmistakeable figure sitting there alone, short, plump, with dark hair and glasses. It was Yioúli Petrea, my old teacher. I dragged Aphrodite over and we introduced ourselves and exchanged news. She was a widow now, retired, no children, but she still gave private lessons to keep herself busy. I told her about my work in Boston.

'Aphrodite calls me a technocrat from hell, the kind of person who is only interested in money and doesn't care about people. As it happens teachers in general don't think much of me! So to punish her I decided to marry her,' I joked.

Bizarrely, Petrea spoke up in my defence.

'Odysséas always cared about people. He had a highly developed sense of justice,' she said.

I looked at her in amazement. 'Don't you remember what an idiot I was in class?'

'Of course I do. Let me buy you both a drink with some of those ill-gotten wages I collected, whether or not you learnt Ancient Greek, Anastasáko!'

'Oh lord, you do remember!'

'Maniots never forget! I shall hold it against you, *maniátika*, as they say.' She was laughing. 'And you too,' she wagged her finger at me, 'you've never forgotten it either!'

'I am sorry for being so difficult. I really don't know what came over me that day. I missed you dreadfully in America. I longed to get back to school and read *Iphigenia in Tauris* and *Antigone* and *Oedipus Rex* all at once.'

We talked over old times and said goodbye warmly. Then I walked arm in arm with Aphrodite along the sea front.

'Was she the teacher you wanted to pour boiling oil on to?'

'She's the one.'

I gazed at her in the moonlight.

'If you had been my teacher, my father would have been summoned for quite a different reason,' I whispered and bent down to give her a kiss. I held her to me, suddenly desperate. '*Melénia mou*, there are things I have to tell you and I need to do it now.'

She pulled away and looked at me imploringly. There was fear in her eyes, I could sense rather than see it, like a dog who knows his master's fear.

'You aren't ready, Odysséa, I can feel it,' she said. 'Nor am I.'

I didn't know if I was ready. Possibly she was right, but I didn't pause to think about it further.

We walked along the water's edge, accompanied by the murmur of the waves, and the distant noise of the taverns along the sea front. She took off her shoes to paddle in the sea and I did the same. Confessions are never easy and there was so much at stake. But this woman was my soulmate. I couldn't possibly keep her with lies or half-truths.

I turned and put my hands on her shoulders. I wanted to see her face. To watch the emotions pass over her gaze, like clouds across a clear sky. To see the shock, the fear, the disgust, the rejection. Now her eyes were dark, like the night.

'I'm a murderer and a coward, *Melénia mou*.'

She looked at me without flinching.

'Tell me,' she said.

I told her everything. How I had left my house on that fateful evening, how I had met little Yiorgís with the gun, and how without meaning to I had killed a child. And afterwards, when my father came, how he had ordered me not to speak and had taken responsibility for it and died, giving his life to protect me. I told her everything that had happened afterwards. How my mother had barred the doorway, and stopped me leaving with my gun. Because she, unlike the blood-hungry women of my homeland, didn't want me to be a murderer.

I told Aphrodite about the *moiroloya* that still rang in my ears, and my first nightmare, the bloody sea in Gytheio. And all the other nightmares that had followed the first and stopped me sleeping. How my mother had arranged for me to leave for America, and the fateful journey to Gytheio that had ended her life. I stopped talking when I ran out of breath. She hadn't turned away; she carried on looking at me in silence with the same inscrutable expression.

'Why did you come back?' she asked.

'Because I couldn't forget it. I felt I owed those people the truth. I needed to tell them what really happened. I owed it to my father's memory. I couldn't be at peace. I was a murderer, I couldn't change that. But I could stop being a coward.'

'Why didn't you then?'

'There aren't many people left to tell. The Haritakaíoi have almost all gone. The boy's mother, Aunt Katerina, is dead. So is her older son, Sotíris. There is a girl, but I don't know where she is. And Michális Haritákos, the man who killed my father, is still in prison. I went to see him.'

'You did?' Her eyes seemed enormous now.

I told her about my meeting with Haritákos. How neither of us had the will to go on with any kind of vendetta. How the tragedy had got the better of us both.

'You don't want to avenge your father, then?'

'The only thing I want, *Melénia mou*, is for my life to be with you, and for us to marry and have children. If you haven't changed your mind.'

I saw her lips tremble slightly. She avoided my gaze.

'Let's go home, Odysséa,' she whispered.

'Aren't you going to say anything?' I asked, and felt fear sweeping through me like the waves on wet shingle.

'I want you to take me in your arms in our bed,' she said, her voice faltering. I held her close to my heart.

'Do you still love me then?'

'I told you. I'm mad about you. Don't ever forget that.'

We went back to the car holding our shoes, our arms about one another. Neither of us spoke. The wave of fear stayed with me. Something had changed and we both felt it. I felt her touch against my leg, but the warmth had gone. I felt suddenly cold. Back at the house, we went straight to bed, but her eyes were troubled. I was afraid.

'Speak to me,' I begged her. 'I want to know what you're thinking, whatever it is. Have you changed your mind?'

She was crying. I kissed the tears from her eyes, tasting their salt. Our lovemaking on that last night tasted of tears. I slept with my head buried in her hair, breathing in her scent.

*** 

In the morning I woke up in bed alone, frigid with fear. I leapt up and searched for her all over the house. She had gone. My mind couldn't function. I dressed quickly, hoping to find her in my uncle's house, but I knew deep down that Melénia wasn't there. Then my mobile phone rang. I grabbed it off the bedside table in the wild hope that it was her. She must have gone out somewhere, to the shops, perhaps, and was phoning to tell me. I didn't recognise the number on the screen and answered it with a strange foreboding.

'Odysséa, thank God, are you all right?'

A man's voice.

'Who is this?' I asked distractedly.

'Kastrinós. Are you all right?'

I assured him that I was perfectly fine.

'Thank God!' he repeated.

He asked me how Aphrodite was, whether she was with me. No, she wasn't with me, I said, she had gone out.

'I'm sorry,' he said and his voice trembled. 'Sorry for what I am about to do to you. I'm crazy about her, you see. She has me round her little finger. She persuaded me not to say anything, but I had to warn you.'

I could make no sense of what he was saying. What the devil was he on about? What could possibly happen to me?

Kastrinós went on.

'Aphrodite isn't called Aphrodite, Odysséa. She is Marina Haritákou, the daughter of your father's murderer. I know it's a shock, but I was just as shocked to find out that the woman I'd planned to leave my wife for was sleeping with you. She persuaded me to help her, but I didn't know we'd be sharing her. When I found out, I almost told you everything, I don't know how I stopped myself. She swore she couldn't bear you touching her. She said as soon as she'd finished with you she would do anything I asked.'

I sat there, stunned.

'Odysséa? Are you there?'

'Yes,' I managed to whisper.

'She set it all up. I want you to believe me. Even the attempted rape. "Who cares about Olympios?" she said. "He's just a spoilt rich kid." We paid off the Georgian. I did, in other words. Just as I've been paying her for the last three years.'

I let the phone fall from my hand. I couldn't listen to any more. Despite my confusion, I could see now that everything made sense. The oil lamp, just lit, and Yiorgis's newly weeded grave. The fact that she was waiting in front of my house that afternoon. The way she always knew exactly what to say and how to win over the old people. The reason she didn't want me to meet her foster mother. Kastrinós saying that he knew her. The muscle that twitched frantically in Kastrinós's face. A multitude of details that made it abundantly clear that there was no Aphrodite.

Then I heard Uncle Nikifóros calling me from outside. I went downstairs and opened the door, empty of all feeling. He wasn't alone. With him was a woman in black, like all *Maniátissa* widows. She was older, but her hair was dyed blonde and the buttons on her shirt undone. Old habits die hard. Potítsa!

'*Koróna mou,*' she cried, falling into my arms.

I hugged her without thinking, my eyes fixed on the old man's ashen face. He knew. My old man knew!

'What a fine man you've become,' murmured Potítsa.

'Leave all that!' he interrupted. 'Where is Aphrodite?'

'I can't find her,' I muttered distractedly.

'You won't ever find her. There is no Aphrodite, my son,' he said in a broken voice. 'She's Marina. Marina Haritákou!'

So it was true! Apparently it was Potítsa who first recognised Marina. Potítsa never forgot a face, and on Saturday afternoon, as we were leaving for Gytheio, she had seen me with Marina, and recognised us both. Potítsa had visited them in Athens, years ago, when Marina was twelve years old and her mother worked for Kastrinós. Marina Haritákou hadn't changed much since then. There are twelve-year-olds and twelve-year-olds, and she had been a real woman even at that age. When Sotíris was killed in a car accident, mother and daughter had left the neighbourhood. Katerina fell ill and the Kastrinoi let her stay in the small house with the garden. From then Potítsa had lost all trace of them. She was expecting her son and his family to arrive from Germany, and had been too busy to tell Uncle Nikifóros straight away. Then, on Sunday morning, while I was still asleep, she visited the old couple and told them everything.

So there was no Aphrodite! There was no Melénia! There was just a slut, who had completely taken me in! She, and her father, and that creep Kastrinós! Involuntarily, I broke into nervous, frightful laughter. That was some revenge! Without guns, without bullets, bloodless! So why did I feel as if my heart was dripping blood?

What exactly had she meant to do? To kill me? She'd had countless opportunities, if she'd wanted to. To take my money? She'd never given me reason to suspect any such thing, and anyway why would she need it with Kastrinós as a lover? Did she want to tear me apart? She'd managed that just fine! She'd sold me love as if I was some greenhorn. And I'd swallowed it. She had talent all right, a first class actress! The virgin, who had been raped and never slept with another man! The more I thought about it, the more I laughed. How ridiculous I must have seemed when I begged her to marry me! And she, with her tears on cue, 'I'm crazy about you.' Making love to me even though she hated me! Even though all she wanted was revenge!

My laughter choked me and I started to cough. I lunged towards the door. My old man tried to bar my way.

'No, *koróna mou*, she isn't worth it.'

I pushed him aside. The tower of the Haritakaíoi stood tall at the entrance of the village as if in mockery. I went through the little door and into the overgrown garden. The low entrance to their tower house was open. I strode across it, fuming with rage, a bitter bile in my stomach.

'Where are you?' I didn't recognise my own voice as it echoed through the deserted house.

'On the second floor. Come up,' she called down to me and there didn't seem a trace of fear in that voice.

I climbed the steep stairs and shut the trapdoor down behind me. Just the two of us now! She was standing tall, beside the battlements. She had seen me from the lookout, she was ready.

Ages before, her people had watched my family's movements from up here and waited. They were ready with the *zematístra* and volleys of stones for a battle to the death. She had preferred to creep up on me on the sly, like a snake, but now the masks had fallen and the enemies stood face to face. Fearless, she watched me, with her head held high, as I blocked her escape. I faced her as if I was seeing her for the first time. She was unbelievably beautiful! Her dark hair loose, the forehead and nose of an ancient *kore*, the stance of a Caryatid. *Maniatopoúles* are very beautiful women, I thought in my raving. Her neck, tender as the stem of a flower. How easily one can snap a stem!

There is a very fine line separating the murderer from his crime. I had already unwittingly killed someone and crossed that line. It would be so easy to cross it again. As I drew near her in the dusty gloom, I felt a deadly hatred, because I loved her so deeply. I stretched out my hand and cradled her beautiful neck, slowly, as I had caressed her once before, and she, shuddering, had kissed my fingers one by one. I felt a shudder now, running through my hand, and the hatred flooded through me like a foaming river. How could she be so false? I closed my fist tightly round her neck and felt its throbbing vein. What was there now to separate me from the crime?

'Did you think you could just get away with it?' I asked her, and the feeling that I held her life in my hands, that I only had to tighten my fingers, gave me a wild, primitive satisfaction.

She lifted her chin proudly.

'Do whatever you have to do quickly.'

'You're prepared to die, just to humiliate me?'

She made no attempt to escape; she looked at me fearlessly.

'There are many ways for a person to die. I am already dead.'

'Why?' I asked curtly, waiting to hear yet another lie. 'Because you were raped when you were eleven?'

Something terrifying appeared in her eyes at that moment.

'That too,' she said drily.

'Why did you do it? What did you want? Money? I would have given you anything you asked …'

'Money?' she said scornfully. 'Who asked you for money? Odysséa, please let me explain. Either that or kill me now.'

'Explain what?' I shouted. 'That you were fucking Kastrinós for money?'

A loud banging on the trapdoor and the voice of Uncle Nikifóros shouting out my name drowned out her answer.

I stroked her neck gently, the way I knew she liked it.

'And your father? Was your father in on the plot too?'

'What plot? My father doesn't know anything. I didn't even know you had been to see him. Just let me explain, Odysséa. And then, kill me.'

'Explain what? That you and your friend Kastrinós framed poor old Stefanos and me? That you bribed the Georgian?'

'What are you saying?' she murmured. 'I didn't tell you who I was in the beginning. And then I couldn't, I was frightened ...'

Her excuses were drowned out by the shouts of Uncle Nikifóros down below.

'Open up, Odysséa!' he shouted, beating frantically on the door with his fist.

'Is it a lie that you slept with Kastrinós? Is it a lie that you took his money?'

She bowed her head. If I hadn't known how well she could sham, I would have said that she was devastated. But she shook her head.

'No, it isn't a lie,' I heard her say clearly through the shouts of the old man coming from the floor below, 'but ...'

My hand was round her neck and the temptation to squeeze it was so great ... Maybe, if I had despised her less, I would have done it.

I pushed her violently away.

'You aren't worth it!' I shouted at her. 'And I am not a murderer. I killed without meaning to. And it wasn't only your family who suffered, even though it seems you've managed just fine with your rich boyfriend. I lost my whole family, just as you did. I shall always be sorry about Yiorgís. But after this at least I know I owe you nothing! What were you trying to do? Humiliate me? Which of the two of us is more humiliated now? I, who really loved you, or you, with so much hatred inside you? You're pathetic ...'

I was back in control. I wouldn't touch her, I wouldn't hit her, she hadn't beaten me, I hadn't lost my ability to think. But then she spoke again, amidst her choking sobs.

'I'm crazy about you, Odysséa ...'

I didn't think. I hit her in the face with all my strength.

She screamed as she fell to the floor.

'Odysséa,' I heard my uncle shouting wildly. 'Don't, my son. It isn't worth you ruining your life for a … Please, open up.'

'And I know you love me,' she said.

'Not you,' I howled, knowing very well that she was right. 'The other one. The Aphrodite you sold me.'

She sat up, wiping a small thread of blood away with her hand.

'The women from our region don't have names, you said it yourself. They exist behind the names of their fathers and their husbands. If you had married me it wouldn't have mattered if I was called Aphrodite or Marina.'

'You're pathetic!' I repeated, through my teeth.

'Kill me!' I heard her shout as I opened the trapdoor to Nikifóros's persistent banging. I left with the vile taste of betrayal in my mouth and her sobbing was obliterated by the sound of the cicadas. I didn't cry. Men don't cry, my father taught me that. Or at least they don't cry openly. They wait their turn and plot their revenge.

# Revenge

I RETURNED TO BOSTON in time for John and Maggie's wedding. I had never been what you would call nice in business, and now the shock of betrayal made me more pitiless than ever. That autumn our company made a lot of money. Colleagues, competitors and subordinates all trembled before me. Even Maggie was careful. But I was fair, and people always got what they deserved.

Since my Uncle Sarándos's death I had kept a close eye on my Aunt Bess's affairs. The shares in her father's business had tripled in value under her husband's management, but she had gradually sold them all. Her beautiful young man had proved extravagant and inevitably the time came for her to sell her house. I had kept an eye on the business through an informant in New York, and when my aunt sold shares I bought them, even if I had to borrow to do so. Kafátos lent me money. He believed the food sector had an excellent future and he was amused by my need for revenge. It was a question of honour for me to rub that woman's nose in the dirt. And the business was a genuine goldmine, if you knew how to work it.

Aunt Bess's house was an old mansion and worth a great deal. I borrowed from Kafátos and bought it through a legal intermediary. Maggie took on the job and completed the purchase quickly and successfully, just after she got back from honeymoon. That same evening my aunt was given notice to leave. The things in the house, all priceless antiques, were included in the sale. I didn't let her keep anything. The Neapolitan housekeeper and the black gardener were informed that they could continue to work there as they had always done. They had been kinder to me than my own relatives, and I didn't want them to lose out. Instead I employed two more members of staff to help them.

'Revenge is a dish that is best served cold,' they say, and I had learned my lesson late. Aunt Bess didn't know the name of the person who had bought her property. Through Maggie, she asked if she could stay in the house for another month until she found somewhere to live. The formal reply, again via Maggie, told her everything she needed to know: Odysséas Anastasákos, the new owner of the house, wished her to leave at once or he would have her forcibly evicted. If she had nowhere to go, there was an old bridge in Brooklyn, where the homeless sleep. He knew it, because he had stayed there himself.

Yiánnis and Maria came to stay with me in Boston for Christmas. I often spoke to my uncle and aunt in Greece on the phone, and sent them money. Yianni had finished the repairs on their house. 'I can hardly recognise my own home,' Nikifóros complained. I tried to persuade them to come over but he wouldn't hear of it. 'I'm an old man. I don't want to die there and leave my bones in a foreign place.'

Autumn came round again. The Greek school asked me to take a look at their finances, a routine job I'd volunteered to do ever since I was a student, to give back to the people who helped me when I needed it. I was overwhelmed with work, but I couldn't say no to the headmaster, Mr Owen, whose gentle manners and integrity I admired. To send one of my colleagues from the office would have seemed rude, and so I promised to drop by there the next day.

I went straight to the headmaster's office and he greeted me very warmly, as always. We chatted for a while and he gave me the data I needed and an office to work in. In the passage I bumped into the Cypriot PE teacher, Anthony Andreou, and we arranged to go out for a drink. A bachelor and a womaniser my age, I hung out with him now and again. It was he who told me about the new teacher.

'She's Greek and she's a doll. Even Owen says she's brilliant at her job. The children adore her.'

'Have you made a move yet?'

'I can't see any way forward …'

It took me a couple of hours to finish the job and say my goodbyes before hurrying back to the office to relieve John. Outside a group of sixteen-year-olds were sitting on the grass enjoying the sunshine. I was about to walk past when something made me turn round and look at the kids again. Was I dreaming? The kids weren't just sitting around; they had formed a circle round their teacher and were listening attentively.

Dark chestnut hair, straight nose, broad, beautiful forehead, proud eyebrows, well-defined mouth. *Méli glykítato!* My heart gave a lurch. She had her hair tied back in a ponytail and was gesturing expressively. *Axion estí to pétrino paizoúli.* I walked over. She hadn't seen me, caught up in what she was explaining: 'Why did Antigone chose death, rather than life and marriage to Haemon.'

'She can always find another man,' she explained, 'and have other children, but she can never find another brother. Her father and mother are already in Hades. In the photocopy I gave you there's a *moiroloy* from my own homeland in the Mani, describing that very thing. *The Poisoner's Moiroloy.* Listen ...'

And then in the old Maniot dialect she recited the *moiroloy*.

'When her husband kills her brother, this woman takes vengeance. She considers it a debt to be repaid. I would like you to compare the thinking of these two women, Antigone and the heroine of the Maniot *moiroloy*. And if you can, look for other examples. Sisterly love has deep roots in the traditions of our country, ever since ancient times. I have noted down the words that you may find difficult.'

A hand went up among the group of students.

'What is it, Steve?'

'I find it spine-chilling, what you just read,' said a thin young man.

'It is. And at the same time it was for centuries the only kind of justice in a wild place. An eye for an eye. I've spoken to you about the vendetta. The duty people owed to wash away blood with blood. Just as Clytemnestra kills Agamemnon to revenge her slaughtered daughter. And Orestes kills his mother to avenge his father's murder.

If you look at the *moiroloy*, you'll see that as soon as the poisoner finishes the job, that is, the murder, she goes to her victims' father and confesses everything. "I did what they did, and gave them their due." Why do you think she does that? Why doesn't she hide her crime?'

'Because the father knows his daughter-in-law was justified in doing what she did,' said Steve.

She smiled and nodded.

'Exactly. But our subject is sisterly love in Greek literature and not the vendetta. So we'll carry on tomorrow. Good work.'

I can see all of her now, the usual jeans, the white shirt. She's wearing a light jacket, even though the children are in T-shirts. She hasn't yet got used to the cold. She's exactly the same. A little thinner, perhaps. She looks up and sees me. She has the sweet, chestnut gaze that I remember so well. The students scatter in the yard. I still don't dare to move. She looks at me steadily and unafraid. She never was afraid of me. She comes up to me slowly. I look at her threateningly, but she isn't put off. Not that I am likely to hit her again. There are many ways you can hurt a person. And that is what I want. To break her. Because my wound, which I thought was healing, is still raw.

'Hello Odysséa.'

I look at her coldly. Indifferently. I try to persuade myself I don't care.

'What are you doing here?'

She shrugs.

'I'm teaching here.'

I involuntarily purse my lips.

'For how long?'

'About two months. I haven't seen you around.'

'It's a big city. Why did you come?'

Her eyes gleam golden and I feel their heat. She's trying to get inside me, to melt the ice in my soul. I won't let her!

'I could say it's for the money. It's a good opportunity. But it wouldn't be the truth. I came because you are here.'

I looked at her coolly.

'And what do you want from me?'

She bites her lip.

'I'm mad about you,' she murmurs the usual refrain. 'A whole year away from you was unbearable.'

That's it! The months, the minutes, are unbearable! Life is unbearable without you and I hate you for that. Because instead of living my life I'm dragging it along, forcing myself to go on. But I'm never going to tell you that. And you're going to pay! Everything on this earth needs to be paid for!

'Why didn't you phone?' My voice sounded icy. 'I could have told you not to waste your time making the trip.'

'Because that's exactly what you would have said. Will you allow me to explain?'

'Haven't you explained enough?' I smile, not hiding my contempt. 'You had your chance, if you'd wanted it. Why do you think I'm interested in it now?'

She looked at me pleadingly.

'Because I can feel it, Odysséa. You do still care. Let me explain. And if nothing changes … I won't bother you again.'

'You're wrong,' I say firmly. 'I'm not interested in what you want to sell me this time. I have my life here, there's no room for you in it. See the sights, go to museums, do your shopping and go back. Kastrinós will be missing you.'

I walk past her and on towards the exit.

'Let me explain …' I can hear her pleading voice behind me.

'I don't have the time, I'm sorry, I'm busy.'

I went back to the office, forced myself to say good morning to Lou, and burst into John's office without knocking. My friend was busy on his computer and started in surprise. When he saw the state I was in he was even more concerned.

'What's happened?'

I threw my jacket angrily down on the chair.

'She's here. Can you believe it? She's here …'

'Who?'

'Her. Aphrodite. Marina. She's working at the Greek school. She wants to spin me another yarn.'

He got up and came over to me.

'What did she say to you?' he asked in amazement.

'Nothing. I didn't let her. I have no intention of letting her destroy me all over again with her lies, like the poisoner.'

My friend listened in confusion.

'The what?'

'How am I supposed to explain it to you,' I growled in desperation. 'The overarching debt of a woman, she says, is to her brother. Sophocles says it in the *Antigone*, and who am I to disagree with Sophocles?'

'What are you talking about, Odysséa?'

'A woman's duty is to her father's clan, that's what I'm saying. She deserves a medal for it, apparently. Because I'm the one who killed her brother.'

'Did she say such a thing to you?'

'She was saying it to the children, she was teaching it.'

'Don't you think you're exaggerating?'

I dumped myself helplessly in the armchair.

'I want to see her,' said John steadily. 'The curiosity's killing me.'

'You'll have your chance. I regularly go to Greek social events and the teachers from the school are always there. Come with me.'

'I wouldn't miss it for anything, my friend. I'll put up with the songs, the dancing, your gossip. So long as I can see her.'

It was a while before John had his chance. I was constantly travelling for work, and my uncle's supermarkets in New York needed attention – three to start with, now four. I had good people working for me, but I still needed to keep an eye on things.

Whenever I was in Boston I could feel Melénia's presence in the air. Despite myself I still wanted her, and it made me harder than ever, cynical and pitiless, both in my work and my relationships with women. What relationships? One-night stands, all of them. It was as if the wound inside me was poisoning all my emotions.

I saw her again on the fifteenth of January at the annual dance of the Greek community. The dance was held at a smart hotel, as it was every year, and everyone was there. John and Maggie came with me as they'd promised, and I invited Lou. I greeted friends and acquaintances warmly, chatted to my compatriots, heard their news. I kept looking round to catch sight of her, even though I knew from the moment I came into the room that she wasn't there. If she had been, I would have felt her. I went back to my table feeling somewhat miffed.

'Where is she then?' asked John impatiently.

I shook my head.

'She isn't here.'

My disappointment was obvious.

The speeches ended, everyone clapped, the band played Hadzidakis and the music overwhelmingly reminded me of that evening in Kalamata, downing beers one after the other while waiting for Aphrodite to get rid of the tourists.

It was only when they'd begun serving the food that she came in. Alone. She was wearing a long black skirt and a diaphanous silver blouse. Her hair was down, the curls framing her face. As expected I sensed her before seeing her. It seemed to me that everyone was looking at her. Dignified and beautiful, she walked to the teacher's table and sat next to Mr Owen, who kissed her hand. I was overcome by a kind of frenzy! I hated her! At that moment I hated her! John saw where I was looking.

'Is that her?' he asked.

I nodded.

'You're right, she's gorgeous!'

At that moment Marina Haritákou looked over to our table, as if she knew we were talking about her. I watched her bend over and whisper something to Mr Owen. She crossed the room proudly, sure of her beauty, knowing that we were all looking at her.

'If you dare to, make a scene,' was what her ironic smile seemed to say.

John got up and pulled a chair over for her to sit down. I didn't blame him for wanting to meet the poisoner, he had heard so much about her.

'What can we get you?'

Primly she sat down and smoothed her skirt, and then looked at us each in turn.

'Nothing, thank you. They're waiting for me at my table. I just wanted to meet you all,' she said apologetically. 'I've heard so much about you.'

'Us too,' replied Maggie bitterly.

Marina smiled that pearly smile of hers and the familiar dimple appeared on her cheek.

'You must be Maggie. And you're John. And you,' she said with admirable coolness, 'you must be Lou. I am Marina Haritákou.'

She fixed me with her gaze. I wouldn't look at her. I pretended to be interested in the other people in the room.

'I guessed that Odysséa wasn't intending to introduce us,' she said sadly.

'Do you blame him?' asked John directly. But Marina Haritákou wasn't put off, and of course I was at fault, having told her details about my friends. She turned to him and her eyes gleamed in the glitter of the chandeliers.

'No, I don't blame him,' she said to John so that I could hear it too. 'He's right. But being right is relative, just like love. You see, to some people loving means forgiving and giving people a second chance. To others, it means selfishness and ownership and playing the tough guy. But if you say to someone, "I am here for you, forever, nothing and no one can part us, everything is going to be all right", what kind of love would you have thought that was?'

'Did you say that?' Maggie asked me in surprise.

'What does it matter whether he said it or not?' Marina went on sadly. 'Since he was lying.'

I knew I had to stay calm. I knew it would hurt her more to think I didn't care, that I had forgotten our affair. That here I was, sitting with another woman.

'Aren't you going to say anything?' she asked me bitterly.

'I'm waiting for you to finish and leave.'

'That's exactly what I'm going to do,' she said. 'I've already finished and I'm leaving. Congratulations on your wedding,' she whispered to Maggie.

She went calmly back to her table. I, who had seen her laugh and joke and cry, I could see the troubled shadows on her face.

'I feel like socking her one,' Maggie spluttered in a vain attempt to lighten the atmosphere. 'What did she mean, "You must be Maggie"? What on earth did you say to her?'

'She is very beautiful,' commented Lou. I stroked her hand guiltily, for having put her through this scene for my own selfish reasons.

'Yes, she is,' John agreed, 'but that's not the only reason she's attractive. Odysséa, maybe you ought to listen to her … I mean …' he muttered bravely, but I gave him a look and he stopped.

I didn't look at her for the rest of the evening. She left with Mr Owen and his wife. The headmaster stopped at our table to say goodnight.

'I hear that you know Miss Haritákou. We are exceptionally lucky to have her with us.'

'I am certain of that,' I said snidely, and wished them goodnight.

***

Another month went by. I went for twenty days to New York, where they informed me that Yerásimos Kafátos had died of a heart attack in the arms of an eighteen-year-old prostitute. He had been a good friend to me. He'd supported me more than my own relatives, and made me think of America as home. I went to his funeral and helped Cathy to deal with his business affairs. To my amazement I learned from the Cephalonian's lawyer that I was to inherit 25 per cent of the various shares he owned and 51 per cent of his businesses. It was a huge fortune. Everything else had been left to Cathy. There was a letter, which the lawyer gave me, written in Greek.

It's Cathy I'm looking after by making this decision. It'll protect her from fortune hunters, unlike your whore of an aunt. Look after her, please. And if you like, fuck her as well. She's been wanting it for years. Don't worry. Where I am, now that you are reading this letter, it won't matter to me. Eros is a total piss-take, my friend. It turns you from a perfectly decent person into a clown.

You're telling me, Yerásimé!

I went back to Boston with my mind in a blur. It wasn't just the death of the Cephalonian, whom I had loved; it was the responsibility he had given me. How would I manage it all? Thank God for John! We would share everything. The work, the profit and the loss.

My Puerto Rican maid Rosa had supper ready for me but I wasn't at all hungry. I poured myself a drink and sat for a long time looking through the window at the park plunged in darkness. I was the inheritor of a huge fortune, my friend had died, but before he died he had once more honoured me with his trust.

I was startled by the sound of the telephone. It was the porter informing me that Marina Haritákou was asking for me downstairs. I thought of sending her away, but immediately decided it would be a chance to finish with her once and for all.

It was snowing gently outside and white snowflakes were melting in her hair. She looked at me in silence, her lips trembling, and fell into my arms. I had mustered all my anger, ready to throw her out, but she took me by surprise. Her confidence had vanished. I didn't have the heart to send her away. She was freezing cold, but the perfume of her hair, her touch, her kisses were warm as ever. I carried her into the bedroom and we made love until my body felt drained. A man's body has its limits, but not his heart. As she followed me step by step on our desperate journey her body was so attuned to mine that it hurt. She murmured that she loved me, it had all been a mistake, a tragic mistake that she hadn't dared to confess for fear of losing me. I didn't want her to talk, I stopped her mouth with endless kisses so as not to hear any more lies. I wanted to bury myself in her embrace and forget everything! Place, time, past and present. And just live in the now. But revenge is a dish that is served cold. And I couldn't forget, even if I'd wanted to. What man with any kind of dignity, whether Maniot, Chinese or Eskimo, could forget that the woman he loved, to whom he had been ready to give everything, had humiliated him behind his back for money? How could I ever forget Kastrinós?

What is the colour of betrayal? I stretched out my hand, took a cigarette from the bedside table and lit it. I took a deep drag and let the smoke out. She was still in my arms, with her head on my chest. I looked at her through the grey veil of smoke. It is one of the last images I have of her. Grey.

'Push off,' I said curtly.

She didn't understand. She stayed completely still, bewildered. I pushed her away roughly.

'Get your things and go. I need space. Space!'

She froze in my arms. She got up slowly and looked for her clothes on the floor. She dressed with hands that were shaking. She couldn't do up her jeans. She couldn't see properly through her tears. She looked at me perplexed, her voice a whisper.

'We just made love, Odysséa.'

I took another drag at my cigarette and blew the smoke in her direction.

'Wrong, baby. I made love to Aphrodite. The daughter of Haritákos I simply fuck.'

She started back as if I had hit her.

'I hate you,' she said. 'For the first time, I hate you.'

'And you are quite right to do so. Let's not complicate things.'

She turned to leave, smothering a sob.

'And by the way, Haritakítsa?' I called after her. 'If you're ever lonely again do feel free to drop by. I won't say no, unless I'm busy with someone else.'

She turned, her glorious eyes full of tears. I could swear, even after all these years, that I saw the salt drops fall to the floor.

'I am the woman who taught Ancient Greek on the stone terrace, and who you stared at for hours. Aphrodite was just a name. I am the girl who played *melissa melissa* with the other girls while you played football with Yiánnis. That was why I reminded you of *méli glykítato*. When did you ever call me Aphrodite? You always called me your Melénia. You wouldn't have loved me if I hadn't always been the girl who reminded you of your childhood. That's why you'll never forget me ever, just as I will never forget you. We are children from the same earth. You said it yourself. And I, like you, have never forgotten that I'm a *Maniátissa*.'

'Did you remember it when Kastrinós had you flat on your back?'

She leant her body against the door frame, as if I had hit her. Her face was as white as a sheet. But her eyebrow quivered, despite the tears streaming down her face.

'Yes, I remembered it! Especially then! And there's something you should know. It wasn't your fault, what happened to Yiorgís. My father had emptied the gun. But Sotíris reloaded it when our mother called him away on some errand, and then he forgot about it, loaded and hanging on the wall. I haven't known for long. So it's no more your fault than it was his. You can go on and live your life free of guilt. You don't owe us anything. Goodbye, Odysséa.'

I heard the front door close. I smoked the entire packet of

cigarettes, and drank almost a whole bottle of whisky until I lost consciousness. I slept a deep sleep full of nightmares. Yiorgákis's head, limp against my father's chest, and Marina Haritákou looking at me with staring eyes and a hole in her chest. How can you tear apart your own flesh? It was the last time I ever got drunk and the last time I smoked again for years.

*I am dead. All around me unknown people, in an unfriendly town. They don't exist, I can't see them, it's as if they are dead. I have passed across the line that separates the upper world from the underworld. Where are my loved ones? I always thought that when I finally arrived at their resting place, my mother would come to greet me and my brothers would call out and jump with joy.*

*'Here, Marina,' my Yiorgís would say. And Sotíris would leave his melancholy and clap with joy. No one is waving at me and so I know that I am alive. Why? What for? Almost all my family are lost in the caves of Ténaros.*

*'You can't leave your father alone, morí!' my grandmother says. 'You don't have the right,' says my mother. 'Why, Mother? Who said I had to go on living and hiding so many guilty secrets in the caves of my soul? Take me with you. You followed your sons to death, after all.'*

*I am tired of suffering in silence. I want to howl. In this frozen city where no one knows me, I can at least howl.*

\*\*\*

Two months later, Marina Haritákou went back to Greece. My life went back to its old rhythm as before. Though of course nothing was the same. But if you've survived the Furies chasing you for so long, as I have, you can survive a disappointed love.

\*\*\*

A year later, I married Lou. Our marriage lasted nearly six months. After it was over, we remained friends and colleagues, and now and again we slept together.

In the meantime my workload had multiplied. We rented a larger office, we took on new colleagues. I shared my time between Boston and New York, worked without stopping, hardly sleeping. John and Maggie had a baby, a beautiful little girl with auburn hair and huge blue eyes. We were crazy about her, she had me wrapped around her little finger and Maggie and I had found something new to quarrel about. I was spoiling the child, she would say! So what! I wish all children had the luxury of being spoiled. One afternoon she came by the office when I was alone, and after the usual chat about Ellen she suddenly cut me off.

'Don't you think the time has come for you to show some pity, pretty boy?'

I looked at her enquiringly.

'That beautiful teacher, I mean. Go and find her, settle your differences.'

I almost choked.

'I can't pity her,' I said drily.

'Not her, you fool, yourself. You need it. Go and find her and beg her if necessary. Otherwise you'll finish up a pathetic, lonely old man who spoils other people's children. Go and have your own children and leave us alone. With her, since no one else is good enough for you.'

'There is no pity, either for her, or for me. Where I come from vengeance is always until death.'

'You're completely insane. When you and I first met I thought you had no feelings at all. I couldn't understand why John liked you. It took years for me to understand what kind of person you really are.'

Who was she to judge my feelings and my decisions?

'And what kind of person am I then, Maggie?' I asked her sarcastically.

'A very gentle and romantic man who loves to the death. And out of stubbornness and wilfulness he lets life run through his fingers. I know that you feel betrayed and that she made mistakes. But who doesn't make mistakes, Odysséa? She came here to find you, to beg your forgiveness. And instead of taking her in your arms and asking her why …'

'I didn't feel like hearing her excuses.'

'Maybe they weren't excuses. No one is perfect. We are people, Odysséa, and we make mistakes. How can such a clever person as you be such a fool in his personal life? Stop and think about it.'

'I respect your concern,' I said curtly, 'but I don't want you to speak about this again. Ever.'

She looked at me angrily.

'I feel like hitting you! Have you asked yourself how she has been all these years? Whether she is alive, whether she's suffering? Whether she's waiting for a phone call or a word?'

'I want her to be alive, so she can suffer as I've suffered. But she's such a whore that she'll have found a way through. I'm not worried about her.'

I left the office and slammed the door behind me. My head was throbbing. I'd had the same thoughts thousands of times. There hadn't been a single day I hadn't thought of her. What if she had been telling the truth? What if she really did love me? But no. She had been sleeping with Kastrinós while she was with me, she had used us both, him for the money, me for God knows what revenge. All I wanted was to shut my eyes and stop thinking. To stop remembering. To stop existing.

\*\*\*

In the years that followed, John and Maggie often tried to persuade me to go with them to Greece, but I always refused. Once and only once I tried to contact Marina. It had been raining again, that thin, infuriating Boston rain that dampens the spirits. I had a work dinner, in a restaurant with a view of the sea, but I didn't feel well. I'd been having my dizzy spells and now I couldn't take my eyes off the sea. It glittered beneath a glorious sun, and I was lying on the sand, watching Aphrodite as she emerged from the water, dripping sunbeams. Or was it her eyes that were sunbeams? She was wearing a sky-blue bathing suit, and came to stand over me, as one with the light shining through my closed eyelids. I was rubbing my eyes to chase the thoughts away, when suddenly everything went black.

I came round in the hospital, but I still couldn't stop the images from the past from penetrating the nightmarish present. We were in the square by the church, in the burning heat, and there were two rows of girls facing one another playing *méli glykítato*. Yiánnis and I walked past, throwing the ball to each other. The girls were too young for us, but we stood there for a while and watched them.

'Look at the *kolaoúzo*,' said Yiánnis. 'She's left Pantelis in peace at last.'

I don't look at the limpet. I look at the little girl on the other team. She is wearing a blue dress and her hair is tied back with a white ribbon. She has sweet brown eyes and long thick eyelashes. How could I have forgotten that image? Revenge, where I come from, lasts until death. That was my next thought and it startled me. I might die. I might die far away from her, without ever seeing her again. My eyes wouldn't open. My head was spinning.

'How many hours of the day do you work, Mr Anastasáko?' asked the beautiful doctor.

'I don't count them.'

'How many hours do you sleep?'

'I do count those. Four, at most. I'm happy if I get three in a row.'

'How long has it been like that?'

'For years. Do you think I might die?'

She smiled at me.

'No, not if you do what I say.'

'Doctor, could you give me my mobile, please? I need to make a phone call and then I'll do whatever you say.'

She put the phone into my hand. I tried to open my eyes, but my head was spinning.

'Could you help me? Could you find a name on my mobile and call it? Aphrodite.'

I spelt it out. The doctor found the name on the list, pressed the call button and gave it to me. A stranger answered. Wrong number. If she hadn't changed her number, if she had answered that call, everything would have turned out differently. But the illness I had wasn't the kind to keep me under for long. It was just a spell of vertigo. I took some pills, was told to rest – which bothered me more than the vertigo itself – and they sent me home.

Time went by. I spoke on the telephone to Uncle Nikifóros in the Mani and to my poor aunt, who begged me to go over and see her. 'I'll come, I'll come,' I kept saying. I couldn't admit that I was afraid to go back. I couldn't let Melénia wheedle her way back into my brain, I couldn't give her the space. I knew from experience that she was like the wind. She could come in through a crack and get inside and once in she would take me over completely.

# Party

MY MOBILE RANG and I ran dripping out of the sea to pick it up. It was John. I had gone to Diro for a swim, and taken a trip into the caves with a local guy who bore a striking similarity to Charon. It was just like this, in a similar boat, that the dead in ancient times crossed the entrance to Hades, but we had all left our obols outside.

'You have to come here one summer,' I said to John. 'I'll give you the key to my house. There's nowhere like the Mani. Nowhere else in the world.' I wanted to share with him the images that fill my vision, the smells I breathe in around me, the soul of this place. My soul. We have shared everything except this. My friend wasn't much inclined to chat, something was up with our subsidiary in Seattle. He should have gone himself, but he couldn't be everywhere at once. I told him to send Takanki. He is capable and trustworthy. With a good bonus, and a nice title – manager of something – he could do the work of ten men.

'He isn't ready yet,' John objected.

'Why don't you send Lou with him, to keep him in check if he needs it?' I had sensed that something was in the air between Lou and Takanki and John confirmed it.

I needed to get back to the office, but I couldn't leave my uncle yet. There were fifteen days to go before the forty-day memorial service. We talked about work quickly and then John asked me about Marina.

'Have you seen her?'

'Yes. She's here. With her father, her fancy man and an illegitimate son, who is a pain in the neck.'

'Have you talked?'

'Yes. She behaves as if nothing has happened. She wants to prove to me that she doesn't give a damn.'

Later as I was driving into the village, an idiot in a BMW jeep overtook me and stopped right in front of her house. It was Aristomenis Ilioupolos, the lawyer from Kalamata, with an armful of flowers and a parcel. I looked at the calendar hanging above the fireplace at my uncle's, where it has always been since I was a boy. The seventeenth of July. Marina *Megalomártyra*. Her name day. That would explain the presents and the flowers, and why the little curtain in the tower house had been changed, and why old Haritákos had been offering Kosmás glasses of ouzo. Even my uncle, deep in mourning, remembered to phone Marina and say *chrónia pollá*. I heard him on the phone, or I wouldn't have believed it: 'May you live a long life, rejoice in your son and be as proud of him as you could possibly wish.'

In Yiánnis's house other things were going on. Effie was about to turn fourteen and they were planning a party. Effie had opinions about everything, from the *mezédes* and the cake to the decorations and obviously the music. But she was having problems in deciding what to wear. Maria had gone traipsing with her all over Kalamata and she couldn't find a thing she liked. Yiánnis was in despair. 'This party is driving me mad,' he confided to me, so I decided to take control of the situation. I did my research and the following evening I arrived at Yiánnis's house carrying a white box with a pink bow. I had been very insistent about the wrapping. It always helps. I adore giving presents. Effie eagerly opened the box and was so surprised, she could barely stammer her thanks. Three different outfits to chose from, with matching shoes. Maria blushed and scolded me just as Maggie would have done.

'Don't tell me off, Maráki. Let me give the child a treat. She's worth it.'

'All this bother just to make sure Alexis fancies her!'

Once she had recovered from the shock, Effie impulsively hugged me and gave me a smacking great kiss on the cheek.

'How can I ever thank you enough, Mr Anastasáko?'

'Cut out the Mr, kid. It makes me feel as if I'm a hundred. Call me uncle, I'd like that,' I said laughing.

***

The great weekend arrived and everything was ready, the cake in the fridge, the *mezedákia* on the buffet, paper plates out, the lights plugged in and the music on the stereo. We went away and left the children in peace. I suggested we all go and eat out somewhere, and take Uncle Nikifóros with us, but Yiánnis wouldn't hear of it.

'I'd rather be near the house. If I see it burning, at least I can run and save something.'

We stayed up late chatting at my house, until little Kostakis fell asleep on Maria's lap and Yiánnis started grumbling that he wanted his bed.

'Take him away, Odysséa, go for a drink or something. He's driving me mad. I'll lie down here with the boy. I'm dead tired.'

Yiánnis agreed, but insisted that we go by his house first to see what was going on.

'What are you frightened of, for heaven's sake?' exclaimed Maria. 'Are you worried they'll have sex? We all had sex when we were young and it didn't do us any harm.'

'I'm going over there anyway. We've got half the fourteen-year-olds in the Mani under our roof. We're responsible.'

'Go with him, Odysséa. Stop him making a fool of himself and ruining it for the kid.'

We went inside through the kitchen door, trying to pass unnoticed. They had changed the music, from Madonna and Lady Gaga to Greek *laiká,* and a blond girl was dancing a sensual *tsifteteli* while the boys clapped and ogled.

I saw young Haritákos across the room take a drag from his cigarette. He was wearing flared jeans and a T-shirt, his hair in a ponytail.

Effie was next to him. I prayed for him to take more notice of the blonde. But no. The *tsifteteli* finished and gave way to a *zembékiko*. Alexis took another drag from his cigarette, and let the smoke out through his nose and mouth. He stubbed it out flamboyantly, looked meaningfully at Effie and walked slowly to the middle of the room.

He put out his arms like an eagle and twirled around twice. The lads knelt in a circle around him and clapped out the rhythm to get him going. There was no need. He leapt and stamped and turned to the rhythm as if he were in touch with another universe. When you dance *zembékiko*, you talk to God. It wasn't just the masterly dance moves, he seemed ecstatic. He had a tall, slim, graceful figure, its firm, masculine lines already formed. Wide shoulders, strong legs, all moving in harmony with the music. He had attitude and class, but passion too, and sensuality. We stood there looking at him transfixed, a golden youth in the dawn of life, as beautiful as the future all kids dream of. I felt a bizarre desire to protect him. Like me at his age, he clearly attracted trouble like a magnet.

As the music came to a stop, Alexis knelt on the ground, and the kids all clapped.

'Let's go,' I said to my friend, pulling him away by the sleeve.

We got into the car in silence, still affected by what we'd seen. It's weird. How the truth can come and hit you in the face at the oddest moments. It can be right under your nose for days, months, years and you can't see it, and suddenly in an instant, from nowhere, it appears and pierces you like a knife, scorches you like a fire.

'Your daughter has a point, Yiánni. The lad ought to be called Michális.'

'After his grandfather, you mean? I'm surprised too. Why did she call him Alexis?'

In fact I hadn't meant his grandfather, I meant that he was like the archangel Michael, who takes souls. How could the poor girls resist him?

'He's an archangel. Didn't you see it?'

My friend took a deep breath and looked at me intently.

'But why did she call him Alexis?' he insisted. 'It's silly, I know. He is only fifteen and you've been away for seventeen years. But I can't stop thinking about it. Every time I see him, he reminds me of you at his age, so much so that I wonder … but then again, he's a year too young.'

I was mystified. My hand stopped midway to the ignition.

'What do you mean?' I stammered.

'Nonsense, forget it,' he said rubbing his eyes, evidently regretting having spoken. 'It's impossible, since he's only fifteen.'

'What do you mean he reminds you of me? I've never danced like that in my life.'

'It isn't the dancing. It's his eyes, his figure, his hands. The way he moves, stands, walks … it doesn't make sense, I know. It's seventeen years since you've been back.'

I leant back in shock.

'I didn't come here, Yiánni,' I murmured. 'She came to Boston.'

# Truth

I WENT UP TO MY BEDROOM but I knew it was hopeless to try to sleep. How could Marina have hidden such a thing? All those years ago, seventeen of them, I had told her I loved her, and that our son would be called Alexis, my father's name. Why would she give that name to anyone else's son? And why would she do what I'd asked, after everything that had happened? Unless she had hoped ... Why was it that my aunt had so desperately wanted to see me when she knew she was about to die? 'Forgive me,' she had said. But for what? And why did the old lady take Marina Haritákou into her house and care for the boy? Why was Marina practically chief mourner at the wake? My aunt must have known about it. So who else knew?

From the window I could still see the light in the Haritákos's tower. Someone was awake. Marina, perhaps. I stayed there looking at that beckoning light, flickering, tantalising.

At daybreak, I went to see my uncle and found him dressed and ready for work.

'I'm going down to take a look at the olives,' he said, eying me anxiously. 'D'you want to come?'

We wandered between the tender olives that my uncle cared for like little children, and then sat down on a rock in the shade. The morning cool felt good. I asked him straight out.

'Do you think that young Haritákos looks like me?'

He looked at me, unsurprised.

'Women are pregnant for nine months, *koróna mou*.'

'I know, but is he like me? Forget the months. Let's say that I was here nine months before he was born. Would you say he looked like me?'

'Were you here?'

I started to feel the first signs of a headache and rubbed my temples helplessly.

'No,' I admitted. 'But she was in Boston.'

The old man lit a cigarette. He blew out the smoke, and then pulled a crumbled piece of paper out of his pocket and gave it to me. Aunt Aretí's last wishes, scribbled in the familiar scrawl she used for writing shopping lists and credit at Kosmás's. He had found it a couple of days ago, in an old chest of clothes to be sorted and given away. 'Nikifóre,' she wrote, 'don't ever touch the boy's money. It isn't ours. It's Alexis's. Give it to him so he can study and make something of his life. And look after his mother. Michális isn't up to much, you know him.'

'As God is my witness,' sighed my uncle, 'from the very first when I saw him I thought he was yours. I meant to tell you, but the months didn't add up. And I didn't know how you would take it ...'

'And *thía*? How did she find out? Didn't it seem strange for Marina to be close to you, after what had happened to her family? I mean to say ...'

'I don't know, my son. Aretí never told me. I came back from the *kafeneíon* one day and found Marina here with the boy. You know your aunt. She could never say no to a child. They both looked as if they'd been crying. The little boy was chasing the chickens in the chicken house. He couldn't have been more than three. It was very difficult to be angry. And from then on she brought the boy over to see Aretí whenever they came down. I asked your aunt what was going on. Many times. She said nothing was going on, and just went on giving her fresh eggs for the child, and whatever else we might have in the house. When Aretí had that first operation in Athens, Marina stayed with her for two days and two nights in the hospital. Like a daughter. It wasn't easy to shut the door on her after that.'

'And Marina? Did she never say anything?'

'She asked how you were. Never to me, to your aunt. We often talked about you and your work, and how well it was all going. She just said "I'm glad" and your aunt didn't think she was lying. But when did she come to America?'

'A year after I left. She worked at the Greek school. She tried to see me and we parted badly.'

'So then … But how could Areti hide a thing like that from me? I can't take it in …'

In fifty years of marriage, he had never had a secret from his wife. Tears came to his eyes and he hid his face in his hands. I wasn't all that surprised. Nothing surprised me about Marina any more. It had begun to get hot and my uncle stood up easily, in one movement, as people who have worked hard all their lives do.

'What will you do?' he asked me on the way back.

'I'll go and ask her, what else?'

Later, Yiánnis and I were sitting together in the cool of the kitchen. The heat outside had become unbearable. Maria was bringing us coffee.

'The seventeenth of November, 1995,' said Yiánnis, 'was when the boy was born. The anniversary of the *Polytechneío*. His mother only just managed to get through the riots to hospital in time. He was nearly born in the taxi. So?'

A subtraction. Subtraction isn't difficult when you have a degree in economics, but it was the hardest sum of my life. I didn't wait for the coffee. I jumped up and ran out into the burning heat. The sun wasn't helping my vertigo, which was well and truly back and had been plaguing me for days. I had no idea what I would say to Marina. I had barely exchanged two words with her since I got back. And I hadn't even thought what I would do if Alexis was really my son.

I walked the eight minutes it took to get to the Haritakos's tower feeling dizzy and sick. Marina's car was parked outside. I went into the yard as I had all those years ago and called out to her as I had then. There was no sign of the abandonment of my earlier visit. Everything was tended and cared for. Marina came out into the blinding sunlight. Barefoot, her hair loose. She was wearing a white, knee-length cotton dress. Christ! Women her age never look like this. She must have made a pact with the devil.

'Don't shout, please. Alexis is asleep.' She didn't seem in the least surprised.

I could feel the cold sweat crawling down my spine. I knew I couldn't frighten her. I never could, even when I was a breath away from killing her. On the contrary, I was the one who was scared. This woman was still a part of my flesh, and I was no longer young or strong.

'I want to talk to you,' I said threateningly, to hide my fear. 'I'm going to ask you a direct question and I want a clear answer. I can perfectly easily find out if you're telling the truth, and I have the money and power to do it. Is Alexis my son?'

She didn't even blink.

'You don't have to pay to find out. If that's what you want, I'll tell you. Yes. He is yours. And if you want to make certain of it I won't stop you. I don't know about him though,' she said provocatively. 'And now that you've got what you wanted, can I ask you to leave quietly. My son is asleep. He hasn't slept properly since the party.'

She turned to go into the house. The blood rushed to my head and I grabbed her by the shoulder. She started, as if she'd been touched by a snake.

'Why? Do you hate me so much?'

'I never hated you, I told you before. Not even when I should have.'

'You knew I would never have left you if I'd known. Why didn't you tell me?'

'Because I didn't want my son to have a father filled with hatred. I'm sorry.'

I couldn't bear to look at her.

'Would you ever have told me? If I hadn't come here and found out?'

'Never,' she said firmly.

I closed my eyes to stop my head from spinning, the world around me wobbled and moved.

'Please,' I whispered. 'Could I have a little water?'

'What's wrong?'

'I get dizzy spells.'

She pulled me over to the door she had just come out of and we went into the kitchen. I collapsed on to a chair, grateful for the cool space, and closed my eyes. She dampened a towel and I pressed it against my flushed face. She put a glass of water from the fridge in front of me. I took a few sips.

'How are you feeling?' she asked formally.

I nodded and opened my eyes by way of answer. I looked around. The kitchen looked homely and showed a woman's touch. On the only window there was a crocheted curtain. It matched the table-cloth and looked like a happy white flag, of the kind they raise for a truce. Let it be a truce then. On the fridge there was a magnet with a tiny photograph of Alexis, around four years old, with a *Don't Forget* list pinned under it. There was a glass plate on the table and on it a starfish, surrounded by a row of shells and pebbles. The sink was spotlessly clean, without a single unwashed cup, and on the wall there hung a framed certificate showing that Alexis Haritákos had won first prize in the 200-metre freestyle swimming competition.

I closed my eyes again and pressed the damp towel to my nostrils.

'What does the boy know?' I asked, with my eyes closed.

'Everything.'

I shook my head.

'So that's why he looks at me like that. He hates me. He thinks I abandoned you …'

I heard her pull up a chair and sit down opposite me.

'He doesn't hate you, Odysséa. He knows it was my choice not to tell you. And even now you don't have to tell him you know. You don't have to be what nobody asked you to be. A father, I mean.'

I was overcome with an incredible rage. How perfectly she had sorted everything out in her tiny mind! Not satisfied with deciding everything on my behalf, even now she wanted it all her own way. A child is a very serious matter; you don't just find out and go on with your life as if nothing's happened. Nobody with a conscience could do it. How could I, when my own father gave up everything for me? But it suited her, of course. To continue the hatred. So that my son could go on thinking of me as a loser who abandoned his mother and didn't care about him. What had the boy said when I tried to persuade him not to go on seeing Yiánnis's daughter? 'No one who calls himself a man would leave the woman he loves.'

'You're crazy,' I shouted at her. 'I can't just carry on as if nothing has happened? I want time with my son. If you don't let me, I'll fight for it.' She knew that I meant it. She had deprived me of the boy for all these years. I would take her to court and take back what was mine.

'Why?' she asked me. 'You don't know Alexis, and you hate me.'

'He is my son, that's why. And it has nothing to do with you.'

'How did you find out?'

'It doesn't matter. Well?'

'I don't want a fuss,' she answered shaking her head. 'It isn't that I'm afraid of you, but I don't want Alexis to be hurt. Anyway you're making a mistake if you think that I can either force or forbid Alexis to see you. Or that he'll listen if he's told what to do by some judge. You don't know him at all. He isn't a child. In three years he'll come of age and be able to vote. He's the one who'll give you the right to see him, not me. Do you understand that?'

I couldn't stifle my anger.

'I understand all too well. Who knows what you've told him about me all these years.'

'I told him the truth. That his father simply spent a night with me and that no man wants to be tied down after a night like that. That if you had known, you would definitely have recognised him as your son and would have contributed as much as you could, because you're a responsible person. But I didn't want to oblige you to do it. I willingly slept with you and afterwards I took responsibility for what happened because I wanted to. I became a mother out of choice. It wasn't the same for you and I didn't want to hear any more insults from you.'

I leapt up and knocked the chair over. It fell to the floor with a crash.

'Was that the truth, Marina?' There was a bitterness in my mouth as if I'd eaten poison. 'Was that really telling him everything? You told him that we met and made love for one night?'

She stood up to face me.

'You know what your problem is? You were an only child and you still think the whole world revolves around you. You never learnt how to share or how to forgive. I'll tell you, if you like, what he knows. When he was little, he used to ask about you. I told him that you lived a long way away, in another country. Vague things. When the questions became more specific, I told him that we separated before he was born, which was true. But as soon as he was twelve, I realised that the time had come to say more. A mother senses these things. Alexis was full of uncertainties and I needed to resolve them before he grew away from me. So I showed him photographs of you and I told him everything. About Yiorgís, about my father and the old vendetta. About how we met again, that we lived together, my lying to you, which you never forgave me, and my trip to America. I told him that I didn't want to see you again, but that if he wanted to get in touch with you, I would help him. He thought about it and said no. He thought it would be absurd for him to phone you and suddenly call you Daddy. "It doesn't bother me," he said. "I like being a bastard."'

'Christ!'

'The last time we talked about it was that afternoon when you brought him home in the car. I had told him to keep away from you. You were still angry with me and I was worried … Then I suggested he speak to you himself, but he refused. He made some remark about your car. "He'll think I want to inherit," he said.'

I rubbed my temples with my fingers. My head was throbbing. She misunderstood my discomfort …

'You can pretend that you don't know,' she said mildly. 'Nothing is likely to change, nobody is going to ask you for anything, least of all him. Even if you tell him that you know everything, but you don't want a relationship with him, he'll understand. He's very mature for his age. He knows that you can't force a person to become a parent.'

Infuriated, I banged my fist down on the table. The plate jumped and the starfish danced about with the pebbles and the shells.

'You think that's my problem?'

'What is your problem then?' she shouted, pacing irritably around the room. 'Why don't you explain it to me so I can understand?'

'My problem is that in all these fifteen years it never crossed my mind there was a boy living here, growing up as a bastard and walloping the village children when they teased him about his mother. You decided to become a mother, you say. And you didn't ask me. You came to your conclusions as to what I felt and you deprived me of the possibility of being a father. And the worst thing is what you did to your son. You let him grow up without a father. Why didn't you go to the trouble of telling me the truth?'

'I gave my son the choice. As for you, the truth you're talking about was always here for you to find out if you wanted to, it wasn't that difficult,' she said sarcastically. 'The truth is that you didn't want to know. So do us a favour and leave us in peace.'

'I want some time with my son. I want to know him and him to know me.'

'I told you …'

'I want you to help me with that, you owe it to me and you know it. Please,' I whispered. 'I'm like you, I don't have another child and I don't think I ever will have one. Do you still think it will harm your son to get to know his father, even now?'

She had a point about some things. Alexis was too grown up for me to force my presence on him. And he didn't like me that much anyway. Only she could help me, because the boy loved her, and I know from experience how much influence mothers have with their sons. I picked up the chair I had inadvertently knocked over and sat down again. I was in a pitiful state and I could feel another dizzy spell coming on. Perhaps my only hope was that she should feel sorry for me.

'Are you all right?' she asked me, more calmly now.

'It's nothing. I suffer from dizzy spells. I'm on the verge of a breakdown, possibly. Will you help me?'

She let out a sigh. She sat down again and put the starfish back on the plate. And then she looked at me with those remarkable eyes.

'I don't like forcing Alexis to do anything,' she said. 'He'll deal with it better if we treat him like an adult, do you see? Go and find him, not here, maybe where he works, where he's alone. Talk to him like an equal and tell him what you want. Be honest. Children have intuition and our child – who isn't such a child any more – also has a brain. Don't take any notice of him if he's rude or abrupt. He'll feel embarrassed, he won't know how to deal with it. But I won't stand in the way, you have my word. And since you ask: No, I don't think it'll harm the boy to get to know you. Far from it. And I want my son to be happy … Will you be all right getting home?'

'Yes. But tell me one thing, what does your father know?'

'The truth, of course.'

'He can't know the truth! He would have persuaded you to talk to me, he would have tried to find me.'

'You think so?' she smiled sadly. 'I thought so too when I told him I was pregnant by you. I wouldn't have let him, of course, but I was surprised. Corydalos Prison is a great school, so they say. More so than Harvard, where you went.'

I looked at her. Marina Haritákou. Aphrodite. Melénia. Beautiful, unbelievably beautiful. Mother of an adolescent son. Ready to protect him, like all mothers. Like my mother. Fearless, calm, decisive. Motherhood suited her. Other women grew uglier. Not her.

'It must have been difficult for you …' I whispered looking into her eyes. 'To hear all that … Kosmás's gossip …'

'Everything has its price. And no price is too high for the happiness Alexis has given me.'

I looked into her face for answers.

'Why did you call him Alexis?'

She bowed her head.

'It's time for you to leave. He'll wake up soon.'

I knew there was no point insisting. Whatever the reason, she would never tell me. Maybe that reason no longer existed. After the shock of our first meeting, her expression was purely indifferent, cold, as you would look at a stranger, not the father of your child. Probably because of Aris, her fancy man. What was I expecting after seventeen years? For her to be faithful as Penelope to the man who had sent her away? And why would Penelope have gone down in history if she wasn't unique?

I stood up, still pressing the wet towel to my face.

'Can I keep it?'

She nodded. When I got home Yiánnis, Maria and my uncle were still there waiting for me.

'Are you all right?' asked Yiánnis, looking at me anxiously. I didn't understand at first why he was asking.

'Why shouldn't I be?' My headache had calmed down and my mind was working with exceptional clarity on the problem that was bothering me now. How to approach the boy.

'You're holding a towel? Did she hit you?'

I'd been clutching the towel to my nose without realising it. It smelled of Marina. Of Melénia. I was flummoxed. She must be given no air space at all. She was still a manageable flicker, but if I blew, even the slightest bit, she would flare up and consume me entirely.

# Finally

I'M STILL IN A DAZE from yesterday. I haven't really taken it on board yet. I dream about it the whole time, day and night. My body feels unimaginably light, like cotton wool, as if I'm walking on air. I sent her a message late last night and four more first thing in the morning. All the same. 'I love you.' I'm happy.

I couldn't believe it when Effie said she had her father's permission to ask me to her party. I'm not Mitsikoyiánnis's favourite person this year. I arrived at the party late, because of work, the little velvet box with Effie's present in my pocket. I hadn't eaten from the previous evening and I haven't eaten since.

Effie looked lovely. She was wearing skinny jeans and a shirt that left her shoulder bare. I told her so, and she said her clothes were a birthday present from Anastasákos. 'He's a very sweet person after all,' she announced, which annoyed me, but I wasn't going to let anything spoil my mood.

'For you, *moró mou,'* I said, handing her the box. '*Chrónia sou pollá.* Open it!'

I know it's not usual at our age to give a ring, but it was symbolic and I meant it. I put it on her finger.

'Do you like it?'

Her eyes sparkled and she gave me a hug. We kissed each other on the cheek.

'One day I'll get you a better one.'

'It's superb, Alexi. I'll wear it forever.'

'So that everyone knows you're mine.'

'I want a real kiss,' she whispered.

'I know. I do too. But it's not the right time.'

I wanted a real kiss very much, I'd been thinking that from the moment the phone rang and she invited me to the party. Those evenings at the tower house, on the millstone, they seemed so long ago it felt like centuries.

We couldn't do much more, so we went and joined the party. I was certain that at some point her father would poke his nose in – there was no way he was going to leave his daughter unguarded for an entire evening. Sure enough, he came in with his best buddy, the creep, to spy on us. I saw them watching me from across the room while Despina danced the *tsifteteli*. And then I don't know what came over me, but I suddenly felt stifled, and I got up and danced. My girl was there and I couldn't touch her, the creep was staring at me with no idea of the relationship we have, Effie's father was present to remind me that I don't deserve to hang out with his daughter because I'm a bastard, and presumably agreed to Effie's inviting me out of pity. 'Don't take any notice of what people say unless you value their opinion,' says my mum. 'People can be limited in their thinking.' Why should Odysséas Anastasákos's opinion have any value for me? Because he happened to be my father? And yet despite myself I couldn't ignore the creep. His opinion bothered me. I felt hopelessly alone at that party, even though all of my friends and Effie were there. It's unbearable to know that your own father thinks you're a piece of trash. He goes on to me about contraceptives and being careful, and it's a big temptation just to go over coolly and ask him: 'Why didn't you use contraceptives? Then I'd have been free of you and my mother and this shitty life.'

I do occasionally have black moods. But then Anastasákos and Mitsikoyiánnis left, and my luck turned. Someone put on an old slow number by the Scorpions and I pulled Effie on to the dance floor. We kept our distance at first, but what with the music and the darkness, her scent, and her bare shoulder where my hand was resting, we were soon close. I don't know how many times I kissed her, I couldn't see whether people were looking and I didn't care. I never wanted it to end. When the music stopped, Effie whispered to me to give her ten minutes and then join her in the room at the end of the passage. Then she left. I needed to drink something cool, or have someone pour cold water over me. It didn't even occur to me to think about the consequences of what we were about to do. I never would have dared to do it if she hadn't taken the initiative.

The next afternoon at Xemóni the creep came in earlier than usual and looked oddly hesitant, as if he wanted to say something and didn't know where to start. I was instantly suspicious that something was up, and because I was obsessed with her, my mind went straight to Effie and what had happened the night before. I tried to stay calm and think logically. If they'd known about us, it wouldn't be Anastasákos, it would be her father Mitsikoyiánnis, coming to string me from the bell tower.

I wiped his table and put down a clean ashtray, ready to take his order, and avoided catching his eye. He was looking at me intently, even weirdly. He was nervously playing with his lighter, tossing it from hand to hand and then flicking it on and off. All the time he'd been coming, I'd watched him without his noticing – since for him I was just the kid who brings the coffees – and I had learnt all his mannerisms. Sure, steady, the confident gestures and measured words of a person with money and power. Nothing excessive, nothing that would just waste time. It wasn't busy, so I took him his coffee quickly to get it over with, and then I sat down with the other kids and we bantered a bit. I was on form. The memory of the night before made me blush and smile, maybe a bit moronically. But we joked and laughed, and even though all the while for some strange reason Anastasákos kept looking at me, I didn't care. After last night, I didn't care about anything. I turned my back on him. I had no intention of having my mood ruined today.

I forgot all about him back there for a while. Finally two couples came in and I went to take their order, and then I saw that he was still looking at me, exactly as before, still playing nervously with his lighter, the glass of water and the coffee in front of him untouched. He hadn't drunk a drop, therefore he hadn't come here for coffee. I thought of Effie and broke out into a cold sweat. She wouldn't answer her mobile, and I still hadn't had any reply to my messages saying I loved her.

I took the couples their order and was about to go back to my mates when I saw him signalling to me. He asked me for the bill and I was counting out his change when he finally dropped his bombshell. He looked at me with that dark, annoying look of his and asked: 'What time are you finishing tonight?'

I told him I was finishing at around eleven and that my mother was coming to pick me up.

'What d'you say if we save her the trouble and I take you home? I'd like us to talk,' said the creep awkwardly. I wasn't used to him speaking to me in that tone of voice. I think I grinned despite myself.

'What about?' I asked somewhat rudely.

'I think you know,' was his answer, and I felt my face go puce.

'What d'you mean?' I stammered, in one last attempt to gain time.

Instead of the list of accusations I was expecting from him, he just said, hesitantly: 'Sit down for a minute. Do you have the time?'

I shot a glance over my shoulder at the kids and my almost non-existent clientele. Even if I could avoid him now, there wouldn't be much point.

I sat down reluctantly, hoping that we would soon be done. My nerves were on edge and I'd had enough.

'I'm listening. Is it about Effie?'

The guy took a deep breath.

'It's not about Effie, son … I'm sorry … I seem to have lost the plot. I don't know how to start. I don't know what to say to you. All this time I've been trying to work out what you've got against me, and why you should hate me. But you're right. I would hate me too.'

I said nothing, relieved that Effie and I had got away with it, and that whatever he wanted it wasn't about us. But my sense of relief evaporated as soon as I saw where he was heading. The guy was freaking out. He hardly knew what he was saying.

'After all these years your father, whom you know only from photographs, comes back and starts making your life difficult. But I didn't know, my boy. If I had known, I'd have been by your side. I know it's not much comfort to a child who's grown up without a father, but that's how it is. We met in a slightly weird way, it's true. But it's never too late. Let's at least get to know one another, my boy, what d'you say?'

It was cheering to see him lose some of that arrogant 'I have everything under control' attitude of his. There's one thing you don't have under control, *my boy*, and it's me. Not with your attitude so high and mighty, nor with the money that you spread around so easily. I could have told him so right there, but there was no way I was going to let the boys see what was going on. My chance had finally come to talk to him face to face. Me and the man who gave me life. Who had the nerve to tick me off for not having contraceptives when my whole existence is due to a forgotten contraceptive. He had the nerve to say I didn't care for Effie and had the nerve to talk to me about consequences. I know the consequences, *my boy!* They're written all over my face in capital letters. CONSEQUENCES. And everyone you see around you can read them. If you think I'm going to hug you now and call you Daddy, you've been reading too many fairy stories.

I shot another look behind me at the lads.

'I'll let my mother know we're coming back together,' I said and got up.

'Okay. I'll come by at eleven.'

He didn't go right away. He finally sipped at his coffee and kept on looking at me. What the hell was going on inside his head? I went back to my friends and my work and ignored him. He had it coming to him. All in good time!

# Back Again

I GRABBED MARINA'S TOWEL, wet it and put it on my face. I breathed in her smell like a drug addict after a long detox. I gave into it, just as years before my alcoholic grandfather had given in to the ouzo and could no longer care less about his humiliation or his pride. Let all the village children run after me, throwing stones and rattling saucepans, I couldn't give a damn! Having said that, I've chosen the right time to make a fool of myself, since sadly there are no children left in this village.

I walked through the empty rooms trying in vain to put my thoughts in order, still reeling from the shock. I have a son! An child who hates me! The hatred was etched on his face that very first evening at Aretí's wake, when I told him that he was more honest than his mother and he punched me in the face. But what did I expect? What would I have done if I had been in his position? In all honesty I hardly even knew what I wanted from the boy. Once, long ago, I had dreamt of a son who would have my father's name, and would be the *noikokíris* of the tower house. We would play and watch football together, and sit side by side looking at the sea. I would buy him toys and clothes, hold his hand, take care of him. We would talk endlessly and I would be right beside him every step of his way. When the nights were cold I would cover him to keep him warm, and in the summer I would teach him to swim. None of that happened, the boy learnt to swim very well without me. He's not a baby any more and he doesn't need me. That's probably what he wants to say to me this evening. But he's my only child, my only continuity, which is a very important thing. I still need him, and I have to admit, like a man, that he's the only bridge I have to his mother. I know I haven't a hope with her. Her indifference is so eloquent that I have no illusions. But even just to see her would be something. The boy … flesh of our flesh, of the two of us … I can't take it in. He looks like me, but he has all the sweetness of his mother.

The image of him dancing *zembékiko* wouldn't leave my mind. The kid is hurting, he's finding love hard, he finds me hard, life seems unbearable. When people are hurting they get angry, I know that well, because that's how I've lived my life. And so this evening I'm ready for anything.

\*\*\*

At eleven I pick him up from work as we'd arranged. He gets into the car without a word. When we first met in the tower house he spoke to me in the singular. Now he's changed it to a cold, formal plural and is calling me *Kyrie* Anastasáko again. I ask him if we could get to know each other better, spend some time together.

'Why should we get to know each other?' he laughs scornfully in my face. 'Don't we know each other already well enough? I met you as soon as you got back here and I don't like you at all.'

He tells me off for leaving it too late to see my aunt, when I knew she was dying, and pretending I had too much work. 'Because God forbid! You might have lost a couple of dollars!' He tells me off for giving Effie such an expensive present for her birthday, just 'to buy her sympathy and distance her from me'. I had no alternative but to agree with him and suddenly found myself saying sorry repeatedly, and trying to explain my good intentions. I only wanted to help him, I say. Because an older and more experienced woman was what he needed, to start off his sex life, and not Effie. She was too young.

'Liar,' the kid hisses through his teeth and gives me a look like thunder. It reminds me so much of the looks my father gave me, that I bite my lip.

This boy, who until recently I didn't know existed, and who has been a pain in the neck sent to bug me ever since I got back, this kid is mine, and I still can't believe it. And all this time, without my knowing it, he has been observing me and noting my weaknesses, my habits and faults, and shown me my own face in the mirror in a way I never imagined I would see it.

I leave him at the Haritákos's tower and am completely in pieces. He says goodnight with a sarcastic smile. I start the car and go home in despair. I must phone John, I must talk to someone. I need someone to tell me that I still have hope. I'm naturally not giving up. I am not a good person, I've said so before, but I'm not the monster the kid thinks I am. I'm not that much worse than anyone else. And whatever his mother has said to him, he has a duty to listen to my version. I don't regret what I am, but if Alexis rejects me, I want him to do it for reasons that correspond to reality.

And there's something else. I like the kid. I liked him from the first moment. He has chutzpah. But he is also living proof that his mother never loved me, preferring to bring him up alone rather than have me as his father.

So now what?

## Just Desserts

ANASTASÁKOS DROVE OFF and I went inside, feeling triumphant and light at heart after decimating the guy who had suddenly decided to act the father. My mother gave me an enquiring look. She had to be back at work on Monday and was about to leave for Athens. She never told me Anastasákos wanted to see me, who knows why she didn't, but it was clear she knew, and now she was expecting me to tell her all about it. I let her stew in her own juice, went up to my room and shut the trapdoor down behind me. The only person I wanted now was Effie. I turned on my mobile and phoned her again. Nothing. She wasn't picking up and I sent her another message, the sixth since the morning. 'I love you. Don't do this to me.' I lay down looking at the wooden ceiling and tried to relive the previous night. My mother was knocking on the trapdoor. A gentle, discreet, slightly guilty knock. I didn't answer.

'Alexi, I'm going. I just wanted to say goodbye.'

'Safe trip,' I called out sarcastically.

'Thank you,' she said, pretending not to notice. 'Goodnight.'

I heard her going down the stairs and then I watched from the battlements as *Pappoú* helped her load up the car. Her shoulders, slumped under the weight of her sadness, made my temper vanish. She'd probably had a rotten day. Poor Marináki! I couldn't let her go off and drive alone through the night thinking about me. I jumped up, unlocked the trapdoor and went downstairs. She'd just got into the driver's seat and she'd been crying. I felt sick with guilt.

'I'm sorry,' I muttered, putting my head in the window. 'Why didn't you tell me that he was coming to see me? Why didn't you tell me he knew?'

'I'm sorry,' she said grimly. 'I thought it would be better if I didn't get involved. It's between the two of you. He came this morning, he'd worked it out. He asked me to give him a chance to get to know you. Not to stop him. I promised I wouldn't. What happened?'

'I gave him a piece of my mind for you. And it was very satisfying.' She gently stroked my cheek.

'Don't be unfair to him, Alexi. Not for his sake, but for yours. He's in a mess too. What did he say?'

'That he wants to get to know me, so we can become best buddies.'

'Think about it …'

'I've thought enough. Now it's his turn to think. Have a good journey, Marináki. Don't cry over him, he isn't worth a single tear.'

'Be careful,' she murmured. 'I'll call you in the morning.'

I promised I would, and stood there watching as the car disappeared along the road to Sparta.

*Look at me. I am transparent as water, don't be angry with me. I'm a mirror, take a look at yourself. I am clay, putty in your hands. I am air, earth, water. I exist because you exist. Don't be angry with me, Alexi mou …*

# Alexis

WHATEVER HOPES I HAD that I would make friends with Alexis evaporated over the next few days. Things were becoming worse than ever, because I was pressed for time. I had already stayed far longer than I'd planned to; there was work to be done back home and John couldn't manage alone any longer.

The kid was flagrantly avoiding me. He didn't even bother to hide it. I went every day to the café where he worked, picking times when it was quiet so that I could talk to him. He would scowl and take my order, and when I asked how he was, how things were, he would answer in monosyllables, frostily polite and sarcastic. One day I plucked up the courage to suggest he come and sit down with me, but he blanked me.

'We don't provide escorts here,' he said rudely and settled down inside with Niko in front of the TV.

I could see that the lad was testing me, he wanted to push me to my limits. And I could understand that he was bitter and if I'd had the time to play his game, it would all have been different, it wouldn't have bothered me. But I was in a hurry. One lunchtime when Alexis was due to clock off work, I waited for him at the usual place to offer him a lift. The lad said no, just like he said no to everything I suggested, and I told him I was leaving soon. It was the worst thing I could have said. Because basically I was saying to the boy that our relationship had a deadline. Everything I'd built up, if I'd built up anything, by patiently trying to get close to him, collapsed in an instant. Alexis pursed his lips and paled. He looked like thunder.

'Are you going? That's fine, don't let's keep you. Who needs you?'

I realised that if I left now, it would take on huge proportions of genuine rejection and abandonment. Of all the goals I had set myself in my life, a relationship with my son was the most important. I couldn't leave and forget the boy, just like I couldn't forget his mother. How could I just go on with my life on the anthill. So, leaving was out of the question. I carried on going to the café and waiting for him after work, and didn't turn a hair when he refused my offer of a lift. I remained hopeful. Marina came back at weekends and if ever we met we exchanged a few formalities under Alexis's watchful eye. He loves his mother very much, he rates her very highly and guards her like Cerberus, ready to intervene if I overstep the mark. It cuts me to the quick that all this time they've had each other and I've been alone. Two of them with me as the enemy. But I like him for standing up for his mother. His furious pride. His faithfulness to the girl he loves. Marina has brought up a great kid. I knew there was nothing I could do but wait.

I told John he would have to cope without me. I had no idea when or how this journey would end. He was totally understanding as always. During all these years when I'd been single I had often taken on twice or thrice as much work to give him more time with his family, so he was happy to help me out.

Alexis had got into the habit of looking over to where I was waiting for him in the car when he clocked off work. He would see me there and then walk off indifferently, while I lowered the window, called out to him, and asked him the same question every time.

'D'you want a lift?'

'Thanks, I prefer the bus,' was his inevitably cold reply. But he would always look, as if he was waiting for the day when I wouldn't be there, because I would have got tired of it and left. So I decided that day would never come.

Time went by. August, and then mid-August, and the lad still showed no sign of giving in. He was stubborn, like the Haritakaíoi and the Anastasakaíoi both. My trial finally came to an end thanks to Aris Ilíopoulos. I didn't take to the *Kalamatianó*, I couldn't stand him actually. I've always had a problem with *-opouloses*, I consider them all wide boys, ever since the day Zafirópoulos sent me away to sleep on the streets when I was fifteen. Aris had a big mouth with fleshy lips and the thought that those lips might be kissing my Melénia drove me wild. But it was he who gave me my lucky break, one evening at Neo Oitylo. Kosmás had been asking me to go out for an ouzo and we finally did – me, Yiánnis, Pavlákos, Leoúsis and Kosmás. We saw the three of them eating at the same taverna down on the sea front. Aris, Marina and Alexis, chatting and laughing, the young lad completely at ease with that stranger, and Marina, smiling, as beautiful as a goddess!

I couldn't bear to look at them. For the first time I thought maybe I'd been wrong to try to get close to the boy. His mother was right, I couldn't force my presence upon him. It would only make us both miserable. No one becomes a father just by sleeping with a woman and getting her pregnant – that isn't fatherhood, it's participation. Fatherhood has to be earned, day after day. With caresses, games, reprimands, conflict, laughter, fairy stories. The way my own father had earned his. And the boy was right – nobody needed me any more. They were getting on fine – he was laughing.

No, I couldn't look at them. I got up from the table, apologised to the others and left without any explanation or excuse. I didn't go home. I walked along on the pebbles beside the breakers. I needed to get back to Boston. That's what I must do. Leave the boy and his mother in peace. I would get my return ticket tomorrow morning.

Then, lost in my thoughts, I weighed a pebble in my hand and skimmed it across the water so it skipped five times. To my surprise, another stone made exactly the same journey before sinking into the water next to it.

'Seven,' I heard Alexis's voice beside me. 'I beat you!'

I was so deep in thought that I hadn't heard his footsteps on the stones. He was standing right next to me, looking at me with those eyes of his. He'd spoken to me in the singular for the first time since he'd found out I was his father. I must have cut a pretty sorry figure – a miserable and lonely old man.

'Why did you leave?' asked the boy. 'You look a sight. You know what they'll be saying now behind your back?'

His voice was a little shaky. As he stood there right next to me, I noticed that he was nearly as tall as I was and he would probably be taller.

'I never care what people say behind my back. Nor in front of me, either. And I'm not at my best, that's true.'

'Because you saw us there?'

'Because I've made a mess of everything. You seem happy, the three of you, like a family. Maybe you're right, I don't fit into your life. I'm trying to force myself into it and making things hard for you. I'm sorry that I've caused you unhappiness.'

Something shone in his eyes and he turned round to look at the sea.

'We're not a family,' he said. 'Since when have we and Aris been a family? He's a colleague of my mother's and I think he's seriously hitting on her. He knows that to get her he'll have to get on with me. He's okay, he makes me laugh. But he isn't my father. You are.'

Now what was he playing at? I couldn't bear it! I opened my hands in desperation.

'What do you want me to do, *paidí mou*? I know I can't erase all those years of absence. I've lost fifteen years of your life. Your first word, your first steps, your first smile, your first day at school. All those firsts.'

The tears welled up, but I didn't try to hide it. 'Be honest with the boy,' his mother had said to me. But I was just tired of hiding things, I didn't care any more.

'Okay, but you haven't missed them all. Who gave me my first condoms?'

He smiled at me with that amazing smile of his mother's, his eyes shining.

'Tell me what you want me to do?' I whispered, on the verge of collapse. 'If you really want me to go, if you're so ashamed of me, if you never want to see me again, then tell me so. I'll do whatever you want.'

He turned and looked at me with tears in his eyes.

'Shall we go for a swim tomorrow afternoon? I'll take you for dinner afterwards.'

'Do you mean it?'

'If you want to, yes. My mother says you're a very good swimmer. But she didn't see how I beat you the other day.'

'Okay,' I said and wiped my eyes. 'But I'll take you for dinner.'

'Agreed. You tomorrow, me the next day. Let's go back now.'

I tried to refuse, I had no desire to go back to Marina's table, but the boy insisted.

'First of all, I want you near me. You've been away long enough. Secondly, it'll throw Aris off his stride. Thirdly, Kosmás won't sleep a wink all night for wondering what it's all about. Me, you and my mother at the same table. He's all of a flutter, just seeing me come after you.'

I smiled at the thought of Kosmás's unquenchable concern with other people's business, and followed Alexis obediently to the taverna. Maybe he was just using me against Aris, but for the first time he had shown signs of relenting and I couldn't risk refusing. We went to Marina's table and I sat down opposite her, with Alexis next to me. She looked at me coolly. The *Kalamatianó* looked astonished.

'I'm sorry, Alexis insisted that I came,' I said, apparently causing Aris Iliópoulos to choke on his ouzo.

'It's true. I don't want my dad to be on his own.'

The only person who wasn't surprised, but merely raised an enquiring eyebrow, was his mother. But even Iliópoulos rapidly regained his composure and soon we were chatting about the appalling economic situation and the measures of the IMF. We didn't like each other, which amused the boy. His mother appeared to be totally indifferent.

An hour or so later Alexis made a move to leave.

'Could you drop me back at home?' he asked me. 'I'm tired and I have work in the morning.'

I agreed, although I would have preferred not to leave Marina alone with Aris. We were both silent on the way back. I stopped the car in front of the tower house of the old enemy clan, with whom I was now bound by the strongest of human ties.

'I hope you meant what we agreed about tomorrow, and you didn't just say it to annoy Aris,' I remarked, suddenly afraid that the boy might just be toying with us for fun.

He lay back in his seat and laughed.

'He's a complete joke!' he said conspiratorially. Then he suddenly grew serious and looked at me. 'I would never have said a thing like that to you and not mean it. You know, when I was little, at nursery and in the first years of primary school, I used to dream that you would come to one of my open days, like all the other fathers, to hear me recite my poem. I'd work hard on it, with all the gestures and the right emphasis in the voice, and my mother helped me get it perfect. One year on Greek Independence Day at school, I played the role of Papaflessa, the priest who defied Ibrahim Pasha at Maniáki in 1825. *Pappoú* was there, and Uncle Vangélis, and Marina, naturally, first and best. And I waited for you. Something told me that this time you would come. My mother had told me you were tall, and I looked for you among all the tall men in the audience. When it was my turn to go on stage I realised you weren't there, yet again, and that the tall guy in the penultimate row wasn't you after all. I didn't say a word, I just burst out crying, right there, in front of everyone. My grandfather was disappointed. They all asked me why I was crying, but I wouldn't tell them. It was then that I realised you were never coming, not to any open day. I stopped waiting for you. I still took part in speech days but from then on I recited the poems as if I was reading out a shopping list. And when Effie first told me that you were coming back, I didn't believe her. Until we met.'

'I'm sorry,' I whispered and bowed my head. 'I didn't know—'

'And it's the same for you. It's as if you've been waiting for me to come all this time, and then this evening, I knew that you'd made up your mind I wasn't coming and you were about to leave. Isn't that right? And it's bad waiting for someone who doesn't come. I would never joke about that.'

I couldn't think what to say to this boy who had suffered so much on my account. If only I had known! But how could that be a comfort to him?

'I'm here now,' I said, as steadily as I could. 'And I'll never stop being with you, whatever happens.'

I had a lump in my throat. He grimaced, as if he couldn't quite believe me.

'That was what you said to my mother,' he chuckled, and opened the door to get out. 'Tomorrow. After work,' he said, slamming the car door behind him.

I watched him disappear into the house. Where was I when my son was born? Where was I when he needed me? Where was I when all the other kids were pushing him to his limits? I was working like a lunatic, unable to sleep, in and out of women's beds. If I had listened to Maggie, I would have been there at that speech day when Alexis was looking for me among the tall fathers in the hall. I would have been in the first row, I would have clapped when my son recited his poem. If I had come to find Marina after that first dizzy spell, I might be with her now, Aris might not have turned up, and I would have got to know my son. But I had been so stubborn and foolish. I thought I had the last word in my relationship with Marina and I was proud of that. But actually she had the last word. When she gave birth on her own and brought up my boy, in utter contempt of me. If Marina had wanted to, she could have stopped work and let me support both her and our child. Instead she took on two jobs to make ends meet. What had she tried to tell me when I wouldn't listen? That it wasn't her fault? That she regretted it? So what if she slept with somebody else behind my back, so what if she was full of lies. I loved her and I would give everything I owned and more, just to have one chance with her. 'I'm tired, Marina,' I wanted to tell her. 'Let's say I've grown old. I can't endure any more years of loneliness and sleeplessness. If only I could bury my face in your hair and sleep, and never wake up again ever. To die breathing in the scent of your hair.'

I don't know how long I stayed there with my head resting on the steering wheel. My life seemed to pass before me like it's supposed to when you're about to die. I would have cried had there been any point. But there was no point. Who could blame Alexis for not trusting me? Children are tough, they don't hesitate to show you your own face in the mirror. I had no room for any more mistakes.

*** 

At three thirty the next day I was waiting for him as usual in the car. He came, as promised, with his swimming things, and I asked him whether he preferred to go to Stoupa which had a sandy beach.

'Since when were Maniots afraid of rock? We're going to Limeni.'

He was an exceptional swimmer. I could match him on the short distances, but on longer stretches I couldn't keep up.

I watched him getting out of the water with his hair dripping, standing tall with his legs apart and his arms crossed. He reminded me of my father during those summers at Gytheio, when after work we would stand like that, side by side, looking at the sea. He was much more fit than I'd been at his age, probably due to the swimming. He had the long fingers and broad hands of the Anastaskaíoi, and black eyes. But his dark, chestnut hair and pearly smile were his mother's. An archangel.

We sat down together in the sun. He was looking at me too with equal interest and was the first to break the silence.

'Mr Anastasáko,' he said and looked at me thoughtfully.

'Yes, Mr Haritáko.'

'I have been thinking. I was thinking last night, and many nights before that.'

'Don't tell me that you've inherited my inability to sleep?'

'No.'

'Thank God.'

'I'm trying to tell you something else,' he went on hesitantly and I didn't interrupt him again. 'That there's no need for you to do all this.'

'What?'

He made a vague gesture with his hand.

'All this … I mean to say, you don't know me. Why should you go to the trouble? I've been unfair to you. You slept with my mother, for whom you didn't have much respect, and then I turned up. No one asked you about it, no one gave you a choice. Why should you be responsible …? I want to apologise for the way I've behaved. But if you look at it from my position … I had to be angry with someone and I can't be angry with my mother.'

He stopped talking and looked away. I coughed to get rid of the lump in my throat.

'You are right, no one gave me the chance to choose, nobody took the trouble to tell me. I don't know why your mother did that, but what's done is done and it can't be changed. You are my son and that is very important to me. I imagine that you know what happened … it's been pretty well broadcast. My father died to protect me. How could I not care about my own son? If you don't hate me too much … I mean … I'm sorry, I'm a bit overwrought … Would you like us to get to know each other a little?'

He looked at me then. We were both on the verge of tears.

'I don't hate you,' he said. 'But I don't want to feel obliged to you, and nor does my mother. That was why she didn't tell you. It's fine by me, but only if you really want it. I'd like to get to know you too.'

Hesitantly, I put out my hand to touch the boy's wet hair. A gesture which came so, so late … when my son no longer needed it. He was already a man.

'On one condition,' I tried to joke. 'I'm not asking you to call me father, that has to be earned and I haven't done anything to deserve it. But don't call me Mr Anastasáko. Call me Odysséa and address me in the singular. I'm not all that old …'

With tears on his eyelashes, he flashed me one of those exceptional smiles of his mother's.

'You said you were going to take me for dinner. Are you going to buy me an ouzo too?'

'You must be joking. Well … maybe one sip, with plenty of water. Your mother would kill me.'

He threw back his head and laughed.

'She's right when she says you're afraid of her,' he said, and got up. 'I'm as hungry as a wolf.'

***

The time I spent with the boy splashing about in the sea, competing at swimming and skimming stones – the kid beat me at both – was a new, fascinating experience. After my first date with Alexis it became a routine to go swimming every day and then eat together afterwards. Marina had gone back to Athens. I followed her advice to 'be genuine'. He was very bright, and I couldn't have hidden anything from him anyway. He told me how curious he'd been to meet me, and I told him how much I'd missed having a real relationship – and how a full wallet isn't enough to rely on. We tacitly agreed on the two things we would never mention again. One was Effie. I knew that the relationship wasn't over – they hadn't kept their promise not to see each other but I preferred to keep out of it and let Yiánnis deal with it if necessary. The other thing was Marina and the past. He never mentioned it and neither did I. The image he had of his mother was sacred and I didn't want to say anything that would spoil it.

I didn't have any dealings with Marina, I saw her rarely and by chance. Nevertheless she was everywhere. At the Haritákos's tower, where I went frequently to see her father and pick up Alexis, her scent was ubiquitous, and I found every excuse to go there. I felt her in the breeze coming off the sea at Limeni, and during my sleepless nights, breathing in the scent of the nightflower that seemed to blossom out of nowhere ever since I stepped back into my father's house. I had never forgotten her and now I was feeling just a tiny sense of doubt. Maybe it was I who had misjudged her. And maybe she still loved me too, if only a little.

After all, if she was such a shallow, vengeful schemer, then how could she have brought up this goodhearted, proud boy? Maybe I was wrong? A number of little things the boy said strengthened my doubts. He knew about the 'list of duties of a Maniot bride' I'd written to tease Marina. He had seen it, his mother had kept it. He knew about my weakness for *koutalídes* and honey, my love of sports cars, my obsession with safety belts and helmets. When I told him about my life in Boston, I could see that Alexis already knew quite a bit. About my apartment looking over the park, John, Maggie and even Lou. His mother had apparently tried to fill the gap of his absent father by talking about me at length. I thought she'd been poisoning his mind with lies, but it wasn't like that at all. 'My mother's been defending you all my life,' he said. In fact 'the poisoner' hadn't said one single bad word against me. No wonder he had granted her a halo and worshipped her like her namesake on the iconostasis in the church.

One Friday evening, Michális Haritákos cooked aubergines *imam* and called me over to eat with them. Just as we finished eating Marina arrived, weighed down with bags, wearing jeans, a T-shirt and trainers. She so much reminded me of Melénia as she came in through the door, I was transfixed. She kissed her father on the cheek and looked tenderly at Alexis.

'May I give you a kiss? Or not?'

'I'll give you a kiss, Marináki.'

He took her in his arms and whirled her round. They both laughed and she took the things into the kitchen as if it was the most natural thing in the world for me to be there. She came out again with a plate and a fork in her hand, and sat down to try her father's *imam*. Afterwards Alexis went to help her in the kitchen and I heard him ask his mother if she minded my being there. He didn't attempt to lower his voice. Either he didn't care if I heard her reply, or he was sure his mother wouldn't mind.

'I don't mind anything, so long as it makes you happy.'

'Do you mind about Mitsikoyiánnis's Effie? I'm going to ask her father if we can go to the show in town together. Odysséas thought he'd like it if I asked his permission.'

'Whose idea was it?' I heard her now turning serious.

'Mine. Effie's father thinks I'm a shifty type who has designs on his daughter. I want to show him that I'm an okay guy who has designs on his daughter. What d'you say?'

'That maybe he doesn't want any guy to have designs on his daughter. I asked you to be careful.'

'Yes, but Odysséas said ...'

'Odysséas doesn't know you,' she said crossly. 'What have you been up to? Speak.'

'Nothing,' said the boy, but he didn't sound particularly convincing. 'Whoever heard, in this day and age, of not being able to take a girl I like to a public event?'

I could hear every word. Clearly Alexis had started this conversation within earshot because he wanted me to take a stand, so I decided to join them in the kitchen.

'I'm sorry if I've put you in a difficult position,' I said.

She didn't try to hide her irritation.

'Right. The first rule when you're a parent is to learn to say no. Otherwise he'll have you on the back foot.'

'I'm sorry,' I mumbled. 'I'll ask you next time ...'

'The first rule, when you have to deal with Marináki,' Alexis smiled at me encouragingly, 'is to not let her frighten you. She does this kind of thing and *Pappoú* calls her the "general".' Then he gave us both a cheeky wink and went out into the garden. 'I'm going to find Mitsikoyiánnis,' he called to us from outside.

She was clearly annoyed, but she didn't want us to quarrel. She sat down with the table between us, like the last time we were there, and motioned for me to sit too. She sighed wearily, probably exhausted after work and so many hours of driving. I let her speak first.

'He's taking advantage of our lack of communication to do whatever he wants,' she said lowering her voice. 'We'll have to watch out for that. It's not going to be easy, but we have a duty to keep a united front on some things, at least the important ones, however hard that may be. We need to keep our personal issues out of it. I told him to keep away from the girls in the village, especially Yiánnis's daughter. He isn't used to not keeping his promises.'

'He's in love with Yiánnis's daughter,' I said. 'Whatever that means. He can't keep that promise, Marina. The night I came back I caught them both at my house. They'd got in by the millstone. I surprised them at it and they thought I was a tramp. Can you imagine? Said if I didn't tell on them they wouldn't tell on me.'

'And you didn't say anything?' she asked me in amazement.

'I promised not to. I didn't know whose children they were. It was they who found out who I was, and Alexis came up to me at the wake in a panic and asked me not to get his girlfriend into trouble. That's why I think it's better if they see each other with our knowledge, since they're going to meet whatever happens. They'll just go underground instead. I spoke to Yiánnis about it, but obviously I didn't tell him about the night at the tower.'

Tight-lipped, she got up and turned on the tap at the sink. Then she turned her back to me and started washing the dishes.

'Maybe you're right, I don't know,' she said uncertainly. 'Maybe you should handle it. I just worry.'

'I understand. I worry too. But I'll keep an eye on them, I promise. Let him go with her to the show, since he wants to. I'll persuade Yiánnis to break the embargo. He's punishing the kid because someone told him they were kissing at the party.'

She turned and looked at me helplessly, with soap suds on her hands.

'I feel so inadequate, so little, sometimes, Odysséa, now that the boy is growing up,' she said, and there was such despair in her voice, such sadness.

'How can you say such a thing? He's a fantastic kid. It's just that it isn't all that easy to say some things to your mother when you're only fifteen. Or to your father. But I'm not exactly his father, I'm a "guest star",' I said, trying to keep it light.

She pursed her lips again.

'I want to tell you,' she whispered, 'how sorry I am. I see you together and I realise that I did something dreadful. I deprived you of each other. But I couldn't …'

Yes, it was dreadful. But she wasn't the only one to blame. Where had I been all those years? Why did I never try to find out whether she was alive or dead? I couldn't look her in the eye and say it was all her fault, not after that night in Boston. She turned her back to me and went on washing the plates, lost in her thoughts. I wasn't sure if it was the right moment, but decided to risk it.

'Marina, I wanted to ask you if I could suggest something to Alexis.'

She didn't speak, but by the way her shoulders were slumped I knew that I had the upper hand.

'I wanted to ask him, if you agree obviously, to come to Boston for the Christmas holidays. I'll stay here as long as I can, but at the beginning of October I shall have to leave. I've already asked a lot of John. I can't come back again at Christmas, and I can't wait till Easter or next summer without seeing the boy. I'll go mad. That's why I'm asking you.'

She carried on washing up with her back to me.

'Okay,' she whispered.

'Really, you agree?'

She nodded.

'Thank you, Marina. I can't find the words.'

She didn't answer or turn round to look at me. I knew that our conversation was over. I couldn't admit what I really wanted, even to myself, so I didn't know what else to say to her. I got up and said goodnight. Her father was sitting smoking in his usual place at the table in the yard, distractedly jiggling his foot. He had heard every word of our conversation, but his face was a mask of serenity. He had no intention of getting involved. I said goodnight to him and went out into the road.

# The Puzzle

AS I WALKED THE EIGHT MINUTES that separated my house from
theirs, I thought of what Yiánnis had told me that morning when
I stopped off at his office for a chat. He had just come back from
Kalamata, where he had gone to negotiate a loan from his bank. He
was acting slightly oddly and I thought maybe something unpleas-
ant had happened to do with the loan.

'It's not about that,' replied my friend. 'It's something else that you
should know about and it's better if you hear it from me. Iliópoulos
has proposed to Marina. He's asked me to do up his house. He says
he wants it to be as lovely as possible for his wife.'

I was speechless. All these years Marina had never married, not
even when Alexis was a baby and she needed help bringing him up.
Why would she decide to do it now? If she married, Marina would
have the last word on our relationship, just when I was beginning to
have doubts, to wonder, to hope, to give in. I was deluding myself
in thinking that seventeen years of separation was a relationship, but
that was how I felt, and it had to do with Alexis. And when another
person is constantly on your mind, the way she had been all those
years, bound to you by love, by hatred, by absence, how else can you
describe it? I'd observed Aris's delicate white hands very closely while
he was holding his knife and fork. It was appalling to think of them
on Marina's body. On the body of my Melénia.

As I was passing Pavlákos's house on my way home, I saw the
former cop unloading some things from his car. He called me to
come in and I couldn't politely refuse. I didn't want to go home
anyway, my mind would just be on Marina. He was alone. His wife
and daughter had gone to his in-laws in Areopolis – he preferred to

stay and watch the football. He had taken the television out into the garden and was enjoying his ouzo with plenty of ice. He offered me one and asked if I had just come from Marina's. News in my part of the world travels fast, he knew all about Alexis and me – we hadn't tried to keep it secret. I myself had made sure to pass it on to Kosmás the *kafetzís*, which was the equivalent of announcing it to the entire Mani in one go. I didn't fancy any more comments about the boy, either in front of me or behind my back, and it was a good way of telling certain people that they would do well to watch out. I wasn't sure I'd be able to keep my cool if provoked and I didn't want to get into a fight.

'So he's yours then, the boy,' remarked my friend, and from his expression I could see that he wasn't in the least surprised.

'You policemen! Nothing escapes you!' I joked.

'We're nothing next to the *kafetzídes*. That was where I got my information from.' He was happy for Alexis, he said, and he meant it. I knew he loved the boy, I'd seen them together a few times – at the funeral and at the *kafeneíon*.

We concentrated in silence on the football, until half time. Then the cop went inside, came out with a plate of *synclino*, cheese, bread and tomatoes, and refilled the glasses with ouzo.

'It's all right for some! Aren't you a bit young to have taken retirement, Pavlákos?' I teased him.

'I never wanted to make money, unlike you,' he hit back. 'It was thanks to that friend of yours that I left early.'

'What friend, Thomá? I don't have any politician friends.'

'You know a few shipowners though. Kastrinós – may he rot in hell. Don't tell me you didn't know?'

Of course. Kastrinós. Pavlákos had been very high up in the police hierarchy when Kastrinós was murdered. He had been blamed for their failure to find the culprit and he had been forced to resign.

'The newspaper said it was a nasty murder.'

'The coroner called it heinous. He also said it was a sexual crime.

Do you know how they found him? On his yacht in Faliro, tied up, butchered like a lamb, with his testicles in his mouth, Mafioso-style. They cut his balls off while he was still alive and then they killed him. Got it? Naturally they didn't mention that in the newspapers. We had to put Marina through the inquest all for nothing.'

The words hit me like a bombshell. I didn't understand.

'What do you mean you had to put her through it?' I asked, confused.

'She was interrogated. She had to be. Witnesses had said that she had tried to kill him when she was just a child. And others said they'd heard her threaten him. What could I have done? I've never forgiven myself. I can hardly bear to look her in the eye. She never mentioned it, it was that other scum who told us. The bulldog he dragged around with him – his "helper". You remember him?'

Of course I remembered him. You could hardly forget him, he was enormous. There was no way you would want to mess with him. But what did Marina have to do with the murder of Kastrinós.

'What are you talking about?' I muttered. 'I don't understand a thing.'

'I'm talking about the abuse, *vre* Odysséa. Wasn't that why you left her? I thought you were a total *malákas* for doing it, naturally, and I imagine she feels the same, but there's no accounting for taste …'

I leapt up. The table with the glasses and the plate of *synclino* fell to the floor with a crash.

'What are you talking about?' I shouted at him wildly. 'What abuse? Have they sold you the same story too?'

'And what story would that be?' he said sarcastically. 'The things she endured when she was an eleven-year-old child?'

'Eleven?' I said angrily. 'Marina was twenty-five when I met her and she was Kastrinos's girlfriend. They set me up together. She hated me because of what happened to Yiorgís. She wanted to get close to me just to have her revenge and she managed it just fine. I would rather she had killed me, Thomá. Maybe I deserved that. But to sell me love on the one hand while selling herself to Kastrinós on the other …'

'Sit down, my friend.'

Thomás was looking at me as if he saw me for the first time. He stood up and pushed me gently back down into my chair. I was shaking.

'I think you have confused things,' he said dispassionately, trying to calm me. 'I don't know why you would believe such a thing, but one thing I do know and I know it for sure. Marina was never Kastrinó's girlfriend. The man was sick. He was a known paedophile, he hid his vice with money. Normally they lose interest in their victims once they've grown up. I don't know why he was so obsessed with Marina. He wouldn't leave her in peace and he paid with his life. Because, you see, he chose the wrong girl to muck around with. To be exact, he chose the wrong girl's relatives. There are people who don't much like it when you hurt their children, you know that for yourself. He wouldn't have got away with it if he were the pope, let alone Kastrinós.'

'Do you mean it was Haritákos …' I stammered.

'If I'd spent my entire life looking for proof, I'd never have found it. A cool operation, set up from inside prison. With messages left to make it abundantly clear: "This is what I do to anyone who touches my daughter." I'm sure that just as the murderer was cutting off his balls and stuffing them in his mouth, he was simultaneously sending his congratulations to *Bárba* Micháli. Why you were let off I can't imagine.'

'It can't be,' I murmured. 'I asked her and she told me …'

For seventeen years I'd had her confession ringing in my ears. 'Yes, I slept with Kastrinós and yes he paid me.' Why would she tell me such a thing?

My friend placed the ouzo bottle in my hand and I took a great, burning swig of it.

'After you finished with her, the kid was in a mess,' said Thomás.

'When she found out she was pregnant with Alexis, she went to see her father in prison. She told him straight out that she was going to have the child come what may and told him about Kastrinós. It was the first and last time she ever spoke about it. I tell you, she didn't breathe a word even at the inquest. The old man decided to act. It wasn't just what he had done to Marina when she was an eleven-year-old child, it was the fact that he was still threatening her and wouldn't leave her in peace. Haritákos was afraid for his daughter. Then there was a breakout from the prison. Three men escaped one night. One by one, silent as mice. And two days later, we found Kastrinós like I told you. I don't know exactly what favour they were repaying Haritákos, but no money changed hands – he didn't have any, and they were empty-handed when we caught them a month later. We grilled them at the inquest, but they didn't breathe a whisper.

'Tell me about the abuse,' I managed to stammer.

And then Pavlákos described, as Kastrinós's bodyguard had described to him, how children came and went from the yacht, and how Marina had fallen into his clutches when her mother became ill.

'Marina at eleven years old was unusually mature and as lovely as ever. A delicious *mezedáki*. And you know what happens to lonely and unprotected *mezedákia*? Whoever fancies one puts out his hand and pops it in his mouth.'

Pavlákos brought out some more ice and refilled my glass. We sat in the garden and he told me everything he knew about Marina's life. Much of it he had heard from Potítsa and Aretí. The rest he had pieced together from his own involvement in Kastrinós's murder case.

\*\*\*

Six months after the arrest of Michális Haritákos, his wife locked her house and put the key in her pocket. She took Marina by the hand and with her teenage son Sotíris slouching along behind her, she went down to Areopolis to catch the KTEL bus to Sparta and from there to Athens. The sun was high in the sky, a strong wind blowing them along as if it was chasing them away. Haritákaina's last glance was towards the cemetery, where under the warm earth her youngest son, her darling, had been laid to rest. Her belongings consisted of just two suitcases – she carried one, Sotíris the other – and a few thousand drachma notes folded in a cloth and tucked into her bodice. She had to pay the lawyer and needed money for the first few days, until she could find work and a roof over her head. So she had sold her dowry at Diro – a few strips of olive trees. If it had been up to her she would have sold their property in the village as well, but Michális wouldn't hear of it. Those olives and the tower house were Sotíris's, he said, he would go back there one day and keep up the family name.

All along the road to Athens, so many kilometres of bad road, Haritákaina, wearing a black headscarf, leant against the window and gritted her teeth. She knew that her eldest son Sotíris was a lost cause ever since the day that evil happened with the gun. It was as if he had sunk into a quicksand of despair and misery and couldn't get out of it, however much she tried to grab hold of him and pull him back to life. She couldn't help him because he wouldn't hold out his hand to her. It was as if he really wanted to follow his brother to the grave. Something was troubling the boy and it gnawed away at him from inside, like woodworm.

In scorching, dusty Athens, Katerina Haritákou put herself and her children into a taxi, her suitcases into the boot, and showed the driver a piece of paper with an address on it. It was a narrow street in Keratsiní, where her cousin, Argyroúla, who lived in a tiny house, was happy to give her refuge for her first difficult few days in the big city. She only had two rooms in all, but friends, relatives and neighbours from the Mani and from her husband's village outside Agrinio, were always welcome to stay when they were driven to Athens by life and by necessity. Státhis, her husband, was open-hearted, shared the crust he worked hard to earn with anyone who turned up, and Argyroúla cooked, fed and put people up without giving it a second thought. They had two boys around the same age as Yiorgís, lively, boisterous and rosy-cheeked. It was hard to be miserable in that house, but the Haritakaíoi could not forget their grief. Haritákaina mourned her lost son and even more her lost life when she saw Argyroúla with her 'Vlach', as the Maniots called him. Her own Maniot husband wasn't worth his little finger, never supported his family as he should, and had proved small-minded, graceless and little.

Sotíris left the house for hours at a time. Nobody knew where he went, he didn't speak to anyone. And when he returned and his mother asked him where he'd been, all he said was 'leave me alone'. Marina was eight years old. As soon as she arrived in Argyroúla's house, clinging to her mother's skirts, a tiny wee thing with a black ribbon of mourning in her hair, she got to work. Endless was the work to be done in her aunt's house, and endless the demands of the men, her uncle, her cousins, Sotíris, friends and acquaintances. Cooking, washing, ironing, piles of laundry to be taken off the line, piles of laundry waiting to be washed. Nevertheless Haritákaina registered her for her third year at the primary school, and never lost a chance to tell her, from morning until night: 'Make sure you learn to read and write, get a certificate, so you can hold your head high and never depend on anyone.' Her mother gave these words of advice with such despair in her voice, it was inevitable that they would find their mark, at least in Marina. Sotíris was another matter.

He had been registered to finish the sixth form at night school, but he couldn't keep his mind on the lessons. With the help of the Vlach, he found a job in the mornings at a petrol station, but his mind wasn't on his work either.

'If I sent that nephew of yours to the sea to fetch water, he wouldn't be able to find it.' The boss told the Vlach, who bowed his head in shame.

'The boy's been through a lot, Theodori, give him a chance …'

'It's you I'm keeping him on for, you know that.' The other guy shrugged his shoulders. 'But the work needs to be done. We all have a living to make.'

They stayed at Argyroúla's house for three months, sleeping on mattresses in the sitting room. At the beginning of the third month Haritákaina found work at a rich house in Palaio Psychiko. The Vlach had managed it again, through one of the friends he had fed and housed in the past, and who 'drank his health with water' as a result. He had come from the same village and lived in their house for three whole years, his first difficult student years in Athens. After that he trained as a shipbuilder at the Polytechnic and did his post-graduate training in London, where he got to know the shipowners. So it was with a shipowner that Haritákaina found work. He was looking for a respectable, clean and trustworthy woman to take care of his house. That was how she was introduced and so she proved to be. Every morning and evening she made the journey from Keratsiní to Palaio Psychiko and back.

Marina's father was sentenced to life imprisonment for the murder of Anastasákos. They took into account his hitherto blameless life, and his shock at seeing his dead son, but his lawyer couldn't do much. It wasn't possible to prove that Anastasákos had deliberately killed Yiorgís. The old vendetta wasn't enough of a motive, and the character of the boy's killer made it seem unlikely. Haritákos had said himself that his son's killer had come like a lamb to the slaughter, and didn't even try to deny the blame. After the sentencing, Haritákos's family regularly visited him in prison. He cut a tragic figure, a shadow of the man he had been in the Mani. Sotíris too, lost in his own world, went about like a silent ghost in the house. And Haritákaina, wrung out by exhaustion and grief, was herself little more than a ghost.

Marináki negotiated her way through this world of ghosts clinging to her mother's black skirts. She held her head high and did all the housework so that her mother could catch a moment of rest. But there were no hugs for poor Marináki, no kisses, and no caresses. Her parents were not dead, and yet she was more or less an orphan.

The family moved to a two-roomed flat a couple of months after Haritákaina got work. The Vlach 'loaned' her the deposit on the flat and she bowed her head and tearfully kissed his hands. The flat was only a block away from Argyroúla's and the cousins continued to see and to help each other. Time rolled on. Her mother and Sotíris left for work at dawn, and then Marina went to school and was first back home. She tidied up, washed, cooked and then opened her books on the kitchen table. At four her brother came back. Marina gathered up her books and served the food. He sat there in silence, fiddled with his food for a while without appetite and then shut himself away in his room, while she cleared the table and opened her books again, waiting for her mother to come back late at night.

One day at about three in the afternoon, when Sotíris hadn't yet come home, the doorbell rang and Marina rushed to open it thinking it was Aunt Argyroúla, with her tinkling laughter and warm hugs. But instead of her aunt, it was Potítsa standing at the door, and the little girl took a step backwards in fright.

She recognised Potítsa perfectly well, of course. She had often come by their house in the Mani, especially when her mother was out, and Potítsa and her father would shut themselves away in the bedroom. Although Marináki was little, she knew very well that this was wrong. If her mother found out she would cry and quarrel with her father again, and Marina couldn't bear to see it or hear it. There was nowhere in the house to hide from the shouting and the wailing. One afternoon coming home from the fields with her mother – it was autumn, they had gone to gather wild greens for a pitta – they had reached the doorstep and heard Potítsa laughing inside. Her mother stood with her hand on the latch, pursing her lips. And then she dragged Marina back to the fields they'd just come from.

'Where are we going, Mother?'

'For greens. We don't have enough for the pitta.'

Katerina knew that Potítsa was sleeping with her husband, and the whole village knew it too. But that was the least of her worries. She needed to keep her children fed, washed and clean, and make sure that nothing was lacking in her home. As for Michális … Theirs was an arranged marriage, as was usual at that time and not only in the Mani. Parents gave their daughter a dowry and an agreement was made. She had seen him just once at a *panegyri*, he was sitting two tables away. 'Do you like him?' her brothers had asked. He wasn't lame and he wasn't blind. He was well built and a hard worker. It wasn't as if she could expect anything better. She agreed, but the marriage never took. They coupled at night, but in daytime they were still two strangers forced to live under one roof. That was why when she found out about Potítsa she wasn't even jealous, she just felt bitter at the ingratitude of the man who shared her life, and with whom she had three children, two sons and a daughter. And she felt ashamed. Very. Both for the children and for herself.

When Potítsa came to their door in Athens, she put out her hand to stroke the child's head, but Marina pulled away. 'How are you, my little bird?' Marina didn't have much to defend her mother with, but what she had she used. She shut the door in the face of her astonished visitor and went back to her homework. She said nothing to Katerina about the visit, and prayed hard that the woman who brought misery into people's homes would never come back. Her prayer wasn't answered, because Potítsa was a neighbour now; she had left the Mani and lived only two blocks away. She visited again when her mother was in, and Marina heard them talking about Alexis Anastasákos and his wife Fotiní. 'I don't bear you any ill for almost destroying my home without a second thought,' Haritákaina said. 'I feel sorry for you, for being led astray by men, and for leading them on – all of them – except for the only man you really cared for. And he wouldn't have wasted his spit on you.' Then Potítsa wept. And Marina's mother just stood there, upright and dry-eyed.

Twenty-two years later, when Marina and her father had made peace with the past, Marina asked him: 'Did Potítsa have anything to do with Anastasákos's murder?'

The old man looked long and hard at his daughter and answered: 'I'd hardly go to prison for a prostitute.'

There was no more to be said. They had no secrets between them. Alexis was three years old by now, Haritákos had come out of prison and went regularly to the Mani, and tried to put what was left of his property into some kind of order. The tower house in the village and the olives. Their first concern was to fix the house, to stop it falling round their ears. They hadn't much money, but Marina managed to secure a reasonable loan to renovate her family home. It didn't have the modern luxuries that Odysséas's tower had, but none of the essentials were lacking. Apart from the money, Marina contributed the innate good taste that made her look like a goddess in a T-shirt and cheap jeans, and her father put in enthusiasm and handiwork. He was good with his hands, and doing up the house was just what he needed to get him back on his feet after so many years in prison. All was not lost. The house in the Mani was upstanding and there was Alexis, who one day would be its master.

Marina tidied up her father just as she tidied up the house. She dressed him in new clothes, bought him shoes, took him to the hairdresser to trim his moustache and cut his hair. She didn't want them going back to the Mani like beggars, it didn't suit them. They had been one of the first families in the area. So what if they'd fallen on hard times, they were still proud. A lion is always a lion. With her son's first lullabies she had taught him to be proud. From the ashes of their tragedy, she had built a protective wall of relatives and foster relatives around the boy. First and foremost herself, then his grandfather, his uncle Vangélis, her foster brother, and two more grandparents – her foster parents whom she still saw – and finally the old folk in the Mani, Nikifóros and Aretí, the chain that linked the boy with his father and his father's roots.

Marina ruled over the men in the family like a true *Maniátissa*, with iron discipline and boundless love. She didn't have a lot of faith in the old man to begin with, but Haritákos pleasantly surprised her, by the way he received the news of his illegitimate grandson and the devotion he showed him. That was enough for a mother to forgive him the 'indiscretions' with Potítsa that had so embittered Katerina, along with everything else. And from the wreckage of their household Marina built the tower house to stand tall again, so she could hand it over one day to her son, as was her duty.

Marina made her peace with Potítsa one afternoon when Alexis was still little, and they were on their way back from swimming at Limeni. She had forgotten to buy water. The boy was hungry and tired, and so out of necessity she went to Kosmás's shop. Until then she had always avoided it, knowing his tendency to gossip. Kosmás was there and he was alone. He gave her half a dozen bottles of water, for which he refused to be paid, and then he stretched out his hands and made a coarse gesture. Perhaps it was the heat, or the tired grumbling of the child in the car, or maybe it was just everything that had been building up inside Marina for years and this was the last straw, but in any case the *kafetzis* found himself face to face with a wild tigress. She attacked him with her teeth and nails with such violence he was almost too shocked to defend himself.

At that moment Potítsa came in to buy orange juice. She saw it all, or at least most of it, and guessed the rest. She had always felt guilty for telling Nikifóros after she'd recognised Marina with Odysséas all those years ago. She hadn't believed for one second that Marináki was capable of plotting vengeance and betrayal and had never forgiven herself for unwittingly splitting them up, as she saw it. And she had known straight away whose child Alexis was, because he looked so like his father as a boy. She had dandled Odysséas on her knee countless times when he was Alexis's age. She joined in Marina's attack on Kosmás without a second thought. She threatened to tell his wife everything and told him not to dare hit on Marina again or he'd have her to contend with.

They left without their water and orange juice, Marina drove back to Areopolis to shop and Potítsa went with her. Alexis had fallen asleep in his car seat. Potítsa stroked his hair.

'The boy has a father,' she said to Marina, 'and his place is here to protect the boy. He shouldn't be thousands of miles away, without a care in the world, leaving you to manage all alone.' Marina didn't deny it, she knew there was no point. She looked into the back seat to make sure Alexis was sleeping, and told Potítsa that she wasn't intending to say anything to the boy's father. A child first and foremost belongs to its mother, the one who has the power of life or death from the moment it starts growing as a vulnerable seed in her belly. 'What is a child to a man?' she asked angrily. 'What would Alexis be to his father? A burden that he's saddled with all of a sudden, to bear for the rest of his life.' There was perhaps no one in the world who understood Marina better at that moment than Potítsa, who had three sons and hadn't bothered to inform any of their fathers of their existence. She swore she would never tell anyone. And yet it was she who had told Aretí Dimákou.

So when Dimákaina stopped Marina after church on Christmas Day and asked if she would bring the boy to visit them at New Year, Marina wasn't surprised, she'd been expecting it. Up till then Aretí had never spoken to her, although Marina had tried to approach the old folk. Aretí blamed Marina for Odysséas's having left them a second time. Now, thanks to Potítsa, Marina had another chance to get close to them, and find out a little more about Alexis's father, and so she wasn't angry with Potítsa for telling Aretí. The secret stayed between the three women. Nikifóros was never told, because he couldn't have kept it from Odysséas. He accepted Marina's presence in the house because his wife insisted, although she couldn't quite explain it. And he was won round by Marina and the way she cared for his old lady and him when they needed help.

Life hadn't been easy for Marina, she had lost her illusions early, but she wasn't a person to give up. Scarcely two years after their arrival in Athens Sotíris was killed, and although he had left them some time before, and had always been more absent than present, his death was more than Haritákaina could bear. She fell ill almost at once and the doctors said it was cancer. They left the flat in Keratsini and moved into the little house in her employer's garden, so that Katerina could go for her chemotherapy in the family's car. The illness lasted for three years and ended with her death. Katerina prayed it would come quickly and release her. She died blessing her 'good' employer who had cared for her and given her his word that he would take care of her daughter. How could she know? Marina was terrified that if she told anyone what was happening to her, her mother would be left to die in the street like a dog. And the shame of it would kill her even sooner, a shame that Marina herself would drag around with her as long as she lived and breathed, just like Odysséas with his Erinyes. So she kept quiet.

But the very same evening that she lost her mother, her abuser visited her again, with the arrogance now of absolute master, and this time she was ready for him – there was nothing left to lose. She took a kitchen knife she'd hidden under the sheet, and did the 'woman's work' that Kastrinós had boasted about – two deep cuts in his thigh. All hell broke loose. The abuser shrieked like a little girl. The 'kind family' threw her out into the street and she was taken in by social services. She lived for a year in a girl's borstal, a year she hardly remembered, except for her black misery and the red blood that hadn't been sufficient to wash away her shame. She had deep burn marks from cigarettes on her body – her punishment for failing to comply when she hadn't been a 'good girl' – and her soul had many more scars. When Myrto Yalanoú, her foster mother, took her on, she was able to see beyond the little girl's lifeless gaze to her own dead daughter, lost to leukaemia six months before. She needed a daughter and Marina needed a mother. Myrto took her in for a trial at first, to the little house in the Plaka, and for weekends at their country house in Loutsa. She often called her by the dead girl's name – Aphrodite – and Marina didn't mind; she liked being the other little girl smiling happily in the photograph beside her bed. She didn't have any scars on her. Death had taken her untouched.

Marina already knew how to help around the house. She lovingly took care of their disabled father, and looked after her new brother, Vangélis, and through the love in that house she gradually healed. Old memories were replaced by new ones, summers in Loutsa, learning to swim and feeling safe under Vangélis's guidance. He took her out to the cinema in Athens – something her own brother had never done – and was proud to have her at his side. Myrto showed her how to lay a fine table and how to make fancy cakes with Chantilly cream. She was a good listener and thirsty for knowledge, so for hours on end she would listen to their crippled father as he translated extracts from Homer, Herodotus and Xenophon. But she never forgot, and the past was always lurking, ready to engulf her. When she first saw Odysséas on the stone terrace she recognised him at once. She remembered him very well, the way younger children tend to remember older ones. However he did not recognise her. She always used the name Aphrodite Yalanoú for work, her dead foster sister's name, because nobody would want a teacher whose father was a hardened criminal. At first Marina tried to keep her distance from Odysséas, but she failed. She could sense that she had nothing to fear from him. He was a victim of the same tragedy that had marked her. That was why she followed him to the Mani and stood outside his family home, and encouraged him to go inside. It was the first time she had found the courage to go back to her own home.

But you carry your past around with you like a tortoise its shell. And when Kastrinós found her at Olympios's house he wouldn't leave her in peace for a second, even though he was now married for the third time. He knew the grim secret of her abuse and threatened to reveal it to her employers – which she hardly minded – and later to Odysséas, who by now had become a part of her life. The thought of it made her feel sick. She was bound in a vicious circle of lies she didn't know how to explain. One thing she did know. She would never again be at the mercy of Kastrinós, or of anyone else and she would rather kill or be killed. She announced to Kastrinós in front of the bulldog that if he made the mistake of coming near her again, he was a dead man. Then Kastrinós, either for revenge or some kind of sick obsession, arranged the attempted rape in the garage and paid the Georgian to persuade Stefanos into it when he was high on cocaine. He didn't reckon on Odysséas, or the two of them falling in love. Nevertheless he managed to wreck everything by telling the young lover a version of the truth, cut and patched to suit his own purpose. A truth that Marina couldn't deny, uncertain where the lies began and ended, and still reeling from the fact that she now found herself sleeping with her younger brother's killer.

One year later, unable to endure her loneliness and the distance separating them, she had forgiven Odysséas everything, and was determined to make one last try, to crawl and beg and plead. By then her father had confessed the truth, that Sotíris had taken the gun on that cursed afternoon and loaded it himself, and left it there waiting, fatally, for Yiorgís. Sotíris, the proud leader of their children's games, had finally told his father during his last visit to prison, before he finally sank into his misery, incapable of coping with the guilt.

But by the time she got to Boston, Odysséas had already forgotten her and was about to start a life with another woman. She came back humiliated, but the child about to be born absorbed all her emotions. Then when she had Alexis, nothing else mattered. She heard about Odysséas marrying the *Japonéza*, and she heard that they separated. At first Marina had waited for him. But clearly she meant nothing to him. She was just one woman among many. She should never have let herself be so exposed. But there is no evil without something good, and she had Alexis. And once whoever it was – may his hand be blessed for it – was persuaded to kill the child abuser, she was able to rest easy.

Men were always attracted to Marina like a magnet, but she had finished with love, as a passion at least. A few casual relationships, to meet the needs of her body, were kept well away from her son and her home. Just sometimes, when loneliness overwhelmed her like a frost, she would allow herself to be led astray by the persistent flirting of some tender admirer, and there were many such, fellow teachers at school, colleagues at the orphanage. But these were rare occasions, and each time she felt more frozen than before, rushing home to warm her soul from her son's black eyes, so like his father's. However much she tried, she never stopped thinking of him and she never stopped hurting.

***

'But why didn't she tell me?' I asked Pavlákos, when he had finished telling me about Marina's life.

'Do you know what it means to be an abused child, Odysséa? Why do you think she works in the orphanage as a volunteer? She told me about a girl called Milena, twelve years old, a little Albanian. She adored that little girl, although the psychologists told her that it was a mistake. Because to really be able to help, you have to keep a distance. To make the right decisions and protect yourself from being worn down by it all. The child had been raped many times by her uncle, who threatened to kill her mother and her younger siblings if she told anyone. Her body was covered in scars. Burn marks. She was still so terrified, she couldn't bear to be touched. She would flinch whenever someone held out their hand to her. Marina saw herself in that child, permanently scarred by her past. And you, instead of protecting Marina, even you left her, for something that had happened without her consent years before. You effectively told her she would never escape it.'

'I didn't know. Kastrinós told me that he was paying her and she admitted it.'

'She told you the truth. He always left her a pile of thousand drachma notes on the table and they were living in his house for free. But Marina isn't that kind of girl. I remember her when she first started coming here. Alexis must have been three then, when her father left prison. She was radiant, a real *neraida*. We all wanted her. Even me. But we were left to want. Because we knew she wouldn't have us.'

I looked at my friend in desperation.

'She's going to marry Aris now,' I muttered.

'And she's right. Aris is a good lad, he'll look after her. Not like some others …'

At this I sprang out of my chair again and almost fell over.

'Cut it out, Thomá. Haritákos isn't the only one to kill a person. I have too. And right now I'm very close to it. All those years wasted! Why didn't you tell me?'

'Tell you what? I thought you were pissed off because she hid it from you that she was Haritákos's daughter. That that was why you didn't want her. She's the daughter of your father's murderer, after all. And because of the old story with Kastrinós. Have you any idea the things I've seen with these eyes of mine? Men who after their wives have been raped never want to see them again.'

I stumbled out into the road and it wasn't because of the ouzo. The pieces of the puzzle where practically all in place. The orphanage for abused children. Marina herself was an abused child. 'You don't know what you're talking about,' she had said when I mentioned Kastrinós. My conversation with Kastrinós on the boat, that muscle that twitched in his face. His expression, when he realised that she functioned with me like any normal woman. The two scars on his thigh. And the look in her eyes, when she realised that I knew about Kastrinós. 'Kill me!' she had said. I had lost my Melenia. No one else was to blame. I was to blame. Because I was so stubborn and I never gave her the chance to explain. I wasn't worthy of the paradise I was offered. I wasn't worthy to be Alexis's father and that was why she never told me about it. I was too small for the gift life had offered me.

I felt dizzy. So many years wasted. So many sleepless nights. So many meaningless embraces, and all the while Melénia had been bringing up our son on her own, waiting for someone who came back far too late.

I went back home and found my bottle of whisky and my cigarettes. Tonight I wanted to get plastered. I went up to the tower, to the bedroom I had shared with Marina when I used to call her Melénia and dreamt that I would spend my whole life with her. Instead I broke her heart and left my son to grow up alone, the village bastard. 'I already know you and I don't like you at all,' he had said. How right you were, my boy.

From the lookout I could see the tower of the Haritakaíoi. Someone was awake. Might it be her? If my mobile hadn't gone off, I would have finished the bottle. I would have drunk myself unconscious. But Alexis's voice at the other end of the line brought me down to earth. 'There is nothing worse than to see your father drunk,' my mother used to say. I didn't want my son to despise me. I wanted him at least to respect me, even if he couldn't love me.

'Odysséa, I've done it, he's letting us go to the dance together,' the boy said excitedly.

'Well done, *koróna mou*.'

'He did say that we weren't to go off alone …'

'Which you were intending to do?'

'To be honest … But I gave him my word and I'll keep it. Will you do me a favour, Odysséa?'

'Anything you like.'

'Will you bring us back home afterwards? My mother is going to Athens on Sunday.'

'Of course I will, my boy, and I'll let Yiánnis know.'

He said goodnight. I picked up the whisky bottle and put it away. I put out my cigarette. There was no room for any more mistakes. I had lost Melénia and the chance that God had given me to be happy. I wasn't going to lose my son as well. I turned off the light, got undressed and lay down on the bed. I closed my eyes and floated away on my memories. Melénia was sleeping next to me, satisfied and happy after making love, her breathing in rhythm with my own. I was holding her in my arms and stroking the velvety skin on her back. Her hair smelled of jasmine. 'I'm crazy about you,' she had said just before falling asleep. And, later, on that cursed morning when Kastrinós phoned and I went to see her: 'I'm crazy about you.' And I had raised my hand and struck her. Tears were streaming down my cheeks. I didn't wipe them away. I let myself cry.

# Why?

'NOTHING IS WHAT IT SEEMS,' my grandfather had said, and it applies to everything, from what I've discovered. Odysséas isn't the person I thought he was, nor is Mitsikoyiánnis. I didn't tell him about me and Effie making love during the party, not because I was afraid he would tell on us – he kept quiet when he didn't know he was my father, he isn't going to give us away now. But I don't want to upset him. Because he would feel bad about keeping it from Mitsikoyiánnis, he would feel responsible and that isn't fair. I haven't seen Effie since the party. Her father got to hear about us kissing during that slow dance. If I knew the wanker who blabbed, I would make him regret it and think hard before opening his mouth again. For two weeks now, Effie has been going everywhere in Areopolis with a chaperone, and we don't dare to meet in the village. Now I have her father's permission to take her out, so there's nothing to worry about. It's true that we'll be in the square with hundreds of people and our friends all around, and I gave my word that we would stay in full view. But still, it's something. We'll be side by side, we'll touch each other, I'll hold her hand. I'm glad because she sounds different and distant on the phone. It's as if what happened between us has pushed us further apart instead of bringing us closer. Did it really happen? I ask myself sometimes whether it was a dream.

I can't get to sleep tonight. I went to the kitchen to get some water and I found my mother sitting on her own in the dark. My grandfather was snoring in the bedroom and the crickets were chirruping outside. I could feel her sadness running like a shudder through my body.

'I'm amazed I ever sleep with two owls for parents,' I said, trying to lighten the atmosphere. 'He doesn't sleep either.'

'It's hot. No one can sleep tonight.'

'Hardly! Grandfather's snoring. And Odysséas has air conditioning. It's not the heat that's stopping him. But what's wrong with you?'

I sat down next to her and stroked her hands. Her eyes were heavy with worry; she couldn't deceive me. She and I are too close for that.

She squeezed my hand.

'*Aléxi mou*, your father has asked whether I'll allow you, if you want to, of course, to go back to Boston for the Christmas holidays. What do you think?'

'He hasn't said anything to me …'

'He hasn't had a chance yet. He wanted to talk it over with me first. Because I was angry about Mitsikoyiánnis.'

'Is that what's bothering you? Is that why you can't sleep?' I took her by the shoulders. 'What are you afraid of, Marináki? Don't you want me to go?'

She hugged me tight.

'On the contrary, I want you to go. It will do you good to get to know your father. You get on well, I can see that. It's just that I'll miss you. It'll be the first time you've ever been so far away from me. But I'm not going to keep you tied to my skirts.'

She's afraid, I can feel it. I don't know what exactly frightens her. Before I met Odysséas it was very easy to say that everything was his fault. The shadows in my mother's eyes, her loneliness, his absence. But it isn't so easy now. I don't know how much he's to blame, but I do know he isn't the total scumbag I thought he was. The more I get to know him, the more I can see that he is a charismatic person, very clever, exceptionally so. But Marina has been and always will be queen of my heart.

'*Ach vre Marináki*,' I said to comfort her. 'Don't be afraid. You know we all only have one mother.'

She was ashamed that she'd let me see her fear.

'I want you to be all right. You. Not me. That's the only thing that matters to me. You won't lose out by getting to know your father. Despite the things that have kept him and me apart, he's a worthwhile person.'

Wonderful Marina. Who always puts herself last. Okay then, Mum. I'll tell him yes. If it's just to see with my own eyes what kind of man it was who turned you down. How this guy, who cries because he has a son he doesn't know, who suffers when I won't let him close to me, whom I've ignored and driven mad, and who insists on making a fool of himself over me even though he doesn't know me, who is terribly busy, but leaves everything so he can wait for me to finish work and offer me a lift home, just so I can tell him to piss off. How a guy like that could have been so hard on you!

# Keep Looking Ahead

MOST EVENINGS WHEN I took Alexis back home from work, I sat with his grandfather in the yard to drink a glass of wine, or share a piece of watermelon, depending on the time of day. The old man liked to talk about Alexis, scrapes he'd got into, things he'd said that showed attitude and brains. Nobody would have ever believed that the kind little old man, besotted with his grandson, had committed two murders. The first in anger. But the second – the atrocity that had been carried out at his command with true savagery – with total awareness and premeditation. He seemed so at peace, so reconciled with life and with his actions. On one of those evenings, Alexis had come out to say goodnight, and when he left us the old man looked deep into my eyes and said: 'I would kill anyone who harmed Alexis.'

He'd said it to me once before, at my Aunt Aretí's funeral. At the time I thought it was a threat, but now I knew that it was a confession, and who better to listen to it than another murderer like himself? I returned his look with equal intensity.

'I would too,' I said, with complete conviction. I had inwardly absolved Haritákos for the death of my father, but for the other murder I felt something more like gratitude. He smiled sadly and patted me on the shoulder.

'I know,' he replied. 'That's why I can rest easy. I'm old, you see, very old. But now that I know you'll look after them, I don't mind if I die. I know that whatever happens, you'll be there for Alexis and Marina. Isn't that right? Don't think badly of her any more, my son. She was a little girl and we left her alone, and she had the bad luck to be beautiful and draw all the vultures to her. What could she do, the poor little thing? And yet, she didn't give up.'

'I loved her very much,' I whispered. 'I swear it, Uncle Micháli. I made terrible mistakes, I know it. If only you had told me about the boy! If she had just spoken to me!'

'She didn't want to tell you. I was still in prison when she came and told me she was pregnant and you were the father. She was white as a sheet from morning sickness, all skin and bone. The lad was lively even when he was still in her belly. She told me she would die if you found out, and I believed her. I've lost two sons, you know. And I wasn't at home to take care of her. I was very afraid. I promised her anything she wanted. "Never you mind," I said to her. "You and I will bring him up together. Who needs Anastasákos?" So she calmed down a bit, she took heart, she told me what had happened, and the rest you know.'

He bowed his head and was silent. And then I told him about my falling in love with Marina, as she sat with the boys on the stone terrace in the garden, and how I'd fought for her and won her. I told him about my first return to the Mani, when she'd been waiting in front of my house, and the night at Kalamata. I hid nothing from him. Not even my first infidelity or what happened afterwards. I told him about Kastrinós, that he had set a trap for us both, about my conversation with Marina when I found out who she really was, and my leaving. I told him about Marina's journey to Boston. I had exonerated Haritákos in my heart and felt the need to make my own confession. And it was true that had he not killed Kastrinós I would have done it myself with my own bare hands.

There was still something that bothered me. I wanted Alexis to have my name and to become my heir. So I informed Maggie to make a few changes to my will and told her I would sign it as soon as I got back to Boston. When I discussed the matter of his name with the boy, however, things went exactly as I had predicted.

'I've been Haritákos all my life,' he said. 'That isn't going to change.'

'But you are Anastasákos too,' I reminded him, and I felt hurt because the distance between us wasn't at all easy to bridge after all these years of absence. Father and son – and yet, two strangers.

'I can't suddenly become a different person,' he insisted.

There was no point in pressing him. At heart I liked it that the boy respected the name of his grandfather and didn't want to upset him, and that he didn't care about his own self-interest and property compared to what he believed to be right. So I found a compromise.

'Would you like us to add the Anastasákos in second place? And you could use whichever one you like? What do you think?'

'And I can have both of them? Not just a Spanish nobleman, an entire train track. After all these years, Anastasakaíoi and Haritakaíoi end up with a joint descendent, me. I like it,' he said.

'Lovely. We'll sort it out tomorrow. Aris can do it, your mother's friend.'

And in fact Aris agreed enthusiastically. Whether to prove himself useful, or because it suited him if the boy was connected to me and there was the prospect of having him out from under his feet, he dealt with our affairs very quickly.

And so my last few days in Greece passed. I left finally at the end of September on British Airways, via London. I purposely chose an evening flight, because I wanted my son to come with me to the airport. I had arranged to return the hire car there, so I passed by to pick up Alexis from home. He had just got back from swimming and I had to wait a few moments for him to get ready. A few moments alone with Marina. She was wearing khaki army trousers and a black strappy top. Barefoot, as she usually was at home. I allowed myself to look at her quite openly. I wanted to take the image of her back with me, her hair spilling over her shoulders, her proud eyebrows, the incredible colour of her eyes. There was so much I wanted to say to her, but it was far too late now. And so we stood opposite one another in silence, just looking at each other, neither of us able to find the words. I look at you and I feel like a moth to a flame. I coughed to clear my throat.

'There's something I need to say to you, it's been bothering me for years. And now that I've met Alexis, even more so. Do you remember our last meeting in Boston? I asked you to leave because I needed space. I want you to know, I never needed space when I was with you. You were my space. And I always made love to you. I never wanted just to fu—'

I couldn't bring myself to say the word I had used then. She looked at me in silence.

'I wanted to say thank you to you for Alexis. For our times together. For you to know how much I owe you. Thank you.'

The boy rushed in calling 'I'm ready,' and I didn't finish my sentence. Marina gave me her hand formally.

'Have a good journey, Odysséa,' she said calmly. 'We'll talk on the telephone about Alexis's trip to Boston.'

'I wish you happiness. With all my heart.'

She nodded.

'You too. *Kalo taxidi.*'

I tried in vain to smile at her, but I couldn't do it. I said goodnight, searching her eyes for any sign of our old love. How could she have forgotten me? I was the traitor and it was my fault, yes. But all these years, even when I'd been living in the belief that she had betrayed me, I had never forgotten her. How could she look at me like that, as if I was a stranger, a guest whom we don't much like, but patiently put up with until he's gone? But of course there was Aris. With his fine delicate hands and big sensuous mouth.

I was in pieces, and on the way to the airport with the boy neither of us spoke. Just before I got on the plane, I reminded my son that I would be expecting him for Christmas and that I would be in constant touch with him. I tried to give him some money one last time, but he refused.

'I don't even accept it from Marina,' he explained.

'Your mother doesn't have enough, I have too much,' I insisted and I put the keys to the tower house into his hand, the contract for the flat in Kallithea, a bankbook and a debit card. 'I don't want either you or your mother to want for anything. I know that she will never accept it, that's why I'm giving it to you. When you go down to the village, I'd like you to go to the house. It's yours.' I put my hands on his shoulders and gave them a squeeze. 'I'll miss you, my boy.'

'Me too, Odysséa,' he said tearfully. 'Have a good journey.'

'Till we meet again, say. I'll be counting the days.'

I hugged him to me with all my strength. It was our first hug. I wiped my eyes and left without looking back. I couldn't bear it.

# Autumn Everywhere

I WAITED TILL I SAW his plane had taken off. Then I got on the metro and went home.

It's been a strange summer. I met Effie, who last year was still a little girl – she had become a real woman, with a body full of promise. And when I finally managed to taste her body, she rejected me as if I'd committed a crime, as if I had forced her to do something she didn't want to. And yet, I would never have dared if she hadn't taken the initiative. No, I would never have dared do it on her parents' bed.

I can't bear it that Effie won't talk to me now. We went to the concert in town with her father's permission and I kept my word. We stayed in the crowd. We didn't go off on our own, not even for a kiss. She behaved as if nothing had happened between us, as if I had dreamt it all. And when I asked what was the matter, she said, 'I don't want us to see each other alone any more.' I didn't understand. 'Tell me why,' I begged her, 'tell me, what have I done wrong?' She said I hadn't done anything wrong. And she took off and gave me back the ring I'd given her for her birthday. I was gobsmacked. It can't be, I thought. Mitsikoyiánnis must have interfered. He must have frightened her. But she assured me that it was her decision and I believed her. Because her eyes had a steely glint about them.

'As you like,' I told her. I have my pride, after all. What is a man worth if he loses that too? We stayed on till the end of the concert in silence and then went to find Odysséas who was waiting for us outside the Xemóni. He knew at once that something was up, the silence made it clear that we had quarrelled and that nothing had gone right. We left Effie at home, waited for her to go inside and shut the door behind her, and then we left. My house is at the entrance to the village, so normally I would have got out first, but Odysséas deliberately dropped Effie off first. He wanted to find out what had happened. I didn't tell him about her birthday night, not because I was afraid of the consequences, but because that's between me and Effie, I don't want to tell anyone else. But I told him she'd given me the boot. I wasn't at my best, but I saw with amazement that instead of being relieved by the developments, as I'd expected, Odysséas took it right to heart.

'I'm sorry,' he said. 'I know you're hurting. I would give everything to protect you from that pain, because I too have hurt a lot.'

'I wish I was like you,' I exclaimed despite myself. 'My mother says that you never fall in love.'

He laughed and his laughter was slightly scary.

'She says that? Don't wish for things you don't understand, I should say. We Anastasakaíoi love only once in our lives and it's forever. I hope in that way you will not be like me, because it hurts.'

This strange summer brought me my father – an attractive fifty-year-old with grey hair and large, strong hands. I'd often tried to imagine him when my mother used to tell me the story of her and Odysséas Anastasakos. A hard, pitiless guy was what I had in my mind, who never forgave, obsessed with making money, indifferent to all feeling. Not that my mother had ever told me he was like that, but what picture could I have of a father who never appeared? And later, the comments in the village, so unfair both on me and my mother, had made me incredibly angry. Why had he left us to endure all that? Where was he? What was he doing? Why had he left us waiting for so long?

But this wasn't the man I had got to know. And although to start with I watched him awkwardly playing his role as a loving father, completely fake as far as I was concerned, and brought on by his sense of duty at what happened one night, in the end I realised that he wasn't at all like that. My father doesn't love me, how could he?

Until just now he didn't know I properly existed. But I do believe that he does really care about me and cares deeply. We get on, he likes me. And I like this guy from Boston, who has nothing in common with most Greek Americans, all swank and no substance. Women can't keep their eyes off him, with his imposing presence and dark, mysterious air.

I arrived home just as my mother was saying goodbye to a glum-looking Aris Iliópoulos, who barely said hello to me. She was looking calm and decided. I knew. My mother had refused his offer of marriage. Although I wasn't in the least surprised, I have to admit that I was relieved. Not that I didn't want her to get married, anything but. But I didn't believe that arrogant narcissist would ever make her happy.

She laid the table and we sat down to eat, the two of us. My grandfather was still away at the village. She didn't seem sad. I didn't ask her anything. But because I remembered my father's words 'We Anastasakaíoi love only once in our lives,' I knew I had her sussed. Whichever of them I took after, I would be in love with Effie for my whole life. Because my mother hadn't forgotten him either.

# Moth

ALEXIS AND I SPENT CHRISTMAS together in Boston, and returned to Athens together on New Year's Eve. Due to the bad weather many people had postponed or cancelled their flights and so we were lucky to find two seats on a plane. Neither of us could wait any longer. I didn't have a particular plan, only a faint hope, and I didn't want to risk losing that hope, or giving anyone else a chance with Marina.

From the airport we went straight to the house. Marina was out. She had told Alexis that she was celebrating New Year's Eve with Stella, her psychologist friend from the orphanage. Better that way, remarked Alexis, because we'd have more time to get ready. Meaning that I would have more time. Alexis arranged to stay with his mate so we could be alone. He had set the stage masterfully. 'You wait for her to get back. *Pappoú* is in the Mani, I'll be at Dimitris's, so there'll be no one to interrupt you. Speak to her. Explain things to her. Say you're sorry. Use your charm. Don't bungle it if she gets angry. She's a general, but a very gentle general. How can she resist you? No woman can. I've seen how they all hover around you.' He said everything he could think of to give me courage, because, if I'm honest, I was in no fit state. I was completely tongue-tied and I felt as if something was pressing against my chest. I was suffocating. I was afraid and I shared my fear with my son. 'Do you really think that I can win your mother round with the usual tricks?' I knew the answer. I would never have any hope with Marina if I wasn't prepared to humble myself completely, and make up for the way I had behaved in Boston. And even then she would find it difficult to believe me, whatever I said, because I had proved myself to be a liar, an egoist and a traitor.

Alexis went, having first had a bath and changed his clothes, and I was left on my own to wander about the rooms. The house crowded in on me. I tried to resist the temptation to go into her room, but in the end I gave in. I opened the door and stood looking at the bed. It was the same bed we'd slept in together in the Plaka. The bedspread, in soft warm colours, matched the curtain and the plain fitted carpet on the floor. Marina always had good taste, even when she lacked money. I suddenly felt very tired, my eyelids were drooping, the bed seemed to be inviting me and I lay down with my feet over the side so as not to dirty the covers. I touched the wooden bedstead. I remembered the feel of the wood under my hand, and I travelled seventeen years back in time.

On the dresser there was an old, yellow envelope. I don't know why I opened it, I'm not normally so crass. And yet I put my hand in and pulled out what was inside. A pile of photographs tumbled to the floor, two articles cut from a newspaper, and a folded piece of paper. I opened the last first and immediately recognised my own handwriting on the list of 'Duties of a Maniot Bride'. One by one I read the silly list of rules that Marina had kept all these years, and the memory of that happiness pierced me like a knife. The articles were much older. They referred to the tragedy in the Mani. The first simply related the events, the second went further. It spoke of a revival of the old vendetta between two ancient Maniot clans in a village in the Middle Mani, our village. It was all in there. Names, photographs. In one of the blurred, black and white photographs, I recognised my mother beside my father's coffin, and myself, standing next to my Uncle Nikifóros. And in another photograph the Haritákos family, all five of them, smiling, before the disaster happened. I put them aside and gathered up the photos that had fallen to the floor. It was what I expected. The photographs of Marina and me taken with that amazing Canon I had at the time. In some it was just me. But in most of them we had our arms around one another. In the Mani, the Plaka, Saronida, Spetses, the Acropolis. I looked at them again one by one from the beginning, and then all over again. Until I eventually turned off the light and closed my eyes. It wasn't hard to get to sleep, in spite of my agony. Her scent was all around me.

I was woken, not by the noise but by the colours on the television screen coming in through the open door. I stayed still for a while, till the feeling in my body returned and my eyes had adjusted, and then I got up. She was lying on the sofa in the sitting room, fully dressed. She was wearing a sleeveless black dress and sheer stockings. She had kicked her shoes off on to the floor and put her lovely feet up on the cushions. Her hair, brushed down over her forehead, was still neat from the hairdresser's. She had it straightened and the ends curled outwards so it looked even longer. I've seen her once before with her hair done up like that and it really suits her, but I prefer it like it was then, when she used to gather up her unruly curls with a hair tie, in that cheeky ponytail of hers. All these years I hadn't been able to forget the girl on the terrace with the beautiful, proud forehead, neat eyebrows, alluring mouth, and now here she was in front of me, the girl I had loved, the girl I betrayed, the girl I had never forgotten, always present in my life in all my moments, even when I was in bed with other women, even on the day of my wedding when I stood with Lou before the registrar and we exchanged our vows.

She hadn't heard me. I stood watching her flick through the channels irritably and then look for her reading glasses on the coffee table. She turned off the television and opened a book. I couldn't stand there any longer, I couldn't wait.

'You look very lovely in those glasses,' I said, idiotically, and she leapt up out of her skin.

I'd frightened her, fool that I am. As she sat down again her glasses dropped on to her nose. She took them off and threw them on the table.

'Why have you taken them off?' I said, softly. 'They suit you.'

'I can't believe you've come all this way just to take the piss. Where is Alexis?'

I sat down opposite her and prepared myself. I had no intention of hiding things from her, and I no longer cared about being dignified. That coffee table was between us. To get to her tonight, I would have to overcome far greater obstacles. I was unable to read the expression on her face.

'Don't worry, he's arranged to go out with Dimitris – I can't for the life of me remember which one.'

'Georgíou.'

'That's him. He's staying over at his house.'

She looked at me with deep suspicion.

'Will you tell me what's going on? What are you up to? Have you two had a row?'

My eyes were stinging and I rubbed them. I had prepared a number of things to say to her. I'd forgotten them all. She pursed her lips and her face grew pale. I saw something in her eyes I'd never seen before. It was fear. And something worse. Panic.

'You can tell me, whatever it is,' she whispered. 'I can take it. Are you taking him away with you forever? Are you going to punish me for hiding it from you? Couldn't you at least wait for one more year?'

She had tried to steady her voice and to appear in control. But the tears gave her away.

'I'm not going to stand in the way of the boy's future,' she said. 'Children are to be cherished and then let free. I'll agree with anything you decide. So tell me.'

'Please don't cry, I can't bear it,' I said, finally managing to speak. 'We haven't decided anything. I didn't come to tell you that I'm taking Alexis, or to punish you for keeping him from me. He's the man of the house and he knows where his duty lies.'

She looked at me, totally baffled.

'What is it then?'

'I look at you and I feel like a moth to a flame,' I whispered, and felt I had said all there was to say.

# Out of the Cold

I GOT BACK LATE in the evening. It was raining outside. I found them sitting next to each other on the sofa, looking at old photographs of me. I looked enquiringly at my father and he gave me a despairing look. My mother was in that kind of mood that can drive you mad. I was dying to find out what was up and when she went to get the supper I had my chance. I sat beside my father and we both watched her go off towards the kitchen.

'Well?'

He shrugged his shoulders hopelessly.

'It's too late,' he whispered. 'It's not my fault. It's nobody's fault, but it's too late. She's not doing it to punish me, she said, but she doesn't believe in it and she can't bear any more suffering. Because … because of me.'

His voice faltered. He seemed broken, and I broke down with him, because I had hoped. All those hours travelling on the plane together we had hoped, the two of us. That he wouldn't be alone any longer. And that I would have what most children had. Both my parents together and loving one another. Marina had brought it all crashing down in one minute. Calmly, like a surgeon taking a dangerous lump out of the patient's body, even though he knew the operation might cost him his life, that was how she took the last hope from my father's heart, knowing that it might kill him. I couldn't bear to see him like that. I hugged him.

'What will you do, *babá*?'

It was the first time I had called him that. I said it without thinking, when I saw how much he was hurting. He shrugged his shoulders again.

'What can I do?'

I didn't have an answer. We sat there in silence, hugging each other, till we heard her calling out to us that supper was ready. He wiped his eyes and signalled to me that we had to get up. The three of us sat at the table. The two of them at either end and me in the middle. My mother had made us an omelette. She had decorated the table. She had put out some wine. She was calm and decisive. We had no choice but to clink our glasses. And then, dazed, I saw that he was smiling.

'Happy New Year, my Melénia. And to you too, my boy.'

He had welled up again, and wiping his eyes he whispered, 'I'm sorry.' And she was no better, her eyes were shining with tears. 'Why?' I wanted to shout at her. 'Why don't you just hug him, forget it all, live together like you dreamt you would?' I didn't speak. Because I know my mother.

She'd got my grandfather's room ready for my father.

'I'll go to a hotel tomorrow,' he remarked, 'and get out from under your feet.' I waited for her to object, if only out of politeness. She didn't say anything. On the contrary, she nodded. And later, when she had cleared and washed the dishes, she went to bed and left us alone. I was sleepy, but I didn't want to leave him. I knew that he would stay awake all night on his own in the dark. Poor thing! He smiled at me.

'Why don't you go to bed? You're exhausted.'

'I'm not sleepy,' I lied, and prayed that my eyelids wouldn't droop and give me away.

'Go to bed, my boy. I'll be all right.'

I brought two blankets and we lay down on the sofas, he on the big one, me on the small one. We were both uncomfortable, but we were together.

'Are you going to leave?' I asked him quietly, so my mum couldn't hear.

'No,' he whispered. 'I'm not going to leave again. Ever.'

I started in surprise. I knew how precious his time was and how essential it was for him to be in Boston. I had seen him at work. There were so many people depending on him. He had stolen a few days to be with me for the holidays, but his commitments were very pressing. John couldn't manage it all on his own.

'What d'you mean?'

He got up.

'I think I need a cigarette,' he said. 'Shall we go out on to the balcony?'

I followed him out. I was no longer sleepy, the cold outside had woken me up completely. At that moment I wanted a smoke too, very much.

'If I were to ask ...' I risked a whisper.

'Your mother would kill me.' He took a long drag. 'I've managed to bring everything in my life under control. The past, my guilt, drink, cigarettes. Everything. Except for my passion for your mother. She's a tough nut. A *Maniátissa*! But so am I. I'm not going anywhere, my boy. I'm staying here. She'll get so sick of seeing me, she'll have no choice, she'll have to say yes.'

'What about your work?' I asked in shock.

'It can go to hell. I'll tell John to sell my shares in the company. And my house. Everything. I've worked for long enough and made more than enough for us to live on. What's the use of it all without you and your mother? I'll be here. With you, beside you, until I win her back. She froze inside – your mother – when I let her down. And I can understand that. I felt the same when I thought she had betrayed me. I'll warm her up again. Let's go and get some sleep. I don't think I'll have any nightmares tonight.'

We went in and lay back down on the sofas. We wanted to be together. We covered ourselves up with blankets and fell asleep.

***

He did as he had promised. After my dad and I returned to Athens, he didn't leave again. He organised the sale of his property in Boston over the phone. For much less than it was worth, I think. He said nothing to my mother. He had found a place in Saronida, but he came to our house every day. We went to the football, the cinema, the theatre. We ate out. My mother didn't come with us on our outings even though he asked her to, so shyly that he seemed more like a teenager than me. She said no, but she kept us company whenever my father came to our house. She kept her distance, always the same, uncompromising. And the time passed. He would often go down to the Mani and whenever I could I went with him. We would stay in the tower house, he gave me his old room and slept in his parents' – my grandparents' – old room. He began to cultivate his olives and helped old Nikifóros.

'What is all this?' the old man would mutter. 'Have you come back to be a farmer?'

He told me that he didn't miss his old life in Boston and I believed him, because he looked happy.

'God granted that I come back to work on my land again, to live and breathe in my own homeland, near my son. To see the woman I love. What more could anyone wish for?'

I didn't believe it.

'Are you really going to do this for the rest of your life?'

He confided to me that he was planning to help Mitsikoyiánnis, whose business had been brought to its knees by the economic crisis. He was going to suggest a partnership and had in mind a hotel complex based around renovated towers. His friend, he thought, rightly, would be the best person for the job. He loved the place. He respected its history.

He played endless games of cards with Nikifóros and *Pappoú*. Marina would arrive home in the Mani on Friday evenings and find them at it. He would look up from his cards and stare at her. As if he couldn't take his eyes off her. She would look away, embarrassed, and hurry on up to her room or disappear into the kitchen, always busy. I was in the middle of it all, watching the tough game that was being played by the two of them. And there were times when I was certain he would win. And then at other times, I was certain he didn't have a chance. *Pappoú* and I prayed wholeheartedly that Marina would finally give in and let 'the enemy' storm the tower of her heart. It must have been the first time a Maniot had wished his clan to be defeated.

Nothing would have changed if my father hadn't been the kind of man he proved to be: patient, stubborn and in love. And in his own way, faithful until death. He let himself go naked and undefended before the woman he loved, shed all his pride and egotism, ignored what people said about him and the ironic looks of the villagers with nothing better to do.

It was a Saturday evening. My father had said goodnight fairly late. He looked at my mother through the open door. 'Goodnight, *Melénia mou*,' he said and went off smiling. I sensed that something was different. I could see it in her face. I decided right away to give her space to think about it. I went up to my room, but I didn't lie down. I calculated how long it would take my father to get home – eight whole minutes on foot – and I saw the light go on in his tower. I stayed there looking at it as if I was hypnotised. And I wasn't the only one. I was certain of that. When I heard the front door closing, I knew. I went slowly downstairs and into the kitchen. My mother wasn't there. On the table she had left a piece of paper with four words written on it. 'I'm going to Odysséas's.'

I looked over at the light again and counted the minutes. A second light went on at exactly the right moment. I breathed a sigh of relief and went up to bed. But first I turned on my mobile to send a text. I couldn't write everything I wanted to say about love, and time going by, and the pride that makes us blind, stupid and unhappy. I didn't want to end up like that. I just wrote three words, scrolled down to Effie's number and sent them.